Ashes to Dust

Also by Yrsa Sigurdardóttir

Last Rituals
My Soul to Take

Ashes to Dust

Yrsa Sigurdardóttir

Translated from the Icelandic
by Philip Roughton

MINOTAUR BOOKS

THOMAS DUNNE BOOKS

New York

This is a work of fiction. All of the characters, organizations, and events portrayed in this novel are either products of the author's imagination or are used fictitiously.

A THOMAS DUNNE BOOK FOR MINOTAUR BOOKS.
An imprint of St. Martin's Publishing Group.

www.thomasdunnebooks.com
www.stmartins.com

Library of Congress Cataloging-in-Publication Data

Yrsa Sigurdardóttir.
  [Aska. English]
  Ashes to dust : a thriller / Yrsa Sigurdardóttir.—1st ed.
    p. cm.
  "Originally published in Great Britain in 2010 by Hodder & Stoughton"—T.p. verso.
  ISBN 978-1-250-00493-2 (hardback)
  ISBN 978-0-312-64174-0 (paperback)
  ISBN 978-1-250-00823-7 (e-book)
    1. Thóra Gudmundsdóttir (Fictitious character)—Fiction.   2. Women lawyers—
Iceland—Reykjavík—Fiction.   I. Title.
  PT7513.Y77A8513 2012
  839.6935—dc23

2011043084

First published in Great Britain by Hodder & Stoughton, a Hachette U.K. company

First U.S. Edition: April 2012

Acknowledgments

I wish to thank all the residents of the Westmann Islands who assisted me as I wrote this book. Foremost among them is Kristín Jóhannsdóttir, who could not have been more helpful. Sigmundur Gísli Einarsson, Ólafur M. Kristinsson, and Árni Johnsen also receive thanks for their helpfulness, as well as the expatriate Westmann Islander Gísli Baldvinsson. None of these individuals is a model for any character in the book.

I dedicate this book to my publisher, Pétur Már Ólafsson, with heartfelt appreciation for his outstanding cooperation and boundless patience.

Ashes to Dust

Prologue

She had often considered death to be a desirable option. Today, however, she hadn't been feeling that way, which was rather unfortunate in light of the circumstances. When her father had died after a difficult struggle with cancer, she'd wondered what the point of everything was. How short and insignificant a life is when all is said and done, she had thought. Her father had been the lynchpin of their little family, but months later she had trouble recalling how he looked without the aid of a photograph. And she had supposedly been one of the closest to him—how quickly were others forgetting him? Once her mother had passed away, as well as herself and her sister, no one would remember him, and it would be as if he had never set foot on this earth. The thought filled her with despair. Now, as she stared her own fate in the face, she realized that her story would never be told. She would never be able to make a clean breast of it as she had intended. No one else could make sense of all this, much less explain the events that had recently overtaken her. Everything was going black, but she managed to snap herself out of it. She knew that when it happened next she might not be able to resist.

If she weren't so weak and confused, she could at least try to defend herself instead of lying here, letting it happen. She must have been given drugs of some sort; this kind of drowsiness didn't occur naturally. On the bedside table stood a bottle of pills that she didn't recall placing there, but by squinting she could see that it contained the powerful painkillers she'd come home with after her last operation. The bottle had sat untouched in her medicine cabinet for months and it was unthinkable that she'd fetched it herself, let alone taken the pills in any large dosage. She had no memory of swallowing them, so it seemed highly likely that they'd been put in her food earlier. She remembered the taste of the pills only too well, and there was no way the wine she'd drunk would have masked it. The foul taste of the vomit in her mouth was not from the pills—but that in itself meant nothing. She retched again and closed her eyes, even though she was afraid she wouldn't be able to open them again. This fear proved unfounded, because they flew open reflexively when a heavy weight descended on her, expelling the breath from her lungs. Her eyes were covered by an ice-cold hand, shutting out the light.

Her racing heartbeat faster still when another hand prised open her mouth and groping fingers pushed their way in. Her feet kicked in impotent protest. Her tongue was yanked out of her mouth and after a moment she felt an agonizing sting. A painful heat spread slowly from the puncture wound, over and through her tongue, and she realized that something was being injected into the soft tissue. When her tongue was released, the hand gripped her nose.

Her thoughts became less distinct, foggier. Was she maybe in hospital, under the hands of a doctor? She couldn't open her eyes and could smell nothing through her nose, which was held shut, but she hoped that this was the case. A low whisper in her ear: *It's almost over—relax.* Was this a doctor or a nurse? She tried unsuccessfully to recall who had been with her before she became dizzy and started vomiting. She was sure she knew, but found it impossible to recall her visitor's name or face. Abruptly, the thought came to her that she still had to buy a birthday present for her sister. What should she give her? A jumper maybe? There were so many beautiful jumpers to choose from. But then she realized that this was neither the time nor the place to think about such a thing. Which reminded her, she not only didn't know where she was, but also what time it was. Was it night or day? How long had it been since the injection in her tongue—if that had even happened? The hold on her nose was released, her mouth was re-opened and the fingers crept back in. She recognized them by their soapy taste. They prodded her tongue, and she could feel that something was wrong. She tried to move her tongue, without success. Maybe she was having a stroke? A stroke could actually manifest such symptoms. What else could it be? She couldn't think. Suddenly the fingers were pressed firmly against her tongue, rolling it and forcing it back into her throat. It made no difference how she fought to free her tongue from this deadly grip—it wouldn't let up. The knees of the person sitting on top of her had trapped her hands at her sides. In despair she tried to remember everything that she knew about strokes, but she could not recall whether paralysis of the tongue was a symptom.

Garbled curses, sounding like they came from inside a barrel or the end of a long tunnel, echoed in her mind. She couldn't tell if she was imagining them, or if they came from whoever was so mistreating her mouth. She tried to say something, expecting her voice to sound the way it did when she attempted to speak at the dentist's—which reminded her, she needed to make an appointment—but all that came out was a moan that seemed to originate in her abdomen. Her tongue still would not move despite repeated messages from her brain, making it impossible for her to change sounds into words. Suddenly the fingers were pressing even harder against it. She could feel her tongue perfectly even though she couldn't move it, and she gagged as it was pushed back into her throat. Her eyes opened wide and she stared at the familiar ceiling panels.

The fingers released her tongue and the weight was lifted from her stomach and hands, but this did not relieve her at all. She tried desperately to catch her breath. Mad with fear, she attempted to think clearly, but could not. Her tongue was stuck fast in her gullet. Her feet kicked, drumming on the mattress in furious convulsions. Her hands clawed at the soft skin of her neck and jaw—maybe she could make a hole for air to come in?

Then everything went black and she was gone, like her father. He had been happy to say farewell to his life, unlike her. The terrible sounds that had emerged from her as she fought for breath had ceased. Her head sunk slowly to one side and she lay in a pool of blood, her eyes full of anguish. Everything was quiet for a moment, then a CD player on the other bedside table was switched on and music started to play.

Shortly afterward the woman's visitor gently closed the bedroom door, showing far more courtesy than he had previously displayed.

Chapter 1

Monday, July 9, 2007

"You're trying to tell me Markús is just tidying the basement? You can't possibly believe that a pile of rubbish is the reason that he didn't want anyone to go down there before him?"

The lawyer Thóra Gudmundsdóttir smiled politely at the man addressing her, an archaeologist called Hjörtur Fridriksson, but did not answer his question. This was getting out of hand. She was very uncomfortable; the smell of smoke and the ash hanging in the air were irritating her eyes and nose, and she was scared that the roof was going to collapse at any moment. On their way through the house to the basement door the three of them had had to make their way around a huge pile of ashy debris where the roof had collapsed onto the intricately patterned carpet, at which point Thóra had adjusted her helmet's elastic chin-strap to ensure that it was fastened tightly. She shuffled her feet and looked embarrassedly at the clock. They heard a dull thud from the basement. What exactly was the man up to? Markús had said that he needed a little time, but neither she nor the archaeologist could guess what his definition of "a little" was. "I'm sure he'll reappear soon," she said, without much conviction, and stared at the crooked door in the hope that it would be pushed open and this business concluded. She glanced instinctively at the ceiling, ready to jump away if it appeared likely to crash down on them.

"Don't worry," said Hjörtur, pointing upward. "If the roof was going to split apart it would have done so a long time ago." He heaved a sigh and stroked his unshaven chin. "Do you know what he's doing down there?"

Thóra shook her head, unwilling to discuss her client's plans with someone unconnected to the case.

"He must have at least hinted," said Hjörtur. "We've been dying to find out about this." He looked at Thóra. "I'll bet this has something to do with pornography. The others think so, too."

She shrugged. That thought had certainly occurred to her as well, but she did not have a sufficiently fertile imagination to guess what kind of thing would be too embarrassing or disgusting to show to a stranger. A film of the homeowner's sexual adventures? Unlikely. Few people had video cameras in the 1970s, and she doubted that the type of film used back then would have survived the destruction that had rained down on the Islands. Besides, Markús Magnússon, who was down in the basement, had been only fifteen when the house had disappeared beneath lava and ash, so he probably hadn't been ready for much in that area. Nevertheless, there was something down in the basement that he'd been desperate to get to before them. Thóra sighed. How did she keep ending up with these characters? She didn't know any other lawyer who attracted such strange cases, and such peculiar clients. She resolved to ask Markús what had inspired him to call her little legal firm instead of one of the larger ones when he decided to demand that the excavation be legally blocked. If he ever returned from the basement. She pulled the neck of her jumper up over her mouth and nose and tried breathing through it. That was a little better. Hjörtur smiled at her.

"You get used to it, I promise," he said. "Hopefully you won't have to, though—it takes several days."

Thóra rolled her eyes. "Damn it, it's not like he's going to move in down there," she muttered through her jumper. Then she pulled it down to smile at Hjörtur. It was thanks to him that things had gone so well until now, in that they'd been able to get by without demanding the injunction. In any case, that would only have been a temporary measure since Markús and his family no longer had any claim on the house. The Westmann Islands owned it along with all its contents, and there was little point in fighting this fact even though Markús had made a concerted attempt to do so. He had focused particularly on Hjörtur Fridriksson, the man now standing next to Thóra; Hjörtur was the director of a project entitled Pompeii of the North, whose task it was to excavate a number of houses that had been buried by ash in the eruption on Heimaey Island in 1973. Thóra had had considerable contact with him by telephone and email since the case had begun, and liked the man well enough. He was inclined to be long-winded, but seemed reasonable and was not easily provoked. Hjörtur had been seriously tested, since Markús so often acted like a total ass. He had refused to give even the slightest clue as to why he was opposed to his parents' house being excavated, had gone on and on about invasions of privacy, and had generally complicated the matter for Thóra in every conceivable way. After trying to reach an agreement but getting nowhere due to Markús's pigheadedness, in defeat she had asked Hjörtur whether he couldn't just dig up some other house instead. There were certainly enough to choose from. But that was out of the question, since Markús's childhood home was one of the few houses in the area built of concrete, and thus was more likely than the others to have withstood the cataclysm in any significant way. The purpose of the excavation was not to dig down to a house that was now simply rubble.

Thóra had already started reading up on how she might best obtain an injunction against the excavation when it transpired that Markús was only concerned about the basement of the house. Finally they could discuss solutions sensibly, and Hjörtur had proposed this arrangement: the house would first be dug up and aired out, and then Markús would be the first person allowed down into the basement, where he could remove anything that he wanted. After some consideration he agreed to this compromise and Thóra breathed easier. Markús had no trouble at all bearing the cost of endless litigation, since he was anything but badly off financially. His family owned one of the largest fishing companies in the Westmann Islands, and even though Thóra would never complain about being paid well for her work, she was upset about working against her better judgment, and toward a goal that would never be reached. She was immensely relieved when Markús agreed to Hjörtur's proposal; now she could start putting the final touches to the fine details of the agreement over how Markús's visit to the basement would be conducted, how they could guarantee that others would not be allowed to sneak in before him, and so on. The agreement was then signed, and they only had to wait for the end of the excavation.

So there they stood, archaeologist and lawyer, staring at a crooked basement door while a man who had still been a teenager in 1973 wrestled with a terrible secret beneath their feet.

"Hallelujah," said Thóra when they heard footsteps on the basement stairs.

"I do hope he found whatever he was looking for," said Hjörtur gloomily. "We didn't think about the possibility of him coming up empty-handed."

Thóra crossed her fingers and stared at the door.

They watched anxiously as the doorknob turned, then incredulously as the door was cracked open only a tiny bit. They exchanged a glance, then Thóra leaned forward and spoke into the gap. "Markús," she said calmly, "is something wrong?"

"You've got to come down here," came the reply. His voice sounded peculiar, but it was impossible to tell whether he was excited, disappointed or sad. The glow from his flashlight shone through the chink and illuminated Thóra's feet.

"Me?" Thóra asked, flabbergasted. "Down there?" She looked back at Hjörtur, who raised his eyebrows.

"Yes," said Markús, in the same enigmatic tone. "I need to get your opinion on something."

"My opinion?" she echoed. When she found herself speechless she had a habit of repeating whatever was said to her, giving herself time to ponder her response.

"Yes, your legal opinion," said the voice behind the door.

Thóra straightened up. "I'll give you all the opinions you want, Markús," she said. "However, this is how it is with us lawyers: we have no need to experience for ourselves whatever it is we're dealing with. So there's no reason for me to clamber down there with you. Tell me what this is about and I'll put together an opinion for you back at my office in Reykjavík."

"You've got to come down here," said Markús. "I don't need a written opinion. A verbal one'll do." He paused. "I'm begging you.

Just come down here." Thóra had never heard Markús sound so humble. She'd only heard him being haughty and opinionated.

Hjörtur scowled at Thóra, unamused. "Why don't you just get it over with? It's completely safe, and I'm keen to finish up here."

She hesitated. What in the blazes could be down there? She absolutely did not want to go down into even darker and fouler air. On the other hand, she agreed with Hjörtur that they had to settle this here and now. She roused herself. "All right then," she conceded, grabbing Hjörtur's flashlight. "I'm coming." She opened the door wide enough to step through and saw Markús on the stairs, looking pale as a corpse. His face nearly matched the white helmet that he wore on his head. Thóra tried not to read too much into it, since the only light was coming from their flashlights, giving everything an otherworldly glow. She gulped. The air there was even more stagnant, dustier. "What do you want to show me?" she asked. "Let's get this over with."

Markús set off down the stairs into the darkness. The beam from his flashlight was of little use amid the dust and ash and there was no way to see where the steps ended. "I don't know how to describe it," said Markús in a strangely calm voice, as he went down the stairs. "You've got to believe me when I say that this is not what I came here looking for. But it's clear now that you have to get an injunction against the excavation and have the house covered over again."

Thóra pointed her light at her feet. She had no wish to trip on the stairs and tumble into the basement head first. "Is there something bad here that you weren't aware of?"

"Yes, you could say that," he replied. "I would never have allowed the excavation to go ahead if this was what I wanted to hide. That's for certain." He was standing now on the basement floor. "I think I've got myself into a really bad position."

Thóra stepped off the final stair and took her place by his side. "What do you mean by 'this'?" she asked, shining her light around. The little that she could discern appeared completely innocent: an old sled, a badly dented birdcage, numerous boxes and miscellaneous rubbish scattered here and there, all of it covered with dust and soot.

"Over here," said Markús. He led her to the edge of a partition. "You have to believe me—I knew nothing about this." He pointed his flashlight downward.

Thóra peered at the floor, but couldn't see anything that could have frightened Markús that much, only three mounds of dust. She moved her flashlight over them. It took her some time to realize what she was seeing—and then it was all she could do not to let the flashlight slip from her hand. "Good God," she said. She ran the light over the three faces, one after another. Sunken cheeks, empty eye sockets, gaping mouths; they reminded her of the photographs of mummies she'd once seen in *National Geographic*. "Who are these people?"

"I don't know," said Markús, clearly in shock himself. "But that doesn't matter. What's certain is that they've been dead for quite some time." He raised one of his hands to cover his nose and mouth, even though there was no smell from the corpses, then grimaced and looked away.

Thóra, on the other hand, could not tear her eyes away from the remains. Markús hadn't been exaggerating when he said that this looked bad for him. "What did you want to hide, then, if it wasn't this?" she asked in astonishment. "You'd better have an answer when this gets out." He appeared on the verge of protesting, and she hurriedly added: "You can forget about the house being buried again as if nothing ever happened. I can promise you that that's not an option." Why was nothing ever simple? Why couldn't Markús just have come up from the basement with his arms full of old pornographic pictures? She aimed her flashlight at him.

"Show me what you were looking for," she said, her anxiety heightened by the nervous expression on his face. "Surely it can't be worse than this."

Markús was silent for a few moments. Then he cleared his throat and shone his light into a nook right next to them. "It was this," he said, not letting his eyes follow the flashlight's beam. "I can explain everything," he added nervously, looking at his feet.

"Oh, Jesus!" cried Thóra, as her flashlight clattered to the floor.

Chapter 2

Monday, July 9, 2007

"To tell you the truth, I don't know whether I should be happy or not that your bizarre discovery of human remains should have occurred before I retired." The police officer looked from one of them to the other. Thóra, Hjörtur and Markús all smiled awkwardly. They were at the police headquarters in the Westmann Islands, where they'd been made to wait for a very long time for the chief inspector, who now sat before them. He'd clearly taken his time in the basement, had wanted to see the evidence with his own eyes before speaking to them. "My name is Gudni Leifsson. I'm almost retired," he added, "after a career of nearly forty years." He clasped his hands together. "I'd like to see others do better." Thóra did her best to appear interested in his remarkable career, with limited success; what she wanted most was to ask what time it was, since she couldn't miss the last plane to Reykjavík. What a waste of time this was.

"But that's the way things go." The police inspector shook his head slowly and clicked his tongue. "I have never seen anything like this." He smiled wryly. "Maybe it's fate playing games with the authorities in Reykjavík?"

Thóra raised her eyebrows. "What?" she inquired, although she had no desire whatsoever to prolong this conversation. "How do you mean?"

"I'm not surprised you have to ask. A lawyer from Reykjavík could hardly be expected to keep up to speed with what happens out here in the sticks." The old man looked at her reproachfully, but Thóra ignored him. "It's only been a short time since the detectives we had stationed here were moved to the mainland in order to cut costs. The trivial crimes committed here didn't justify the expense." He smiled broadly. "Until now." He looked at Markús meaningfully before continuing: "Three bodies and one head." He tutted again. "You were always up to mischief as a boy, Markús, but isn't this taking it a bit too far? It's quite a leap from stealing rhubarb to mass murder."

Markús leaned forward, his expression open and sincere. "I swear that I know nothing about these bodies. They're nothing to do with me." He sat back again, seemingly satisfied, and brushed dust off the arms of his jacket.

Thóra sighed deeply and decided to interrupt Markús before he got the chance to say that he'd only had something to do with the head. "Before we go any further, I would like to ask where this is going. Is this a formal interrogation?" She thought—but did not say—that if it were it would be ridiculous to interview Markús and Hjörtur together. Their interests were completely at odds. "If so, I wish to state that as Markús's lawyer, I question your procedures."

Inspector Leifsson pursed his lips and sucked air through his teeth as if trying to clean between them. "It may be that you work differently in Reykjavík, Madam Lawyer," he said coldly. "There, you presumably go 'by the book,' as they say, although one never actually knows which book they mean. Here, on the other hand, I'm in charge. If I want to speak to you, as, for example, I do now, then I shall do so. It can't hurt anyone, can it? Least of all your client, Markús." He smiled at Thóra, but it did not reach his eyes. "Unless you think he's got something on his conscience?" He looked at Markús. "The bodies appeared to be quite old. Perhaps he killed all of them, back when he was a spotty teenager?" He paused, regarding her levelly. "But my heart tells me it isn't so. I think we'll find some sort of logical explanation for this mess, which I was hoping we could just clear up without having to go through formal channels. And I'm happy to take the blame for that."

Thóra placed a restraining hand on Markús's shoulder. "I wish to speak with my client before we go any further, and afterward we will go by this famous 'book,' so that everything is aboveboard."

Gudni shrugged. He seemed to be in good shape for a man his

age, as far as Thóra could tell; fairly trim, and with a good head of hair. She couldn't shake the impression that he looked like Clint Eastwood, and she had an overwhelming desire to stick a toothpick in the corner of his mouth to get the full effect. He stared at her for a moment as if he knew what she was thinking, before turning to Markús. "Is that what you want, Markús, my friend?" he asked the other man, who sat mutely at Thóra's side.

Markús squirmed uneasily in his chair. In front of him sat the authority figure of his youth, who remembered him stealing vegetables from people's gardens, or whatever it was that the old police officer had mentioned at the start of their conversation. "I haven't done anything," he muttered, glancing sideways at Thóra. "Is there really any reason why we have to go through all this official stuff?"

Thóra drew a deep breath. "Markús, my friend," she said calmly, hoping that the words would have the same effect on him as when the inspector had used them. "In the basement you asked for my help, and now I'm giving it to you. Come out into the corridor here with me for a moment, where we can speak privately. Afterward you can decide what you want to do. In other words, you'll be free to go home with Inspector Leifsson and let him question you at his kitchen table, in the presence of his wife and cat."

"My wife is dead," Gudni said coldly. "And I have a dog. No cat."

Throughout all of this Hjörtur had been waiting on the sidelines, quietly following the conversation. Now he finally spoke up, but what he said made Thóra think that he was the type who hated conflict, even as a silent observer. "Wouldn't it be best for everyone if you two went off on your own for a bit? Then I can tell you about the things that concern me," he said, glancing hopefully at Gudni. "It would really help me if we could do this quickly. If I don't get back to my office soon my colleagues will think something has happened to me. They know that I was in the house that you've cordoned off, and they must have heard something's going on there."

Gudni stared at Hjörtur without replying. These silences must be his secret weapon during interrogations, thought Thóra. Perhaps he hoped that people would start speaking, to fill the embarrassing pause. The archaeologist did not fall into his trap. There was a brief silence, then Gudni's face broke into a chilly smile and he said: "Fine. I don't want your colleagues pulling out their pens and writing obituaries about you, my dear Hjörtur." He looked from the blushing archaeologist to Thóra. "Suit yourselves. No one will disturb you in the corridor outside the office." He waved them to the door. "We'll be here if you decide to honor us with your presence." As Thóra and Markús reached the door they heard him say to their backs: "But you'll not be coming to dinner at my house."

"What are you thinking?" muttered Thóra through gritted teeth, once they were outside the office. "You go there to fetch a severed head, and then think you can sit and chat with the police without having any idea of your legal position. Do you realize how much trouble you could end up in?"

Markús looked angry for a second, then his anger gave way to resignation. "You don't know how things work here. This man is the law in the Islands. Him alone. There might be other policemen, but he's the one who calls the shots. He often settles cases without making any trouble for those involved. I think it would be best for me to just talk to him, and after he's heard what I have to say he'll make things easier. Especially since I didn't do anything wrong."

Thóra wanted to stamp her foot in frustration, but she clenched her fists and settled for knocking lightly on the wall for emphasis. "This case will soon be taken out of Gudni's hands. Corpses and severed heads aren't a matter for small police departments, no matter how powerful particular officers may be in their own jurisdictions. He might be able to solve cases his way when they concern stolen rhubarb, but this is another matter entirely. It's my understanding that in the light of the seriousness of this case, and because of the unusual circumstances, it won't go to the Criminal Investigation Department in Selfoss, which usually handles such cases here in the Islands. It'll go straight to the Reykjavík police and their Crime Lab, and you can be sure that they won't conduct themselves like Gudni. So it's all the same to me what you do, but it'll work out much better for *you* if things are done in the proper way. When you're being questioned informally, he can use everything that you say in court. And to make matters worse, Hjörtur would be able to confirm everything that you said. It's completely crazy."

"But didn't he say that the Criminal Investigation Department had shut up shop here in the Islands?" asked Markús, who to Thóra's relief finally appeared to be showing some concern.

"The Westmann Islands are not outside the jurisdiction of the CID and the Crime Lab, even though they no longer have offices here. The detectives will simply hop on an airplane and start snooping around."

"I see," Markús said softly.

Thóra sighed. She couldn't help but feel for this man, who was so unlike her. It seemed as though all the stubbornness, short temper and rudeness he had previously displayed were now gone. He had clearly been badly shocked by what he'd found in the basement, and she believed him completely when he said that was the first time he'd seen the bodies, and even the severed head that he'd gone to fetch. Thóra had had no time to ask him about this strange paradox in the commotion that had arisen when they'd come up from the basement and told Hjörtur to call the police. The sight of the bodiless head's contorted face—which had almost looked as if it were sticking out its tongue—had made her feel so claustrophobic that it had been out of the question to speak to Markús down there. "How about you tell me why you were so eager to get to the basement to fetch a head that you say you didn't even know was there? I've tried to come up with an explanation for it, but I have to admit defeat." She paused for a moment and looked Markús in the eye. "After I've heard your version of the story we'll wait here quietly for Hjörtur to come out, then we'll go in and let Gudni decide whether he wants to question you formally or leave it to whoever takes over the case."

"Fine," replied Markús, taking a deep breath. "You're probably right."

Thóra was pleased with his change of heart, but wasn't certain it would last. "You have to understand that if you say something to him and I interrupt you, you keep quiet and let me do the talking. The same goes if I advise you not to answer a particular question."

"Okay," said Markús. "You're the boss." He smiled ruefully at her. "Where were you when the big rhubarb case came up? They made me pull up chickweed in the school garden every night for a month."

Thóra smiled back and looked around to make sure that none of Gudni's subordinates were listening in. "So, tell me about the head that you went to collect without knowing anything about it."

Gudni leaned back in his chair and took the last page out of a battered electric typewriter. He placed it carefully facedown on the other pages that had been piled there, then lifted them and shuffled the stack into order. He put the pages on the table so that Thóra and Markús could read them. "Just as the law prescribes. Read these through, then I would be very happy if you could verify your statement with your signature, Markús, so that all the formal details are in order and your lawyer can breathe easier."

Thóra flashed him a pro forma smile. She couldn't care less if he were dissatisfied with the procedures, as long as the interests of her client were guaranteed. In the end, everything had gone quite well for her. Markús had been questioned as a suspect, but that was to be expected considering the circumstances. The main point was that he hadn't got himself into any more trouble by saying too much too soon. Thóra jerked her chin in the direction of the report. "Doesn't it match what was stated? You haven't added anything, have you?" she asked, enjoying a small moment of revenge.

"Yes, in the main, this is what was stated," replied Gudni sarcastically. He clasped his hands and leaned forward. "To summarize the police report, I understand the sequence of events to have been as follows," he said, looking at Markús. "Late on the evening of 22 January 1973, Alda Thorgeirsdóttir contacted you and asked you to get rid of a box for her. You had a crush on Alda, who was by far the prettiest girl in the Islands, so you took the box without any further discussion. You brought it to your own basement, thinking you could hide it better later. That didn't happen, since the eruption started that same night and you were woken by your parents and put on board a ship that sailed with you, your mother and your siblings to the mainland. On the boat you met Alda again, and when she asked whether you'd got rid of the box and where you'd put it, you told her the truth; the box had been left in the basement in the rush. You didn't ask Alda what was in the box, since you didn't want to displease her, her being so pretty, et cetera." Gudni grinned at Markús, who reddened. "Then nothing happened for around thirty years, until the Pompeii of the North project made the news and Alda contacted you. She implored you to prevent the house from being dug up from the ashes, because of the box that was there, and you still didn't ask her what was in it. Maybe you've still got a crush on her?"

Markús blushed again. "No, it's not that. It just didn't come up in our conversations."

"Never mind," said Gudni, and continued with his summary. "In the end it was agreed that you would get to go down to the basement and take from there whatever you wished, and when she heard the news Alda calmed down. You planned to fetch the box and take it to her as requested. Then something happened: you finally decided in the basement that you wanted to know what was in the box, and out rolled a dried-up severed head. At the very same moment, you clapped eyes for the first time on three corpses that were not there that fateful night."

"Actually, the head didn't roll out," replied Markús, looking oddly affronted. "I was so shocked when I saw what was in the box that I dropped it. Then the head fell out and bounced to the spot where it is now. It didn't roll. I actually think that I may have kicked it in my hurry to get out of there, but I'm not certain. Anyway, it stopped right next to the bodies and that's when I noticed them. I hadn't noticed them before, since it was dark down there."

Thóra interrupted Markús before he got any further with his description of the head's travels around the floor of the basement. "Well, I think it's best that you read this over, Markús, despite this fine summary by Gudni, and then we've got to get going. The police have other things to take care of in the light of your statement. I assume that you'll want to speak to this Alda, who appears to know more about the origins of the head than Markús does." She looked at the clock. If God and good fortune were with her there was still a chance that she'd catch the last flight home. It looked as if Markús would be cleared of all charges, even though the CID would probably want to speak to him later. She hoped Alda would verify his statement. If she didn't, then his position would worsen considerably, both regarding the head and the three corpses. But Alda would surely confirm his story and explain about the head. Thóra glanced at her watch out of the corner of her eye, and then at Markús. He was still working his way through the first page of the police report. She hoped her flight had been delayed.

Chapter 3

Tuesday, July 10, 2007

Some days in Thóra's life were slightly worse than others; on a bad day, for example, she would need to stop on her way to work to go back and turn off the coffeemaker, or she'd get a call from the school asking her to fetch her daughter Sóley, who had got a bloody nose at break time. Other days were even worse: bills were overdue and the cash machine was broken, petrol got pumped into the family car which ran on diesel, and so on. On those days nothing went as it should, neither at home nor at the office. It was not yet noon when it became clear to Thóra that this was going to be one of those unfortunate days. It started with a long search for the car keys, which finally appeared in the mess in her son Gylfi's room. The refrigerator turned out to be nearly empty, and the bread that Thóra had planned to use for Sóley's lunch was moldy. Thóra had wanted to go shopping on the way home from the airport the night before, but the plane from the Islands landed so late that the shops were closed. Things were no better at the office, where everything was topsy-turvy: the computer system was down because of "router upgrades" by the Internet service provider, and there was no phone connection because an overzealous electrician who had been making repairs on their floor had accidentally fiddled with a wire that he ought to have left untouched. So for the greater part of the morning they had no connection to the outside world apart from their mobile phones. This upset the secretary, Bella, who refused to use her mobile phone for office work since the office didn't pay her phone bill. Bragi, Thóra's business partner, had lent her his mobile with desperation in his eyes. God only knew how the girl would treat callers, since she was not known for her amiable disposition.

As soon as the telephone connection was restored, Markús rang. After exchanging pleasantries, he got to the point.

"Alda isn't answering my calls," he said. She could hear the anxiety in his voice.

"You weren't supposed to try to contact her until the police had finished questioning her, Markús. It could look as though you were trying to influence her testimony, and that's the last thing we want." Thóra knew full well that he wanted to make sure the woman would verify his story, but she doubted that a phone call from him would change Alda's testimony. She would either tell the truth, or lie to save her own skin. And when the chips were down, most people chose self-preservation.

"But it's so strange," said Markús. "We've had quite a lot of contact recently and she's almost always answered as soon as the phone rings. Even when she doesn't answer right away, she generally calls me back pretty much immediately. She's never ignored me like this." He hesitated for a moment before continuing: "Maybe she's avoiding me because she doesn't want to back up my story. What do you think?"

Thóra was fairly certain he was right, but didn't want to worry him even more. Of course there could be another explanation, but it seemed unlikely. "I think we should keep calm until we know something for sure." She looked at the clock. "I imagine that the police have already contacted her, although they probably haven't questioned her yet. If she doesn't substantiate your story then they'll call you back in, and you have the right to have me there to support you. They will want to talk to you again, whether she verifies your statement or not, so you should just keep calm if they contact you."

Markús took a deep breath. "Alda wouldn't throw me to the lions."

"I'm sure you're right," replied Thóra, thinking that Androcles had probably said the same thing about the Romans in the old days, right before he was shoved out into the arena. "Of course, I could phone our friend Gudni and try to find out what's going on.

There's no guarantee he'll tell me anything, but in the light of his dislike for formal procedures, you never know—he might let me in on something."

"Do you think he's still in charge of the case?" asked Markús hopefully. "I could always phone him myself."

"No, absolutely not," Thóra said quickly. "I don't want you speaking to him on your own. God only knows how that would end. I'll talk to him. Even though the police in Reykjavík are involved in the investigation, they'll certainly keep him informed of any developments. It's his home ground."

"Shouldn't I keep trying to get hold of Alda in the meantime?" said Markús.

"You should forget about that," replied Thóra firmly. She thought for a moment, then asked: "When did you last speak to her?"

"I spoke to her briefly by phone the evening before last," answered Markús. "The night before we went to the Islands. I told her that I was finally going to be allowed into the house."

"I see," said Thóra. "One final question before I phone Inspector Leifsson: do you think that Alda knew about these three corpses, or played any part in their deaths or the death of whoever owned the head?" Thóra wasn't sure she'd ever asked a more ridiculous question.

"There's no way," said Markús. "We're the same age—making her fifteen in the year of the eruption. She wouldn't hurt a fly. Neither then nor now. So she could hardly have expected that I'd stumble onto three corpses as well as the box in the basement. If she'd known about the bodies or been connected to them in any way I'm sure she would have pushed me even harder to have the excavation stopped. Warned me, at the very least."

"Yes, one would have thought so," Thóra said thoughtfully. "It's just a bit of a coincidence that a box with a severed head and three corpses should be found in the same place."

"Well, stranger things have happened," said Markús, seemingly insulted.

"Are you sure?" Thóra retorted. She could think of nothing even remotely as bizarre. They said good-bye and she went to get herself a cup of coffee. She could use a bit of refreshment before phoning Inspector Leifsson.

Gudni Leifsson turned off his flashlight as he went down into the basement. The lights that the Reykjavík CID had set up there were pointed at the area where the bodies had been found, but were strong enough to light the entire basement space. He went over to the man leading the investigation, a discomfortingly young man who had introduced himself as Stefán when the gang of police from Reykjavík had disembarked from the little plane late yesterday evening. It was obviously time to retire. It was happening far too frequently that he met colleagues who had still been in their mothers' wombs when he himself had started his career. Gudni stared straight ahead. "What do you think?" he asked calmly, without wasting words on pleasantries or even looking at his colleague.

Stefán turned around to see who had addressed him. His expression immediately changed to one of irritation, which confirmed what Gudni already knew: the policemen from Reykjavík wanted the country yokels to leave them alone to investigate the scene in peace. This Stefán had scarcely deigned to listen to Gudni's account of recent developments as they were driving to the house yesterday evening along with several nameless, even younger men. These accompanying officers had not spoken a word the entire time, as far as Gudni had been aware. "Isn't it a little better than it looked at first?" he asked now, not letting the young man's irritation trouble him.

"We don't know anything yet," Stefán replied, turning away from Gudni to watch the men working. "How could this possibly be better than it looked?"

"Well," said Gudni calmly, "I just wondered whether these might be the earthly remains of some unlucky thieves who got trapped here in the eruption and suffocated. People who had perhaps intended to take advantage of the emergency situation and do their looting undisturbed. This house wasn't buried under the ash the first night, so unscrupulous individuals would have had time to come here from elsewhere and make a clean sweep of the neighborhood. The eruption made worldwide headlines at the time."

Stefán stared at Gudni. "You can't be serious," he said, pointing at the three corpses where they lay, side by side, on their backs. "How do you see that happening? The air became so bad that the burglars ran down to the basement to lie down and take a breather? They could hardly have thought that there were any valuables down here." He turned back to his subordinates' work. "People who suffocate are generally found lying on their stomachs, unless they were sleeping when it happened. They try to crawl away. They don't lie down nicely in a row, any more than their heads fly off their shoulders." He pointed at the place where the head had lain, but it had already been removed from the scene.

"You'll discover one day that there are no absolutes in this life," Gudni replied, perfectly unperturbed. This wasn't the first big city upstart he'd sparred with. "Otherwise, hopefully this Alda has an explanation, at least as far as the head is concerned. Have you spoken to her?"

"As far as I know, no one's been able to get in touch with her," replied Stefán, without looking at Gudni. "We're going to keep trying, and hopefully we'll reach her today. Then I'll have a better talk with this Markús Magnússon, who came here to pick up the bonce."

"The head, I expect you mean," corrected Gudni. "We're talking about a human head here—not a 'bonce.'"

Stefán shot Gudni a look that was anything but pleasant. "Head, bonce, noggin—what difference does it make? I very much doubt that this Markús has told the truth, the whole truth and nothing but the truth about what happened here. I find his statement in the report both untrustworthy and ridiculous."

"That's because he's an imbecile," Gudni replied. "Always has been." He switched on his flashlight and turned toward the stairs, without saying good-bye.

Dís honked the car horn and pulled herself up over the steering wheel to look out through the windscreen. The little end terrace appeared to be empty. She leaned back again in her seat. What was Alda thinking? She hadn't come to work for two days in a row. There was nothing too mysterious about that, anyone could catch the flu, but it was unlike her not to call in and let people know, or to answer messages. Alda was conscientiousness personified; she always came to work on time, and was always willing to work late if necessary. In a nurse this was a rare quality, and Dís knew that without Alda she and Ágúst would have it much tougher at work. They paid her well, and up until yesterday her work record had been spotless. So they couldn't understand at all why she hadn't called in to let them know that she couldn't make it yesterday morning, especially since four operations had been scheduled. Dís and Ágúst, both doctors, had had to assist each other, performing the operations together instead of taking them separately with Alda's assistance. Because of this they'd had to cancel a number of patient consultations, and even the anesthetist they'd called in had had to help out, which was bad for their reputation. No, there was something very peculiar about this, so Dís had decided to make a quick trip to Alda's house during her lunch break, to see if she was home. She looked out again through the glass and wondered whether something could have happened to the woman. Alda was single and childless, so it was entirely possible that she had passed out at home without anyone knowing. Dís got out of the car.

She walked up to the garage that connected Alda's terrace house to the next one and peered in through a gap in the brown-lacquered door. She thought she saw a reflection from Alda's new green Toyota, but could not see it clearly enough to be sure. Nevertheless, this was a bad omen. Alda could hardly have got very far without her car, and if she was at home it was extremely odd that she hadn't contacted anyone. Dís went to the front door of the house. The sound of the doorbell came from within as she rang it repeatedly. She stopped pushing it and put her ear to the door in the hope of hearing Alda, but could not make out any audible sign of human activity. Still, she was fairly certain that she could hear a radio. She pressed her ear even closer to the door and covered the other one. Yes, yes. She could even hear the tune. It was an old cheesy pop song, about a boy calling out to his father. Dís straightened up and knitted her brow. It occurred to her how strange it was that even after working with Alda for seven years, she had no clue as to what sort of music she liked. Somehow it had never come up in conversation. She grabbed the doorknob and tried the door. It was unlocked.

"Alda!" she called through the doorway. No answer—only the

melancholy voice of the now-forgotten singer, asking his father to wait for him. Dís pushed on the door until it opened fully. She went in and called out again: "Alda! Are you home?" No answer. The song finished, but started again several seconds later. It must have been on a CD, with the CD player set to repeat. Radio stations hadn't yet stooped to playing the same song over and over again. Dís walked slowly up the stairs to the first floor. If Alda had been taken ill, she was most likely to be in her bedroom upstairs. Dís had only been to the house once, when Alda had invited her and Ágúst, along with their spouses, to dinner earlier in the year, and then they hadn't left the ground floor. The dinner had been impeccable, as expected: good food and delicious wine, everything very tastefully presented. Dís recalled how amazed she'd been that Alda hadn't been in a steady relationship since her divorce, which had actually been over and done with by the time she'd started working at the plastic surgeon's office. She was a particularly pleasant woman, approaching fifty; she had kept herself in good shape and was warm, cheerful and courteous. Dís called Alda's name one more time before climbing the stairs. No answer. The music, on the other hand, became clearer with every step. She walked as quietly as she could, hoping that Alda would be lying there asleep with the melancholy music playing.

The singer's emotional voice came through the half-open door. Dís repeated Alda's name, more softly. She didn't want to startle the woman if she was simply sleeping, or even getting dressed. Through the gap in the doorway she could see the sun shining on a corner of the embroidered bedspread. Dís pushed the door with one foot and put her hand over her mouth as she looked into the master bedroom. The music was coming from the CD player on the bedside table, and next to it was an empty wine bottle, an open prescription bottle and a syringe. In the middle of the bed lay Alda. Dís didn't need her medical degree to realize that there was little use in trying to resuscitate her.

Chapter 4

Tuesday, July 10, 2007

Thóra leaned back in her chair and sighed, trying to decide who to ask to pick up her daughter Sóley—for the second day in a row. Her mother was out of the question. She had helped out the previous evening when Thóra had been delayed in the Westmann Islands, and besides that, her parents were on their way to the theater. She would never hear the end of it if her mother missed the play she'd been looking forward to for months. It was some sort of drama-tized documentary about the injustices women suffer in the mod-ern world. Thóra smiled to herself. Her father would be eternally grateful if she rescued him from this theater trip, but she decided not to ruin their plans. Her mother's disappointment would last far longer than her father's gratitude.

She decided to call her ex-husband. Hannes would not be best pleased. The work of an emergency physician was no less demand-ing than that of a lawyer, and the days were longer and harder. He took the kids every other weekend and sometimes asked to have more time with them when it was convenient, but in general he was not receptive to taking them at short notice. Hannes had a new wife, and his life now revolved mainly around the two of them and their needs. Thóra's, on the other hand, revolved around everyone but herself; lately all of her time had been going into her work, her two children and her grandson, who had recently turned one. The grandchild actually came part and parcel with a fourth child—her daughter-in-law. Sigga was seventeen, a year younger than Thóra's son Gylfi, but there was not much difference between them in terms of maturity. Somehow the young parents had managed to keep their relationship going despite their belly flop into the deep end of adulthood. They stayed with Thóra every other week, and in between the girl went home to her parents with the little boy—without Gylfi. The relationship between Gylfi and Sigga's parents was a chilly one; they seemed unable to forgive him for their daughter's untimely pregnancy. This was no secret to anyone, least of all Gylfi, so Thóra was happy when he decided to stay at home while Sigga was with them. In this way she managed to keep her son to herself a little longer and continue with his upbringing, which had been cut short when he had accidentally increased the human population.

Thóra put the receiver under her chin and adjusted a framed photograph of her grandson as she selected the number. The little boy had been christened Orri, after countless other proposals by the young parents that still made Thóra shudder. He was irresistible; blond and big-eyed, and still with round, chubby cheeks even though he had long since stopped bottle-feeding. It warmed Thóra's heart to see him, and she was looking forward to taking care of him next week even though the household's stress levels increased perceptibly when mother and son were around. She smiled at the little boy in the photo and crossed her fingers when the phone was finally answered. "Hello, Hannes. Could you do me a small favor? I won't be able to pick up Sóley . . ."

The girl watched from the playground as the ambulance drove up to the house. She twisted in the swing and let it turn her back in a semicircle. She was happy that the sirens weren't on because if they were, that meant it was serious. Maybe the lady had just fallen down and broken her foot? Once her friend broke her foot and then an ambulance came to get her. Tinna puffed up her cheeks then let the air leak out while she thought about all of this. Fat cheeks. Skinny cheeks. Fat cheeks. Skinny cheeks. She stopped playing bellows with her cheeks and sat deep in thought. Here was proof that you didn't need to eat to become fat. Air could make you fat. She stiffened. Everything was full of air. It was everywhere, and there was nowhere to hide. She would have to try to breathe less.

A dull thud came from the ambulance and Tinna directed her attention back there. She was hoping that someone would come out of the house so that she could find out what had happened, but the bustle around the ambulance was better than nothing. The house was more interesting—maybe they'd arrested a criminal inside, but the walls blocked her view. If they were thin walls maybe she could see through them, just as it would be possible one day to see through her. She squinted in the hope of seeing better, but it didn't help. Yet something was going on: the first police car to arrive had had its sirens on. No police car had come when her friend broke her foot in the school playground, so it was unlikely that they'd come to the lady's house because of an accident. If it was a robbery, then Tinna hoped that the police would put the robber in jail. She was a nice lady who didn't deserve anything bad to happen to her. The swing creaked. The girl watched as two men stepped out of the ambulance and took a stretcher from the back. She sighed. This wasn't good. When was she going to meet the lady now? Maybe she'd be in the hospital for a long time. Last time Tinna went to the hospital she didn't get to go home for forty days. But that didn't change anything. This could always wait. She'd often waited longer than a few months for something. For things that were really important.

Tinna stood up on her swing to get a better view. She held on tight, dizzy from standing up so quickly. When she closed her eyes the unpleasant feeling passed, as always. She reminded herself that it was a good sign to get dizzy, it was almost equal to passing out and that meant the body was burning fat. When Tinna opened her eyes again the men with the stretcher had gone into the house and there was no movement to be seen outside it. The ambulance was parked right in front of the house, blocking her view of the door. She stretched herself as high as she could, trying to see if the door was open, but with no luck. Should she go home or wait for the lady to be carried out? She was in no rush to go home; no one was there, her mother worked until five and didn't get any break even though it was a staff day at Tinna's school. There was nothing waiting for her at home.

She bent her knees and swung standing up, without particularly intending to do so. It was good to feel the air playing through her hair and she sped up a bit, only to slow down immediately when she remembered that the air was not her friend. Her heart pounded in her chest as she tried to settle the swing. As soon as it stopped she felt immediately better, and wondered what she should say to the lady, how she could put into words that she knew who she was for real. Tinna smiled to herself. The lady would be surprised and was sure to be happy, too. It was still stuck in her memory how sad the lady had been when her father had reacted so terribly to what she was trying to tell him. Her dad was a real idiot. A grumpy, drunken idiot who didn't understand Tinna, any more than her mother did. She was a lot worse, talking constantly about food, food, food and how Tinna had to eat, and sometimes she even cried. So Tinna always preferred to go to her father's every other weekend because he didn't expect anything from her. He told her she ought to eat but then didn't pay any more attention to whether she did or not, unlike her mother. That was fine by her. Her dad was so uninterested in Tinna that he hadn't even caught on that she'd heard everything that had passed between him and the lady the night she came to visit. Tinna had let herself in without her father or the visitor being aware of it, and the anger in her dad's voice made her even keener not to draw attention to herself. She knew how to make herself inconspicuous, especially since that was her goal: in the end, she would become invisible. If she had already reached that goal she would have been able to step between them and watch the lines on their faces and their body language as they argued. But she wasn't quite that good yet, so she settled for sneaking to the sitting-room door and listening in on their conversation. When they finished she went out again and pretended to be arriving just as the lady was leaving the house. Her father was unusually sulky when he let her in, but she acted as if nothing were wrong and in the end he returned to normal, not caring about anything but the game on television.

The lady had no more idea than her father that Tinna had listened in; perhaps she had no idea at all that she even existed. Unlike Tinna's father, however, she would be happy to discover that Tinna had heard what had passed between them and would no doubt want to get to know her better. Tinna had got her name and telephone number from a note that she'd left behind on the table for Tinna's father, so that he could contact her later. That had turned out to be a work of patience since her dad had torn the paper to pieces and thrown them on the floor, so Tinna had to piece together the tatters just to be able to read what was written there. Once she had the woman's name and telephone number it was easy to find her address. Tinna had sometimes come here just to watch the house without particularly knowing why or what she was hoping to find. The evening before, things had finally been different, and Tinna had watched with great interest. In fact little had actually happened, but maybe all would be explained later. She thought about the note that had blown away on the wind and got stuck in the shrubbery. Tinna had taken it and hidden it at home. It mattered. She knew that for sure—just not why or how. But it would come to light someday.

She sat back down in the swing and hooked her delicate elbows around the brown chains. The smell of iron on her palms reminded her of last summer, when she had tried to swing right over the bar, certain that by doing so she would burn a thousand calories. She still had an ugly scar on her right foot after the attempt failed miserably. The air then hadn't made her fatter, but thinner. It made it all so difficult—the rules kept changing, and Tinna had to be constantly on the lookout if she didn't want to become fat, fatter, fattest.

She pricked up her ears as the sound of men's voices came from across the street. She stood up again in the swing to see if the woman would be carried into the ambulance, but was careful in case she got dizzy and fell off. She didn't want to miss this. First a policeman appeared, walked ahead of the paramedics and opened the door to the ambulance. They followed with the stretcher, and the girl stiffened. She squinted and shook herself. Maybe there was an explanation for this? Maybe the woman was ill and they didn't want her to get cold? She jumped from the swing and ran over to the pavement. The policeman who stood there holding open the back door of the ambulance noticed her and waved her away. "There's nothing to see here. Go home," he called.

Tinna didn't answer. In general she was afraid of male authority figures, whether they were doctors, headmasters, bus drivers, or others who wanted to boss her around in some way. Now, however, she felt as if the policeman was not actually there, had nothing to do with her. It was almost as if he were a 3D image on a screen, less real than the paramedics she was staring at. Tinna stood openmouthed, her eyes glued to the white blanket covering the woman on the stretcher. She didn't move. The woman didn't have a cold. She was dead, and with her Tinna's hope of another, better life in which she was beautiful and adored. The woman could make people beautiful. She had said so. Tinna turned on her heel and ran away, without thinking where she was going. If she ran fast enough she could maybe go faster than her thoughts, and get rid of the uncomfortable idea that her father might have done the woman some harm. It would not have been the first time. Or else it had been the visitor who had snuck out of the house, the one whose note it was. Tinna pushed everything from her mind except for the thought that she was now burning calories. Burn, burn, burn.

"Dead, you say," repeated Gudni, frowning thoughtfully. He closed his eyes and rubbed his forehead. His interlocutor was on the phone, so he didn't need to hold his expressions in check, although he had been taught at the start of his career to remain as poker-faced as possible, and never to give any indication of his thoughts. For Gudni this had never proven to be especially difficult, but sometimes it was still good to be able to sit alone and allow disappointment, or more rarely, happiness, to find its natural outlet. "How did she die?"

"The autopsy hasn't been done but it looks as if she committed suicide," replied Stefán. It wasn't possible to tell from his voice whether he thought this tiresome or tragic, or indeed whether it affected him at all. Perhaps such things were bread and butter for the police in Reykjavík. "We'll find out tomorrow, I suppose. I just heard and thought I should let you know. I obviously didn't go to the scene myself, so I don't know anything more at the moment. I'm leaving tomorrow and then hopefully I'll get some more news."

"Where was she found?" Gudni asked. He would not have considered Alda likely to resort to such desperate measures, but then again he had only known her as a child and a teenager. She had had everything going for her then, both beauty and intelligence.

Naturally, though, things could have changed, and perhaps her life had taken a turn for the worse. He hoped this was not the case, but if it turned out to be so, he sincerely hoped that her fate was not tied to events in the Islands long past.

"At home," said Stefán. "Her colleague found her, I understand. Went to find out why she hadn't shown up at work."

"This muddies the waters of the basement case quite a bit," Gudni said. He paused for a moment before adding: "Not least because Alda now can't verify Markús's statement."

"No," came the curt reply. "We didn't get a chance to question her. We couldn't reach her, but when the time of death becomes clear, we might wonder whether she was trying to escape questioning."

"If that were so then one would expect her to have left behind a note, or something that would clear Markús of all suspicion," said Gudni. "It would be cruel to let him take the blame if she had dirty laundry to hide. They were good friends, I understand, and it must have been clear to her that she alone could have confirmed his story. Is it possible she knew nothing about his statement and the discovery of the bodies?"

"I have no idea," snapped Stefán. "I've always tried to avoid filling in the blanks with speculation at the start of an investigation. We don't even know the cause of death. As it is, she appears to have died by her own hand, but who knows, maybe it was something entirely different—an accident, or even worse. Tomorrow we'll search her house, and who knows what we'll find."

"Hopefully not more bodies," said Gudni. "Unless maybe we find the torso that goes with the head." He smiled. "Don't forget to go down to the basement." He hung up and stared at the phone on the table. None of this made any sense.

Thóra put down the bag of groceries and fumbled for her mobile phone. The ring tone was muffled and she tried to remember whether she had put the phone in the right or left pocket of her jacket, or stuck it in her handbag. She finally found it in her left pocket, among coins and old VISA receipts. She saw Markús's number on the screen and decided not to answer. He could wait until morning. She set the phone on the table and started to put away the food that she'd bought on the way home. Hannes would arrive shortly with Sóley; he had come to Thóra's rescue, even responding cheerfully to her request and offering to take their daughter swimming. She hoped that this was the shape of things to come: that her relationship with her ex was finally starting to take a friendlier, more relaxed form.

Her phone bleeped. Instead of picking it up and reading the text message, Thóra finished putting away the groceries and turned on the oven. She read the directions on the frozen lasagne package and threw it into the cold oven, contrary to the manufacturer's recommendation. Ultimately it all ended up the same: the food would be warm whether she put it into a preheated oven or a cold one. Then she took her phone, went into the sitting room and threw herself onto the sofa. The message was from Markús. *"Alda is dead. The police want to meet me tomorrow. Please call me."*

Thóra groaned. It looked like Markús would be her client for a little longer. She sat up and dialed his number. He was either the unluckiest man in the country, or something else, something far worse, was behind all of this.

Chapter 5

Wednesday, July 11, 2007

Markús dragged his hands frantically through his hair. This was not the first time that Thóra had sat in her office with a desperate client, so she knew how to deal with it. It was of little use to tell him everything would be all right, that he needn't have any worries, this would soon be finished, and so on. Such talk was often far from the truth and only postponed the inevitable. They had just come from being questioned by the police, which could have gone worse, but it could also have gone better. Markús had responded frostily when they'd requested biological samples from him, but in the end he calmed down and gave the police samples of both saliva and hair.

"The positive side of this, Markús, is that they asked you very little about your previous relations with this Alda. Either they think her death occurred naturally, or else they don't suspect you of having caused it." She looked at him sternly. "The negative side, on the other hand, is that now Alda cannot substantiate your explanation of the head in the box."

"You don't say," growled Markús.

Thóra paid no heed to his sarcasm. "Are you absolutely certain that you two never discussed this by email or in others' hearing? For instance, your co-workers?"

Markús managed a company that dealt in components for ship engines and machinery, and although Thóra did not understand anything about how such businesses worked, she knew it was going well and that he had several people working for him. They seemed to be very conscientious employees, because Markús appeared to be anything but indispensable, and had never had to postpone or cancel a meeting with Thóra or anyone else involved in the case because of work.

"No one heard anything," answered Markús determinedly. "Alda and I spoke mainly by phone and I do that in private. We met fairly irregularly, almost never with anyone else present, and we didn't discuss this topic in the few instances when there were others around. And I only use email for work. I'm not one of those people who gets emails with jokes or pictures of kittens."

It had never crossed Thóra's mind that he was. "And there were no witnesses to your conversations?"

Markús shook his head, disgruntled. "No."

"When you told the police that Alda had rung you the night before we went to the Islands, they were extremely excited. Considering how much they asked you about that telephone call, it must have occurred shortly before she died." Thóra flicked through the copy of Markús's statement that she'd been given following the questioning. "You said that Alda had sounded peculiar, was unusually bad-tempered and distracted, and you'd thought she'd either been anxious about your visit to the basement the next morning or that someone was with her, making it impossible for her to speak freely with you. Besides that, you were driving, so you weren't able to speak to her for very long."

"I just got that feeling. She didn't say anything to suggest that there was someone with her—it just sounded a bit as if there was."

"The reason I'm asking is that perhaps someone overheard this final conversation of yours and could confirm she'd mentioned your visit to the basement. That could help us, especially if she mentioned the box and said something about having given it to you." Thóra smiled encouragingly at Markús.

He scowled. "Of course I don't remember the conversation in detail, but I'm fairly sure she didn't say any such thing. She asked me not to mess this up and said that I should take a bag with me in case the box had rotted." He shuddered. "She could have given me a better idea of what it was that I was going down there to get. I don't know how she ever thought I could put the head in a bag and walk out of there with it as if nothing had ever happened. I wouldn't have even been able to touch it."

"Considering how much you'd done for her already, without asking any questions, she doubtless thought you'd just continue in the same vein," replied Thóra.

"I was just a kid," said Markús heavily. "Things have changed since then." He straightened up in his chair, and she could not deny that he did not look like anyone's fool. He undeniably possessed a degree of masculine charm. His face was anything but delicate, its strong lines almost coarse. Thóra suspected that he dyed his hair, since there was not a single gray to be seen even though he was nearly fifty years old. This suggested he was preoccupied with his appearance, which fitted with the impeccable and obviously expensive clothing he always wore.

"Yes, I understand that," Thóra said. "But maybe she hadn't actually ever realized it." She put down the report. "I'm going to ask the police department if they have any information about whether Alda had visitors that night. Maybe we'll be lucky." She looked at Markús. "Of course the fact remains that you say you didn't know about the corpses down there. What are we supposed to do about that?" She leaned back in her chair. "The only person who objected when they were going to excavate the house was you. One would assume that whoever put the bodies there would have tried to prevent the excavation in one way or another." She thought carefully about how to phrase what came next. "It's my understanding that your parents are still alive. Could one of them have encouraged you in your efforts to block the excavation?"

Markús stared silently at Thóra for a moment. "If you're suggesting that they had something to do with this, you're out of your mind."

"You didn't answer my question," Thóra said calmly. "Did they encourage you or not?"

Markús smiled bitterly. "My father has Alzheimer's. He's in no shape either to encourage or discourage anyone. Mum, on the other hand, has all her spark plugs firing, and her feelings about the excavation were the opposite of mine. She was even really excited about it. She was hoping to recover some fine dinnerware from the house. Even though Dad had managed to get most of what we owned out of the house before it disappeared, he still left quite a few things behind. He hadn't given much thought to the dinnerware."

Thóra nodded. The man had no doubt put a lot of effort into saving the home's stereo system and such like. Of course, Markús's mother's excitement about the excavation did not rule out her husband as a suspect; he could very well have put the bodies there without his wife knowing. "Someone put the bodies there, that much is certain. Does anyone come to mind?"

Markús shook his head. "I don't actually remember every single person who lived on the Islands at that time, but it's completely ridiculous to think that any of the people I do remember could have killed those three. Everyone here was normal; just your typical Icelandic fishermen's families." Markús started running his hands through his hair again. "My best memories are of my friends, and naturally they were all just dumb kids like me."

"Are you absolutely certain your father couldn't have had something to do with this?" asked Thóra. "It was at your home, and I find it unlikely that someone would have broken in there to hide bodies."

"Broken in?" echoed Markús. "They wouldn't have needed to break in. It was all unlocked. People were asked to leave their houses open so that the rescue crews could go in and out of them as they needed." He brightened. "Naturally, the place filled up with people arriving from the mainland after the night of the eruption. I don't know any figures, but the rescue crews needed a lot of manpower and the majority of those who lent a hand weren't from the Islands. Our house wasn't buried immediately."

Thóra considered this for a moment. "So you think it more likely that one of those people put the bodies there?"

Markús shrugged. "What do I know? The only thing that's completely clear to me is that I had nothing to do with it."

Thóra hoped that this was indeed the case. It was always more comfortable to fight for a just cause. "We might be getting ahead of ourselves with this kind of speculation. We should wait for the results of the forensic autopsy on the bodies and head." She smiled weakly at Markús. How was an autopsy performed on a head? "Who knows, maybe these people simply died of natural causes or suffocated in the basement. Wasn't that what happened in the only death to occur during the eruption?"

"No one died in the eruption," said Markús angrily, almost as if he were defending the eruption's good name.

"Really?" said Thóra. "I always thought that one person died. And in a basement, no less."

"Oh, him," said Markús. "That doesn't count. He was an alcoholic."

The confused look on Thóra's face forced him to explain this a little better. "He went down into the pharmacy basement looking for spirits. The eruption had nothing to do with it."

Except that the poison gases which killed him came from the eruption—but Thóra had no desire to waste time explaining this. She picked up the report again and leafed through it. "This is odd. Am I right in thinking that you've never been asked whether you thought you'd seen any of the dead people before?"

Markús jerked his head to one side in surprise. "They didn't ask me that because the bodies are hardly in a condition for anyone to be able to identify them. And I couldn't really see very clearly there in the basement."

"In other words, you think you've never seen them before?" If it were possible to identify these people, it would be easier to determine what happened to them.

Markús shook his head slowly. "No, I'm almost sure I haven't," he said. "But as I said, it's possible that they're people I knew. I would have to be able to see them again under better conditions, although I doubt that would make any difference."

Thóra thought of the dried-out, dusty corpses and knew that it would be difficult to identify them except in the lab of a forensic pathologist.

"They must be foreigners. Even though there are cases of Icelanders vanishing without a trace, it's out of the question that three people disappeared at the same time without attracting attention." She hurriedly corrected herself: "Four, I mean." The head was still so unreal to her that she kept forgetting to count it along with the bodies. She thought for a moment. "Maybe they were sailors?" she asked. "They could have belonged to the crew of a wrecked ship."

"And how would that crew have ended up in our basement?" asked Markús, puzzled.

"Well, that's another question," said Thóra, and smiled at him. "We should wait for the autopsy. I suppose the police will call you in again for questioning after that, and after they've gone over the medical examiner's report. Until then I'll try to find some witnesses or anything else that could possibly support your statement about Alda and the box."

Markús stood up and snorted. "Like that's going to happen," he said sulkily as he left. "She was the only one who could possibly have backed me up."

Thóra tried unsuccessfully to look encouraging. This looked bad; the only hope of Markús getting off scot-free now was if it turned out that the people in the basement had suffocated. Again she had forgotten the head. How in the hell was it possible to explain that?

Stefán put down the phone, closed his eyes and counted to ten. He shook himself. "That was the medical examiner," he said to the policeman sitting across from him, and pinched himself to keep calm. "He doubts that Alda committed suicide. The autopsy revealed several details that need further explanation." He paused for a moment. "How could you possibly not have investigated anywhere but the bedroom? Are you completely useless when I'm not there?" He tapped the stack of papers on the table with his index finger for emphasis. The young officer reddened and Stefán wondered whether it was from shame or anger. He continued: "How did you leave the scene? Is the house marked in any way that would let the relatives of the deceased know they can't go roaming about in there, or did you just shut the door and drive away?"

"Uh," said the young police officer, his cheeks even redder.

"Uh," parroted Stefán. "What does 'uh' mean?"

"We didn't mark the house in any particular way," replied the young man. "It looked like suicide. I've seen several of them," he added, in a slightly more confident tone.

"Don't you get arrogant with me," hissed Stefán. "I couldn't care less whether you've seen three suicides or three thousand. It's this one particular incident I'm unhappy about, and I'm not about to listen to the medical examiner scold me for the working methods of my men." He took a moment to calm down. "According to him there are various things lacking: you took almost no photos of the scene and your report on the search of the house doesn't cover any other room but the bedroom. What's more, he says that blood is never mentioned in the report, even though the corpse's injuries suggest there must have been blood present."

"There was blood," muttered the young officer, his own face bloodred. "There were small pools on both sides of the head, from injuries to the woman's cheeks and neck."

"Oh, now you decide to tell us?" hissed Stefán loudly. "You maybe want me to fix the report for you? Something like that was certainly supposed to go in it! I'm so bloody amazed, I'm almost speechless." Various words could be used to describe Stefán's state at that moment, but "speechless" was not one of them.

"We were told that the woman's injuries were self-inflicted. I think there was blood and skin under her nails." The young man straightened up. "I want it put on record that the doctor who came with the ambulance ruled this a suicide at the scene. It was also him who deduced this about the blood, and that's why I didn't feel there was any reason to write it down in the report. We proceeded with our work under the conviction that this was a suicide, since there was nothing to suggest otherwise." He looked curiously at his boss. "What exactly was discovered in the autopsy?"

Stefán scowled. "It appears she didn't die of poisoning. The doctor tested her blood and stomach contents for the active ingredient in the drugs found on the bedside table. It wasn't present in any life-threatening amount."

The young officer raised his eyebrows. "Then how did she die?"

Stefán had calmed down completely. He was relieved to hear that a doctor had declared it a suicide at the scene, since this mostly cleared his men of any blame for ruining the case. "Of course it'll probably be necessary to conduct further tests before it's possible to confirm it, but the doctor thought it most likely that the woman suffocated."

"Suffocated?" echoed the young police officer. "Choked?"

Stefán shook his head. "It's still uncertain. The examiner hasn't ruled out illness as the cause, but he says he wants the home of the deceased searched better in order to determine whether a person or persons unknown might have played a part in her death."

"I see," said the young man, utterly relieved that Stefán's disposition appeared to have returned to normal. "Our shift is finishing—do you want us to go back there first thing in the morning, or . . . ?"

Stefán's eyes narrowed. "No. You'll go now. Immediately." He dared the young man to object by staring directly into his eyes. "You'll go over every square centimeter and then write a detailed report, as if you were investigating a murder scene. I want a copy of the report waiting for me on my desk tomorrow morning." He waved his hand at the door. "I would hurry up if I were you, before your colleagues go home—and you're left in the lurch." The younger man opened his mouth as if to object, but stopped. He walked to the door. When he was standing in the doorway, Stefán added: "Take note of all the calls to or from her home phone and her mobile. Since she probably died on the Sunday evening, calls from that particular time are naturally the most important."

"Will do," replied the young man, with a touch of bitterness in his voice. What a fucking mess. He was tired after a long day and completely ready to throw himself onto the sofa and stare at the television. It wasn't an attractive thought, having to comb through an entire house in search of God knows what.

"One other thing," called Stefán as the door was closing.

"Sir?" The young man stuck his head back through the doorway.

"I am particularly interested in knowing whether Alda called the mobile phone of Markús Magnússon that same night, and how long the phone call lasted. Understand?"

"Understood."

The door closed. Stefán stared at it and thought things over. He knew that he should call his colleague in the Westmann Islands and inform him of these developments, but he really had no desire to do so. It could wait. He was going to go down to the National Hospital, meet the examiner, and have a look at Alda's body. He stood up. He had to admit it wasn't just because of his job that he wanted to go there: the examiner had mentioned that the woman had been rather significantly enhanced—a word Stefán couldn't understand until he got a better explanation for it. Stefán's wife was always complaining that she wanted to get breast enhancements, so he wanted to see some for himself. Who knew, maybe he would give her the green light if he liked what he saw.

Chapter 6

Saturday, July 14, 2007

The only guests at the prizegiving that Saturday morning were the children who had won and their parents. Sóley sat between her mother and her brother Gylfi, smiling broadly. The competition had been part of the Arts Week at the City Library and involved drawing pictures of home appliances that made a family's life easier, and Sóley had spent an entire afternoon conscientiously drawing and coloring. To Thóra's great surprise her daughter had won; up until that point Sóley had displayed limited talent in the arts. The girl who had won in the oldest age group walked back to her seat with a little bouquet and a check from the sponsors of the competition, one of the largest electrical equipment companies in the country. The city librarian called Sóley, who took her place next to the woman, red-cheeked.

"Congratulations on your victory," said the librarian, taking Sóley's small hand. She pointed at the girl's picture, which was hanging in a special display along with the other illustrations that had been entered in the competition. There were actually not very many of them, just as Thóra had suspected when she received the news that Sóley had won. "I have to say, this is a very artistically drawn picture of a steam iron that you've done," said the librarian as she handed Sóley a large envelope and bouquet.

Thóra knitted her brow. Why had Sóley drawn a picture of an iron? Her ex-husband had taken it with him when they separated, because none of Thóra's clothing required ironing. She doubted that Sóley knew what it looked like, but it seemed she'd done a decent job even without a model. Thóra looked proudly from the picture to her daughter, whose cheeks were even redder than before as she stood there next to the librarian with the prize in her arms, staring at her toes. Sóley seemed on the verge of tears, but she clenched her teeth.

"It's a snowmobile. Not a steam iron," said Sóley, chewing her bottom lip.

Now it was the librarian's turn to blush slightly, but to Thóra's great relief she resolved the problem successfully by saying that she'd misread her notes. On the other hand, Gylfi's burst of laughter did not help, and as they stood there afterward in front of the picture he continued to giggle.

"It looks exactly like an iron," he said. "How did you ever get the idea of drawing a snowmobile? Do you think it's a household appliance?"

Thóra leaped to her daughter's rescue. "Of course it is. In the countryside snowmobiles count as home appliances." She tightened her grip on her daughter's hand, while Sóley hung her head. "Don't listen to him. He has no idea what snowmobiles look like." The same actually went for Sóley. "I'm going to buy you ice cream in honor of your win." She looked from the snowmobile to the other pictures. "Sóley. Yours is by far the most beautiful. Stands head and shoulders above the rest."

"No, it's ugly," said the child. "I should have drawn a door, like I was going to at first."

Thóra realized that she would have to explain to her daughter at a better time what the words household appliance meant. "There there," she said. "You won and that was no accident. You drew the most beautiful picture. Steam iron and snowmobile both start with the letter 's.' That's why the woman got mixed up." She kissed Sóley on the cheek and gave her son the evil eye, since he appeared to be on the verge of bursting into laughter again. "Do me a favor and find me a book about the eruption in the Westmann Islands," she said to him. This would get Gylfi thinking about something other than the snowmobile-steam iron and she would benefit from reading up on the events of 1973, which she actually knew very little about. While he went to find the book Thóra used the opportunity to cheer up her daughter, although she didn't actually smile until they were sitting down with huge glasses full of ice cream with whipped cream on top. Thóra's mobile phone rang just as she was finishing her ice cream, but she decided not to answer for fear the world would crumble around her daughter. She changed her mind when she saw on the screen that it was Markús calling. His world truly was crumbling around him, and ice cream would do very little to improve his situation.

Thóra hung up on Bragi, her partner in the legal firm, and sighed. She was exhausted after a long day, which had gone differently than she'd planned. Markús had been called in for yet another round of questioning, now under suspicion of involvement in the untimely death of Alda and of being party to the death of the people in the basement. The phone call from Markús had been urgent, so Thóra ended up at the police station after finishing her ice cream, instead of going to the cinema or doing something else with her children. She had had to listen to the same questions put to her client as in the previous interviews, along with a few additional questions about Alda. They all concerned whether he had been at her home on the Sunday evening when she was thought to have died. Markús had denied this and stuck to his story that they had only spoken on the phone. At first he absolutely denied having gone to her house for weeks, but later admitted that he had in fact been there—not on the night they were asking about, but the night before. He had stopped there for a short time and had a glass of wine.

Thóra felt like screaming when Markús let this slip. She was disappointed in him, mainly for trying to keep quiet about his visit, especially since his meeting with Alda had occurred outside the time in which the police were interested. As such, this only increased their suspicion toward him. Thóra thought it likely that he'd been so stubborn about not admitting his visit because he feared being charged with drunk driving. This was not unusual—many people hid insignificant details from the police if they involved illegal actions, and tended to focus on keeping them secret even if they were suspected of much more serious crimes. The police's attempts to tie Markús to a murder didn't seem to bother him, but he was like a cat on a hot tin roof when attention turned to his possible motor vehicle violation. He was obviously clinging to the childish belief that in the end his name would be cleared of the murders without his needing to put any great effort into it.

When the police came to the end of their list of questions concerning Markús's visit to Alda, Thóra felt that the interrogation had run out of steam and that Markús had withstood the worst of it. She was wrong. Markús responded furiously when the police eventually said they wanted to question his closest relatives. For a time Thóra thought that Markús's protests would end with his being arrested, but she was finally able to calm him down before it came to a scuffle. After leaving the office Thóra pressed him on the cause of this violent reaction: he said that he was worried about his elderly parents, although they probably weren't the only ones who would be called in for questioning; the police also wanted to speak to his older brother, Leifur, who ran the family's fishing company in the Islands. Markús had demanded that Thóra be present during all of the interrogations, and had a hard time understanding that she was prohibited from doing so due to conflict of interest. She also tried to explain to Markús that the police were simply fishing; they weren't just on the look-out for whatever would tighten the rope around his neck, but also for anything that could cut it loose. The purpose of the investigation was to gain a clear picture of events; this was not a government inquisition aimed at pinning everything on him. She had her doubts that Markús would accept all of this, but in the end he settled for her explanations.

There was something else, however, that was worrying Thóra— her imminent trip to the Westmann Islands. There she planned to search high and low for someone who could shed light on the discovery of the corpses in the basement, and perhaps even bear witness to the exchanges between Markús and Alda in the days before the eruption. Around two-thirds of the residents of the Islands had returned home after the eruption, and they formed a group that might conceivably have witnessed something significant. Although this plan was far from fail-safe, it was the only idea that Thóra could come up with at this stage of the case. Markús had agreed to it without objection, and even liked it. He was desperate to free himself from his current situation, and since the case had by now been reported in the media, it was clear to him that it was only a matter of time before his name would be dragged into the discussion. But as things stood now, it appeared that the reporters had received little information from the police, even though the case had naturally aroused a great deal of interest. Thóra felt it her obligation to acquaint herself with the coverage and she could only admire how creatively some reporters had managed to liven up their articles on the case, even without any new information. This, of course, would not last long, and soon the police would have to release information concerning the investigation in order to save face. Markús's name would not be included in their press releases, but there was a risk they would have to announce that one person was already being questioned as a suspect.

Then the game would be up and finally his name would be leaked. It was therefore imperative to try to clear him of all suspicion, as soon as possible, but Thóra could do little to speed up the investigation before the autopsy report and the findings from the crime scene were available. After she received these reports there would barely be any time to go to the Islands to speak with possible witnesses. So it was now or never. This was why it wasn't the trip itself that was bothering her—the Westmann Islands were beautiful enough, of course, and it was nice to visit there. No, what annoyed her was that it had turned out that Thór, the firm's junior lawyer, was too busy to go with her. Thóra thought it important to have a second set of eyes and ears with her in the Islands and the only ones that were available belonged to her secretary, Bella. Bragi had rightly pointed out that it mattered little whether Bella sat at the telephone or was somewhere else, making it convenient to bring her along as an assistant. The others at the firm were actually set on working when they arrived in the mornings—so it was either Bella or no one.

Thóra sighed and scrolled through her contacts list for her secretary's number. She wished she could phone Matthew and ask him to come to Iceland. He would certainly come if possible, but calling him would break her resolution to leave him in peace while he contemplated the future. An Icelandic bank had recently bought the German one for which he worked, and as a result he had been offered the position of supervisor of security at the main branch in

Iceland. Soon he had to make a big decision. The work was similar to what he was doing now, and the pay was much better, which hadn't surprised Thóra as much as it had him—the banks were locally notorious for paying ridiculous salaries. So the decision was not the job itself, but the move to Iceland. He knew no one there but Thóra and her children, so she didn't want to interfere with his decision. If she encouraged him to come, she would be morally bound to maintain their relationship. If she discouraged him, he might think she didn't care. A long time ago she had realized that any potential life partner would have to live in Iceland, so her relationship with Matthew depended on his decision. If Matthew did not come to Iceland, their relationship would be finished. They were hardly ever together, and that simply didn't work. Thóra blushed at the thought of phone sex, which they had tried unsuccessfully. It seemed clear that for sex she needed a flesh-and-blood man, in the same room as her, and therefore it was better to be with someone who did not live many thousands of kilometers away. On the other hand, she hoped that he would come; she liked him and enjoyed being with him. There also seemed to be a shortage of attractive men of the right age. She didn't like any of the ones that had recently tried it on with her, not even after her fifth glass. And that said a lot about them. The men who attracted her attention were either far too young, already taken, or gay. Before shaking off these thoughts it struck her that perhaps there was an overabundance of men in the Westmann Islands. One could always dream, and it didn't hurt to have Bella in tow, especially since compared to her secretary, Thóra resembled a *Playboy* centerfold. Enough of that for now, she thought, and turning to the matter at hand, she called Bella's number.

After Sóley had gone to sleep and it was clear there was nothing worth watching on television, Thóra decided to have a look in the book *Memorable Events 1971–1975*, from the series *Our Century*. She had acquired the collection after her grandfather died, and although she didn't open the books very often, they had occasionally come in handy. The book wasn't thick and obviously contained far from all the newsworthy events of the period, but Thóra thought that the disappearance of four people must have found its way into the book, assuming it had made the news at the time. She flipped quickly through 1973 until she reached the summer of that year and the eruption in the Westmann Islands was finished. Markús's childhood home had actually been buried some time during the first month of the eruption; nonetheless Thóra wanted to make sure that nothing got past her so she didn't stop reading until she came to the headline "*Eruption Finished!*" from 4 July.

Upon reading, she found little that could conceivably be connected to the corpses in the basement. The airplane Vor, with five people on board, had crashed at the end of March north of Langjökull Glacier, and in the first article about the incident, the crash site had still not been located. A later article about the accident stated that rescue crews had found it, as well as the plane's passengers, who all turned out to be dead. Another article that caught Thóra's attention was from the end of January, concerning the loss of the British smack *Cuckoo*, along with its four-man crew. It had sailed from Thorlákshöfn in the middle of the month, but nothing was heard from it or its crew after that. Thóra sat up on the sofa as she read this article, but lay back down again when several pages later she read that wreckage from the ship had been driven ashore along with remains of one of the crew's bodies. The smack was thought to have capsized with all hands in a storm that hit shortly after it left the harbor. Thóra's attention was captured again later in the book when she read that a group of six hikers had got lost after setting out on a trip from Landmannalaugar. The group had consisted of four foreign geologists and two Icelandic guides who were supposed to have been very familiar with the area. Thóra did not need to waste any time trying to imagine how part of the group had sought shelter in a basement in the Westmann Islands to get away from bad weather on the mainland, because immediately on the following page there was a report that the men had been found hounded and cold in a little emergency hut in the highlands. They had got lost in the drifting snow and could thank their lucky stars that they had stumbled on the hut. Thóra then read one report about people who had disappeared and were never found. In February, the *Seastar* had sunk southeast of the mainland with a ten-man crew. The passengers boarded two rubber life rafts but were never found. The group had consisted of nine men and one woman: five Icelanders and five Faeroese, and despite repeated searches through the articles Thóra could not discover anything about whether the crew had ever been found. The only problem was that Markús's home had probably already been buried in ash by the time the ship perished, and it was an enormous distance to the Islands from the place where it had sunk.

Despite her disappointment Thóra continued reading, then found an article that reawakened her hope. It concerned the huge number of foreign reporters that had come to Iceland to cover the eruption. Of course there was nothing in the article about any of them disappearing, much less four of them. Although it was unlikely that any full-time journalists or reporters had failed to return from Iceland without it ending up in the news, it was possible that things might have been different for freelancers. Some of these reporters might have traveled to Iceland without letting anyone know of their plans. They would perhaps not have been searched for here when their disappearance was discovered later in their homelands.

Little else had occurred in the first part of the year that could shed any light on the identity of the corpses. The Cod War raged, but Thóra could find no indication anywhere that anyone had disappeared or been considered lost at sea in connection with the conflict between the British and the Icelanders over the extension of Iceland's territorial waters from twelve miles to fifty. Several other articles mentioned deaths or disappearances, but they were never groups of people, always isolated individuals. Thóra thought it too unlikely that the corpses were a collection of people that had all disappeared or died under different circumstances at different times, so she didn't read these latter articles in any detail.

She also thumbed through 1972, since there was a possibility that the bodies had been in the basement before the eruption started. That year, however, turned out to be as lacking in significant detail for her purposes as 1973. A photo of a sinking ship raised an eyebrow, but the accompanying article said it was a trawler that was thought to have hit a mine. However, further investigation of the sinking revealed that the ship's owners had exploded dynamite in its hold in the hope of an insurance payoff. No one appeared to have died or disappeared in connection with the incident.

Another headline to draw Thóra's attention stated that eighty British trawlers were speeding toward the Icelandic fishing grounds. The article was dated at the end of August 1972, which was a bit early; however, this case involved a huge number of men, making it possible that four of them might have disappeared without being noticed. In fact nothing was mentioned about the disappearance of any of them, but the article succeeded in capturing the tone of relations between the two nations during the Cod War. The end of the article quoted a British trawler captain, who stated that if the Icelanders tried to board a British ship within fifty miles and outside twelve, they would be met with boiling water and sacks of pepper. Thóra found the mention of the pepper quite amusing, the boiling water less so, but the statement indicated that those involved had been prepared for anything—even physical injury.

After her reading Thóra was little closer to discovering anything than she had been before, except for her feeling that the bodies might be connected to the Cod War in some very vague way. After all, to Thóra's mind the word "war" meant devastation and death.

She slammed the book shut and hurried to pack for her trip the next morning.

Chapter 7

Sunday, July 15, 2007

Thóra took her seat next to Bella in the plane. She thanked God that the flight would take only half an hour—she had a terrible fear of having to keep up a conversation with the girl in such close quarters. In the end Bella chattered the entire trip without pause, the gist of her monologue being her desire for Thóra to bring a lawsuit against the state for the ban on smoking in public places. Thóra smiled uncomfortably but didn't dare interject. She even nodded noncommittally when her secretary said that after smoking was prohibited in airplanes the majority of passengers had started to get sick after long-haul flights because the air on board was changed much less frequently. Instead of breathing smoke the passengers breathed germs and bacteria from people who came from all over the world and who therefore, according to Bella, could have the Ebola virus or bird flu. Thóra doubted that people who had contracted these diseases traveled much to the Westmann Islands, but nevertheless tried to breathe less than usual. When they landed she gulped down fresh air at the door of the plane and enjoyed the feeling of the warm breeze playing about her face. Bella hurried past Thóra and out of the airport to have a smoke.

"Well," said Thóra as she dragged their suitcases over to Bella, who stood by the ash bin, enjoying her cigarette, "shouldn't we try calling a cab?" She looked around but there was no taxi to be seen. She felt worse when she saw that some of their fellow travelers appeared to be getting ready to walk into town. Maybe there weren't any taxis in the Islands? Just as she was on the verge of going back into the airport to ask about this, a new Range Rover jeep pulled up. Thóra had recently been told how much these cars cost, but the figure was so high that she still thought it must have been a misunderstanding. The dark windowpane slid down into its slot and a middle-aged man stretched out through the open window and called to them.

"Are you Thóra?" he said, looking at Bella. His voice was deep.

"No, that's me," Thóra called back quickly, rather displeased that her secretary should be mistaken for her. Although Thóra did not consider herself a great beauty, the difference between their appearances and clothing was like night and day. Thóra always tried to dress smartly: in tasteful jeans and a sporty outdoor jacket that had cost far, far too much, while her secretary looked more as if she were on her way to the stage to act in a play about the Baader-Meinhof terrorist gang. To make matters worse, the girl's makeup made her look like a vampire. Thóra stepped closer to the car.

"Hello," said the man, and reached over to open the passenger door. "My name is Leifur, I'm Markús's brother. He called me and said that you were on your way, so I thought I'd come and pick you up."

"Thanks," replied Thóra immediately. "My secretary is here with me, is that all right?"

"Yes, of course," replied Leifur, as he stepped out of the car and put their suitcases in the back. "You're staying at Thórshamar Hotel, I expect?" he said, after they'd all piled in.

"Yes," replied Thóra, and she took the opportunity to examine the man better. She could see a distinct resemblance between the brothers, and thought they must both have been very handsome in their younger years. Leifur was slightly older than Markús, probably in his fifties. He carried his age well, like his brother, and had the air of someone who is used to being in charge and getting his own way. She wasn't attracted to much older men, but she could see that the brothers were good-looking. Leifur's smart clothing suggested he was a man who appreciated good quality, and this fitted with his choice of car, although Thóra knew that clothing did not tell the whole story. Bella, for example, was neither a terrorist nor a fat vampire, although people might be forgiven for thinking otherwise.

———————

"The hotel is in an excellent location," said Leifur as they drove off. "In the center of town, not far from the harbor."

"That's good to hear," said Thóra, and wondered what she should say next. She had no idea how much he knew about the case, and wanted to avoid telling him anything he didn't already know. It wouldn't look good if he started quoting her at police interrogations. She glanced around in search of something to talk about. "Great weather," she said, and then reproached herself for the cliché. "Is it always so nice here?"

Leifur turned toward her and smiled. "Sure, I guess so."

Much to Thóra's regret, no lively discussion of the weather ensued. No one said anything for a few moments and she used the time to look around. There was little or no traffic on the roads, just like last time she had been here. The landscape was just as magnificent, and she was about to mention this when Leifur started speaking again, now less upbeat than before: "It's terrible, this thing with the bodies," he said, glancing over at Thóra. "I presume it's okay to talk about it in front of your secretary?"

"Of course," said Thóra. "Nonetheless, I'm unable to discuss details of the case with you. At least, details that you don't know about already."

"No, I'm not going to try to get anything out of you," replied the man. "That's not what I meant. I was just so shocked that they were found in our house. My family has enough to deal with right now."

Thóra's ears pricked up. "Oh?" She looked around the jeep and recalled how Markús also seemed to have quite enough to get by on. Financial concerns could hardly be overburdening the family.

"Ah, well," replied Leifur, sounding dejected. "It's a lot of little things combined with a few larger problems. Dad's illness is the biggest."

"Yes, Markús told me about it," said Thóra. She always found it difficult to speak to strangers about illness or death. "You have my sympathies. It's a terrible disease."

"Thanks," he said. "No, you needn't worry about me. Markús told me his side of the story and I have to admit that although it might sound improbable, I trust him. It was a bit odd how he chased after Alda all those years ago. She stood head and shoulders above the rest of the girls in those days, but still. He would have done anything for her—actually, he did enough stupid things even without her."

"Yes, it's all very peculiar," Thóra said. "I was hoping I could find something that would shed light on the subject while I'm here, but perhaps that's unrealistic. Too much time has passed."

"Yes and no," mused Leifur. "The eruption, and the time that followed, are still fresh in the memories of those who experienced it. It was a terrible ordeal."

"I can only imagine," said Thóra. She pointed at the stone arch over the entrance to the cemetery. "Isn't this the gate that was in the famous photo?" She was referring to a picture taken during the eruption. In it the cemetery was completely covered in ash and the only thing standing out from the pitch-black blanket was the arch, with the Biblical inscription *I live and you will live*. In the background a column of fire stretched up into the sky. It was a very stirring image, and the photographer had managed to tell an incredible story. "I didn't realize the cemetery had been dug out."

"A lot of things were dug out of the ash after the eruption. For a while they were removing nearly ten thousand cubic meters of ash from the town every day. Landa Church was partly buried," said Leifur, pointing in the direction of the imposing but unostentatious chapel standing next to the cemetery. "A few houses were dug up, next to the ones where the current excavation is taking place." It was clear to Thóra that she had to learn more about the eruption if she didn't want to waste all her time uncovering facts that were already common knowledge. She had brought the book Gylfi got from the library, and could start reading it in her hotel room that evening. Leifur continued: "I actually don't know why the houses on our street weren't uncovered then. I'm sure there was a logic to it, as with anything else. They'd doubtless been considered ruined, and quite rightly. I can't imagine anyone bothering to try to make the ruins they've already dug up inhabitable again."

"I know I couldn't be persuaded to live in any of those houses," said Thóra. "My trip the other day was enough, even without what was found in the basement."

"My wife and I were thinking of inviting you to dinner tomorrow night," said Leifur as they pulled up at the hotel entrance. "Both of you, I mean," he added when he realized that he'd forgotten Bella. "Nothing fancy, but easier than you having to trek off to a restaurant. There actually aren't many places to eat in town, so I expect you'll be glad of the change."

Thóra looked back at Bella, who shrugged indifferently. She turned again to Leifur. "That would be lovely," she replied. "What time?"

When everything was settled regarding dinner, Thóra and Bella said good-bye, but Leifur insisted on carrying their suitcases into the hotel and took his leave only after each of them had received the keys to their separate rooms. "Don't hesitate to get in touch if I can help in any way," he said. "I know this place like the back of my hand and I can help you out if you need it. As you can imagine, I want to do everything I can for my brother." He handed Thóra his mobile number, turned and walked away.

"There's something strange about that man," said Bella, as she and Thóra stood by the large window in the hotel foyer and watched him get into his car.

"Why do you say that?" asked Thóra in surprise. She had found him extremely pleasant, if a little distant.

"There's just something spooky about him," said Bella, and walked toward the stairs without any further explanation.

Adolf turned onto his side and his stomach churned. Without opening his eyes, he knew what he would see in his bed. The odor that filled his nostrils was a blend of perfume and sour alcohol. The turbulence in his stomach grew but he fought against it, breathing through his mouth so that he wouldn't throw up. When the discomfort had almost passed he wished he had just puked over the woman in his bed, whose name he couldn't remember for the life of him, and thus ensured that he would never see or hear from her again. He looked at her and tried to recall what he had found attractive. It wasn't her nose, which from close up he could see was completely covered with blackheads. Her thick black mascara had run, making it look as if he'd woken up next to Alice Cooper. Adolf considered pulling the covers down carefully to look at the rest of her naked, because it was still possible she had a great body. The shape under the duvet didn't seem to suggest she was very fat, rather the opposite: she seemed to be very thin. It actually didn't matter whether she was fat or thin, though—it had been a stupid mistake to bring her home. It had never been more important that he kept himself to himself. He screwed his eyes shut, full of self-loathing. Why couldn't he ever stick to the plan? Have two beers, then stop. Go home. Alone.

The girl shifted in her sleep, and Adolf held his breath in case she woke up. He needed a little more time to compose himself before talking to this bird he could barely remember. What did she do, how old was she? He wasn't too bothered about what she was called—he never remembered people's names. People rarely had conversations in which their names played any real part, as he knew from long experience. On the other hand, he had to prepare himself for the unwanted affection she might show him, and at the same time work out how to get rid of her without hurting or insulting her. As it was Sunday it was ludicrous for him to pretend that he needed to go to work, so he was in trouble. He wondered what time it was. Was she likely to wake up soon? He tried to look at his alarm clock on the bedside table, but had to lift his head to see over the girl. He took care not to make the bed springs squeak. It was only ten thirty. He breathed a little easier. He couldn't really remember when they had got home, let alone what time they had fallen asleep. The smell in the room suggested that it hadn't been all that long since they'd finished. He also felt sure that he'd kept drinking late into the night.

Why the hell hadn't he taken his lawyer's advice? What was so hard about staying away from girls for a few months? The time would pass quickly, and it wasn't as if he would actually miss them. Surprisingly, he was even getting bored with how easy it was to get them. All he needed to do was go to a club, sit down at the bar and pretend to be lost in thought. Within minutes some drunk girl would appear next to him and start chattering away. It wasn't exciting anymore, if it ever had been. It was about as challenging as fishing with a dragnet at a fish farm. The psychologist they'd forced him to see said that he was one of those men a particular type of woman found attractive, and with that came a great deal of responsibility.

Oh, sure. Why should he have to shoulder the blame? They could do that themselves. It wasn't his fault he sent out some sort of involuntary primal signal that charmed the opposite sex.

Anyway, clearly the worst-case scenario was that more women would start to press charges, or even just blog about him. Even so, he couldn't resist temptation. He had to get a grip on himself. The money was within reach, so close he could hear it rustling. If he could just think of that and let it suffice whenever his longing for women crashed over him. He would have little use for money if he was found guilty. And how would he get women then? Waste all his money on prostitutes? He was flooded with self-loathing again, and his headache intensified. He let out a moan, and to his horror the wretched girl's eyelids flickered. Adolf held his breath and waited. She didn't wake up, and he relaxed slightly—but not for long, as suddenly her eyes opened and she stared straight ahead, still woozy with sleep. He watched her eyes dart around as she tried to figure out where she was. Finally they came to rest on him, and her face broke into a wide smile as she pulled herself out from under the duvet.

"Good morning," she said, her voice slightly hoarse.

"Good morning," he replied. "How do you feel?" He tried not to let his voice betray the fact that he couldn't care less.

"I've felt better," she admitted. "Do you have any Coke?" She gave him a look that was doubtless meant to be seductive, but which stirred no feelings in him bar irritation. He might have found it cute if she'd looked better, but the smudged makeup and lack-of-sleep-face didn't do much for her. Maybe she was good-looking under normal circumstances; for her sake, he hoped so.

"Absolutely," he said as he half raised himself off the bed. He swept his feet over the edge but had to wait for the dizziness to pass before standing up. He must stop drinking. Or at least cut down. He stood up and had to wait another moment before he could walk steadily into the kitchen. He knew without looking that the girl was staring at his naked body, and it aroused him despite how poorly he felt. On his way through the room he looked around for a cigarette and spotted a half-crumpled pack on the coffee table, next to an overflowing ashtray. As he fished a bent cigarette from the packet he made a mental note to buy a bigger ashtray. His lighter lay in a dried-up pool of red wine on the table. After several attempts he finally conjured a flame from it and lit his cigarette. He inhaled hard and let smoke leak from his mouth without exhaling. Now all he needed was a Coke, and things would start looking up. He went into the kitchen with the burning cigarette in his mouth and pulled open the refrigerator. Coke was one thing that he always made sure he had, in bottles of all different sizes. He took the top off a two-liter bottle and gulped down the cold soda, which would help to settle his upset stomach.

As the refrigerator door swung shut he noticed a note that he'd stuck there a long time ago but hadn't remembered to throw away when it no longer served its purpose. *Alda—6:oo Weds.* Adolf tore it off, crumpled it and threw the ball of paper in the direction of the open rubbish bin, where it hit the rim and rolled back across the floor. It stopped at his feet and rocked there for a moment. Adolf looked down at it for a second then kicked it, sending it skimming across the floor into a corner. It was best to forget everything about that woman, as soon as possible. He had seen to it that she would leave him in peace from now on.

Adolf turned away from the ball of paper and focused his mind on the present. He couldn't remember whether they'd used any contraception, and considering the fog that surrounded his memories of last night, he doubted it. He would have to take his own precautions. It was bad enough paying child support for one love-brat. They were pretty hefty, those payments. He reached into the kitchen cabinet for a glass. None of his glasses were the same; he'd collected them from here and there. He rummaged around until he found what he was looking for: a thick dark blue tumbler, almost opaque. Next he pulled out a drawer and grabbed an envelope from inside. From the envelope he took six little white tablets which he ground with a spoon on a cracked saucer. Four was probably enough, but he felt more confident using six as he would be in no position to make sure that the girl took the second dose, which was recommended for twenty-four hours later. He stirred the powder into the Coke and looked down into the glass, happy with the result. Only a tiny bit was left floating on top. He fished out the white speck with his index finger and licked it off. It could hardly do him any harm. Adolf picked up the envelope to close it, and felt it before he stuck it back in the drawer, discovering much to his sorrow that there were only two tablets left. He would have to get more, right away.

Adolf screwed the plastic cap shut on the Coke and held the bottle in one hand. Then he lifted the glass and tilted it as if he were toasting an invisible friend, before turning back into the bedroom. On his way in he wondered how best to get rid of the girl without any repercussions. The morning-after contraceptives in the glass would only win half the battle; he would also have to throw up a blockade against their getting to know each other any better. He didn't have much time to think things over, so he decided to use an old excuse that had served him well. He would say that he was getting over a difficult breakup and that he couldn't commit to anything right now. He would conclude by asking her whether he could phone her after he'd sorted his head out, since he felt there was something really special about her. She would swallow this hook, line and sinker—everyone wanted to be special. If she only knew how incredibly average she was. By tonight he wouldn't even remember the color of her hair. He stubbed out his cigarette in the overflowing ashtray, which pushed two other stubs onto the table. Christ. Maybe he could trick her into helping him clean up, or even better: get her to clean up without him having to help at all.

"Coke," he said, waving the glass to and fro. He stood in the doorway and leaned against the doorpost. "Would you like a drink?"

The girl looked up and licked her dry lips. "Oh, yes, please."

She smiled and sat up, making the bedcover fall from her breasts. She did nothing to try to cover them. Adolf smiled back. Nor was there any reason to hide such beautiful breasts. He sat on the edge of the bed next to her and handed her the glass. She took big gulps as if her life depended on it and Adolf watched her chest rise and fall. She removed the glass from her mouth and took a deep breath. "God, I'm so hungover." She handed him the nearly empty glass. "You want some?"

He took the glass but did not drink. Instead he placed it and the Coke bottle on the bedside table and moved closer to the girl. Now it would be fun to find out what she was like in bed—he recalled so little about last night. Afterward he could give her the speech about how emotionally handicapped he was at the moment. He was, after all, wasting his last tablets on her. A little smile crept over his lips. The story wasn't exactly a lie. He *was* emotionally damaged. His dealings with that bitch Alda proved it. A nasty giggle slipped out and he saw from the girl's expression that she wasn't completely sure what to do. How ridiculous. As if this girl had any choice. No meant no—he was completely prepared to accept that. The trick was to suppress the no before it emerged, prevent it from being said. He kissed the helpless girl on the forehead and placed his hand lightly over her mouth.

Chapter 8

Sunday, July 15, 2007

"Do you know anything about the volcano?" Thóra asked as they walked out of their hotel into the warm air.

"No," replied Bella. "Nothing except that it erupted."

"Yes, as usually happens with volcanoes," said Thóra, wondering why she had thought it was worthwhile to bring her secretary. "Well, you'll learn more about it later. The man we're going to meet knows everything about it, Markús says."

"Can't wait," drawled Bella, pulling a pack of cigarettes from her jacket pocket.

Thóra paid no heed and kept walking as the secretary stopped to light up. Bella didn't hurry to catch up after her cigarette was lit, so they walked the rest of the distance to the harbormaster's office a few paces apart. Thóra used the time to think about what she wanted to get from this Kjartan Helgason. Apparently he had been out at sea a great deal in his day, and Markús considered him to be among those best informed about the eruption and the rescue work following it, and had said that as Kjartan had been a friend of his father, it should be easy to get him to open up. Thóra had little hope that much would come out of this interview, but she and Bella would at least know a bit more about the eruption afterward. Maybe he would even have some thoughts about who the men in the basement might be, and could point Thóra in the right direction. She was well aware that the police were working day and night to find out precisely the same thing, and that they had connections out in the world with which Thóra could scarcely compete, despite her owning the whole series of *Our Century* books. On the other hand, it was clear to her that identifying the bodies would speed up the investigation significantly, as well as provide clues as to who they might have had dealings with and what they had been doing in the Islands. How people live influences how they die.

Kjartan welcomed them on the steps outside the harbormaster's office, where he was having a cigarette with another, younger man. He introduced himself when Thóra arrived and shook her hand firmly. The top bone of his right index finger was missing, and his palm was rough. He appeared to be approaching retirement age: a few dark hairs could still be seen on his otherwise white head. He limped slightly as he showed them in, and told them unexpectedly that he still hadn't recovered after being struck by a boom nearly twenty years ago.

"That's why I stopped going out to sea," he said, smiling ruefully. "You can't tread the waves very well with a gammy leg." He slapped the top of his thigh.

"And did you go straight from that to working here?" asked Thóra as they made their way up to the second floor.

"No, my dear," replied Kjartan, stepping up one more stair with great effort. "I've done this and that from the time I became a landlubber. I've only been here for five years."

"And you can't get an office on the ground floor?" she exclaimed, surprised that a partially handicapped man should be forced to hobble up the stairs.

"Yes, I'm sure I could," replied Kjartan. "But I don't care about that. This bother with the stairs is worth it." He opened the door to a small office. "I have to have a sea view," he said, and pointed out of the window to where the harbor and Heimaklettur Peak appeared. "I'm like a puffin. I can't take off unless I've got the sea in my sight." He waved his hand around the room. "I'd get nothing done."

It seemed to Thóra from the piles and scraps of paper covering the room that the man's accomplishments were scarcely exemplary, despite his view of the sea. "I live by the sea, too, and I know the feeling," she said, lifting a strange-looking device from the nearest chair. "Can I put this somewhere else?" she asked, looking around to find a secure place. Although it looked like it might be a piece of junk, it could just as easily have been valuable, hence its place on a chair rather than on the floor like most other things in the office.

"Just throw it on the floor," replied Kjartan as he took his own seat. Thóra placed the object down carefully and sat in the chair. Bella pulled another chair over to Kjartan's desk and also sat, after removing a plastic bag that appeared to contain some glasses or cups. She put the bag down quite roughly, and Thóra had to wait until the glasses stopped clinking before she started to speak. "I hope we're not dragging you away from home to meet us," she said. "Markús said that you would be here, but since it's Sunday I wasn't sure."

"My dear, don't worry about it," replied Kjartan. "I needed to work this weekend. There's only the two of us here trying to catch up with everything because of the reports that need to be done this week. Yet another ridiculous inspection is about to begin."

Thóra relaxed a bit, but at the same time sympathized with the man, who certainly appeared to have a lot of work to do, considering the condition of the office. "Okay, good," she said, then turned to the matter at hand. "Markús has perhaps explained to you my business, which is to say, I am assisting him in a case that appears to be connected to the eruption," she began. "He told me that you knew everything about everything." She added quickly, hopefully: "And everyone . . . ?"

"Is that what they say?" said Kjartan, with a pleased smirk. "I don't know about that, but I am familiar with this case of Markús's." He did not take his eyes off Thóra. "This is a small place. Every single person here knows pretty much everything about the discovery of the bodies, both what's been written about in the papers and the aspects that aren't being discussed in public."

Thóra smiled reluctantly. It was to be expected. The Westmann Islands were inhabited by nearly four thousand people in approximately thirteen square kilometers, so the story must have circulated very quickly. Now she just had to hope that the same had occurred with the story behind the corpses. "What exactly happened here in the Islands the night of the eruption, and the day before Markús's home was buried by ash? Markús has told me what he remembers, but naturally he was just a teenager, so he was sent to the mainland straight away that night. I understand that he didn't return to the Islands until some time had passed, and by then his house was gone."

"I suppose you're hoping to hear that someone besides Markús went down into the basement?" asked Kjartan. He rocked back and forth on his office chair, which creaked.

"I'm interested in knowing whether it might be at all possible to rule out such a thing," answered Thóra cautiously. She had to be careful not to let the old man turn the meeting into an opportunity to satisfy his own curiosity. "If you could perhaps explain to me how all this happened, and try to remember anything that might be important for Markús's case?"

"I don't know whether what I remember could help Markús in any way." Kjartan leaned forward quickly. His chair creaked again. "I would hope so—I like the boy. His father and I were great friends. He was never called anything other than 'Krúsi króna' here in the old days, since he used to go on and on about money."

Thóra smiled. It had been decades since Markús had been a boy, but in the mind of this man he seemed to have stayed at that age. "Still, it would be good to hear your side of the story. One never knows what details will be revealed," she said. "How did it start? As far as I know, the eruption began without warning."

Now it was Kjartan's turn to smile. "The eruption on Surtsey was a clear warning, in my opinion." He reached out to the wall behind him and took down a framed map of the Islands. The map was faded and dusty; Kjartan blew most of the dust off, then pointed at Surtsey and ran his finger along the islands that lined up in a horseshoe from Surtsey to Heimaey itself. "It doesn't take a genius to realize that the volcanic belt is located here. It isn't a great distance," he said, placing his little finger on Heimaey and his thumb on Surtsey. "About thirteen, fourteen nautical miles." He laid the map on the desk in front of him. "The Surtsey eruption began in 1963, and Eldfell blew in 1973. Ten years is a short time on the scale of geological history."

"Perhaps," said Thóra. "But it's still quite a long time for human beings. So the inhabitants of the Westmann Islands stopped worrying about eruptions some time after the upheaval on Surtsey ended?"

"Yes, yes, that's right," said Kjartan. "Actually the only warning that people got was several small earthquakes the evening before the eruption started. No one paid much attention to them, since people thought the tremors came from the area where they'd recently finished constructing the Búrfell power plant. Now I'm no specialist in quakes, but I was told that one of the three seismographs set up to record the movements of the earth's crust was broken, making it impossible to determine their epicenter with any great precision. Not a single person put two and two together when they felt the tremors." Kjartan paused. "There were actually various other signs that no one paid any attention to," he added, avoiding her eyes. "A woman who lived on the edge of town, at the place where the eruption began, was amazed to see that the elves were packing up and moving out two days before it started."

"Elves?" repeated Thóra carefully. "I see." She decided to keep her opinion to herself where elves were concerned.

"Yes, and several days earlier, a little girl told her parents that an eruption was about to happen at the place where the fissure was formed." Kjartan shrugged. "There are other stories like this, about unexplained events just prior to the disaster, but one never knows how much store to set by them. An amateur painter, for example, did a painting of the area showing the volcano and lava before these events occurred. I actually believe that some people can somehow sense catastrophes before they happen—just as animals seem to. However, I'm not one of them."

Thóra silently thanked God for that small mercy. "Then the eruption started in the middle of the night?"

"Yes," said Kjartan, seemingly relieved that Thóra didn't want to talk about the supernatural. "The fissure opened at two o'clock in the morning and started spewing lava. It wasn't more than two hundred meters from the nearest farm, so it's a miracle that everyone was saved."

"People must have been terrified," said Thóra. "I've never been near an eruption, but the noise must have been incredible."

"It might be hard to believe, but there wasn't that much noise," he replied. "Most of those who lived nearest the site were woken by the noise, but many people who lived farther away had to be woken up. Police cars, fire engines and other vehicles drove around the streets of the town with their sirens on, to warn people. A little later the decision was made to evacuate the Islands, and people were asked to go down to the harbor. Most people didn't need to be told twice, and for some reason most of them had flocked down there anyway. A few people, however, had to be persuaded to leave."

"Didn't they realize the danger they were in?" asked Thóra. "I'd have thought a spouting volcano in your back garden might be pretty persuasive."

"Of course it was the middle of the night, and people were still a bit sleepy. Some people thought there was a fire; the first person to see the eruption called the police and reported one. He was the farmer in Kirkjubær, and the fissure went through his farm. Just over two kilometers long, if you can imagine it." Kjartan appeared almost proud that this hadn't simply been a little tourist eruption. "Now, others thought that some sort of war had broken out. The Cold War was in full force by then—as was the Cod War, of course. And keep in mind that the present-day landscape is deceiving and you can't really tell what happened from how it looks now. The Eldfell cone didn't exist at that time—it was formed in the eruption. It was just flat land, and suddenly a row of lava spouts appeared out of the earth. From a distance they could very well have appeared to be burning buildings, or a big grass fire. And of course, everyone reacts differently in a crisis." Kjartan smiled to himself, remembering. "I ended up talking a woman out of her house, which was very close to the fissure vent. She had got up and started making pancakes! We had a hell of a job persuading her to put down her pan."

Thóra laughed. She noticed that Bella was sitting there as if fossilized; she'd not moved a muscle since sitting down. Thóra didn't know whether that was good or bad; either the girl was paying rapt attention, or she was miles away. "But in the end you got everyone off the Islands?"

"Yes, we did. We managed to get everyone up and on the move in about an hour, and people made their own way down to the harbor. The weather had been unfit for sailing the day before, so the entire fishing fleet was in the port. Otherwise enormous carnage would have occurred, since it was only a short time from the start of the eruption until red-hot ash and debris started raining over the town. Tephra, it's called. That made everything much more dangerous." Kjartan leaned back. "Those of us on the rescue crews really had to run for it. It looked as if the lava would close the harbor, since the fissure reached all the way down to the seaward approach at Ystaklettur Cliff. We were in a really tight spot—we needed to get five thousand people out of there. Not to mention the sheep and chickens."

"Sheep and chickens?" echoed Thóra. "You sent farm animals to the mainland by boat? What about the dogs and cats?" She hadn't thought about that. Naturally there had been other living things on the island besides people.

"Dog ownership was forbidden at the time, but most of the cats were left behind. There was no chance to round them all up. Most of them died as the eruption went on, from the toxic fumes. The sheep, on the other hand, were sent immediately to the mainland on helicopters from the American base, while the chickens were transported by ship," replied Kjartan. He stopped suddenly. "Even though I watched my own house disappear beneath the lava, the hardest part of the eruption was when the cows from Kirkjubær were led down to the harbor to be slaughtered. It was horrific. The farm was the first building to disappear, since the volcano was on that farmer's land, and he was quite old and in no position to start farming again. There was no other option, but it was pitiful. Natural disasters affect animals terribly, and to make matters worse I think the cows sensed that this trip down to the harbor would be their last." He cleared his throat. "The farmer went to the mainland the next morning by plane. Everything that he owned fitted into a little box that he held in his lap the whole way."

Thóra pushed the image out of her mind—Markús's box was enough for her. "In other words, everyone abandoned the town?" she asked.

"Somewhere between two and three hundred men remained behind to try to salvage whatever they could. Everyone else—among them the women and children, of course—was sent to the mainland. It was God's mercy that the fleet was in the harbor. It would not have gone so well if the boats had been out fishing, I can tell you that." Kjartan looked out for a moment over the harbor before turning back to the two women. "People were piled up on board the boats and packed in everywhere they could fit. The seasickness was awful. It's no fun to be tossed about on the waves, surrounded by the stink of fish, if you're not used to it. Not to mention if you're sleep-deprived and suffering from shock." Bella obviously *was* listening, because out of the corner of her eye Thóra saw her grimace.

"Were there any other boats in the harbor apart from the ones from the Westmann Islands?" she asked. "Foreign vessels, for example?"

"No, none," replied Kjartan immediately, glowering at her. "Out of the question."

Thóra decided not to pursue this, although she had hoped that a foreign boat might have been moored there. "Do you remember anything about Markús that night, or Alda, his girlfriend?"

"No," replied Kjartan, without hesitation. He fell silent, clearly unwilling to elaborate.

"Are you absolutely certain?" asked Thóra, surprised at the swiftness of his response. "He wasn't there with his father, your friend?"

"I must have seen his father, although I don't specifically remember it," scowled Kjartan. "He worked on a rescue crew and was in the Islands during the days following the eruption, although I don't recall whether I met him that night. I don't remember the boy at all, nor Alda for that matter. There was a crowd of people there. They all had their arms piled high with whatever they had decided was most valuable at the moment they were forced to head to the harbor, the most incredible collection of things. In most cases what truly mattered was left behind; photo albums and other keepsakes were forgotten in the mad rush to save new standard lamps or other worldly goods that would soon become worthless."

"But are you sure you fully realize which Alda I'm talking about?" persisted Thóra. She thought it peculiar that Kjartan hadn't hesitated at all when she mentioned her name. Perhaps he'd heard Markús's explanation for the severed head and had already remembered who she was. She hoped this wasn't the case, because it would mean Markús had been very indiscreet.

"There was only one Alda in the Islands at that time. She was the same age as Markús, and her father was one of our friends. His name was Thorgeir and he died recently. He was one of those who stayed behind to assist the rescue crews along with me and Markús's father Magnús."

"Did you know Alda died this week?" asked Thóra.

"Yes, I heard about that," he replied. "Her mother and sister still live in the Islands, and I know both of them. The whole thing is, in a word, tragic, and I don't understand what causes people to take such desperate measures. Her mother is devastated, understandably." Kjartan glanced very quickly out over the harbor before continuing. He seemed to wish to change the subject, clearly finding it difficult to talk about sensitive issues, like so many men of his generation. "But I don't remember either Alda or Markús being there that night. Try to imagine five thousand people milling about out here. It was utter bedlam, and there was no time to talk to shocked teenagers."

"Markús said that he'd been evacuated to the mainland on the same boat as Alda, and that they'd spoken onboard," said Thóra. "Is it possible to verify this? In other words, are there records of who went on which boat to the mainland that night?"

Kjartan shrugged. "I simply don't know. The Red Cross took down the names of those who landed and arranged for people to be sent to Reykjavík from Thórlákshöfn. I think they also recorded which people were taken in by relatives and so on. Whether the records say which ships people traveled on I don't know, and if they did who's to say if such papers were even preserved?"

"They're probably in the National Archive," cried Bella, suddenly. She blushed slightly when Thóra and Kjartan looked at her in surprise. They had both forgotten her. "That's where I would put them, anyway," she added, before abruptly shutting up.

"There's also an archive here in town," said Kjartan. "On the first floor of the library. They might have those papers there."

"If not, then they're probably in the National Archive, as you suggested, Bella," said Thóra, pleased with her secretary's interest. This was a possible assignment for the girl while they were here, she thought. Bella could search for the documents in the town's archive and dig through them until she found Markús's and Alda's names. If they didn't show up in the search, Bella could continue in Reykjavík later. There was a lot at stake, because although such documents would not suffice in themselves to clear Markús of all suspicion, they would at least provide some support to his story. He had told Alda on the ship that the box had been left behind in the basement, and since Alda was no longer living, Markus was in dire need of anything, no matter how small, to help support his statement. Thóra turned to Kjartan. "The men who remained behind to do the rescue work," she said, "could they travel between the Islands freely, or was there some sort of system in place?"

Kjartan shook his head. "For the first two or three days there was no organization at all. People just worked like mad on their own initiative, salvaging what they could. And then it changed and started becoming more orderly. Although attempts were made to control the operations, it was actually nature that controlled everything according to its whims. It also wasn't long before more rescue crews came from the mainland, but unfortunately I don't have any precise numbers available on their size or how they were organized. I do recall that there were three or four hundred people here at the height of the rescue operation." Kjartan looked Thóra in the eye. "If you're asking whether any of them could have gone into the house and put the bodies there, or killed those people in the basement, the answer is absolutely yes. It wouldn't have been at all difficult. The houses that they're digging up now weren't immediately buried by ash—at least two weeks passed from the start of the eruption until the ash covered them. I wouldn't have wanted to enter them myself at that point because they were so close to the vent, but someone may well have been desperate enough to take the risk. About four hundred houses were covered by lava and obviously those couldn't be saved. That row of houses, on the other hand, was buried under ash, which doesn't have the same destructive power as molten rock. If I'd been hiding bodies I would have put them in houses that clearly would have been covered by lava, but of course that would have taken an enormous amount of courage. Lava doesn't flow that quickly, but there are few sights more terrifying. It doesn't spare anything. And it wasn't just the burning lava that would have held most people back, but also the toxic gases it produced."

"Do you have any idea who these people were that were found in the basement?" asked Thóra. "Do you know whether anyone went missing? From the rescue crews, for example?"

"I have no idea," replied Kjartan. "As far as I know, they all returned home in the end. No one died in the eruption."

"Except the man in the basement of the pharmacy," said Thóra.

"That wasn't the eruption," he replied. "He was an alcoholic."

Thóra was speechless. This was clearly the accepted view in the Islands. Alcoholics didn't count. She was determined not to let this put her off. "But you must have wondered who these people were?" she continued. "The Westmann Islands aren't very large, so naturally it's most likely that these men had some kind of tie to them."

"Not a clue," said Kjartan, and he tightened his lips. "From what I've seen in the news, no one knows who these people are, or how they ended up in the basement."

"That's correct," said Thóra patiently. "But it doesn't hurt to wonder. It occurred to me that this might be connected to the Cod War, that they were sailors who died in an accident at sea or in some quarrel between the Icelanders and the British. I guess I'm assuming that they're Englishmen."

"I doubt that," replied Kjartan. "There were various difficulties at the time, but they never developed into anything like what you're suggesting. Besides, it couldn't have been kept secret if something like that had happened. We would never have been able to kill four Brits without it becoming a huge incident. I have no idea who these people were, unfortunately."

Thóra decided not to press any further, but was surprised that the man might not at least have considered the possibility that the dead people were foreigners. It was absolutely indisputable—four Icelanders simply could not have vanished without being missed. An uneasy feeling came over her. The man before her knew more than he wanted to reveal. He'd been more than prepared to chat about unimportant things. She looked at Bella and stood up. "Well, this was informative." She shook Kjartan's hand. "Maybe we'll get a chance to disturb you further, if anything else occurs to me."

On the way out she noticed a framed photograph on the wall next to the doorway. It showed five people with their arms around each other's shoulders. They were all wearing helmets, while in the background a jet of ash stretched to the sky. One of the men was clearly Kjartan in his younger years. All of them looked exhausted, and none smiled at the camera. "Is Markús's father in this photograph, perhaps?"

Kjartan walked up to it and pointed at one of the men. "That's him. Magnús. And then there's Geiri, or Thorgeir. Alda's father."

"This is clearly you here, but who are the other two?" Thóra asked.

Kjartan snorted rudely. "That's Dadi," he said, pointing at a rather ugly man who was a good deal shorter than the others. "A boring bastard who was married to an even more boring woman." He moved his finger. "And this is Gudni."

"The policeman?" asked Thóra, turning to Kjartan. "Was he one of the friends that you mentioned?"

"*Was* is the operative word," replied Kjartan.

Chapter 9

Sunday, July 15, 2007

Bella relaxed with a cigarette as they stood outside Café Kró, a little harborside restaurant they had come across in their search for supper. Thóra stood next to her, which was against her natural instincts, but the weather was so good that being in a bad mood seemed impossible. She felt completely relaxed after the meal, and the sea breeze had perked her up. The air had grown colder in the evening, even though the sun was still in the sky as if nothing were more normal. Even Bella's smoke, which drifted over Thóra's face every now and then, could not ruin the beautiful evening. A small boat sailed out of the harbor, several seagulls following it from the jetty. Otherwise the wharf was calm, except for two men who were repairing the pilothouse on a small fishing boat tied to the pier just below where they stood. The repairs were proceeding at a leisurely pace since the men spent more time chatting than working, and Thóra admired their relaxed attitude. Perhaps it was the extreme beauty of the surroundings that had this effect on people. As Thóra watched the lively bird life around the steep sides of Heimaklettur Peak she could feel her stress dissolving, and she thought she could have sat there sipping her drink for the rest of the evening.

"So, how many bodies were there?" said Bella, rudely interrupting her reverie.

"In the basement?" said Thóra, even though Bella could hardly have meant anything else. "Four. Or more correctly, three and a quarter. One of the corpses was just a head. Haven't you followed the story in the news?" she asked, astounded.

"No, I don't read that rubbish." Bella put her cigarette in one corner of her mouth and exhaled a great cloud of smoke. She watched thoughtfully as it floated upward, spread out and disappeared. "Who kills four people at once?" she asked, frowning. "One I can understand, maybe two. But four is too many. Is it possible that this wasn't murder?"

Thóra had to admit to herself that they were thinking along the same lines. "I haven't got the results of the autopsy yet; maybe it isn't finished. It could well be that three of them died by accident, or poisoning, or by some means other than human hand."

Thóra breathed in the scent of the sea, which still overpowered the smell of her secretary's cigarette. "The head, on the other hand, is harder to explain. If the men weren't murdered—what about this head? Who would decapitate a corpse, and why?"

Bella shrugged. "Maybe he was in an accident and the body was separated from the head. It does happen."

"But how did the head end up in the box? And the box, along with three bodies, down in Markús's basement?" Thóra was surprised to find that she was enjoying talking this through with Bella. She had no way of knowing where the case was heading, and she wondered how to make the most of her trip to the Islands. She might as well head back to Reykjavík if there was no useful information to be gained here.

Bella frowned, and Thóra was relieved to realize that it was a sign of deep thought rather than anything Thóra had said to insult her. "This woman who gave your client the box," she said, taking a drag on her cigarette, "do you think she killed those people?"

"No, I can't see it," replied Thóra. "She was a teenager, hardly capable of killing four men. Not alone, anyway." She leaned against the wall and basked in the mild evening sun. "I've got to find a way to meet her mother, because she's the one most likely to know something about where the head came from—if not more. It's rotten luck that her father's dead. I imagine that he's probably involved somehow. But whether Alda's family is connected to the case or not, they must know *something*. Teenage girls are good at hiding all sorts of things from their parents, but I don't see Alda strolling casually around town with a man's head in a box. If nothing else, her mother could tell me who she spent time with after the disaster.

Maybe she confessed to a friend, or friends, later on? Markús lost all contact with her after they came to the mainland, so he's no use."

"Her mother still lives in the Islands, remember," said Bella, looking around as if she expected the woman to be living in one of the warehouses at the docks. "That old man today said so, anyway. You should phone her, or go and see her."

"She may be living here," said Thóra. "Still, I don't think it's right to visit her on this trip, in light of the circumstances."

"Isn't it exactly the right time to do it?" asked Bella, flicking her cigarette into a barrel a short distance away. "She's sure to be vulnerable after losing her daughter, and ready to open up."

Thóra shook her head. "No, that's no use. If she's in shock she might refuse to speak to me. I'll ask Markús's brother about Alda's family tomorrow evening, and if he knows anything he can maybe tell me how I ought to proceed. Hopefully he'll know how her mother is holding up."

Bella didn't seem to be listening to her. "Do you remember the cemetery we drove past?" she asked suddenly. "With the arched gate?"

"Yes," replied Thóra, wondering where Bella was going with this. Did she want to go and look around the graveyard?

"Could the bodies be from there?" the other woman asked. "Maybe a relative or someone else had been trying to save the bodies from disappearing in the eruption? The cemetery was buried and dug up later. Maybe whoever disinterred the bodies wasn't sure that would happen?"

Thóra looked at her secretary in surprise. "Digging up corpses just to put them in the basement of a house that was going to go the same way as the cemetery? I highly doubt it."

Bella shrugged. "Maybe whoever did it regretted it, or didn't have a chance to move the bodies again."

Thóra wanted to put a stop to this idle speculation, but couldn't think of any clever way, so she just said, "Shouldn't we get going? I'm happy to get an early night, so that we can get plenty done tomorrow."

Bella looked at her watch, then regarded Thóra quizzically. "Are you kidding? I haven't gone to bed this early since I was three years old."

Thóra's cheeks reddened slightly. "I'm not necessarily talking about going to sleep right away. I need to phone my children and a few other people first."

Bella shrugged again. "Suit yourself." She looked around. "I'm going to go for a wander and see if I can't find a bar or two."

Thóra thought this was a bad idea, but knew perfectly well that she had no say in how her employees spent their free time. "Don't do anything I wouldn't do," she said with false cheer. "Tomorrow I'm going to visit the archaeologists overseeing the excavations, and then we should stop by the archive. And then you never know what might come up. In other words, we've got a busy day."

"Don't worry about me," said Bella, as she set off in the opposite direction from their hotel. "I'm not the one who's always late."

Thóra couldn't help letting Bella's retort get under her skin. You could say what you liked about her secretary, but she always got to work on time. Thóra, in contrast, was usually late because it took so long to get herself and the children ready in the mornings. Although the situation was far from ideal when she only had her own children at home, it was a sight worse when her grandson and future daughter-in-law were added to the mix. "You realize that you can't count this pub crawl as a company expense," she called after the girl. "The accountant will refuse to pay it." No sooner were the words out than she regretted them deeply. Could she have thought of a more ridiculous comeback?

Bella did not turn around, but as she walked away she lifted one hand in the air and gave Thóra the finger.

Chapter 10

Monday, July 16, 2007

Thóra was furious to find Bella at breakfast ahead of her. The secretary had taken a seat by the window and on the table in front of her were plates piled up with high-calorie foods. She had such a smug look on her face that Thóra briefly considered taking a seat elsewhere, but she swallowed her pride and sat down opposite Bella.

"Well," she said as she pulled the coffee pot toward her, "did you have fun last night?" She herself had gone straight to her room and phoned home, since her parents had gone out of their way to house-sit and babysit in her absence. This arrangement was much less trouble than taking the whole gang over to their house, including Orri and his mother. Thóra's father was in high spirits having set up camp in her garage, which he'd been itching to fix up for a very long time although her mother hadn't been too keen on the idea. In her opinion everything at Thóra's had gone to the dogs: the filter in the washing machine was blocked, a flood of clothing poured from the wardrobes every time she opened them in search of an outfit for Sóley, and in the farthest corner of the fridge there was a jar of jam that had expired last century. Thóra therefore had to endure a half-hour lecture about what a terrible housewife she was, but she didn't need her mother to tell her that. At the end of the call she'd been allowed to speak to Sóley, who told her happily that she was wearing Gylfi's huge socks because Grandma couldn't find any of hers. Gylfi then came on and muttered into the receiver that she had to come home—Grandma was driving him completely crazy and Sigga was depressed. Before hanging up Thóra promised him that she would fix everything; she'd been affected by the thought of her daughter-in-law's depression. She turned on the television and flicked through the channels without finding anything that appealed to her. She ended up watching men in sunglasses play poker, but finally fell asleep before figuring out how the game worked.

"Crazy," said Bella, and she took a large bite of bread and jam. She'd spread the jam so thickly that it was more like jam and bread, causing one corner of the slice to break off from the sheer weight and leave a purple jam stain on her chin. She was completely unperturbed, wiping off the jam with her index finger and sticking it in her mouth. "I met some great people."

"Good," said Thóra, pouring milk into her coffee. "Were these people the same age as you?"

"I didn't ask for ID," said Bella, lifting her own coffee cup to her lips. She regarded Thóra over the rim and wiggled her eyebrows. "I slept with someone."

Thóra choked on her coffee. "What did you say?" she spluttered.

"You heard," said Bella proudly. "It was brilliant. Sailors really know what they're doing."

"*Sailors?*" said Thóra, still aghast. "Were there more than one?" How could this girl get herself a bedmate, or mates, as if it were nothing, when Thóra felt like she herself would have trouble finding an interested party in a men's prison? Actually, that wasn't entirely true: more often than not she was the uninterested one, rather than the men she met. Still, she felt irritated.

"No, it was just the one," said Bella. "Not for any lack of opportunity—I certainly *could* have had two."

Thóra was speechless, and indeed said nothing for the remainder of breakfast. That hardly mattered, because Bella gave her such a comprehensive account of the events of the previous night that Thóra wouldn't have been able to get a word in edgeways.

Dís hid her head in her hands. "What do we do now?" She was still recovering from the shock of finding Alda's body. The first night after the discovery she had lain in bed, exhausted but unable to fall asleep. She kept wondering if her colleague Ágúst could have overlooked some clue that the nurse had felt ill. All of their interactions with Alda that she could remember had to do with work, the next

operation or the state of the little storeroom. If there had been any
clues, they weren't making themselves known. In the early hours of
morning, just before sleep was finally merciful to her, she com-
forted herself with the thought that time healed all wounds. But
mental scars took much longer to heal than physical ones, and it
wasn't getting easier to come to terms with Alda's death as time
went by. If anything, Dís thought that she felt worse now than the
day she'd discovered the nurse's body. She knew she'd remember
that moment forever; after reporting the death, she had waited in
the bedroom. In hindsight it would have been wiser to wait down
in the living room or the kitchen, or even out in her car, but at the
time she'd felt it would be disrespectful to the deceased, so instead
she had sat down at the little dressing table at the end of the bed.
Barely ten minutes had passed between the end of the emergency
call and the ambulance arriving, but those ten minutes had been
the longest of her life. For most of that time she had sat stiffly looking at Alda's body, at the staring eyes directed at the doorway as
if there were some great truth to be found there, the gaping mouth
that appeared to be contorted in a scream of anguish. Judging from
the evidence on the bedside table this was a suicide, although the
appearance of the body suggested otherwise. Dís was not familiar
enough with pathology or forensic medicine to know how a body
should look after overdosing on the type of drugs by the bed, but if
the pills *had* killed Alda it was clear that she hadn't chosen well.
Her fists were clenched, and to Dís it looked as though her usually
flawless cheeks had been scratched deeply enough to draw blood,
enough blood to form the dark pool in which her head lay.

"What do you mean? We can't *do* anything. She killed herself,"
replied Ágúst coldly. "We'll bring flowers to the funeral. A wreath
or whatever." His voice gave no indication that he was upset by
Alda's death, although she had worked for them for a decade.

Dís pulled her hands from her face and sat upright. "What's
wrong with you?" she asked sharply. "A nurse who has worked with
us dies before her time and your idea is to say good-bye to her with
flowers—or 'whatever.' That's pretty cold." She glanced around the
room and asked herself why she was surprised. Ágúst's office was a
reflection of his personality: cold and soulless. Although her own

office was not all that interesting, his was so bereft of any luxuries and so tidy that in an emergency an operation could be performed on his desk. There was nothing in it that didn't have a purpose, not a thing displayed simply because it was attractive or amusing. Even the framed pictures on the walls, which depicted the most common plastic surgery techniques, were there for a purpose. Just after hanging them up Ágúst had told Dís that they would frighten patients who were reluctant about operations. His logic was that such individuals would thus be forced from the start to determine whether they actually trusted themselves to undergo an operation just to look better. Ágúst had recently told Dís that after the photos went up, last-minute cancelations had decreased noticeably.

Now he rocked backward in his seat, clearly surprised. "Huh?" he said, then fell silent. He sighed. "I know this may sound cold, but I'm not one for public displays of emotion." He reached across and took Dís's hand, which was resting on the edge of the desk. "You know how highly I valued her. I just haven't been able to get my head around this, I think. All I can think of is how we're going to find a replacement nurse for the operations that we have coming up." He smiled sadly. "It's easier to deal with the small things."

Dís returned his smile sympathetically. "I know," she said. "It's not as if I haven't been thinking about that too." She pulled her hand away from his and placed it in her lap. She found it uncomfortable to touch his skin, which was silly considering their latex-covered hands touched all the time during operations. "This will all be fine," she said, and pushed her chair back. "Things have a way of working out." She stood up. "I think I would feel better if I hadn't been the one who found her."

"Of course," replied Ágúst. "Try to stop thinking about it. Remember Alda as she was in life. She deserves to be remembered that way."

Dís nodded. Then she asked: "Do you think she might have been murdered?"

"Murdered?" asked Ágúst, flabbergasted. "Who would have had any reason to murder her?"

"Oh, I don't know," said Dís thoughtfully. "Some rapist out for revenge?" she added.

"For God's sake, I don't think so," said Ágúst, frowning. "I'm sure the rape association keeps better control of things than that."

Dís smiled. "They're called the Emergency Reception Unit Support Team for Rape Victims, and I'm not entirely sure that they do have things under control. I know Alda had had enough of them when she left her job at the A&E."

Alda's decision to give up her part-time job had come out of the blue several months earlier. She had been volunteering in the local A&E several nights a week and on the weekends, and among other things had earned a good reputation for her support and assistance of rape victims. She had seemed to enjoy this work, and perhaps her decision to quit was the clue that Dís had been trying to remember. Who knew, maybe the horrors Alda occasionally witnessed there had finally been too much for her to handle. "Maybe it was someone else entirely," she said cautiously.

"Like who?" said Ágúst in irritation. "Mickey, Goofy and Pluto?"

"No. Like you, for example," said Dís calmly, pulling a little paper bag from the pocket of her scrubs.

Ágúst stood up. He didn't seem angry, just surprised. "Me?"

Dís went over and put the bag on the desk in front of him. "I took this from the table beside her bed. Judging by her body, her death wasn't painless. Not at all what one would expect if sleeping pills had killed her."

Ágúst looked Dís in the eye, stubbornly. "And this makes you think that *I* killed her?"

"Look in the bag," she said softly. "I haven't completely lost my mind."

Ágúst looked down at the bag and grabbed it. He glanced quickly back up at Dís.

"Be careful not to touch what's inside," she said calmly. "This might have to go to the police." She saw Ágúst's expression harden and hurried to add, earnestly: "If you were connected to this in some way then it goes no further. If not, then I've got to turn this in somehow. I took it from her bedside table." She pointed at the bag. "But that's a problem for later. First we've got to get this cleared up." He looked at her. "Don't look at me like that until you've seen what it is. Take a look."

Ágúst pulled the plastic down carefully with his index finger. He didn't need to open the bag the whole way, as he recognized the contents as soon as they appeared. "Fucking hell," he said quietly, and his head drooped. "What do we do now?"

"All I know is that no one raised a single objection against the excavation except for Markús," said Hjörtur, walking over to a shelf that appeared about to break under the strain of folders and a tall stack of papers. The archaeologist placed the pages he was holding on the top of the stack and turned back to Thóra and Bella. "Not his parents, and not his brother. And I can assure you that this Alda you mentioned never got in touch with me. She might have discussed things with someone else here in this office, but if she did no one has mentioned it."

Thóra nodded dejectedly. "Would you be willing to ask? If she had, it could make a difference."

Hjörtur gave her a look that combined pity with irritation. "I will, but I doubt it'll lead anywhere."

Thóra sensed that she would have to tread lightly in her dealings with the archaeologist so that he wouldn't block her out. He wasn't obliged to answer her questions or assist her in any way. "Thank you very much," she said humbly. "I know the discovery of the bodies threw a large spanner in your works, and I expect you're just as eager as I am for the case to be solved. One might say we share a common interest."

Hjörtur didn't take the bait. "I certainly hope that the police conclude this as soon as possible, but I'm not in as much of a rush as you are. What's waiting for me has been there for thirty-five years, so several days or weeks ahead or behind schedule isn't going to change the overall picture. We're not comrades." He crossed his arms. "If there's nothing else I can help you with, I would really prefer to keep working. I'm using this downtime to finish several reports that have been hanging over my head. We're not just sitting here twiddling our thumbs because the area is temporarily closed."

Bella snorted, and Thóra hurried to say something before her secretary butted in. "I wanted to ask you a couple of questions, and I promise to be quick," she said. "You'll be rid of us before you know it." She smiled and hoped for the best, but Bella was staring stonily at the archaeologist.

Thóra wasn't sure if it was her honey or her secretary's vinegar that moved Hjörtur, but he agreed to sit down with them for a few minutes. They followed him into a small conference room. "Has anything been found in the excavation that could possibly be connected to the discovery of the bodies?" Thóra began. "Something that might have had no particular significance when it was found, but might now, in the light of what was in the basement? I'm not confining my question to Markús's parents' house."

"No," replied Hjörtur. "I don't remember any such thing. Nor have I given it much thought."

"I expect you log and store everything that you find," said Thóra. "Is there any chance of us being allowed to have a look at those things?"

He shook his head. "No, I can't imagine we'd allow you to do that. The plan is to let the owners of the houses go over the items with us in the later stages and try to reach an agreement on what happens to them," he said, pushing his empty coffee cup aside. "The idea is to set up an exhibition of these items on the site of the excavations, and hopefully in the houses themselves. As you know, the Westmann Islands Municipality owns everything that comes out from under the ash; on the other hand we would certainly want to try to appease the original owners of these items. Something that might mean nothing to us could be invaluable to its former owner, for sentimental reasons." Hjörtur took a deep breath. "Many people have contacted us because of this, mainly looking for photo albums and suchlike, although there have been some inquiries about things like graduation caps, trophies and wristwatches. We do log everything that's found, and it's stored in such a way that it's easy to trace which item came from each house. It would be a huge undertaking to go through all that, so we can't allow it at this stage."

"Haven't the police made a request to search through the items?" asked Thóra. "One would think they would at least have some interest in whatever was found in Markús's house."

Hjörtur shook his head. "Not yet, and hopefully they won't

want to. A lot of work has gone into our system and it would be a huge pain to have to tamper with the boxes."

"Do you have anything against my going through the item log?" asked Thóra. "That might be of some help to me."

Hjörtur's lips thinned. "I'll have to check," he said tightly.

Thóra decided to back off a little. "Might someone have had access to the basement before Markús?" she asked. "Was the door open or closed while the ground floor was cleaned?"

"Are you asking whether the corpses were put there before or after the house was excavated?" said Hjörtur.

"Yes, actually, I am," replied Thóra. "It would certainly increase the number of people who could have links to the case."

"I believe we shut the basement door as soon as we reached it, and you were quite satisfied with how we did it, as I recall," he said, stony faced. "It wasn't more than a couple of hours from when we dug out the door until it was nailed shut. Everything was in accordance with our agreement. Of course anyone who wanted to go down there *could* have, but it's out of the question that anyone took a corpse down into that basement since the excavation."

"But how can you be sure?" asked Thóra. "Don't get me wrong— I'm not suggesting that you or your people had anything to do with it."

"I went down there with the police after the corpses were found, and it didn't take much archaeological expertise to realize that they'd been lying there for years or even decades, rather than several days."

"Wouldn't it be possible to make it look that way?" persisted Thóra. "To throw dust over the corpses, or something, making it appear as though they'd been lying there untouched for years?"

"No," said Hjörtur resolutely.

"Do you have any guesses as to who the people lying there were?" she said. "You're from here, aren't you?"

Hjörtur smiled into his beard. "The volcano erupted on my third birthday, so I can't tell you anything about the event or the people who lived here," he said. "However, I think it's out of the question that these are men from the Islands. Everyone escaped the eruption, so four people couldn't have disappeared."

Thóra decided not to mention the man who had suffocated in the basement of the pharmacy.

"Still, you must have thought about it?" she said. "Who those people were? As an archaeologist, you must be curious about your own dig?"

"Of course I've thought about it," agreed Hjörtur. "But I don't have much imagination so I didn't really get anywhere. I can tell you one thing, though," he added. "Just out of curiosity I looked over the newspapers from that time period—we have them here on old-fashioned microfilm—and I found nothing about missing persons, either Icelandic or otherwise. So they appear not to have been missed, which is very odd." He cleared his throat. "I don't know how well you could see when you were down there but they'd set up floodlights by the time they came to get me. It looked to me as if at least two of the men were wearing wedding rings. What sort of men were they if their wives didn't even look for them?"

An unpleasant thought about her ex-husband crossed Thóra's mind, but she pushed it away. "Good question," she settled for saying. Then she asked: "Did you notice anything that would indicate the men were sailors? I was sort of toying with the notion that this could be related to the Cod War."

Hjörtur shook his head slowly. "As far as I could see and can remember, they weren't wearing waterproofs, or anything else you'd expect to see on sailors at that time," he said. "That's not saying much, though, since sailors aren't always dressed in their work clothes, any more than anyone else is." He smiled and looked down at his scruffy jeans.

"I understand," said Thóra, who had been hoping for a different answer, perhaps even that the men had been holding ropes and nets. She thought for a moment before continuing. "Do you think someone might have got confused and put the bodies in the wrong place?" she asked. "Was the eruption bad enough at any point to make visibility that poor?"

Hjörtur shrugged. "Well, I don't know," he said. "It seems unlikely, but I can't be a hundred percent certain." He scratched his head. "There's also the possibility that the house where the bodies were supposed to have been put had already disappeared, and Markús's house was chosen instead. There's an excellent Web site about the houses that disappeared, both the ones in the area the lava swallowed and those that were buried in ash that we're digging up. Maybe you'll find something useful there."

Thóra smiled at him as he scribbled down the Web address. He had made an excellent point; it was possible that the corpses were not supposed to have ended up there at all, and the whims of the volcano had determined where they could be buried. Why would a man put bodies in his own basement if there were numerous other houses available? Had the bodies and the head ended up in the same place by accident? This riddle about the bodies was starting to infuriate Thóra. She had to uncover the story behind them. Mostly for Markús's sake, but also to satisfy her own curiosity.

Thóra sat with a steaming cappuccino in the same restaurant that she and Bella had eaten in the night before. She had noticed they had computer access for customers, so she could kill two birds with one stone by having a cup of coffee and looking online. They had split up their to-do list: Bella would visit the archive, while she looked at the Web site Hjörtur had recommended. Thóra knew her task was nicer than Bella's—she got to sit in a cozy environment with a cup of coffee while Bella searched through dusty files for two names—but she felt this division of labor to be a small come-uppance for the uneven distribution of luck with men the night before. Although Thóra had in part sent Bella away to get her out of her sight, she really hoped her secretary would accomplish her task, although the chances of this were slim. Thóra had sent her to the archive without first checking to see whether files transferred to Reykjavík the night of the eruption even existed there, but since Bella hadn't contacted her it seemed she'd found something to rummage through. Either that or the archivist happened to be a man, and Bella had seduced him.

Thóra scanned the text on the screen. She quickly found information on Markús's house and its residents at the time, and recognized the names of his parents and brother. She noted down the names of their nearest neighbors, and then those of the residents of the other ten houses on the street. All the names told her was that Kjartan, whom she and Bella had met at the harbormaster's office, looked to have lived in the house next to Markús's. At least, the name of the family head was Kjartan Helgason. There could have been two men with the same name, but no other information on him was to be found on the Web site.

Thóra clicked on the next link, Residents of Sudurvegur Street, and found short biographies of four residents. Luckily, one of these biographical blurbs was about Kjartan Helgason and, even better, the article was accompanied by a photograph. Thóra recognized him immediately. On the downside, his biography didn't tell her much except that Kjartan had had a long career at sea, then worked in various jobs before taking up his current position as harbormaster. He had married and had four children; they were all adults now. Upon finishing this article Thóra skimmed through the other biographies, but found nothing that seemed likely to help Markús. The only thing that drew her attention was how many children there had been in each home. Apart from one couple that appeared to be childless, Magnús and his wife Klara had had the fewest children, just their two sons Leifur and Markús.

Thóra finished her coffee and phoned Bella to check on her progress—and set her mind at rest about the archivist's safety. Her secretary was sullen. The files were obviously in the archive, but Bella hadn't yet been able to discover which boat Markús had traveled on. Thóra regretted not having asked Markús what the boat was called, since the files were arranged by name of vessel. Thóra did her best to be encouraging and tell Bella how important her task was, then she said good-bye and informed her secretary that she was going back to the hotel, where they would meet and decide how best to take advantage of the rest of the day until their dinner with Leifur and his family.

The weather was so pleasant that Thóra decided to make a detour and enjoy the sunshine. She walked past a souvenir shop and went in to buy a statue of a puffin for Sóley, as well as a tiny pair of woolen mittens for her grandson Orri. Just as the saleswoman was ringing up the items, Bella called.

"Guess what I found out?" she said proudly. "Markús and Alda took the same boat to the mainland."

Thóra thanked her, hung up and smiled happily at the saleswoman as she handed her her credit card. They'd cleared the first hurdle.

Chapter 11

Monday, July 16, 2007

"Could you please pass the salt?" asked Thóra, trying to sound nonchalant. On a beautiful porcelain plate in front of her was a light blue egg, flecked with brown, which she had cracked open halfway. Doing so had exposed an almost transparent white, even though the egg was supposed to be hard-boiled. Thóra wasn't very adventurous when it came to food, and a wild bird's egg wasn't very high on her list of delicacies. Normally she would have refused it politely and waited for the main course, but at a dinner with unfamiliar hosts she had no other choice but to salt it well, swallow it and smile. Leifur grinned at her and handed her the saltshaker. "It's not for everyone," he said. "You don't have to eat it if you don't want to."

Thóra smiled back. "No, I would really like to try it," she lied, and shook the slender shaker over the grayish albumen. Then she handed the salt on to Bella and watched as her secretary did much the same. Bella peered out of the corner of her eye at Thóra, clearly suffering the same dilemma.

María, Leifur's wife, was watching them closely from the opposite end of the table. She was visibly displeased. She looked away from the two women and turned to her husband. "I don't know why you always have to force this on your guests, especially as we have visitors so rarely," she said, lifting her glass and gulping down her white wine. "It stopped being clever a long time ago." Her glass banged loudly on the table when she put it down, and it was embarrassingly clear that she'd had a bit too much to drink. She was an extremely good-looking woman who had probably been a great beauty in her youth, but she was painfully thin and Thóra would have bet anything she'd had medical assistance to keep herself looking so good. Her clothing was impeccable and appeared to be mostly brand-new, although it wasn't the latest fashion. Her outfit was classic, a knee-length beige skirt and cream silk shirt that matched her pale suede high heels. Since María had very fair coloring, she looked so monotone that Thóra thought she'd be invisible if she walked in front of a haystack.

"Maybe you'd have preferred to serve your famous burned French onion soup, dear," said Leifur, shooting his wife a look that was anything but loving. He did not seem to be dressed as formally as her, although he wore a shirt and smart trousers. Perhaps the casual impression came from his gestures and facial expressions, since he was in every respect more relaxed than his wife.

"Have you always lived here in the Islands?" asked Thóra, in an attempt to lighten the mood. She had experienced her own marital troubles and hindsight told her that incidents like this were the reason others had started to decline her and Hannes's dinner invitations before they finally divorced. There had been no need to serve half-raw wild birds' eggs to drive away their guests.

"God, no," snapped María.

"María isn't from here, as you might've guessed," said Leifur, smiling sarcastically at his wife. "We met when I was studying in Reykjavík and lived together there for two years until my graduation. With the exception of my school years I've always lived in the Islands." Leifur set aside the empty shell of one egg and reached for another. "I always wanted to study to be a sea captain, but ended up in business." His experienced hands broke the shell off the top of the beautifully colored egg. "It was clear that my father's fishing company was growing and I felt a business degree would be of more use to the family and the company."

"And you turned out to be right, isn't that so?" asked Thóra. She knew from Markús that the fishing company was doing very well. She stuck her spoon into her egg, scooped out some of the hard congealed stuff and tried to swallow it quickly.

"Yes, I suppose I did," said Leifur. "I actually doubt that my education makes much difference. We've been lucky with the catches, and have very experienced captains. Actually I have been able to strengthen the company's foundations, but that's only part of the picture. Things are getting a bit tight now, what with the quotas being curtailed, not to mention the instability of the króna."

Thóra nodded and decided not to get into a deeper conversation about the exchange rate or finances. There was little more boring to her than money talk, and there was a risk that she would display her own ignorance if the conversation continued on its current path. "And Markús hasn't been involved with the fishing company at all?" she asked.

"No, he's gone his own way," replied Leifur. "Luckily, maybe," he added. "It's never a good idea to run a company with two directors. Since father retired I've been running the show alone, and doing well. Markús doesn't complain, and it wouldn't matter if he did. He's happy with his share of the profits."

María snorted. "You would've done even better if you'd sold. You're not the only one with a degree in business administration in this family, and I know very well how much you can get for the quota and the ships. Magnús says that we could live perfectly well off the interest alone, Markús included." She took another gulp of wine. "But God help us if the quota and the company were to be sold."

Thóra didn't know which Magnús she was referring to, but was fairly certain that she didn't mean Leifur and Markús's father. Whoever she meant, Thóra thought she knew where the root of the disagreement between the couple lay. María wanted to sell the company and move to Reykjavík. Yes, that's where Laugavegur High Street was, with shops where one could spend all one's money. She would fit perfectly inside a terribly expensive penthouse in 101 Reykjavík, the downtown district, where she would look out over the blue bay past a single lily in a vase as she sipped café au lait. Leifur, in contrast, would clearly feel about as welcome in such minimalist surroundings as a patchwork quilt. He clearly wanted to hang on to the company and live in the Islands, where he could continue to work in the fishing industry. Perhaps moral obligation played a part too; if the quota and the fishing company were sold, how could he continue to live in the Westmann Islands? His must be a difficult position, bearing the responsibility for the jobs of so many workers in such a small community. Although Thóra was no specialist on the Islands' community after two short visits, she felt that it reflected certain characteristics of the whole of the country in the not so distant past. Iceland before the age of capitalists. Iceland when most people were on almost equal financial terms and the wealthiest men were the pharmacists. Leifur and María's house was no different from any other house in the neighborhood: large and well kept but far from luxurious. It must feel strange to have that much money but never spend it, especially for María, who obviously appreciated the finer things in life. Thóra thought it best to change the subject. "Do your parents still live here?" she asked Leifur, taking another mouthful of egg. It seemed never-ending, and she couldn't imagine anything but an ostrich laying one this size.

"Yes," replied Leifur. "They live in this street, a few doors down, but we're not sure for how much longer. Dad has become extremely difficult and Mum is so old and tired that she can hardly cope. María has been helping her but they're getting to the point where they'll need specialist help, which is hard to find here in the Islands."

María received unexpected Brownie points from Thóra for this. She looked at the woman and decided that despite her cold manner she must have a warm heart. It wasn't so difficult to put yourself in her shoes, an empty nester with not enough to do, while her husband was rushed off his feet. If the woman was from Reykjavík, her support network must be there; old girlfriends could hardly stop by for coffee here. "You have children, don't you?" she asked, addressing María. "Do they live here?"

"No," the woman replied sadly. She added quickly: "I mean, no, they don't live here, but yes, we have children. Two, Magnús and Margrét." She sat up straighter. "Margrét is abroad, doing a medical degree, but Magnús is a business administrator like his father. He works for one of the big banks and recently became director of property management." She glanced at her husband. "So it's foolish to think that one of them could take over the business. Magnús already makes twice what his father does."

"Now, it's not that simple," said Leifur to his wife. "You know that." He turned to Thóra. "Even though our children have followed other paths in life, one never knows whether things might change. And Hjalti, Markús's son, is very keen on the sea and the company. He's with us more or less every summer and a lot of week-ends during the winter. He would be very disappointed if the company changed hands." Once again it appeared as though the conversation were heading in the direction of the couple's unre-solved conflict.

Thóra heard Bella sigh softly. She must be tired of the conversa-tion, although it could just as easily have been the egg that still lay half eaten on the plate in front of her. "Do you remember anything about the eruption?" she asked Leifur in a desperate attempt to re-lieve the tension.

"Of course, my dear," replied Leifur, pushing his plate away. "It's hard to forget."

"Did you go to Reykjavík on the same boat as Markús?" asked Thóra. "I'm trying to find someone who could verify that Markús and Alda spoke to each other during that journey."

"I was on board," replied Leifur, thoughtfully. "I must admit I don't particularly remember Alda being on the same boat, but that doesn't mean much. Alda was the same age as Markús, two years younger than me. At that age I didn't pay much attention to kids." He took a sip of wine. "However, I can assure you that if Alda *was* there, Markús wasn't far behind." He put down his glass. "I don't think he ever actually got over his crush on her, not even as a grown man."

"That's certainly my understanding," said Thóra, as she tried to push the egg down into its shell so that it would look as though she had finished it. She put down her spoon and wiped her mouth with a napkin to complete the illusion. "Is there anyone else who might possibly remember these interactions? What about your mother?"

Leifur shook his head. "Not Mum. She was very seasick and had enough to worry about. I doubt she even noticed Markús." He twirled his glass on the table. "Let me think about this a bit. Maybe I can remember some other people who were there. It would mostly have been Markús's childhood friends who would have noticed anything; the whole class had a crush on Alda so maybe they can remember something."

Thóra reached into her handbag, which was hanging on the back of her chair, and took out a photocopy of the report that Bella had found in the archive. "Here's a list of the people who came to the mainland on that boat. Maybe you'll recognize the names on it." She handed it to Leifur.

Leifur looked over the list, which was handwritten and totalled four pages. Suddenly his face brightened. "Jóhanna, Alda's younger sister. She still lives in the Islands and works at the bank where I do business. Maybe she can help, although she might not remember the evacuation. I'll talk to her tomorrow if you think it might help."

Thóra thanked him. She saw Bella give up on her egg and place her napkin over it with an uncharacteristically dainty hand movement. "Thank you," she said quietly, pushing the plate away slightly. "Very unique flavor," she added, without looking up from the tablecloth in front of her. María smiled at them, but only with her mouth. She stood up and started clearing the table. Then she went, arms full, to the kitchen, where they could hear her preparing the main course. Thóra crossed her fingers in the hope that no more special dishes would be served, but genuinely feared that the woman was about to appear with a platter of grilled starfish. "Haven't the police come round to take statements from you?" she asked Leifur, setting aside her concerns about the menu. "Or your parents?"

"I received a phone call the other day from Reykjavík and I told them I knew nothing about it," he replied. "I doubt they'll let it go that easily because the man I spoke to asked a lot of questions about my future travel plans, as well as about Mum and Dad. He also told me they'd be back in touch, and that we'd be subpoenaed. I pointed out to him that it wasn't possible to question my father, and described his illness. This was on Friday, as I recall, but I haven't heard any more from them." Leifur shrugged, almost dismissively, although Thóra couldn't tell if his lack of interest was genuine. "They'll come when they come. We've got nothing to hide."

"You have nothing to worry about," Thóra reassured him. "But what explanation do you have for the bodies in the basement? You must have given it some thought."

Leifur gestured noncommittally. "Of course I have," he replied. "I wish I could say I was able to come up with an explanation. I have no idea who these people were or how they ended up there, of all places. It does seem pretty obvious to me that they were foreigners, though. Four Icelanders could never have disappeared in the eruption without anyone noticing it."

"And were there any foreigners here at that time?" asked Thóra. "And by 'that time' I mean during the eruption, as well as before it started."

"Hmm," he mused. "Before the eruption there were always foreigners around, though not as many as now. They were mostly sailors and people working in the fishing industry, not tourists like they are these days." He smiled apologetically at Thóra. "I have to admit I don't know whether any foreigners were here during the eruption itself. I suppose there were some who helped out during the rescue operation. Soldiers from the base, maybe."

Thóra, who hadn't thought of this, made a mental note to ask about disappearances from the Keflavík Naval Air Station at the time. She hoped that all the information hadn't been spirited away on the departure of the Defense Force.

"Would there be any way for me to speak to your father?" she asked cautiously. "Maybe he still remembers this, even though the old days might be slipping from his memory?"

Leifur looked forlorn. "I'm afraid there wouldn't be much point. Even though Dad has good days it's been a long time since it was possible to have a decent conversation with him. He talks, but the words he strings together are usually meaningless and unrelated. Mum, on the other hand, is sharp as a tack." He regarded Thóra closely. "What are you getting at? Do you think my father had something to do with this?"

To Thóra's relief Leifur did not appear to be angry, just curious. "No, not necessarily. I was hoping he could give me some information about people's visits to your house, or hazard a guess at who the bodies belonged to," she said. "It's reasonable to suppose he would have paid closer attention to his own house. The other rescue workers no doubt had less interest in it."

"That's a good point," said Leifur. "But he won't be able to help you. It's a shame. Mum won't be much help either, since she wasn't here doing salvage work. However, she may remember something about any foreigners in the area just before the eruption." He shook his head. "I don't know what else she might know. It may be that she doesn't remember a single thing about any of it. It's been decades. I can only remember bits and pieces myself."

A faint smell of smoke drifted in, and Bella wriggled in her seat. "Can I smoke here?" she asked hopefully.

"María smokes in the kitchen," he replied, and waved Bella to the kitchen door. "Please. She'll be delighted to have company." Bella did not need to be told twice.

"Did you not know Alda at all?" Thóra asked after Bella had left. "She appears to be a key player in all of this if your brother's story about where he got the severed head holds up. My instinct tells me that the corpses and the head are two branches of the same story. Anything else would be too much of a coincidence."

"I agree with you there," replied Leifur. "Unfortunately I didn't know Alda at all well. Of course I knew who she was, and there was quite a lot of contact between our parents in those days; but as I told you, she was younger than me, so I didn't pay much attention to her. After we went to the mainland the friendship between our parents pretty much fizzled out. They moved to the Westfjords, if I remember correctly, while my father kept on fishing in the South."

"But doesn't her mother live here in the Islands?" asked Thóra. "That was my understanding from Kjartan at the harbormaster's office, and he also said her father died recently." She added in explanation: "I met Kjartan yesterday at Markús's suggestion."

Leifur nodded. "As I said, I know that Jóhanna, Alda's sister, still lives here, but I'm not certain about their mother. To tell the truth, there was no love lost between me and my father's old friends. Especially not after I took over the business."

"Oh?" responded Thóra. "What happened?"

Leifur rolled his eyes, exasperated. "I thought Dad was much too sentimental about them. It was as if he felt he owed them something, particularly Geiri, Alda's father, even though all of the negotiations were perfectly aboveboard."

"Now I don't understand," she said. "What negotiations are you talking about?"

"The purchase of the first ship," replied Leifur. "They bought it in partnership, Dad and Geiri, Alda's father. That's how the company worked at first, it was co-owned by the two of them." He pointed out a painting of a ship hanging on the wall behind her. "That's the boat, *Strokkur VE*, a hundred-ton motor trawler. The painting was in Dad's office. I removed it when I took over, since to me it was so closely connected to him, and I wanted to make it clear to everyone that a new skipper was at the helm. I still wanted to be able to see it, just not at work." Leifur smiled. "It wouldn't be considered an enormous ship today, but in its time people thought it was quite something." His expression was oddly proud and affectionate, although the painting couldn't exactly be called a masterpiece. "They hadn't owned the ship for more than a year before the eruption, and Dad disagreed completely with Geiri over further operations. He wanted to keep the fishing company going after the eruption, but Geiri simply gave up and let Dad buy him out."

"I saw an old news report from the period about a trawler that had been sunk to collect insurance money," said Thóra. "That suggests the industry hadn't exactly been easy for everyone."

"Very true," said Leifur. "It was terribly hard for a while. Luckily we never had to resort to the desperate measures you describe, but we were no doubt not far from it when things were at their worst."

"Was your father a wealthy man before he started the fishing operation?" asked Thóra, turning from the painting to Leifur. "I know less than nothing about ships, but I expect they cost quite a bit."

Leifur smiled. "No, he really wasn't wealthy at all. He put everything he had into financing his half, and even that came nowhere near the total cost of the boat. He and Geiri took out a large loan to make the purchase, and mortgaged everything they owned. The ship also had a huge mortgage, of course. Because of that, Dad only needed to pay Geiri back what he'd contributed originally, but there was no profit foreseeable in the operation during those first few years and it was unclear whether it could keep going after the eruption. Part of the collateral disappeared with our house and that complicated the family's finances a great deal." Leifur took a sip of wine. "But Dad didn't give up even when things were going really badly; if anything, he became more enthusiastic. He managed to keep the ship, and trumped that by buying the only processing plant here at the harbor for peanuts, while the eruption was still happening. It had been written off by its former owners when he took the chance on it, but he got it going again, even before the eruption stopped. No one would have believed it when the deal was made, because at the time people thought all the property in the Westmann Islands would be worthless."

"How did your father actually pay his debts?" asked Thóra. "Was it possible to fish, despite the disaster?"

"The Westmann Islands fleet had a record catch that winter. Dad caught more fish than he ever had before, but he didn't land his catches in the Islands until after he'd purchased the plant. Dad was hardworking, but he was also lucky. Good catches and inflation that ate up the loan over time helped him start raking it in. When the processing operation got off the ground, slowly but surely he was able to build up his own fleet of ships, and over time he added a trawler, then another and so forth. He also laid the foundations of the company as it exists today during the eruption. His boldness when everything appeared hopeless worked to make him wealthy, while his friend, who lost his courage during the hard times, was left behind with nothing to show for it."

"I saw a photograph of your father, this Geiri and others at Kjartan's office," said Thóra. "One of them was the police inspector Gudni Leifsson, whom I understand was one of your father's friends. As I understand it, their friendship was severed at some point."

Leifur shook his head. "No, Father and Gudni have been friends their whole life. But Kjartan took offense when he was connected to a case of liquor smuggling. He thought that Gudni should have turned a blind eye to his part in it, in the light of their being friends. Dad wasn't involved in that, luckily. I don't understand why Kjartan is still going on about it, since the case was dismissed and he never suffered at all because of it."

Leifur cleared his throat and fiddled with a button on his shirt. Thóra got the impression that he wasn't telling her the whole truth, but didn't think he was lying, exactly. He looked quizzically at her. "Is Gudni making life hard for you?"

"No," said Thóra halfheartedly. "At least, not yet. Hopefully this investigation will be over before he can."

Leifur's jaw clenched and he seemed on the verge of saying something, but at that moment María and Bella reappeared, trailing smoke behind them, so he stopped. Much to Thóra's relief, the main course was leg of lamb. She was sure Leifur hadn't told her everything. Those who are not used to hiding the truth always give themselves away.

Chapter 12

Tuesday, July 17, 2007

Thóra put down her mobile phone and heaved a sigh. "No answer," she said regretfully to Bella. "That was the last one." They were sitting in the hotel lobby, where Thóra had gone online to look for the telephone numbers of women Markús thought had been friends with Alda when she was young. Thóra had called him shortly after she got up to tell him that she was making no progress in the search for anyone who could back up his story about the box. Markús had told her some names, and judging by the list Thóra had scribbled down Alda had been extremely popular. Unfortunately Markús had difficulty remembering surnames, so after a long search Thóra ended up with only five names. Three had answered and they all told the same story. They had been great friends with Alda in the old days but hadn't kept in touch, since unlike them Alda had moved to the Westfjords after the eruption and hadn't returned to the Islands with her parents after a year.

According to the women, the majority of the refugees had lived in and around Reykjavík, but for some reason Alda's family ended up out in the countryside. They didn't know whether this had happened because of relatives or work, since they never spoke to Alda at the time, although they had all tried to find her. She hadn't been in the "Eruption Class" that was put together in the Bústadur School for teenagers from the Islands, nor on the trip to Norway the summer after the eruption, to which all of the children from the Westmann Islands between six and sixteen had been invited. One of the women thought this was odd, saying that Alda had often spoken of how much she wanted to go abroad. None of them recalled Alda having entrusted a secret to them right before the eruption, nor had any of them been on board the same boat to the mainland as Alda on the night of the evacuation. So they could not bear witness to any conversation between Alda and Markús, although they all remembered Markús very well, and they all even mentioned how much of a crush he had had on her. The only thing that came out of these conversations was that one of the women professed herself amazed that Alda hadn't accompanied her parents back to the Islands when they finally returned, instead choosing to move to Reykjavík and attend junior college there under the protective wing of her father's family. The woman even thought it likely that Alda had never again set foot in the Islands after the eruption.

Thóra switched off her phone and put it into her handbag. "If it's true that Alda never came back here, that's a pretty good indication that something happened," she said.

"Such as what?" asked Bella indifferently. "What happens to make someone end up carrying around a head in a box?"

"Good question," said Thóra. There was certainly something to what Bella said. What sequence of events had to take place for a teenage girl to come into possession of a human head? "In any case, I still find it very unlikely that she murdered someone at such a young age."

"Why?" asked Bella. "I've never been *more* likely to kill someone than during my teenage years." She stared at Thóra. "I could probably have done it quite easily."

Thóra smiled reluctantly. "Hardly," was all she said, although in her heart she did not agree. She was in no doubt that Bella was capable of such an act, both then and now. Thóra had no time to consider this any further, because someone tapped on her shoulder. Behind her stood a woman of around forty. She was dressed in a blue trouser suit, and the name tag on her lapel read *Jóhanna Thorgeirsdóttir.* This must be Alda's sister. Leifur had certainly stood by his word from the night before.

"Hello, are you Thóra Gudmundsdóttir?" said the woman in a low voice. Her eyes were reddened and her face haggard. "The woman on reception pointed you out to me."

Thóra stood up and shook the woman's hand warmly, but the expression in the eyes that met hers was anything but friendly. "Yes, hello. You must be Alda's sister." She squeezed the woman's hand. "My condolences for the loss of your sister." She released her hand, since the woman only held it limply. "I didn't expect you to come and see me, and I hope that Leifur didn't press it on you."

The expression on the woman's face tightened another notch. "I didn't speak to Leifur. He spoke to the branch director, who sent me here. Leifur's a close acquaintance of his, and close acquaintances get good service. As I understand it, he's not to be offended."

Thóra swallowed her irritation at Leifur. She had understood his words to mean that he knew Alda's sister, and that he himself would speak to her. She hadn't expected a woman who had recently lost her sister to be sent to her like a pizza delivery boy.

"I am sincerely sorry," was all she could say as her anger subsided. She paused a moment. This degraded woman standing before her deserved better. "You don't have to speak to me if you don't want to. I understand that you're suffering and I don't wish to take advantage of Leifur's insensitivity or that of the man you work for. They don't run my errands."

The woman looked up and squared her jaw. "The branch manager is actually a woman." She looked around. "And actually I'd be happy to sit down for a moment. Two of the four clerks called in sick this morning, but the bank's work regulations stipulate that there must always be two cashiers out front. I'm one of the two who came to work today." She pointed at the sofa in front of the reception desk. "Let's sit down there. Then my manager can decide whether she or the cleaning lady will fill in for me."

Thóra smiled approvingly at Alda's sister. "Good idea," she said. "But can I suggest that we sit in the cafeteria instead? It's quieter and we've got a better chance of getting coffee there." She sent Bella away and they sat down over cups of coffee at a little wooden table in the farthest corner of the cafeteria.

"First of all, I should warn you that I still haven't recovered from the news about Alda," said Jóhanna as she took her seat. "Although there were eight years between us, we were very good friends. We weren't in daily contact, but we were close nevertheless." She took a sip of coffee, placed the cup back awkwardly on its saucer and adjusted it carefully. "I don't believe she committed suicide. She would never do that. It must have been an accident, or something worse." She looked up. "I expect everyone who experiences a relative killing himself or herself thinks that way, but it's not like that. Alda wasn't the kind of person to commit suicide."

Thóra realized that the woman didn't know why she'd asked to meet her. "I didn't ask to see you to discuss Alda's tragic death." She took a deep breath. "I'm afraid I don't know the circumstances so I can't comment on it. I'm working for Markús, Leifur's younger brother. He's in a rather difficult position, you might say, because three bodies were found in the basement of his childhood home. Alda's name came up in the investigation and I was hoping that you could either tell me something that might help Markús or point me toward someone who can." Thóra stopped and waited for the woman's reaction. She thought it highly likely that she would thank her abruptly and say good-bye.

Jóhanna looked at Thóra, apparently quite surprised. "Of course I've read the news and heard people talking about the bodies. It's a hot topic here in town, understandably." She seemed slightly embarrassed as she continued. "They said Markús was involved, but I thought it was just gossip since he hasn't been mentioned in the papers. I've never heard Alda's name mentioned, I've only heard that they were British people who had probably been murdered before the eruption."

"British?" exclaimed Thóra. "Do you know where that story came from?" Could her hypothesis about the Cod War have been correct?

"I haven't really tried to find out," replied the woman. "I've had other things to think about. But I seem to recall the autopsy uncovered that."

Thóra stiffened. Was it possible that the majority of the town's residents had heard about developments in the investigation before those involved had been given the information? She tried not to display any emotion, but she was itching to rush down to the police station and give Inspector Leifsson an earful. "I haven't heard that so I don't know if it's correct," she said. "Whether it's true or not, the case is in the hands of the police and the investigation is still in its initial stages. As it is, I only have knowledge pertaining to my client, and Alda's death was a hard blow for him to bear. She was privy to information that could have kept the investigation afloat and shed light on his innocence."

Jóhanna shifted in her seat, breathing quickly, her pupils dilated. "Do you think that someone murdered her to keep her quiet?" she asked breathlessly. "That must be the explanation." She placed one hand on her chin. "Could the man responsible for the deaths of the people in the basement have killed Alda?"

"Let's not get ahead of ourselves," said Thóra calmly. "As I said, I'm not sure how Alda's death is connected to the case, if at all. I'm trying to figure that out." She didn't want to say that this case might explain Alda's suicide—if indeed she had committed suicide. Similar things had happened, when someone didn't trust himself to stare his own misdeeds in the face, and instead chose the unknown. "It's entirely possible that there is a connection. At the very least, it's a strange coincidence."

"What do you want to know?" asked Jóhanna resolutely. "I want to help in any possible way I can."

Irritation at Leifur overwhelmed Thóra. If he had responded in the right way, she would have been better prepared. She asked the first question that came to mind: "I know that you went with your mother and sister to the mainland the night of the eruption. Do you remember seeing Markús and Alda speaking to each other on board the ship?"

Jóhanna's eyes widened. "It's strange, but I remember the sea voyage as if it happened yesterday. I was only seven years old but that night was an experience I've never been able to forget. I thought war had broken out."

"And did you happen to see whether Alda and Markús spoke?" asked Thóra patiently.

"Actually, I think I did," replied Jóhanna. "I held tightly to my mother's hand on one side and to Alda's on the other, and I remember I didn't want to let go when she tried to walk away. I'm pretty sure that it was with Markús. They went off somewhere but I don't know where, or how long they were gone. I just remember that I cried the whole time she was away, because I was sure she wouldn't come back."

"Are you happy to declare this to the police?" asked Thóra, trying to mask her delight. This was all going very well.

"Yes, I think so," replied Jóhanna. "My mother might remember it too, and she's probably a better witness, since she was older than me when it happened, naturally." She fiddled with her teaspoon on the saucer. "She's not in any fit state for an interview at the moment, because of Alda, but she'll get over it, hopefully. Dad died quite recently after a long struggle against cancer, so she's suffered a lot this year."

"I understand," said Thóra. "I heard you moved to the Westfjords after the disaster. How was Alda at that time? I realize you were young, but do you remember whether she changed in any way? Did she behave differently or seem depressed at all?"

Jóhanna shook her head. "No, I don't think so. Alda went to boarding school soon after we moved west, so I didn't see her much. Like everyone else in the family she'd been uprooted, so naturally she may not have been quite herself. I think Mother would know better than me."

"What school was she sent to?" Thóra asked. Maybe she could look up some of Alda's schoolfriends.

"I'm pretty sure it was Ísafjördur Junior College," said Jóhanna.

Thóra tried not to reveal her surprise, but this didn't sound right. "I understood from her girlfriends that she went to Reykjavík Junior College? Was that not the case?"

"No, not at all," Jóhanna replied. "She changed schools in the autumn, wanting to be in Reykjavík rather than the west, since we'd all gone from there back to the Islands."

This didn't add up. How could Alda have started school in the middle of the winter term, a year above the one she should have been in? Markús had been the same age as Alda and her classmates, and he was still in secondary school the year of the eruption. "Was Alda a good student?" she asked.

"Yes, very good," said Jóhanna. "She was always incredibly conscientious and hardworking. She actually enjoyed learning. Not like me." She smiled, but it faded quickly. "It's funny," she said, although she didn't look at all amused, "I've lain there thinking about what could have happened to Alda but it never crossed my mind that this could be connected to the bodies in the basement. I was so certain that it had something to do with her work at the A&E, that one of those disgusting rapists had broken into her house and killed her."

"Well, there's no evidence that that's what happened," said Thóra. "So maybe this case of the corpses *is* connected to Alda's death in some way."

"Yes, I'm convinced it is," said Jóhanna determinedly, crossing her arms.

Thóra knew that people who were grieving often held on to the slenderest threads of hope, clinging to illogical theories and explanations. It was a way to focus their minds on something other than the grief and guilt they would feel for the rest of their lives.

"I'm sure the truth will come out," said Thóra, although she didn't feel sure at all. "These rapists you mentioned, did Alda have much contact with them? I would have thought she'd have dealt with the victims, not the perpetrators." Markús had told Thóra about Alda's work for the Emergency Reception Unit.

"When you put it like that, I suppose it doesn't make much sense," replied Jóhanna. "To my knowledge she didn't ever meet them, but I was imagining that one of them could somehow have found out her name and set out for revenge. She'd had to testify in at least two cases. She'd actually had enough, and she'd just resigned from the unit when this tragedy happened. Something came up at work that she never had time to tell me about. She was planning to fly here next weekend to stay with me; she said she needed to tell me something and wanted to do it face-to-face."

"She was going to come here?" asked Thóra. "From talking to her childhood girlfriends, I thought she never came back after the evacuation."

"That's true, she didn't," agreed Jóhanna. "The eruption affected her so badly that she never trusted herself to return. Also she was at school, and worked every summer. I'm not sure that it was a conscious decision of hers, it just turned out that way. She might have wanted to cut her ties to the Westmann Islands, although she never said anything like that to me. What was really tragic was that after the disaster, kids from the Islands never wanted to say where they came from. We were looked down on and made to feel as if we were parasites feeding off the rest of the country. You can't accuse Icelanders of being sensitive to the needs of others, even their own countrymen. Their compassion doesn't reach very far. Alda might have wanted to put some distance between herself and the Islands because of that."

Thóra doubted that was the reason. It seemed more likely that whatever had led Alda to ask Markús to hide the severed head had made it impossible for her to imagine returning to the area. "This thing she wanted to discuss with you, did she say what it was about?" she asked.

Jóhanna shook her head. "She was being a bit weird about it. She said she should've sat down with me a long time ago to get it off her chest." She stopped, seeming on the verge of tears. "That's how I know she didn't kill herself; she wouldn't have done it before we had a chance to talk. She was so insistent that we meet face-to-face, she couldn't tell me on the phone."

"When did you hear from her last?" asked Thóra.

"The day before she died she phoned to tell me that she'd bought her ticket, and she seemed happier than she'd been in the previous phone call." Jóhanna rubbed at her right eye. "It was as if she'd received good news or had a load taken off her shoulders. I don't know what had happened."

Thóra suspected that what had cheered Alda up was the knowledge that Markús was going to remove the head from the basement. She must have been nervous while the status of the excavation was still unclear, which would explain her mental state in those conversations with her sister. When it looked as if everything was going to work out she had felt happy again, but this lasted only a short time before everything went as badly as it possibly could. "Hopefully it will all become clear," she soothed.

"She said one thing I didn't understand," said Jóhanna thoughtfully. "She asked me under what circumstances I would get a tattoo. She was in such a good mood that it didn't seem to matter to her that I couldn't answer the question. And then there was some rigmarole about how one should be careful of judging others and that she wouldn't make that mistake again. She said she would explain it all the following weekend, but I felt like the tattoo question was somehow connected to her cheerfulness."

"Tattoo?" Thóra frowned. How could something like that be relevant to all this?

Chapter 13

Tuesday, July 17, 2007

Thóra was pleased with Bella. The young woman stood at her side, her arms crossed over her chest and a thunderous look on her face that was making even Inspector Leifsson squirm in his seat. "It absolutely beggars belief that one should hear of developments in a police investigation out on the street," continued Thóra. "Since you're in charge of the station, and since the information must originally have come from here, I have no choice but to hold you responsible for the leak." The thundercloud next to her nodded its head emphatically.

Gudni was completely silent for a moment, as was his wont. He rocked back and forth in his chair and then leaned forward, placing his elbows on the desk. "I haven't leaked anything," he said calmly. "Six police officers work here in addition to me, not to mention the receptionist and the cleaner. Any one of them could have blurted something out without me having had anything to do with it. So you'd better think twice before you start accusing me of a breach of confidence."

"Accusing you?" snapped Thóra. "I'm not *accusing* you of anything. I've come here to demand a copy of the autopsy report, which I understand you have. I wish to inform myself of its contents first-hand rather than relying on street gossip."

"I understand," said Gudni quietly. He was clearly unhappy about this new development, but trying not to show it. Thóra noticed some small muscles twitching around his mouth. "I don't have any objection to you seeing the documents. Should I check and see what *the book* says about such things?"

"Kindly do so," she replied, knowing he wouldn't have the first idea where to look for the laws regulating access to files in a criminal case. She actually doubted that a copy of the relevant regulations existed in Gudni's office, and he probably wouldn't even know where to find them on the Internet.

"But I don't see what purpose it will serve," said Gudni, as he stood up. He picked up some papers stapled together in one corner and waved them at her. "No doubt you'll get hold of this soon enough, because I have trouble believing that Markús won't be arrested very soon. The autopsy does not look good for him."

"How do you mean?" asked Thóra. She longed to tear the report from the man's hands and start reading it.

"I mean that it provides, for the first time, clear evidence that these men were murdered. In other words, this is now a murder investigation. In addition, the report contains indications of the men's nationality. They are probably British, and contact has already been made with the British police, asking them to investigate who these men might have been. So no doubt this case will soon be all over the British newspapers, and when that happens I can promise you that the police department will be a hive of activity, and the demand for answers will ensure that Markús will be taken into custody. He is the only suspect we have at this stage." Gudni stared straight at Thóra. "The autopsy does not implicate Alda."

"No, we didn't expect it to," said Thóra. Although she was disappointed, Gudni did have a point. She sighed deeply. The only people who could have explained things and cleared Markús's name were either dead or demented.

"It doesn't help that these British men were murdered during the Cod War," said Gudni. "Certain individuals in particular social groups still harbor a grudge over that dispute, both here and in Britain. The British press are sure to play up that angle."

"Do you think that these men were murdered because of fish?" cried Bella. "Because of *cod*?"

Gudni gave her a reproachful look. "The codfish is money with fins and gills. You shouldn't underestimate its importance."

Bella was about to defend herself so Thóra hurried to interrupt her. "Were they fishermen, then?"

"That is not stated directly, but you can read this at your leisure and draw your own conclusions," replied Gudni. "It's best that I go and make a copy of it." He walked past them without another word.

Bella scowled at him, then looked around the little office. "Fucking idiot," she said, seemingly more to herself than to Thóra. She went over to Gudni's desk and ran her eyes over the things lying on it.

"For God's sake don't start looking at anything," Thóra hissed exasperatedly.

"He wouldn't have left us alone if there was anything here he didn't want us to see," said Bella as she bent toward the desk. She turned one of the pieces of paper on the table faceup. "When did the volcano erupt, again?" she asked.

Thóra moved closer. "January 1973. The eruption started on the night of the twenty-third. Why?"

"This is an old report," said Bella. "It's dated the twentieth of January 1973. Don't you find it a bit odd that he's got such an old report on his table?"

"What does it say?" asked Thóra anxiously. She looked over at the doorway but there was no one to be seen. How long did it take to photocopy ten pages? "Quickly!" she whispered.

"Wait," said Bella, as she picked up the page to get a better look. "It's a report about signs of a fight or injury at the pier. The police were called out by the harbormaster, who found a lot of blood on the pier on the morning of Saturday the twentieth of January. He couldn't think of any natural explanation for it and called the police, thinking that a crime might have been committed. He said the harbor had been unsupervised from midnight on Friday evening until he turned up for his next shift, at eight o'clock on Saturday morning." Bella ran her finger down the page. "The police officer examined the evidence, which was compelling, and asked the harbormaster what ships had been moored there. It turned out that no boat had been moored there for several days. The police also checked whether anyone had gone to the hospital with injuries that night, but no one had been admitted after midnight except a married couple with a sick baby." Bella looked up at Thóra. "Couldn't this be linked to the bodies?" she asked.

"I don't know," Thóra half whispered. "Quickly, keep reading." She glanced at the door out of the corner of her eye, but all was quiet. "The police interviewed several people in the wake of this, and two witnesses reported seeing Dadi Karlsson up and about early in the morning. One of them said that he'd been docking in a dinghy, and the other that he'd been at the place where the blood was found. The police officer spoke to Dadi but he denied this and said he hadn't been there. He claimed he'd been at home sleeping and said his wife could verify that, which she did. The officer then boarded the trawler that Dadi piloted but found nothing unusual there. The case was considered unsolved, but plans were made to investigate whether the blood could conceivably have come from an animal or an illegal catch that had been landed under the cover of night." Bella looked up from the report. "That's all there is."

"Which police officer wrote the report?" Thóra asked hurriedly, and waved her hand to indicate that their time was running out. Footsteps could be heard approaching in the corridor.

"Gudni Leifsson," said Bella, and hurried to put the paper back in its place. No sooner had she done so than they heard Gudni walking through the door behind them.

Thóra turned to him, trying to look innocent. She couldn't be certain, but if this report wasn't connected to the case, why would he be looking at such an old document? She also had a feeling that Gudni was not investigating a cold case in cooperation with his colleagues from Reykjavík, but working on it alone. Whether that was a good thing or a bad thing for Markús, she'd have to wait and see. "Well," she said, and walked up to Gudni. He handed her a copy of the medical examiner's report and looked inquisitively at Bella, who was still standing very close to the desk.

"Do you need something?" he asked her coldly.

Bella looked back at him, equally impassive. "No, why do you ask?" Her glare dared him to accuse her of prying.

Gudni did not fall into her trap, but frowned for a second before turning back to Thóra. "There's more there that will catch the attention of the media if and when the report's contents are made public," he said. "It's about the head, and the evidence is indisputable." He smiled nastily. "Which comes as a surprise in a case I thought had already reached its dramatic peak."

"There are a lot of surprises still to come in this case, it seems to me," said Thóra, against her better judgment. There was something about this man that ruffled her feathers. However, she avoided glancing at the papers on his desk as she said this. It was better to leave him wondering what she meant.

Thóra put down the papers and drummed her fingers as she tried to gather her thoughts. She'd finished going through three of the four sections; a specific report had been written for each of the bodies, as well as for the head. The sections she had read concerned the three bodies, which turned out to be of two men in their thirties and a man of around fifty. The men were Caucasian and all the bodies were extremely well preserved, owing to the unusual conditions in which they had been stored. The heat of the eruption was thought to have played a large part in protecting them, along with the lack of humidity in the basement and the fact that heavy toxic gases had destroyed all insect life down there.

Even though the text was hard to read, every other word being an incomprehensible medical term, it was clear that the men had not been killed by toxic gases. Although no conclusion was reached on the exact cause of death, it was strongly suggested that the three men had all been victims of violence. They all had peculiar wounds on their hands that appeared to have healed long before, and which were therefore unconnected to the events that had led to their deaths. They seemed to be scars from deep scratches whose origin was unclear, but it was considered unlikely that they had been made by tools or knives because of the irregularity of their shapes. Two of the men were thought to have died from head injuries, since their skulls had been smashed, seemingly by the same unidentified blunt weapon. The nose of one of them had been so badly broken that the cartilage had been driven into his brain, although the medical examiner could not determine whether he had died from this injury or from his fractured skull. The report further stated that while the third man's head injuries were minor, he had both a broken back and three broken ribs, which had punctured one of his lungs. The report concluded that the latter injury had caused bleeding into the chest cavity and lungs, which would eventually have caused the man to drown in his own blood. Thóra shuddered, but it was clear to her that a teenage girl on her own could not have done so much damage to a group of men.

The examiner's conclusion concerning the men's nationality was supported by various factors. It was noted that each taken on its own would not be enough to determine the men's origin, but together they lent sufficient weight to the hypothesis that the men were British. It was also noted that the person or persons who had transported the bodies to the basement had seemed not to expect them to be found, since no attempt had been made to remove the dead men's clothing or anything else that could be used to identify them. This had proved useful in determining the men's nationality, since the brand labels on their clothing and shoes were still partly legible and turned out to be mostly from British companies; the brands of the oldest man's clothing were more expensive than those of the younger men. The material in the younger men's fillings turned out to be the one British dentists had used around 1960, and one of them also had a steel pin in his ankle from an old injury, stamped with the trademark of a British manufacturer. Other things were taken into account; the two younger men were both tattooed with the initials *HMS*, which if taken to stand for *Her Majesty's Service* would suggest that they could have served in the military for a time and had wished to commemorate this in ink on their skin. Two of the men also had British pound notes in their pockets, and one had an elderly packet of British cigarettes.

Thóra wondered if the tattoo that Alda had mentioned to her sister could conceivably have been the same as the ones mentioned in the report. What had she said again? *Under what circumstances would you get a tattoo?* Could she have been talking about entry into the military? Thóra shook her head instinctively—it couldn't be that. She was sure it had nothing to do with the case, but marked the text to make it easier to recall that particular detail if tattoos came up again.

The report made for melancholy reading as a whole, but Thóra was pleased to read that the bodies had probably been put there after the eruption started. This was based on the discovery of traces of ash on the back of the men's jackets—the corpses had been lying on their backs. The fine layer of ash that slipped in through the chinks in the house and covered all the surfaces in the basement could not have got in underneath the bodies after they'd been laid on the floor. In addition, there were tiny burn holes in the men's clothing, which indicated that they'd either been alive and walking around during the eruption and been hit by the small embers that had rained from the sky during that time, or that the same had happened while the bodies were being carried to the house. No embers could have got into the basement, since its few windows had been boarded up, though fine ash had managed to slip in through all the cracks. In other words, the men had been on the move during the eruption, alive or dead. This meant, to Thóra's great relief, that Markús could not have taken the corpses there.

When she started reading the section of the report that focused on the head, she was even more relieved. It began by describing the box Markús said had contained the head, and it concluded that the evidence indicated this had indeed been the case. Long-dried-out remains of blood and other biological matter at the bottom of the box indicated that the head had been inside. There were also no traces of ash in the hair, which was taken as an indication that the head had been enclosed in something and had not got dusty like everything else in the basement. This, too, strengthened Markús's defense, and Thóra took a moment to mark this section in the margin. Unfortunately, analysis of the fingerprints on the box revealed nothing of significance except that only one set could be distinguished. The prints in question were recent, and at the time the autopsy report was written they had not been compared with Markús's prints, which were not yet on file. Thóra knew that he would now be called in for fingerprinting, but was unconcerned as his prints on the box would fit perfectly with the sequence of events he had described. These were the only legible prints: any others that may have been on the box had not been deliberately erased, but rather had faded due to the unusual conditions and to the time that had passed before the box was discovered. This was unfortunate, since Alda's fingerprints on the box would have been particularly useful. These results were not considered conclusive, so the report stated that the box would be sent to a laboratory overseas that was better equipped to analyze such things. There were similar plans for the analysis of the men's back molars. Thóra hurriedly scribbled a note to herself to remind her to phone and request that fingerprints be taken from Alda's body if more prints were found on the box, although she imagined that would happen as a matter of course.

Then there was the head itself. Thóra still hadn't come across anything to explain Gudni's snide hints about Markús, so she steeled herself to find something here. The autopsy breakdown started quite innocently with notes on the age of the teeth, which indicated that the head belonged to a young man, probably around twenty years of age. Then the report turned to the cause of death, which was impossible to determine in the absence of the body. The evidence suggested the head had been removed postmortem. This conclusion was drawn from the saw cuts, which were unnaturally even, suggesting that the man could not have been alive while they were made. Thóra looked up from her reading and wondered whether this meant that a living man, even unconscious, would have moved around while his head was being sawn off. As before, a surreal feeling came over her when she thought about the severed head. None of her law tutors at university could have thought to prepare their students for anything like this, and in fact Thóra doubted any level of tuition could have prepared her either. She kept reading. The head was thought to be male based on measurements of X-ray images of the jawbone, as well as other size ratios of the skull. In addition, stubble was still perceptible around the chin. There were no dental fillings, so no attempt could be made to determine the nationality or even the race of the head. This was bad, in Thóra's opinion. If it had been another British man, that would suggest that the head belonged to someone from the same group of men, with whom Markús had no provable connection. Then she could easily have argued that Markús had become accidentally entangled in a serious matter of which he had no knowledge, and therefore had been ignorant of its significance when he put the box in the basement. As it was, this was not ideal.

She turned the page and read on. She hadn't read more than two more lines when she clapped her hand over her mouth. This was what Gudni had meant. She looked up at the ceiling and drew a deep breath. The thing she had seen in the head's mouth in the basement, and thought to be a tongue, was something very, very different.

Chapter 14

Tuesday, July 17, 2007

Adolf reread the brief message he had typed before pushing *send*. He was lying on the sofa at home, with one eye on a golf tournament whose location and name he didn't know. He didn't like golf, but was oddly fascinated by how boring it was on television. He stared as if hypnotized as one white ball after another was whipped into the air, vanished against the pale sky and then reappeared, bouncing and rolling along the manicured grass. Adolf wondered if he'd forgotten to turn his phone's ringer back on when he left his lawyer's office. But he hadn't, and the message he'd just sent had definitely gone out.

He put down the phone, sat up on the sofa and reached for the newspaper. He had to find something to do this evening, since his friends weren't answering his calls or texts. This didn't really surprise him: people with jobs were usually busy on weekdays. He himself had been laid off after his arrest, and had made no effort to find himself another job. He had enough to deal with after the death of his mother. When all this trouble with the court case was over he would apply for a job somewhere else, but it wouldn't really work right now, as it wouldn't look good to start a new job and have to ask for time off to go to court. He opened the paper and turned to the cinema listings. If no one wanted to do anything tonight he would go and see a film. He couldn't imagine sitting at home alone, fighting against his anxiety. Plan B was much more sensible: go to the gym and work out until he was exhausted, then go and take in one of the summer blockbusters that demanded nothing of him except that he stay awake. He wondered whether he should take his daughter along; it would do her good to get out of the house, and he would have someone to talk to during the trailers. Although he was well into his thirties he still felt uncomfortable going to the cinema alone, though it wasn't quite as unthinkable as it had been when he was a teenager. He might have to reconsider his trip to the gym if he took Tinna along, though, since she hardly had the strength to lift her towel after a shower, much less any weights.

Fuck the gym, he could go there later. He called his daughter and she agreed to go and see a film with him that evening, her choice. There was neither interest nor uninterest in her voice, and he had the impression that she'd agreed to see him out of a sense of duty. It had always been hard for him to understand her. He had only been with her mother for one night and had never had a good relationship with her. So he didn't know whether it was just he who had difficulty connecting to her emotionally or whether the same went for her other relatives. In truth, he suspected he wasn't the only one. The poor girl had always had some sort of mental trouble, but it was only recently that she'd started acting so depressed that you couldn't help but notice it. Thinking about it reminded Adolf that he still hadn't told his lawyer about Tinna's illness and this was probably a big mistake. Maybe he could gain the judge's sympathy if she testified? He had always been pretty good to her, looked after her every other weekend since she was tiny—after the paternity test was performed, of course. Even though he'd more often than not left her with his parents, he'd heard that children benefited from being around their grandparents, and no harm had been done to her even though you'd be hard pushed to find another couple as boring as them.

When his father died two years ago, Adolf had hoped his mother's condition would improve somewhat, that her mood would brighten and she would somehow change into another person. His parents had always squabbled over stupid little things for as long as he could remember, and had managed to scare all their friends and relatives away. Actually one or two of his relatives had occasionally dropped by out of a sense of familial duty, but they had always been scared off by the oppressive atmosphere in the house. The only words the couple had spoken in the presence of others had been poorly concealed potshots at each other or rants against the rest of society. There had been no news topic so mundane that they couldn't find a way to turn it on its head and complain about it for hours at a time. Adolf shuddered slightly at the memory. He didn't know whether the root of this behavioral pattern had lain with his mother or his father, since he couldn't remember them being anything apart from terribly unhappy. If the problem had been his father, then his mother had been so worn down by the time he finally died that her true nature had been erased. She continued to grumble, but now just directed it into thin air. So it hadn't been a day of great mourning for their only son when she had died recently. Adolf thought this seemed appropriate: they had both chosen their own unhappiness over everything else, including their own child, and didn't deserve to have anyone grieve for them.

What had that Alda said about them, again? That they had applied for a divorce early in their marriage? If that was true, there was no doubt in his mind that they would have been better off going through with it than ruining what was left of their lives and making each other unhappy. He couldn't fathom how two such different people came up with the idea of marrying, unless something had happened after the marriage that had changed them so much that they couldn't change back. He didn't believe that, but thought they had simply been thoroughly unpleasant people by nature and had raged and ranted at each other in the hope that two negatives would make a positive. Instead they had lived in utter misery and hostility until the end. He did not intend to finish up like that. If he was that negative too, he wasn't going to make things worse by living with or marrying a female version of himself. Again he thought about the pending court case. Maybe he could also get the judge's sympathy via the story of his upbringing? Of course he had wanted for nothing in material terms, since his parents had been quite well off, but he had lacked affection. He was so pleased with this idea that he decided to write it down to give to his lawyer. This was bound to work, especially if Tinna could be called upon to testify and persuaded to say that he was her main guardian. No judge with a trace of humanity could sentence him to prison after hearing a testimony like that from a sick child. Adolf was glad she still looked like a child, even though she was now sixteen.

He wondered briefly whether he should phone his lawyer and speak to her—that always made him feel better. She always managed to come up with something to quash any negative thoughts he was having about the case. Sometimes she did this by telling him good news about the other case that she was handling for him, making the hospital in Ísafjördur realize that unfortunately they would not be able to wriggle out of paying Adolf compensation for his mother's death. He smiled just thinking about the sum she'd mentioned. He couldn't complain about his financial situation; he had inherited his parents' mortgage-free house and everything that they had managed to scrape together in the course of their lives, for the most part unconditionally, if you didn't count that wretched inheritance tax. The additional compensation would just be the icing on a delicious cake that had pretty much landed in his lap. Nevertheless, he decided not to call. She would probably start talking about Alda and he didn't want to hear it right now. He'd gladly never hear her name again, especially right now. He didn't want to think about what had happened when they'd met. Nor did he want to have to explain to his lawyer that Alda would not be testifying for him as they had been hoping. Not a hope in hell of that, now.

"Tomorrow," replied Thóra, in answer to her daughter's usual question: *When are you coming home?* "Early, in fact. Probably before lunch."

"Good," said Sóley, happily. She dropped her voice to a whisper, so Thóra had to strain to hear her. "Grandma's making those disgusting meatballs wrapped in leaves."

"Aha," said Thóra, smiling to herself. Cabbage balls hadn't been her favorite either when she was Sóley's age. "I'll make you something for lunch. Don't worry." She said good-bye to her daughter, who told her that Gylfi wanted to talk to her. Her son's husky voice took over.

"Can you find me a place to stay in the Islands for the festival?" he said, without saying hello or wasting time on small talk. Ah, the August Bank Holiday festival, thought Thóra. She'd forgotten that was coming up. The Westmann Islands were famous for it.

"Everything's fully booked and I can't stay in a tent with Sigga and Orri," he went on.

"I would have thought the main obstacle to staying in a tent would have been you," replied Thóra. Gylfi was hardly an outdoors man. "And it's out of the question that you take the baby to the festival with you. He's far too little." She looked up at the ceiling. "In fact, you're too young yourselves." It was extremely unfortunate that the human body matured so early. It had no doubt been a benefit when people died around thirty, but it was absurd for longer lifespans. "It's a bad idea for you to come here."

"I thought maybe you'd come with us," said Gylfi quickly. "We could rent an apartment for all of us to stay in, including Sóley. Then you could look after Orri if Sigga and I need to go off somewhere, food shopping or whatever."

At first Thóra was amazed and pleased to hear that Gylfi wanted to have her with them, but then the penny dropped. She was supposed to pay to rent an apartment, do the cooking and cleaning and take care of Orri as well. She had to hand it to Gylfi: she could hardly say he'd been sneaky about it. He'd got straight to the point, at least, which was a definite plus. "I'll see what I can do, but I think it's pretty much impossible to find an apartment here now," said Thóra after thinking for a moment. She could think of far worse things than a little holiday with her children for the Bank Holiday weekend. Mind you, she was pretty sure she wouldn't have been invited to go with Gylfi and Sigga if they hadn't had the baby.

"Awesome," said Gylfi. "Check on a flight for us too," he added, as a parting shot. "It looks like they're all booked too."

Thóra rolled her eyes and said good-bye. In the wake of this call she made several unsuccessful attempts to find accommodation for the weekend in question. She was in her hotel room, so she started by ringing reception in the hope that two rooms might be free. Her question was actually met with laughter, and the same occurred when she tried other accommodation in the Islands. One woman who ran a guesthouse felt sorry for her and offered to check on whether there were still any apartments open. There were always people willing to rent their apartments that weekend, to families rather than groups of teenagers. She took down Thóra's number but told her not to get her hopes up. Thóra didn't feel like checking on flights or sea crossings until it was clear they could get accommodation. It wasn't much good being able to come to the festival if they'd be out on the street. She was getting ready to go down to meet Bella for something to eat when the phone rang again. It was Matthew. His voice sounded cheerful even though he hadn't yet decided whether he would take the job in Iceland. Reading between the lines, Thóra thought he was waiting to see if she would make his decision easier: he would come if she encouraged him, but would stay put if she indicated that she would rather he didn't.

He seemed to have resolved not to discuss his decision, although it made conversation embarrassing and awkward. She wanted him to come, but was nervous about how it would go if their interest in each other started to dwindle over time. She decided to change the subject so that there would be no danger of her giving in and asking him to take the job. "Why would you cut someone's genitals off and stuff them in their mouth?" was the only thing that she could think of saying. The part of the autopsy report concerned with the head was preoccupying her. It had stated that the mouth of the severed head had contained a man's reproductive organ, likely from the same person. That was the unexpected element Gudni had hinted at.

There was a long silence at the other end of the phone.

Finally Matthew spoke: "I'm just wondering what it is you wanted to say, whether I've misunderstood. I can't come up with anything, so I'm starting to think I didn't mishear you at all."

"No," said Thóra. "You didn't mishear me. At the moment I'm working on a case that concerns, among other things, a head in that very same condition."

"A head?" said Matthew, clearly baffled. "I see you haven't yet switched over to divorce cases, like you were thinking of doing. Or is this one of them?"

"I wish I knew whose head it was," replied Thóra sadly, before running through the case swiftly with him. When she had finished she repeated her original question. "If I knew what would drive a murderer to do such a thing, perhaps I could narrow down the number of possible suspects."

"It sounds to me as if this case is one of those that will never be solved," said Matthew, tacitly declining to discuss the mutilation. "So much time has passed that I doubt you'll get anywhere."

"That would be bad news for my client," said Thóra. "He doesn't want this allegation hanging over his head for the rest of his life, which is what might happen if the truth doesn't come out." She paused before adding: "I mean, it's the best he could hope for in the event that the guilty party isn't found. He could very well be charged or sentenced. For the moment there are no other suspects and this investigation has all the makings of a media circus. It's not the kind of case that brings out the best in the police or the justice system."

"You take on the strangest jobs," said Matthew. "Is that deliberate?"

"No, far from it," said Thóra emphatically. "At least I have to believe it's not. I didn't go searching for the man. When I took this case on I expected the worst, but not that heads would roll, literally . . ." She exhaled. "But you haven't answered my question about the way this head has been treated. Have you ever heard of such a thing?"

"Well, I'm no expert," replied Matthew, and Thóra could hear his voice taking on a more serious tone. "But of course I've heard and read about similar cases."

"Of *course*," said Thóra. "It happens all the time, silly me."

Matthew sounded insulted. "You know what I mean. These things aren't unheard of in wartime; in fact I wouldn't be surprised if it happened in prehistoric times. Its purpose is almost certainly to deprive the victim of his masculinity, and at the same time to display the perpetrator's revulsion toward the individual in question. The Mafia also used to do it to traitors."

Thóra raised a sarcastic eyebrow, although Matthew couldn't see her. "I doubt the Mafia had anything to do with this. This is a small community dependent on fishing, with little to interest the Mafia."

"I imagine there's a harbor there?"

"Yes, as a matter of fact there is, but I still don't think this has anything to do with the Mafia," said Thóra confidently. She had seen photos of the Westmann Islands taken around the time of the disaster, and cigar-wielding Mafiosi in suits would have fitted into them about as naturally as astronauts in full spacesuits. "True, the Cod War between Iceland and Britain was in full swing at the time, but it wasn't a war in the usual sense, so this is unlikely to be related to any battle."

"I think this type of treatment also occurs in hate crimes, when people are killed because of their race, religion or sexual preference. Would that fit?"

"I don't know, damn it," replied Thóra. "The bodies haven't been identified, which makes the case impossible. Hopefully that will be resolved soon, since I'm sort of stranded here until I know more."

"I know this much, Thóra," sighed Matthew, "what this person has done displays enormous hatred, spite and cruelty. If whoever did it is still alive, I don't like the look of this. They won't be too happy about people digging around in the past."

Thóra tried to lighten the mood. "Ah, bless you. The culprit is either six feet under or a senior citizen. I don't think I'm in any danger."

Matthew was silent for a moment. "You can't grow out of hatred. Not that kind of hatred, Thóra. You should watch your step."

After the phone call she sat for a moment, staring into nothing. She tried to imagine herself cutting off a man's penis and putting it in his mouth, but she couldn't. She realized that there was a lot of truth in what Matthew had said. This crime showed unbelievable hatred; the kind of hatred only possible in someone who no longer held company with civilized men. But what could cause that?

Chapter 15

Wednesday, July 18, 2007

There was no one in reception when Thóra came to return the keys. Bella was nowhere to be seen, so she sent her a text message telling her she ought to hurry if they wanted to catch the plane. Thóra had no interest in missing the morning flight and having to wait until evening for another, since there was so much waiting for her at home and at work. She threw her key forcefully onto the table in the hope that the receptionist would hear her, but in vain. Spying an old-fashioned bell, she rang it loudly. It didn't take long for the young woman who seemed to be on duty at the reception desk around the clock to appear with a smile on her lips and check Thóra out. However, there was still no sign of Bella. Had she perhaps gone out again last night, and was still asleep next to some random sailor? Looking at her watch Thóra saw that there was no reason to panic yet, so she plonked herself down in an easy chair and grabbed some newspapers. They turned out to be from the day before, but that was good enough for her.

After a while Alda's sister Jóhanna walked into the hotel lobby and came over. Thóra quickly put down the paper she was reading and greeted her.

"Oh, good," said Jóhanna as she shook Thóra's hand loosely, trying to catch her breath. "I was so sure I'd missed you. You're taking the morning flight, aren't you?"

"Yes," replied Thóra, looking over at the clock again. "The girl who's with me is a bit late. Luckily, because otherwise I'd be at the airport." She smiled at Jóhanna. "Did you want to talk about something in particular?"

"I found something last night. After talking to you I started to think about Alda and what you said about the bodies in the basement. If my sister was murdered then I want to help in any way I can." She lifted a plastic bag that she'd brought with her and held it out toward Thóra. "That's why I went looking for these. I want you to see them."

Thóra looked down at the bag, surprised. She took it from Jóhanna. "What are they?"

Jóhanna looked apologetic and rubbed at her chin. "Alda always kept diaries and I knew they were kept in storage, with other things, at Mother and Father's. Our house was one of those that wasn't buried completely and was dug up later. After Father died, Mother put the house up for sale, but no one was interested. I helped her go through stuff and throw some of it out, so the house could be shown without her feeling ashamed of all the junk in the basement and the garage. I found these among some of Alda's things that she left behind in the evacuation. I was going to bring the diaries to our meeting last weekend." She smiled apologetically. "Mother is in Reykjavík because of Alda's death, and she doesn't know I took them. I'm not sure she'd remember them, in all honesty."

Thóra could have kissed the woman, but restrained herself. It was clear to her that she shouldn't accept the diaries, which could be used as evidence in the police investigation, but equally she knew that if she turned them over she wouldn't get to see them again any time soon, and even then she'd probably never get to read every word. However, as a lawyer she had an obligation to do the right thing. "The most proper course of action would be for these diaries to go to the police," she said, holding the bag out to Jóhanna. "It's possible that the diaries contain information they have the right to receive."

Jóhanna's expression hardened and she stopped rubbing her jaw. "I won't give these to Gudni and his colleagues. It's out of the question. These are my sister's private thoughts from her sensitive teenage years, and I don't want them being made public for strangers to rip them apart."

"Have you read them?" asked Thóra, still holding out the bag.

"No," said Jóhanna, shaking her head. "I can't bring myself to do it. At the time these diaries were the holiest things that Alda owned and she wouldn't let me near them, even before I could read. I don't want to know her secrets, no matter how trivial they might seem today." She looked imploringly at Thóra. "I trust you, although I don't know you at all. You know how it is to be a young girl, and besides, you will be able to judge whether there's anything relevant to the bodies and to Alda's murder."

"It's not definite that Alda was murdered," said Thóra, mainly as a formality. Jóhanna had clearly fixed the idea in her head and right now nothing Thóra could say or do would change that. "And even if the diaries shed some light on the case, that doesn't mean they'll explain her death."

"I understand that," replied Jóhanna, although her expression said otherwise. "Maybe there's absolutely nothing there. But there might be something. We'll just have to see." She took Thóra's hand. "Could I ask you to read through them for me? If there's nothing in them of interest to the police, then I could have them back and no one would need to know anything." She paused for a moment. "If you do find something, then I suppose that particular diary would go to the police, and that would be fine with me. I just can't disrespect my sister by handing these over to the police if there's no need for it."

Thóra looked at the woman standing before her. She was, as before, wearing the plain uniform of a bank clerk, and the green blouse she'd chosen to go with her blue suit didn't match at all. There was a white spot of toothpaste at one corner of her mouth. Fashion and grooming are naturally not uppermost in one's mind during times of grieving, and Thóra couldn't help but feel sorry for her. "I'll read these, but I'll have to hand over everything that I think pertains to the case." She looked at the bag. "It would, of course, be best if you read them yourself."

Jóhanna shook her head briskly and her hairstyle, if you could call it that, went completely askew. "No. I don't want to. You might think me silly or cowardly but it's more than loyalty to my sister that stops me reading what's in them." She inhaled through her nose and exhaled slowly. "Something went wrong between Alda and Father. I don't remember them ever speaking, or meeting up.

I'm too scared to find out what caused it, in case Father did something unforgivable to her. I want to remember them both as they were, and it's too late to change anything. They're both dead."

Thóra nodded. She got the picture. Incest cases were reported far too often, so of course Jóhanna was afraid this was the case. She said: "I understand. You can rest assured I won't hand over anything that's not directly related to the case. And I'll get in touch with you before I give them anything."

Jóhanna smiled, relieved. "Good." She looked at the large clock hanging in reception. "God, I've got to get going. I'm really late."

Thóra watched the woman walk out through the hotel door and trudge off in the direction of her work, her eyes following her until she disappeared around a corner. The bag hung heavily from Thóra's clenched fist, and she was itching to read the diaries. She sincerely hoped there was nothing in them that might cause Jóhanna unnecessary pain, but she feared there would be. Anything relevant was bound to be both negative and painful for the woman. What Matthew had said about hatred echoed in her mind, and Thóra asked herself if she really wanted to know how this tragic series of events had started.

Bella plonked herself down next to Thóra at a table in the airport. She jerked her thumb over her shoulder, in the direction of the refreshment kiosk. "Load of rubbish. They don't even stock it." She twisted around in her seat, and it looked to Thóra as if she were giving the cashier the evil eye. "And they call this an airport."

"The flight takes twenty minutes, Bella," said Thóra irritably. "I'm sure you can survive without nicotine gum." Now the evil eye fell on her so she looked away, in the direction of the boarding gate. "They'll probably announce the flight soon," she said, just to have something to say. It wasn't just Bella's nonsense that made her impatient to get going, but the fact that she was waiting anxiously to dive into the diaries. She was in a hurry to read them, not just from excitement over what they might reveal, but also because if she had to hand them over to the police, it would obviously look better if she did so quickly. The police would be annoyed with her no matter how promptly she gave them the books, but it would reduce the damage if she did it as soon as possible after getting hold of them. If she could read through them today, it would be possible to make photocopies of them and return the diaries tomorrow.

"They're in no hurry," muttered Bella. "We've paid for our tickets and they can't leave without us." She stood up. "I'm going out for a smoke." Thóra felt relieved to be left alone again, and her relief grew when she heard the call to board their flight to Reykjavík. She went to fetch Bella from the airport entrance, where she was leaning up against a statue honoring the visit to Iceland of Gorbachev and Reagan and blowing out one stream of smoke after another. "Come on," she said. "I don't want to miss our plane."

"It's not going anywhere," said Bella confidently, but nevertheless took one last drag and stubbed out the cigarette. She pointed at the inscription on the statue's base. "Who are these guys?"

"Come on," said Thóra, not caring to tell the girl the story behind the world leaders. "They're just some former big shots who don't matter anymore." She hurried inside, even holding the door open for her secretary to chivvy her along, but they were still the last to board the plane and take their seats. As soon as she had fastened her seat belt, Thóra took out the diaries.

"What are those?" asked Bella in surprise when she saw the multicolored, slightly battered books in Thóra's lap. She raised her pencilled eyebrows. "Diaries? I had some like that when I was a kid. Whose are they?"

The tracks of Reagan and Gorbachev might have been covered over by time, but some things survived from generation to generation. Thóra had kept diaries herself, not unlike those lying at the top of the stack. "Oh, this is something that I need to go over," replied Thóra, not saying anything about who the diaries belonged to. "I don't think they're anything important." Thóra had hit the nail on the head, judging by the first diary. It was from 1970, and at first glance nothing in it appeared relevant to the investigation. Alda's handwriting was typical for an adolescent girl: big rounded letters, the letter "i" sometimes dotted with a heart. There was often a whole week between entries, which was perhaps the reason Alda had been able to keep her diaries going for years. Thóra had given up keeping a diary after six months, when the entries started to show her in black and white just how little happened in the life of an eleven-year-old, and she decided it would be better just to note down special events. She would have given a lot now to have the chance to peek into the mental world of her own childhood, which was now almost entirely lost to her.

Thóra closed the first book and put it at the bottom of the pile. She found the diary from 1973, which stood out as it was the most tattered of all, and the spine cracked as she opened it. She turned to the first page and read the entry for New Year's Day, in which Alda welcomed the new year and listed, with numbers, what she wanted to accomplish in the next twelve months. Thóra smiled as she read the girl's resolutions:

1. Go to a foreign country
2. Do homework
3. Get a record player
4. Get a boyfriend
5. Stop thinking about my hair—it will grow

Although she didn't understand the last item, the rest perfectly suited a fifteen-year-old girl taking her first steps into the adult world. Today this might seem more like a thirteen-year-old's voice, but in 1973 things clearly moved a bit slower in a teenager's life. Thóra went on to read about what a drag Alda's parents had been after the party the night before, and how her little sister Jóhanna still hadn't got over her fear of the fireworks, which had been even more beautiful than last year. This was followed by a short paragraph in which Alda talked of her concern about fireworks in the Islands, clearly torn between her delight in them and their negative effect on animals. The entry ended with a promise to be sure to make each day exciting enough to deserve a write-up in her new diary.

Thóra read on, through a description of how that long-ago January had been spent. School started again after the Christmas break and Alda appeared not to be disappointed at all, even seeming to look forward to it, according to the diary. She had a crush on someone called Stebbi and had started to think it was mutual, but seemed not to have any interest in Markús except as a friend. It wasn't clear to Thóra whether the girl had realized how much of a crush he had on her, but all the entries mentioning him were positive and appeared to be written with platonic affection. The fifteenth of January turned out to be a huge watershed, because Alda had kissed Stebbi outside the shop; this page was scribbled all over with hearts and flowers. The next day was less enjoyable because the family kitten went missing, an incident that escalated in drama over the next few days until it was finally found after an extensive search. Thóra wondered if the kitten had been one of the numerous cats left behind in the Islands, their numbers dwindling little by little as the eruption continued. From time to time there were also further reflections on hair that made no more sense to Thóra than the reference at the start of the year. The best that Thóra could come up with was that Alda had cut her hair short and been unhappy with the outcome, but she didn't completely grasp why this seemed to be of such great concern to her.

At the start of the third week of the month Alda appeared to be very excited about a school dance that was in the offing. It was clearly a big deal, and although Alda didn't describe it in any great detail she appeared to be looking forward to it and dreading it in equal measure. There was a reference to something all the kids in her class were going to do, but Thóra couldn't fathom what it was. When it came to the nineteenth of January Thóra was slightly startled. The date had been written at the top, but beneath it the page had been crossed over so heavily and repeatedly with a ballpoint pen that in some places there were holes in the paper. The facing page had been subjected to the same violent treatment. Something had happened, and no matter how Thóra scrutinized the scribbles she couldn't make out what was written underneath. Perhaps Stebbi, the boy Alda had liked, had jilted her. However, the marks had been made so forcefully that Thóra found this explanation unlikely, even though the writer had been a teenager with raging hormones. She put the diary on her lap.

"What's this mess?" said Bella, pointing at the scrawls. "Did a little kid get into the diary?"

That hadn't crossed Thóra's mind. It was possible that Jóhanna had scrubbed these lines out in her sister's book in a fit of pique or a tantrum. "I don't know," she replied truthfully. "Up until now it has all been rather tidy." Bella snorted disbelievingly. "Yeah, right." She stared at the scribbled-out pages and Thóra couldn't help but do the same. The flight attendant announced over the tannoy that they were commencing their descent into Reykjavík and that they should return their seats to the upright position and fasten their seat belts. "Have you ever read about a plane crash in which the only ones who survived were those who put up their tray tables or had the backs of their seats in the upright position?" asked Bella, loud enough for others to hear. "I think they're just trying to protect the trays and seats if we crash. It's bullshit." The passenger sitting across the aisle gave Bella an affronted look and fastened his table against the seat-back in front of him. Thóra busied herself looking straight ahead and acting nonchalantly. She turned to the next page, which turned out to be empty. There were no entries for the twentieth of January or the twenty-first. "Damn," she thought; up until now there had not been a single word that might relate to the head and box. The diary had been left behind during the evacuation, so Markús's only hope was that Alda had written something significant in the entry for the twenty-second, the night the eruption started. Hopefully that page wasn't empty. Thóra drew a deep breath and crossed her fingers before turning the page.

Luckily, the next page was neither empty nor completely crossed out. Still, it looked as though Alda had been on drugs or had had a fever when she wrote the entry for that day. Thóra couldn't make head or tail of the text which, unlike Alda's previous entries, was written in waves all over the page instead of following the lines. The entry was composed of repetitions of the word *disgusting disgusting disgusting* and several instances of *why did I go out? why? why?* as well as *I want to die.* These sentences were all strung together and Thóra couldn't discern any particular order in them. On a line below this jumble was the sentence:

I'm not going to write anymore. I'll do this for God and Mum and Dad and then I'm going to kill myself. I'm not coming back here.

This appeared to have been written in a calmer state, because the letters were straighter and better formed. There was nothing else.

The pen had been dragged down along the margin and at the bottom of the page there was a single word in writing so tiny it was barely legible:

Markús

Thóra lowered the book and sighed. Why couldn't Alda have been clearer? However, this did show something: it strongly suggested that the girl had experienced a shock. If Thóra used her imagination, Markús's name might be interpreted as a declaration that he could help Alda. On the other hand, her client's name on the page did not substantiate his statement. After this entry, the diary consisted only of empty pages.

Chapter 16

Wednesday, July 18, 2007

Thóra put down the newspaper. She could take comfort in the fact that the photo on the front page could have been any prosperous fifty-year-old man. There were enough of them around. Hopefully that would be of some consolation to Markús, who stared at her from the grainy image like a convict. The press must have searched high and low for a photograph showing her client with a cruel expression. Although his face was quite blurry, the photo seemed to show a man who was capable of anything. The headline *Four Dead—Autopsy Suggests Murder*, was positioned in a way that made it quite clear Markús was being portrayed as a criminal. The accompanying article barely elaborated on the headline except to say that Markús Magnússon, Reykjavík businessman, was helping police with their inquiries. A short biographical summary, in a separate box at the bottom of the page, pointed out that Markús had resided in the Westmann Islands at the time the men seemed likely to have been murdered. However, no mention was made of his youth at the time. Markús seemed not to have got around very much, because the photograph from the front page also accompanied an article later in the paper, along with two photos of the excavation site and an aerial photo of Heimaey. It was clear the newsmen hadn't acquired a copy of the medical examiner's report, and they still hadn't connected Alda to the case. The main body of the article was a review of everything that was already known about the case of the discovery of the bodies, but with the addition of Markús's involvement and the case becoming a murder investigation. Surely the media would soon make the connection and drag Alda's name into it.

Thóra felt it was important to thoroughly investigate the nurse's role in all of this, but as soon as the media became interested in Alda, lots of doors would close. She thumbed through her notes and went over the little she'd written about Alda. She decided she ought to contact Ísafjördur Junior College in the hope of tracking down her schoolfriends, speak to the plastic surgeon's office where Alda had worked, then interview the employees of the A&E department where she'd taken evening and weekend shifts. Thóra wondered whether she should speak to a doctor there whom she knew quite well—her ex-husband—but decided not to so that she wouldn't owe him a favor. Experience had taught her that the saying "an eye for an eye" fit their relationship well.

She looked up the number of the college and crossed her fingers, hoping someone would answer. It was midsummer, so she couldn't be sure anyone would be there. Luckily, the school's office was open and she spoke to the secretary, who was extremely obliging.

Thóra agreed to hold while the woman went to look up Alda, in case she couldn't get through to her again. After a long wait the woman returned to the phone.

"Well, you know what, there was no Alda Thorgeirsdóttir registered here during the winter of 1972–1973," said the woman, sounding apologetic. "Could she have gone by any other name? These are just paper records, in alphabetical order. We were supposed to have gone paperless a long time ago but never had the time to do it, which is why I'm afraid I need to have a full name."

"No, I don't think so," replied Thóra. "Could she be missing from the file because she started studying there after the new year? At the end of January, after the eruption in the Islands?"

"That wouldn't change anything," said the woman, still sounding regretful. "Of course it's possible that someone here made a filing error, but I find that rather unlikely. The school's public funding is based on the number of students, so we've always been careful with our records. Although many things are done differently now, that's one thing that hasn't changed."

Thóra thanked the woman and hung up. Had Alda gone there

under another name, or did Jóhanna simply misremember which school her sister attended in the wake of the disaster? It must be the latter, since Jóhanna's story didn't fit in any way. Teenagers didn't jump up a class and start a new educational level in the middle of term. Wondering who could help her unravel this mystery, Thóra concluded that she would have to speak to Alda's mother. She would be sure to know the details of Alda's schooling, and Thóra could use the opportunity to try to find out other information, too. In her notes she had Jóhanna's mobile number, but when she rang to ask her to arrange a meeting with her mother, there was no answer. Jóhanna was probably at work, which meant Thóra had no choice but to try again later. She also wanted to tell Jóhanna that nothing in the diaries suggested anything out of the ordinary in Alda's relationship with her father.

She decided to ask Alda's childhood girlfriends again about her whereabouts following the evacuation, in case by some chance they had remembered anything further. Only two of them picked up the phone, and it was clear from their tone that they feared her telephone calls would become daily occurrences now they'd made the mistake of humoring her the first time she rang. Both of them were noticeably less friendly this time, and neither of them could remember anything beyond what they'd already told her. Both stood firmly by their assertion that Alda had attended Reykjavík Junior College, though they didn't know when she'd started there or whether she'd completed her studies. At the end of their conversation, the first woman muttered something about being late and said good-bye without giving Thóra a chance to ask any further questions, but the second wasn't as crafty and Thóra managed to ask her about a number of things she'd been mulling over since reading the diary entries. "Could something have happened to Alda just before the eruption, and was she acting any differently from usual?" asked Thóra.

"God, it was such a long time ago," replied the woman, sounding as if she thought the phone call would never end. "If she was, I don't remember it."

"No depression, irritability, nothing like that?" urged Thóra.

"I don't remember anything," replied the woman, but then paused for a moment as if something had occurred to her. "Actually, we had all ended up in a little bit of trouble the previous weekend— I'd completely forgotten about that."

"What happened?" asked Thóra anxiously.

"Oh, just typical teenage stuff," said the woman. "We tried alcohol for the first time the Friday before the eruption. We got completely wasted, and things got a bit crazy. I was grounded because of it and wasn't supposed to go out for two months, but that fell apart after the volcano, of course. If Alda was in a bad mood, it was probably because her parents were so angry with her."

"Where were you drinking? At someone's house?" asked Thóra, thinking back to her own youth.

"No, it was a school dance," replied the woman. "It was actually stopped and we were all sent home, even though not everyone had been drinking."

Thóra pressed her for more information but got little for her trouble. The kids had made plans to steal alcohol from their parents; each of them had filled a Coke bottle with whatever they could get their hands on, and most had taken small amounts of many different spirits so as not to arouse suspicion. Some strange cocktails had resulted and everything got out of control, as might be expected. The woman Thóra was talking to had got sick herself, which meant that she was one of those whose parents were called and asked to come and pick them up, vomiting and crying. Thus she had no idea if Alda had managed to get herself home, or whether she had also had to be collected. She couldn't remember anything from the latter part of the night, because of her drunkenness. Thóra decided not to press her any further about this, but to take it up with Markús in good time. Hopefully he hadn't been as badly affected and could remember more details.

"There's just one more thing and then I promise to let you go," she said. "Do you know why Alda was unhappy about her hair?" Thóra expected the woman to be baffled, but she wasn't.

"Oh, that," she said sadly. "That was horrendous."

"Did something happen to her hair?" Thóra's mind spun with all the horror stories she'd heard over the years about hairdressers

who accidentally burned the hair off their clients with perming solution or hair bleach that was too strong.

"It was all cut off," replied the woman. "Our class stayed over in
the gym one night after our exams, before Christmas. When Alda
woke up in the morning someone had hacked off her hair, presumably while she slept. They never found out who did it."

Thóra frowned. "Who was there, or had access to the gym?"

"The whole class was there, as far as I can remember. Of course
there were a couple who either didn't want to come or were off
sick, but most of the kids came. There were also two teachers there,
and the teaching assistant. There might have been other adults, but
I don't remember who. I would probably have forgotten it if it hadn't
been Alda's hair. Naturally, she was hysterical, because she had
particularly beautiful hair, long and blond. It had been hacked off
with scissors and it was such a mess afterward. Of course what was
left was tidied up at the hairdresser's immediately, but it still looked
pretty ridiculous. Far too short, like a boy's."

Thóra thanked her and hung up. She was dumbfounded, since
she well remembered how sensitive adolescents could be about their
hair. She doubted this ugly event could be connected to the case in
any way, but you never knew. Yet another detail to ask Markús
about, along with what the woman had said about the teenagers'
drunkenness the weekend before the eruption—the night before the
blood was found at the pier.

Thóra turned her attention to the doctor's office where Alda had
worked. An Internet search revealed that it was run by two plastic
surgeons, Dís Haflidadóttir and Ágúst Ágústsson. Thóra thought
she recognized Ágúst's name, having heard it mentioned in her sewing circle when they'd discussed beauty treatments. Those of her
friends who thought they were in the know said he was the best
breast man in town. There were even unconfirmed stories about
people who'd traveled all the way from Hollywood to go under his
knife, but Thóra remembered thinking that sounded ludicrous. If
you couldn't find decent breasts in Hollywood you were hardly going to get them in Reykjavík. Surely practice made perfect? Dís
hadn't been mentioned, though; if people flocked to her from the

other side of the world for operations, no one in Thóra's sewing circle knew about it.

The answering machine informed Thóra that appointments could be made before noon on weekdays. Those who needed to speak to the doctors about operations that had already taken place could call the phone number printed in their aftercare pack; this emergency number was clearly not up for grabs. Thóra left a message.

That left only the A&E, whose number Thóra knew off by heart thanks to a long marriage to a doctor who often worked past the end of his shifts. Those nights had always seemed to drag on and on. She recognized the voice of the woman who answered, even though she and Hannes had been divorced for around five years. The woman on the other end clearly had no such recollection: Thóra's voice appeared to ring no bells with her, nor did her name awaken any friendliness. Thóra tried to console herself with the fact that the staff was large and her name was quite common. After asking to speak to Alda Thorgeirsdóttir's supervisor, Thóra was informed sullenly that the phone call would be transferred to the head nurse on call. She tried to thank the woman, but before she could do so the call was transferred and Thóra's eardrums were assailed by a frightful, tinny tune that sounded like nothing she had ever heard.

Several minutes later a chilly female voice announced itself as belonging to Elin, who sounded as if she had no overwhelming inclination to relieve the suffering of the sick and wounded.

Thóra introduced herself and explained her business. She said she was seeking information about Alda Thorgeirsdóttir, and asked whether she might stop by and speak to her former colleagues about a case concerning a childhood friend of the recently deceased nurse. "I'm familiar with the workings of your busy department, and I promise to trouble you as little as possible," she concluded hopefully. These people had enough to do, and no one knew this better than Thóra. She fully expected to have to interview the hospital staff over open wounds.

"Alda Thorgeirsdóttir was no longer working here when she died," said the head nurse. "She was never actually a full-time employee; she just took shifts on weekends and the occasional evening. She worked at a clinic in town, so perhaps you should try them."

How helpful, telling Thóra something she already knew. "Of course I'll be doing that," she replied, echoing the woman's frosty tone. "But I would also like to speak to your staff."

"I can't see how that would help," came the reply. "Firstly because there is nothing to tell, secondly because I'm not sure such a thing would be proper, and thirdly because we simply have no obligation to speak to some lawyer who appears from out of the blue. We value propriety very highly here."

Propriety? How old was this woman—a hundred? A hundred and fifty? "Naturally you're not obliged to speak to me," Thóra replied, "unless of course I were injured. If you prefer, I could always have you subpoenaed to find out whether you have any information that might count. Might that be the best solution, do you think?"

"Subpoenaed?" exclaimed the woman, sounding noticeably less assured than before. "That's completely unnecessary. I told you she wasn't working here anymore." She hesitated. "What is this about, may I ask? Alda's death?"

"It's a case I'm working on for a man who knew Alda," replied Thóra, enjoying holding the cards.

"Is this about the rape case?" asked the woman, her voice now full of suspicion. "We have no comment. We're not protecting anyone, and you'll find nothing out by snooping around under false pretenses. The case is on its way to court, where guilt or innocence will be determined and our part will be finished. We follow the rules for such cases, and there's no leeway for letting a lawyer in off the street to chat about God knows what."

Now it was Thóra's turn to hesitate. Rape? She had to be careful not to get involved with something unconnected to Markús's case. Actually, the nurse had been quite correct; the hospital had no obligation to her or to Markús, and the interests of those who came to them for assistance naturally took precedence. "No, this has nothing to do with a rape. That I can promise you," said Thóra earnestly. "Unfortunately it seems as though this can't happen, so we'll have to leave it. You have enough to worry about."

Thóra hung up. She hadn't given up her efforts to speak to the

staff of the A&E out of respect for the hospital or the Hippocratic
Oath. She simply planned to make her way in through the back
door. Swallowing her pride, she dialed her ex-husband's number.

As Dís listened to the message on the answering machine the smile
she usually wore after a successful operation vanished. Now what?
A lawyer who wanted to speak to them about Alda? Not the police,
as she had feared, but the lawyer of some childhood friend of
Alda's, someone Dís had never heard of before. She listened to the
message again and tried to read more into it, but without success.
The voice was soft and courteous, seeming to suggest neither that
the speaker felt Dís and Ágúst were hiding something nor that this
was a formality unrelated to who they were. Dís wondered whether
she should fetch Ágúst, who was finishing up a consultation with
the last patient of the day: yet another young man who wanted to
have a scar from a fight removed. She decided not to. Ágúst tended
toward the melodramatic, and she had no desire to nourish her
own anxiety with his paranoia. She felt sick thinking of the one
court case their work had involved them in. Ágúst had rendered
himself almost incapable of working with the stress of the case and
his wild flights of fancy about what might happen. By the time a
settlement was finally reached, Dís was on the verge of offering up
her soul along with the damages they were ordered to pay. It would
be a small price to pay for peace of mind at work.

Dís scribbled down the lawyer's number then erased the message, resolving to phone and arrange to meet her tomorrow, when
Ágúst would not be at the office. This was undoubtedly something
unimportant, probably concerning her estate; whether Alda had
had life insurance from the office, or somesuch. Dís could take care
of this herself, and in the unlikely event it was about something
else, she would get Ágúst involved—but not until she had to.

She went over to Alda's tidy desk, which was conveniently located behind a partition separating it from the waiting room. Alda
hadn't had an office of her own like Dís and Ágúst, since she
mainly assisted them in the operating room and only a tiny bit with
paperwork. Dís looked over the well-ordered workspace, which in
that sense resembled Ágúst's office. However Alda, unlike Ágúst,

had given her little area a tiny bit of personality: on the table was a framed photograph of a woman whom Dís recalled was Alda's younger and only sister, and there was also a little daintily painted flowerpot containing a cactus which seemed to be thriving. Poor little thing, thought Dís. Neither she nor Ágúst had the ability to keep so much as a weed alive, and it would take a lot for the receptionist to tear herself away from Facebook to look after a plant. Dís was about to throw the plant into the rubbish bin to avoid having to watch it wither away, but she couldn't bring herself to do it, for Alda's sake. She would try to remember the plant and nurse it as best she could. At least she would have tried, even if the cactus died. Out of respect for Alda, she didn't want to throw out something she had cared about.

Pleased with her noble thoughts, Dís sat down and started to scrutinize Alda's desk and computer. It didn't occur to her that such a thing was inappropriate. She owned the company that owned the computer, like everything else in the office, and if Alda kept any secrets that she wouldn't have wanted to come out at work, then it was best if it were Dís who uncovered them. Ágúst was a gossip and the receptionist, at best, a simpleton. Both of them lacked the maturity to respect others' privacy.

As the computer was firing up, Dís looked through Alda's desk drawers. In the top drawer the stationery had been so tidily arranged that Dís wouldn't have been able to recreate the layout if her life depended on it. In Dís's top drawer everything was a jumble: pens, paper clips, stamps and anything else that ended up there for want of its own particular place.

The other two drawers had little in them, although there were some files that Dís had trouble understanding. Among them was the autopsy report of an older woman who had died in the hospital in Ísafjördur. She skimmed through it and could see nothing in it connected to Alda or to her work in the office. She didn't recognize the woman's name, and when the computer was ready she tried running it through their database. The woman hadn't been one of her or Ágúst's patients. She shrugged, assuming the woman was a relative or friend of Alda's, although the age difference between them did not suggest the latter. Dís put the report on the table so it wouldn't end up in a box with other things for disposal or storage. Maybe she could find an explanation for this somehow. The death had occurred quite recently, so perhaps it would help explain why Alda had killed herself. Dís suppressed a shudder at the thought that the cause of death might be something other than suicide. Although suicide was awful, there were many things worse, and Dís wouldn't hesitate to share any information that supported Alda's having died by her own hand.

The drawer also contained a photograph of a young man Dís did not recognize. The photo was very artistic, and the subject clearly wasn't aware of the photographer. He sat slouched on a chair, looking out into space, solemn but not scowling. He had the look of someone who wasn't scared of anything. Dís couldn't tell where the photograph had been taken, as all you could see was the man, a yellow wall and the chair, but something made him look very distinguished. Before Dís put the photo down she frowned and tried to figure out what it was she found so attractive about him. She couldn't, but wondered whether Alda had kept this photo because she felt the same.

She shut the drawer and turned to the computer, smiling when she saw what Alda had chosen as her desktop wallpaper. It was a kitten that had been Photoshopped and now smiled idiotically at her with a set of human teeth. Dís thought she'd have nothing against owning a kitten if it were possible to make it look like that, and idly wondered whether she could use her expertise to do the work. She was obviously tired after a long day.

She quickly gave up reading through the files on the computer, which were countless. After opening several at random she found nothing that drew her attention, so she went online and out of curiosity checked which pages Alda had bookmarked as favorites. As she read the list her mouth dropped open in amazement.

She clicked on one link after another in the hope that they wouldn't be what their names suggested, but unfortunately they were. A succession of pornographic sites popped up. Dís gaped. Alda had been a completely different person than she appeared. Could this be connected to her work at the A&E, and the rape cases that they sometimes had to deal with? The more Dís saw, the clearer it became that this explanation didn't hold up. Here she saw the entire spectrum of sexual relations: sadomasochism, homosexuality, conventional sex between a man and woman, and numerous other variations. Dís breathed easier when she had ascertained that children were not included. What had Alda got herself into? Was this the reason she wasn't in a steady relationship: that she didn't know what she wanted?

She logged off the Internet and felt almost abused herself, although it had been her choice to look at the material and she had known what she was getting into. It wasn't the contents of the pages that upset her so much as the fact that she'd looked through a door into a part of Alda's world that she hadn't known existed. Ugh, it would be very difficult to write the obituary now, and Dís cursed herself for not having even started it. She exhaled and considered whether she should just leave well enough alone and turn off the computer. But curiosity overruled her better judgment, and she went into Alda's email. She vowed to herself she wouldn't open any message that could possibly be connected to Alda's sex life, but she allowed herself to arrange the messages according to the senders and recipients in order to see what had gone on between Alda and the people she knew.

Messages from Ágúst were at the top of the list, and Dís only had to open a few of them to realize what had been going on. She leaned back in her chair. The Web sites were nothing compared to this. She fervently hoped that whatever this Thóra Gudmundsdóttir wanted, it didn't have anything to do with this.

Chapter 17

Wednesday, July 18, 2007

The booklet about rape was certainly informative, but it did not hold Thóra's interest for long. There was no other reading material in sight, and after rearranging everything in her handbag there was nothing else for Thóra to do. She was sitting with her legs crossed in an uncomfortable chair in an empty hallway in the old City Hospital, and had started to swing her feet to and fro in boredom. She couldn't read the booklet a third time. Hannes had arranged for her to meet a nurse who had known Alda, but the problem was that the woman wasn't certain when she could get a break and had suggested that Thóra come and take her chances.

Thóra was about to give up when she heard footsteps approaching. A middle-aged woman in a white gown and matching trousers came around the corner. She held a stack of papers tightly to her chest. The woman slowed down as she approached Thóra.

"Are you Thóra Gudmundsdóttir? I'm Bjargey. Sorry to make you wait," she said, extending her hand. She wore no rings and her nails were clipped tidily short. "I was in a meeting that I thought would never end." She pointed with her chin toward the door next to Thóra. "We can sit down in there. It's in a terrible mess but at least it's quiet."

Thóra had certainly had no shortage of quiet in the last forty minutes, but she smiled and stood up. "Fine," she replied. "I won't take too much of your time."

They walked into a little office and the nurse turned on the light with her elbow. "It's my understanding that you worked with Alda

Thorgeirsdóttir and might be able to help me," said Thóra after they'd sat down.

"Yes, I can try," replied the woman calmly. "There are of course limits to what I'm allowed to talk about, but since I don't entirely know what this is regarding, we'll just have to see whether I can help you or not. I should probably point out that I'm meeting you as a favor to Hannes. We work together a lot."

"I fully understand, and I'm very grateful to both of you," replied Thóra. "I'm not fishing for information about patients or anything else here in the hospital, but I'm looking for someone with whom Alda might possibly have discussed personal things." She levelled her gaze at the woman. "Alda left behind secrets that can't be bottled up any longer. My hope is that she trusted someone with them, possibly a colleague of hers."

"That's a good question," said Bjargey. "Alda wasn't really the chatty type, although she was always kind to everyone, staff as well as patients. But no one in particular comes to mind." She smiled weakly at Thóra. "Alda only worked here on weekends, but she also took extra evening shifts when she could. They always needed staff then, because most people want evenings and weekends off." Realizing she was still holding the stack of papers, Bjargey put them down on top of a similar pile on the desk before continuing: "Alda worked somewhere else during the day, she didn't often share shifts with the same people, so she wasn't part of a group like the rest of us."

"So she didn't work with anyone in particular?" asked Thóra. "With you, for example?"

Bjargey shook her head, causing the hair-clip keeping her fringe out of her eyes to come slightly loose. Her hair was cut short, but had grown out a bit. She lifted one hand to catch the clip, without missing a beat. "I do the scheduling and other admin for the nursing staff in the A&E, so I know it didn't work like that. I worked with Alda sometimes, and liked her." Bjargey pushed her hair back up and refastened the clip. "To put it mildly, I was very surprised to hear that she had killed herself. I didn't think she would do that, to tell you the truth."

"Hadn't she stopped working here?" said Thóra. "I understood from the head nurse I spoke to that Alda resigned shortly before she died."

"Yes, in fact she had," replied Bjargey, clearing her throat. "That matter is actually still being investigated, both here in the hospital and elsewhere, so I can't say much about it."

"Do you mean that Alda didn't leave on good terms?" said Thóra. "That's actually what I was led to understand in my conversation with the head nurse."

"Good and not so good," said Bjargey, enigmatically. "A particular situation came up that she and the department couldn't see eye to eye on, which led to an agreement that she should take a leave of absence until the matter was resolved." She fiddled again with her hair-clip, although it now appeared to be securely fastened. "The decision was reached without acrimony. I'm convinced that Alda would have come back if things hadn't gone as they did."

"I see," said Thóra. "You said the investigation was ongoing both here in the hospital and elsewhere. Are you talking about a police investigation, or a liability claim?" She tried to imagine crimes one could commit in a hospital. "Did Alda make a mistake in her work? Did she steal drugs? Or . . ."

Bjargey had fallen silent and appeared to be wondering how best to reply, if at all. When she finally spoke again it was as if she were weighing every word carefully. "Alda wasn't accused of a work error and she didn't steal any drugs. The case wasn't about anything like that. It's debatable whether she behaved in an appropriate manner, but all the allegedly unusual conduct took place outside work hours, and therefore should not concern this institution. However, circumstances arose that made it wrong for her to continue working here during the investigation."

Thóra could make no sense of this. "I don't understand what you're getting at," she said, and smiled confidingly. "Is there any way you could explain more clearly?"

"No," replied Bjargey, now without any hesitation. "This has nothing to do with Alda's death and I can't see how whatever you're trying to dig up could relate to this in any way. So I would prefer not to discuss it any further." She avoided looking Thóra in the eye as she said this, but then directed her gaze at her and added: "I'm sorry. It's a sensitive matter."

Thóra realized it was useless to pursue this any further. "No problem," she said. "But to return to my errand—can you think of anyone Alda might have known well on her shifts, even if they weren't actually friends?"

Bjargey gave Thóra a patronizing smile. "Have you visited the A&E in the evening or at the weekend?"

"No, actually I haven't, but I came here several times with my children when they were younger. As it happens, it was always in the daytime."

"There's no comparison," said Bjargey. "Alda worked all the difficult and tiresome shifts, when the A&E filled with puking pissheads who had injured themselves, or with their victims, who came here either beaten up or cut up. Try to imagine yourself working with such a demanding bunch. Drunk people are incredibly impatient and if a lot of them are made to wait, the situation in the waiting room can be borderline dangerous, not to mention how unpleasant it is to have to listen to all their arguing and complaining. So there's really no time or space for chatting or making friends, I can tell you that much."

"Oh dear," said Thóra, understanding only too well how horrible a workplace full of drunk people could be. She had heard many stories from Hannes over the years, so what the woman said didn't surprise her. "Alda must have been an extremely hard worker," she said. "Did she have any particular role, or did she do all the general nursing duties?"

Bjargey looked again at Thóra as if she were reluctant to answer. "Alda took on pretty much everything. She was an outstanding nurse and had a great deal of experience in closings because of her work at the plastic surgeons'. The doctors used to ask her to assist them in stitching and such like. She was also very compassionate and mature, which made her popular when there was a need to calm or comfort people in distress, or to fill out incident reports. She was particularly good with women," said Bjargey, glancing at her watch. The message was clear: *enough*. She looked up again at Thóra. "Luckily, there are fewer women than men here on the weekends, but the gender ratio is balancing out more and more with every weekend that passes. Unfortunately."

Equality appeared to be making more strides in the underbelly of human activity than in the workplace, but Thóra refrained from saying so out loud. "Her sister told me she'd been involved with a few rape cases, and among other things had to testify in court because of it. Is that right?"

Bjargey hesitated for a moment, then replied: "As I said, Alda was here mostly in the evenings and on weekends, and those are precisely the times most violent crimes are committed. Since her manner was particularly kind and gentle, she often took part in the examination and care of girls and women who had been subjected to such appalling acts. She also participated a little in the follow-up care of the victims in the cases where trust had developed between them and her. It's much better for the women not to have to discuss what happened with too many people."

"Of course," said Thóra. "What form does this follow-up care take?"

"It varies," said Bjargey. "It isn't always possible to arrange counseling sessions, since some of the women are psychologically unstable and have difficulty keeping appointments. Of course attempts are made to proceed with face-to-face therapy, but in worst-case scenarios the cases are discussed by telephone. Alda was one of the few who didn't mind giving her telephone number to the women, and she often provided counseling and support by phone." Bjargey added quickly: "Naturally she was paid for it, and she wrote down every phone call and filled out the appropriate paperwork." Bjargey looked at her watch again. "Is that everything?"

"Yes, just one more thing before you go," said Thóra. "Did Alda ever talk about the Westmann Islands or the volcanic eruption in 1973?"

Bjargey frowned thoughtfully. "No, not that I recall," she said. "I actually worked with her over the Bank Holiday weekend last year and the Islands came up in our conversation. She told me that she was from there, I recall." She quickly added: "Unlike other weekends, the Bank Holiday is relatively quiet in Reykjavík, as you know. So we had a peaceful shift and got to speak to each other a bit."

"Do you remember what you talked about?" asked Thóra cautiously. She was certain that the woman would end their conversation there and then if she started talking about a lopped-off head. "Did she mention at all why she never went back to her hometown?"

Bjargey shook her head. "No, I don't think so," she said. "She was simply reminiscing about what the festival was like for the residents of the island. Told me about the Islanders' white tents, and things like that. I don't remember her saying she rarely went there." Bjargey seemed to be on the verge of standing up when she suddenly stopped. "Actually," she said, "I asked her whether she wanted to go, since I could easily have found another nurse to fill in for her."

"And?" asked Thóra. "What was her reply?"

Bjargey's brow furrowed. "I remember I found her reply and the tone of her voice quite peculiar and very unlike her," she answered. "She said her heart wouldn't let her go even if her head wanted her to." The nurse looked at Thóra. "Then she laughed as if it were some hilarious joke." She stood up. "I didn't get what was so funny."

Stefán found the song on the radio quite inappropriate, so he turned it off. He was sitting in his office, but should have been on his way home. One more day in which he didn't make it home on time. He sighed deeply. Tomorrow it would happen again. His promotion within the police department demanded more of his time than he had originally expected, and it was starting to take its toll. His wife thought he was messing around in his office all evening, and was in a bad mood every night. Stefán was getting very tired of the situation at home, particularly the fact that it seemed to take at least an hour to get his wife going in bed on the occasions when he was in the mood. Tomorrow he would be home by five at the very latest. Definitely. Yet it seemed that whenever he entertained thoughts like this he would suddenly be hit with a flurry of urgent business. Where were all these people with all their burning issues between nine and five? Just earlier, for instance, the forensic pathologist had phoned at five sharp with the results from the second drug test on the dead nurse. He had asked Stefán to wait a little while he took care of something in the autopsy lab, but promised that he would phone again when he was back up in his office, where he had left the report. So Stefán had waited, but as experience advised he had phoned home and explained why he would be late. His explanation fell on deaf ears. He did not expect to be welcomed home joyfully tonight. It was six thirty when the doctor finally rang and Stefán noticed that the same cold tone had crept into his own voice as he had heard in his wife's.

"Keep it short," he said. "It's getting late."

"You don't need to tell me that," replied the doctor, just as irritated. He paused and there was a brief riffling of papers on the other end of the line before he got straight to the point. "As you recall, the first test revealed nothing to indicate the cause of death so another test was performed. I don't know how familiar you are with these cases, but the lab first tests only for the things that are specifically requested. Of course we asked them to test for the active ingredients in the tablets found on the bedside table, then we also had them look for several common substances, but with no result. However, for the current test we widened the scope. I also took several tissue samples and had them tested."

"Which tissues?" asked Stefán. What he knew about forensic pathology could fit on the back of a stamp, but he didn't want the doctor to realize this. He hoped it wasn't too stupid a question.

"I mainly took samples from the usual areas, but I was most eager to see the results from the woman's tongue," replied the doctor, who Stefán could hear was still flipping through his papers. "I've never seen a corpse with a tongue like that and I suspected something unnatural was going on."

"And?" asked Stefán impatiently. The tone of the doctor's voice told him that he was going to say something important and he wanted to relish the moment. Stefán had no time for games.

"And, I was right," said the doctor triumphantly. "This woman was murdered and the proof is in her tongue." The rustling stopped suddenly. "Very unusual. Very."

Stefán took a deep breath and counted to three in his head. He couldn't spare the time to count up to ten. "Might you consider telling me about this amazing discovery, or do I have to guess?" he asked calmly.

"Guess?" repeated the doctor, laughing. "You could never guess this, my friend. The woman's tongue was injected with Botox and then shoved down her throat." When Stefán said nothing he added, "Tasteful, don't you think?"

Stefán spoke up again: "Botox, isn't that antiwrinkle medicine?" He wasn't particularly interested in plastic surgery, but his wife ruined all the television shows they watched with a running commentary about this or that actress having surely had Botox injections. "Paralyzes the skin or something like that?"

"It actually paralyzes the muscles," the doctor replied. "This drug, if you can call it a drug, is closely related to botulism, or food poisoning, but it can also cause lethal paralysis. Botox prevents messages being sent from the nerve ends of muscles to the upper part of the face, thus inhibiting it from contracting. The muscles in question are technically paralyzed, so they can't form wrinkles in the skin. It only lasts for a few months at a time, so people need to repeat the injections if they want to maintain their youthful appearance. It's an ingenious substance, although in this instance it has been used in a very unpleasant and unconventional manner."

"So her tongue was paralyzed?" asked Stefán, even though the answer was obvious. "It fell back into her throat and choked her, did it?"

"That was the idea, I imagine," said the doctor. "However, the problem is that it takes Botox several hours to work perfectly, even up to a few days, although muscle movement is restricted almost immediately. I think the murderer got tired of her struggling, so he shoved her tongue down her throat. She wasn't able to pull it back up again because the tongue's muscular actions were impeded. She had a faint bruise on her upper arm that could suggest she'd been held down." The doctor stopped. "I need to go over everything again in the light of this new information. It may well be that I'll find other evidence that can be used to get a good picture of what happened."

"But you're convinced that this was murder?" Stefán asked. "She was a nurse, and could have done this to herself. People do strange things when they're unbalanced."

"It's out of the question that she could have done this herself," said the doctor stubbornly. "The marks on her arms don't suggest that she intended this conclusion for herself. I have the feeling that someone wanted to make this look like suicide, but panicked and wasn't careful enough. The drugs themselves might have been enough, but the vomit found in the room suggests that her stomach couldn't bear them and tried to expel the poison."

"And then it just happened that the murderer had Botox in his pocket," said Stefán. His head was spinning.

"As you say, she was a nurse and no stranger to plastic surgery, judging by her body," replied the doctor. "Maybe she had the Botox at home, which the murderer used to his own advantage. Maybe the idea was to prevent the vomiting by blocking its way out."

"I don't know whether you realize, but she worked at a plastic surgeon's office," said Stefán. "Maybe she got the Botox from them, to keep in her first-aid kit if wrinkles suddenly appeared."

"Maybe," said the doctor thoughtfully. "I think it's rather doubtful that she got her own supplies from them, though. This isn't a substance to be used at home. On the other hand you never know, maybe the plastic surgeon she worked for dropped by?" He snorted. "Now is not the right time, nor is it my job, to ponder who may have done this. My task is to uncover the cause of death, and I now think I know what that is. Premeditated murder by a most unorthodox form of choking. My report will be on your desk by noon tomorrow. I'd better get to work on it."

Four murders plus one made five. Stefán said good-bye and sighed heavily. He wasn't going home for quite some time, that was for sure. He switched on his radio but switched it off again when he heard not music, but loud and obnoxious adverts. When he had turned down the radio earlier, a song about sex had been playing. He'd been hoping that it was still on, because he had absolutely no hope of the real thing any time soon. He sighed again and dialed his home number.

Chapter 18

Thursday, July 19, 2007

After the longest stretch of warm weather Thóra could remember, dark, heavy clouds now filled the sky. The light was yellowish and the horizon was all gray. She pulled her thin cardigan tightly around herself and realized that she hadn't dressed for the weather at all. It only took two weeks of warm weather to make you forget what Icelandic summers could be like. Thóra felt as naive as the foreigners who tried to fend off the horizontal rain with mere umbrellas. She quickened her pace and flung open the door to the police station, where she was supposed to meet Markús. He had been called in for yet another round of questioning. Thóra had phoned the police officer, Stefán, to ask him what they wanted to talk about, but he had deflected all her questions and she sensed the case had taken a more serious turn. She shook most of the rain from her hair and brushed it from her clothing.

She was ten minutes early. She took the opportunity to smarten up in the toilets, thinking to herself that it was difficult to respect a woman whose face was smeared with mascara. When she was more or less satisfied with the effect she walked back to the lobby. Markús stood there wearing a dark blue rain-jacket, sensible shoes and a hangdog expression.

"Well," said Thóra as she walked toward him, "are you ready?" She received only a grunt in reply. They both walked to the interrogation room in silence. Thóra was happy not to speak to Markús when he was in such a mood, since now was hardly the time to wonder what the police were planning to ask him. He had been summoned with just over half an hour's notice in the early afternoon, but before Thóra had dashed out to her car she'd managed to shove the relevant files into her briefcase.

Nevertheless, as they reached the door Thóra paused for a moment to reiterate to Markús that he should answer according to her advice and not say anything outside the scope of the questions, at least not without consulting her first. Markús nodded in agreement, still with the same sullen look, and they walked in. Thóra had to remind herself that people reacted differently to pressure: some became absolutely unbearable, like her client in this case. Could he be grieving for Alda so much? Everyone agreed that he'd been in love with her. True, Alda hadn't felt the same, but it was possible that he had taken her death very badly. His eyes might not have been swollen with weeping, but perhaps he was someone who dealt with grief through anger and lack of communication. Thóra resolved to be nicer to him.

Stefán was already in the interrogation room with another officer, who was leaving when Thóra and Markús arrived. The officer greeted them gruffly on the way out, and once again Thóra had the feeling that matters were about to come to a head. She crossed her fingers, hoping Markús wasn't on his way into custody. Apart from the discomfort and shock he would experience, it would put increased pressure on Thóra, demanding more time from her than she actually had to give.

Stefán opened the questioning by announcing that Markús remained a suspect, and that now the murder of Alda Thorgeirsdóttir was being investigated in addition to the murders of the four unidentified men in 1973. Thóra tried to look impassive but nonetheless dropped her pen on the floor. Markús didn't have as much self-control, but seemed at first to be taking it very calmly. When Thóra sat up again, though, his face was flushed dark red and his breathing heavy.

"Are you telling me that I'm suspected of Alda's murder?" he said, quietly but angrily. "Are you nuts? Didn't she kill herself? What the hell is this?"

Thóra put her hand on his shoulder. "Let's let Stefán talk. This must be a misunderstanding we can sort out." She looked at Stefán.

"How did Markús come to be a suspect in Alda's murder, and when was it actually revealed that she was murdered?"

Stefán appeared completely unaffected by Markús's reaction. "The results of the drug test on her blood and soft tissues revealed that it wasn't suicide. In the interests of the investigation I can't discuss these results right now. I need to ask Markús a few questions concerning his relationship with the murder victim, and I strongly recommend that he answer them." Stefán's face was stony, making it impossible to read anything from it.

"In the light of my client being considered a murder suspect, I insist on seeing these particular test results," said Thóra. "As well as the autopsy report."

Stefán smiled mockingly. "The report you got from the police in the Westmann Islands?" He leaned forward slightly. "I know Gudni let you see the autopsy report on the bodies in the basement. That won't happen again. If you want further files you have to acquire them through the proper channels." He straightened up again.

Thóra would have to explain herself, as Markús could not afford to have Stefán and his colleagues against him because of the autopsy report—there was enough pressure from the media and police authorities to solve the case as quickly as possible. "It's true that I got the report from Gudni without submitting a special request, but it must be borne in mind that I had already heard about its contents on the street. It can't be considered natural that information from the case files is on the lips of everyone but the parties involved."

Stefán looked at Thóra, but said nothing. He turned again to Markús. "Where were you this past Sunday evening, the eighth of July?" So they had confirmed the time of death; Thóra scribbled it down.

"I don't know," replied Markús sharply. "How am I supposed to know that?"

"If I were you I'd try to remember. You have previously stated that you were on your way to the Westmann Islands, and you were there the next morning, as is now well known." Stefán flipped through some papers on the desk. "You said you left Reykjavík at about seven, and by eight thirty you were at your summerhouse on the banks of the Rang River. From there you went down to Bakki early the next morning, from where you caught a flight to the Islands. Is that correct?"

Markús appeared confused. "Yes, yes. I just didn't remember the date. If you had asked about the evening prior to my trip to the Islands I would have answered immediately."

"In other words, you're sticking to your statement?" said Stefán.

"Of course," snapped Markús. "Why wouldn't I? That's how it happened. Check with Westmann Islands Air. They must have a record of it."

"I'm not asking about your movements on Monday morning," said Stefán. "I'm asking about Sunday evening. It only takes two hours to drive to the airport at Bakki, so the fact that you were there the next morning doesn't tell us anything." Stefán looked up from the report. "Can anyone verify your story? Did you stop for petrol or food along the way?"

Markús rocked in his chair and seemed to be trying to remember. Thóra sincerely hoped that he'd stopped for both petrol and something to eat at some shop or other. Her hope was not realized. "No," he said. "I stopped for petrol on the way out of town, as far as I recall." He exhaled disappointedly. "A lot of time has passed. But I think I stopped at the Orka petrol station on Snorrabraut Road."

"At what time, do you suppose?" asked Stefán.

"Around seven, a little earlier. I don't know," replied Markús, then added in irritation: "Can't you see it on my credit card account? I pay for almost everything by card."

Stefán did not reply, but Thóra knew that the use of a card in a self-service petrol station didn't amount to an alibi. "Sorry," she interjected. "Couldn't you show that Markús was present at the scene rather than make him struggle to remember an evening from eleven days ago? I'm sure he would have paid better attention if he'd known what that evening had in store." Now it was Thóra's turn to give Stefán a sarcastic smile. It felt good, but not for long.

"That's precisely what we think we can do," said Stefán. "Prove that Markús was at the scene on the evening in question." He looked from Thóra to Markús.

"What?" gasped Markús, completely deflated. "That isn't possible," he said simply. He seemed too astonished to be angry. "That just isn't possible," he repeated.

"And yet it is," said Stefán. Thóra hoped he was referring to the bottles of tablets in Alda's home, or something else Markús had already explained. She was out of luck. "We have a witness who claims to have seen you there around the time that Alda was murdered, as well as biological evidence on her body. Comparison of this evidence and your DNA, which you gave willingly in connection with the corpses in the basement, proves it unequivocally."

Markús was clearly not going to be heading home after this interview.

Tinna lay in bed, her eyes wide open. She was tired, but she knew that you burned fewer calories in your sleep than you did while awake, so it was out of the question to take an afternoon nap. Through the closed door she could hear her mother tidying up in the front room. Things were unbearable since she'd left her job to look after Tinna, because it made everything so difficult. When her mother had been gone the whole day it was easy to say that she'd eaten food that she'd actually thrown away. That wasn't possible now, because her mother watched her so carefully. On a normal day, Tinna would have been out there drying the dishes or helping tidy up, but she didn't feel like it. She was angry at her mother, and it would be boring. Her mother had found her at the computer earlier, reading one recipe after another in utter fascination. Mum had lost it, saying Tinna would be better off eating some food than staring at it on the screen. The exchange ended with her mother starting to cry, and Tinna had disappeared into her room. Her mum would never understand how she felt, and it was useless trying to explain. Tinna longed for the food on the screen, craved it even. However, she never gave in to the temptation of making or buying any of it, since she felt better denying herself than succumbing.

The vacuum cleaner started again outside, and Tinna put her hands over her ears to block out the noise. It was an old Hoover that a friend of her mother's had given her when the last one broke. Tinna tried to guess how long it would take for her mother to finish and leave. She always did the floors of the little apartment last, so she must be nearly finished. Then she would go to the shops, but before their falling-out she had asked Tinna to come with her. Tinna certainly wouldn't be going now, and the thought actually made her extremely happy. Instead she could use the opportunity to have a long shower, and then wipe away the water in the bathtub to cover her tracks. Her mother must never know that she had taken another shower, or she might call the hospital again and have Tinna readmitted. She knew now that Tinna took showers to wash off the calories and that the more often she washed, the more calories she got rid of. She felt the longing to start scrubbing herself grow stronger, especially since the disgusting drink that the doctor had given her was still in her stomach. What she wanted most was to puke it up, but she knew she wouldn't get away with it. No, it was better to send this nasty nourishment down the plughole.

She knew it hadn't been that long ago that she'd avoided showers like the plague in case the water allowed calories to pass through her skin. She pushed away this thought, since she found it uncomfortable to compare the two theories. Which was right? Was it a mistake to wash too often? She pressed her eyes closed again and lay with her hands over her ears. By neither seeing nor hearing she could clear her mind. Despite the noise of the Hoover she managed to make herself feel as if she weren't there. She would just lie here and lose weight. Maybe then she could finally become what she wanted to be: slim. Nobody else understood her, not her mother or the doctors. Her father was the best of them, because even though he often said she was too thin, he didn't seem interested enough in her to force her to eat. So with him, she was able to choose for herself how much she ate. She'd often been able to stay with him a whole weekend without actually eating anything. He just didn't notice. Her mother, on the other hand, was more observant, and it was after one such weekend that she got some sort of court order to prevent Tinna from staying with her father. Now she could never be with him for more than four hours at a time.

Images kept springing into her head. The lady visiting her father. The lady's house. The visitor who had sneaked out. The note. The lady carried out to the ambulance beneath a white sheet. The lady who could have helped her so much. The lady God had sent from Heaven to make Tinna slim. The lady who made others beautiful, and would have loved Tinna however she looked. The lady who would have understood her. Tinna tried to avoid thinking about it. She had to shut out everything. One, two, three . . . she focused on meaningless numbers and didn't know whether she was saying them out loud or silently. She had counted up to thirty-four when someone grabbed her shoulder and shook her. She opened her eyes but kept her hands over her ears.

"Come on, Tinna," she heard her mother say, and Tinna relaxed the pressure on her ears. "You're coming with me to the hospital."

Tinna shook her head and closed her eyes again. She felt her mother pull her clawed fingers away from her ears, forcing her to listen. Her mother was much stronger than she was, so resistance was futile. After Tinna became as slim as she planned to be, she would also be incredibly strong, and then no one would be able to force her to listen when she yearned for silence. "No," said Tinna quietly, but realized as soon as the word fell from her lips that she'd shouted it.

"Yes," said her mother, her eyes sad. "You can come with me or I'll be forced to call an ambulance. It's up to you." She let go of Tinna's hand and looked at her. Suddenly she ran her fingers through her daughter's hair and several tears rolled down her cheeks. "Get up, darling," she said, without doing so herself. "You've got to come with me."

Tinna wondered whether she could say anything to change her mother's mind, but realized almost immediately that it was no use. This was not the first time this had happened. Maybe her mother would let her stay at home if she told her what had happened between her father and the lady. Especially if she told her the lady was dead, and that her father might have played a part in it. Maybe he knew the visitor who had slunk out of the lady's house. It might be possible to use the note to find out. It had been blown out of the car. Tinna's mother couldn't stand her father and would definitely want to hear the story, but Tinna decided to say nothing. Even though her father didn't pay much attention to her, he was generally good to her and had promised to buy her some clothes. He was expecting to come into a great deal of money, and then they could go shopping in town. If Tinna told anyone what she knew, he wouldn't get any money and she'd get no new clothes. Her mother would never keep the secret, and it was no fun having a secret everyone knew. No, it would be better to get up and go to the car. She could act as if everything was fine and hopefully the doctor would just scold her mother for wasting his time. Tinna knew exactly what she was doing. If not, then she could point out again that it was her body and that it only belonged to her. Not to her mother and not to this doctor who peered so closely at her. She straightened up and swung her feet over the edge of the bed. Her mother started crying even harder.

"Look at your legs, sweetheart," she said, and swallowed. She stood up and walked out of the room. "I'll get the car keys. Put on your parka. It's raining." Her voice cracked and she sniffed.

Tinna stood up carefully. She felt dizzy but she mustn't under any circumstances faint. Then they'd put her straight into the psych ward and keep her there for a long, long time. She breathed slowly and took several hesitant steps, picking up the English dictionary her aunt had given her as a confirmation present. It was heavy, so Tinna would lose weight on her way out to the car. She cheered up. At the hospital she would get to take a shower, and then another when the shifts changed. Maybe it wasn't all bad.

Adolf put down the phone and wondered about this strange disease afflicting his daughter. He couldn't understand it at all. The girl had never been chubby; before she got sick she'd had a bit of baby fat but nothing you'd notice. Now she was a walking skeleton who refused to eat, and at this rate no man would want her even if she offered to pay him for it. It wasn't that he thought of her in that way—she was too young and besides, she was his daughter. But this appeared to be the life that awaited her if she carried on with this nonsense. Tinna's mother had been hysterical on the telephone and insisted that the girl was mortally ill. He didn't quite agree with that—he was sure that in the end she would be so hungry that she would have to eat something. He did vaguely recall a headline in some gossip magazine about a famous model who'd died of anorexia, but that was different. That woman had starved herself because of work, but Tinna had no reason to do so. In the end, she would come around.

He stood up from the sofa and went into the kitchen to look for coffee, but to no avail. All he found was a little jar of instant granules that had expired several months earlier. Nevertheless, he prepared a large mug of the slop and gulped it down at high speed, black and sugarless. He needed to perk up a bit and be wide awake when he spoke to his lawyer. He found that since he'd lost his job he was paying less attention to the world around him and was generally more apathetic. It was probably because he had too much time on his hands, which meant that he dragged things out until the last minute. He shook himself to speed up the effect of the caffeine in his blood. He didn't remember who had recommended this method, but it always seemed to work. He phoned his lawyer.

"Did you know that the nurse who wanted to meet me is dead?" was the first thing she said.

"No," lied Adolf. He'd seen the death notice several days earlier and had felt relieved. "Does it matter?"

His lawyer cleared her throat. "I would have thought so, yes," she said. "It was my understanding that she had information that might have helped you. You needed her, I can tell you that much."

"I didn't rape the damn girl," snarled Adolf. This was all bullshit. They'd never pin it on him.

"You don't need to keep telling me," said his lawyer, with a hint of fatigue in her voice. "If this Alda had been able to testify in your favor, it would have meant a great deal. Your position is bad enough as it is."

"How can someone be accused of rape after more than twenty-four hours?" he said heatedly. "If I had raped her for real she would have gone straight to the police or the hospital. Not home."

"That does work in your favor, but it's actually not uncommon, and therefore doesn't suffice in itself. I remember that she had some injuries and unexplained bleeding from her genitals." Adolf didn't feel like saying anything, and she continued, "Of course you already know all this, there's no use going over and over it." She paused for a moment but was met by more silence, so she started again: "When this Alda called me, she said she wanted to speak to you before she came to meet me. I tried to get her to change her mind, but she insisted. Did she contact you?"

"No," Adolf lied for the second time. "She didn't."

"That's too bad," said the lawyer. "Are you absolutely sure?" It was clear from her tone that she didn't believe him, so perhaps to cover this she added: "It's just that Alda treated the girl when she went to A&E, so whatever it was that she wanted to say would probably have made a great deal of difference. As it stands now, the hospital report is very bad for you."

Adolf knew all this. "I told you, Alda didn't come."

"What you actually said was that she hadn't contacted you, but it doesn't matter." The woman sounded unconvinced. "You let me know if you suddenly remember a phone call or a visit from her that slipped your mind."

Adolf let her question go in one ear and out the other. "That's not going to happen." He hesitated slightly but then continued, "I'm not in the mood. My daughter is ill and she's been admitted to hospital. As a matter of fact, her life's in danger." To judge by the silence on the other end of the phone this surprised his lawyer, who was usually imperturbable. "Still, I'm sure she'll recover. Maybe she could even testify . . ."

Chapter 19

Friday, July 20, 2007

Yesterday's stormclouds had disappeared and been replaced by thin wispy clouds in an otherwise clear blue sky. It was as if God had been puffing on a cigar and exhaled in the direction of Iceland. Thóra sat outside on her veranda, enjoying the morning. The pages of the *Morgunblaðið* daily newspaper lying on the table in front of her rustled in the breeze and steam drifted up from her coffee cup. She closed the paper and took a sip of coffee. Mercifully, *Morgunblaðið* had gone easy on Markús in its report on his arrest and the detention order pending trial. This was perhaps no surprise, since the judge had been on the fence. For a while Thóra even thought that he would deny the state prosecutor's request. However, this did not happen, although he did reduce the recommended custody period from three weeks to five days. Thóra's objection and her remarks on evidence that pointed to Markús's innocence may have helped. For the first time in her life she wanted a cigarette, or at least to smell cigarette smoke. Passive smoke from Bella was probably to blame, unless she was losing her mind. Thóra hoped that it was the former. She couldn't afford to fall apart today, since the High Court would rule on the detention order this afternoon.

Understandably Markús had wanted to appeal the district court's decision. In fact only three days of the five had remained when the decision was announced, but she did not blame him. Three days felt like a thousand: no innocent man wanted to sit behind bars. She looked at the clock and saw that it wasn't even eight yet. If she left the house within the next hour she might have time to find something else that could rebut the court's decision. Yet she had no idea what exactly that might be. Without doubt, it was Alda's diary from 1973 that had influenced the district court judge's hesitation over Markús's guilt. Thóra had handed it over to the police immediately after Markús's interview. Stefán had reacted angrily and accused her of concealing evidence from the police, and Thóra had tried unsuccessfully to explain herself. When the prosecutor had tried to devalue the importance of the diary in court, the judge took Thóra's side and said the handover hadn't been delayed unnaturally in light of the circumstances. Another small victory had been won when the judge had asked numerous questions about the evidence that suggested the three bodies had been placed in the basement after the eruption had been going on for some time, which meant that Markús couldn't have been there. The police didn't have much on Markús as far as the bodies in the basement were concerned, if you didn't count the head.

Alda's death was a different story. Here there was very little in Markús's favor: both a witness and evidence suggested that he'd been at the scene. The witness turned out to be a boy who had been distributing flyers for his sports club's tin-can collection on the evening that Alda was murdered. The police had found one of the flyers in Alda's house and tracked down the boy, who had given a description of a man who had shown up there at the same time as the boy had been walking away from Alda's house, around seven thirty. The description fit Markús perfectly, and the boy had then selected a photo of him from a group of several he was shown. The boy said that the man had walked up to the house, but he hadn't seen him get out of a car, nor did he particularly remember anything about cars on the street that evening. Thóra tried to point out that Markús's car was a model that any normal healthy teenage boy would certainly notice, but to no effect. It was pointed out that Markús could easily have parked elsewhere, especially if he had come there with criminal intent and hadn't wanted anyone to notice him. Thóra's objection that Markús had an extremely average appearance and that the description could easily have applied to countless other men was also of little use, as, for that matter, was the fact that the boy could have selected Markús's photo from the stack at random. However, Thóra hoped this assertion would find better support after she examined the photos that the boy had been shown, because the police could easily have given him a selection in which Markús alone fit the description. She would be allowed to see them later, and she also hoped that a record of calls to and from Markús's phone, as well as Alda's, would be turned over to her at the same time. Thóra clung to the hope that this log would reveal that Alda had called Markús as he was driving eastward from Reykjavík, as he insisted. That would strengthen his testimony a great deal; Alda would hardly have rung Markús if he were at her house.

Thóra had more trouble finding an explanation for the DNA sample on Alda's body, which proved to be from Markús. This was a hair discovered upon combing out the woman's pubic hair. It was compared with hair that Markús had provided, and turned out to be from his head. The autopsy hadn't revealed any recent sexual intercourse, so Alda's genitals had been swabbed in search of Markús's saliva, which had not been found. What his head had been doing between the woman's thighs was thus left undetermined, and Markús could not shed any light on this detail, since he insisted vehemently that he had not been at Alda's home, much less between her legs. The only conclusion that Thóra could reach on this subject was that the hair could have come from toilet paper, or something else Markús had come into contact with during his visit the previous evening. Such a thing was not impossible, but this explanation would not be taken into consideration at this stage of the proceedings. On the bright side, if it came to trial, the prosecution would be required to prove unequivocally that the hair had been brought to the scene that fateful night and in connection with the murder; not before that night, and by accident.

Markús had taken the court's decision incredibly calmly. He was unhappy with it, but understood that he had to swallow it and wait for the High Court's decision. Thóra praised him for his courage and said that she would let his family know, among them Hjalti, Markús's only son, who lived with Markús's ex-wife when he wasn't in the Islands with his uncle Leifur. The phone call proved to be difficult for Thóra: Hjalti was a little older than her son Gylfi, only nineteen and he seemed very upset at the news. He asked over and over whether his father would be sentenced to prison, and it didn't matter how much Thóra tried to reassure him that this was unlikely—he wouldn't be convinced. He only calmed down a little when Thóra gave him Markús's message that everything would be all right and not to worry at all. Out of pity for the poor boy, Thóra told him at the end of the conversation that he could phone her if he had any questions or wanted to talk to her about his father's case. She fully expected him to take her at her word and keep in touch, especially now that his father's name was in the papers.

Thóra took another sip of coffee and stood up. She looked out over the calm swell and shaded her eyes, then closed them and breathed deeply through her nose. She considered how best she could spend her spare hours, without reaching any conclusion. Markús's detention made it more difficult for her to determine a possible witness. It was clear that Alda's mother and sister would hardly welcome her with open arms. And although Alda's colleagues hadn't been as close to her as her relatives, they would undoubtedly view Thóra with suspicion. Nonetheless, Thóra decided to start with them. Yesterday she'd received a message from Dís, one of the plastic surgeons at the office where Alda had worked, saying she would be willing to meet up. Who knew, maybe she had some useful information. She might even know the real reason behind Alda's resignation from the A&E. Alda's sister's theory that her murderer was a vengeful rapist was starting to sound more convincing, in the absence of more plausible options.

Thóra reopened her eyes and looked out at the placid sea, so much nicer to look at than the overgrown garden. This was the summer that Thóra had intended to sort out her garden, but now it was almost over. She'd ticked almost nothing off the list, apart from mowing the lawn. The hedge had grown to the height of a man or taller, which Thóra wasn't proud of. Its branches reached up to the sky, utterly neglected. The flowerbeds had succumbed to weeds. She could certainly see how entire cities could disappear beneath a rain forest's lush greenery, considering how quickly vegetation could sweep over things even in a polar climate. She went back inside. The garden could wait until next year.

Of the four people in the waiting room, Thóra felt she was the one who could most use the services of a plastic surgeon. There were two young women who were attractive by any standards, although their bleached blond hair did little for them. The other occupant was a young man, and Thóra couldn't think for the life of her what he might need fixed. On behalf of all Icelandic women she sincerely hoped he wasn't planning on having a sex change complete with breast implants.

The waiting room was plain, but the fixtures and fittings looked expensive. It made the little closet that served as a waiting room at her legal firm look ridiculous, which suggested a plastic surgeon's time was worth far more than a lawyer's. That was no surprise: people were more concerned about their looks than their reputations. Thóra looked at the clock and hoped that it would soon be her turn; she was getting uncomfortable sitting there, knowing the others were regarding her and wondering what work she was having done. She was on the verge of pointing out to one of them, who had glanced once too often at Thora's chest, to mind her own business, when the receptionist appeared and informed Thóra that Dís would see her now. Thóra stood up and followed the slender woman. She was wearing a short dress, and such high heels that Thóra's toes ached in sympathy. Again she compared this to her legal firm's office setup, where Bella steered clients into the harbor of the waiting room like a squat little Gothic tugboat, the tattered hem of her floor-length dress trailing behind her.

"Through here, please," said the dark-haired girl, her snow-white smile gleaming. "And I hope it all goes marvelously for you." She opened the door to the office, turned and left.

Dís was on the telephone but indicated that Thóra should take a seat before putting down the phone, standing up and extending her hand. She was wearing a white fitted shirt and black jeans that hugged her slender waist, as well as a thick belt that clashed with an otherwise conservative outfit. Thóra thought they were about the same age, and noticed that the doctor was in very good shape. Her body didn't look like it had been sculpted with a scalpel, but rather by blood, sweat and tears—probably requiring several hours a day with a personal trainer. It must be important for a plastic surgeon to look good.

"Hello," said Dís, who seemed aware of Thóra's scrutiny of her body. She sat back down. "I'm sorry to have made you wait; I didn't expect to be so busy. It's usually quite calm here before lunch."

"That's fine," said Thóra. "I'm just grateful that you were available to meet me at such short notice."

"I gathered it was important," said Dís, smiling hesitantly. Her face was not dissimilar to Thóra's, with high cheekbones and a wide mouth. The main difference was that Dís had nicely styled hair and flawless makeup, whereas Thóra usually dragged her hair into a messy ponytail and wore only mascara. "Of course I want to do anything I can to help apprehend whoever did this to Alda. I saw in the paper that a man had been taken into custody. I hope the sentence fits his disgusting crime."

Thóra cleared her throat. "Ah, yes. I forgot to mention that I am actually representing the suspect." She could see this information was not well received. The doctor's friendly face hardened. "He says he's innocent, and it's indisputable that the police don't have much to go on. His custody period is unusually short given the seriousness of the case, which reflects the judge's doubts about my client's guilt. There is a lot of evidence that actually supports his plea of innocence. I'm looking for information to back him up, and at the same time I want to find out who actually did murder Alda." She drew a deep breath. "No one who cared for her will want to see the wrong man punished."

Dís said nothing. She gazed thoughtfully at Thóra, who looked resolutely back. Then Dís's expression suddenly seemed to relax. "Of course I don't want that," she said. "Nobody wants an innocent man to be found guilty. So shall we say that I'm prepared to help you in the unlikely event that this man didn't do it?"

Thóra decided not to spend any more time defending Markús to the doctor. She hadn't come here to argue, and it wouldn't strengthen her position to antagonize her informant. "Okay, thanks." She turned to her list of questions, determined to make the most of her time since she didn't have long. One of the people sitting outside was probably waiting for a consultation with the woman about some urgent operation. "When you heard that Alda had been murdered," she said, "did you wonder how such a thing could have happened, or who could possibly have wanted to harm her?"

Dís didn't take time to think, but replied immediately. "I must admit, the first time I heard it was murder was this morning, when I read about the custody order. As you know, I was the one who discovered Alda, and I thought at that point that she'd killed herself. Suicides don't often make it to the papers, so I was very surprised this morning when I saw her death had been reported. I actually have no idea what else has gone on since I found her body. No one's told us anything about the progress of the investigation." She added hurriedly: "Of course, we didn't even think that there *was* an investigation."

"You say *we*," said Thóra. "Who do you mean?"

"Oh, yes, of course," Dís replied. "I mean myself and Ágúst, my partner in the clinic. He's a plastic surgeon too, and Alda worked with both of us."

"I understand," said Thóra. "But when you saw this morning that it was a murder investigation—did anyone come to mind as the culprit?"

Dís's cheeks reddened slightly and she muttered a negative, before inquiring: "A thief, maybe?"

"Well, I don't know about that," Thóra replied. "Would anything in Alda's house have been particularly attractive to thieves?"

"No, nothing I can think of," said Dís. "But are burglars that picky? I suppose Alda had everything one might imagine a petty thief would steal—television, stereo equipment, some jewelry. Maybe these things weren't top of the range, but I would imagine anyone poor enough to take others' property isn't very fussy."

"That's true," conceded Thóra. "But they're also not usually into killing people and making it look like suicide."

"No, I don't imagine they are," said Dís. "It's just that Alda had no enemies I'm aware of, so that was the only thing I could come up with."

"No ex-husbands or boyfriends who had been bothering or harassing her?" asked Thóra.

"Nothing like that," the woman replied. "Not to my knowledge.

As a matter of fact she was divorced, but as far as I gathered the divorce was amicable, and they hadn't had any recent contact. As far as boyfriends were concerned, she kept that to herself, if there were any. She never spoke to me about men."

Thóra found it incredible that the woman hadn't been in any relationships. The autopsy report stated that she had had breast implants, signs of a face-lift, Botox in her forehead and scars where the bags under her eyes had been removed, along with evidence of stomach stapling and several other minor operations. Why would she undergo such ordeals if not to attract a man's attention? "Could she have been in relationships that she chose not to talk about?" she asked.

"Yes, yes," replied Dís, and her cheeks flushed again. "That's quite likely. Alda didn't confide in people much, although she was always pleasant and friendly."

"Did she ever mention why she never went to the Westmann Islands, or talk about a bad experience she'd had around the time of the eruption there?" Considering that Dís had described Alda as the shy, retiring type, Thóra didn't expect much of an answer to this question.

"She never talked about the Westmann Islands," said Dís. "She tended to change the subject if conversation ever turned to anything about the Islands, which wasn't often." She looked curiously at Thóra. "What experience are you referring to?" she asked. "Alda never mentioned anything."

Thóra chose not to answer the doctor's question, since she didn't know what had happened. She smiled at the woman and simply said "Botox," then waited for Dís's reaction. She clearly couldn't expect any useful theories on Alda's murder or insight into her life, so she might as well change the subject.

Thóra didn't have to wait long for Dís's reaction, though it was somewhat baffling. The woman leaned back in her chair and said nothing for a moment. She looked straight at Thóra, who would have given a lot to know what she was thinking. "What about Botox? Are you thinking of getting some injections?" She pulled out a pen. "If so, you need to make an appointment like everyone else."

Thóra smiled fiercely, so all the possible wrinkles in her face would show themselves. "No, actually I'm not," she said. "Not right now, anyway. The forensic pathologist's tests revealed that Botox is one of the likeliest causes of Alda's death."

"What?" muttered Dís, not completely convincingly in Thóra's opinion. "How could that be? Botox isn't life-threatening."

"Not in the forehead," said Thóra. "I can't tell you what the report said, other than that the Botox was used in a very unconventional manner." She could see that the doctor was almost biting her tongue with the effort not to blurt out questions. "Could Alda possibly have had Botox at home?" she asked, before Dís's curiosity could get the better of her.

"What, *Alda*?" asked Dís. Thóra said nothing, allowing Dís to realize the stupidity of her question. "No," she said. "Alda didn't have any Botox, to my knowledge. Of course she had access to it here, but we keep close track of all our supplies and it's out of the question that she took drugs from this clinic. We're particularly careful about all our work here and would never have let her take the substance for her own use. Where else she could have got it from, I couldn't say. The A&E doesn't keep a supply of it, I know that much."

"Where do you get the Botox you use in this office?" asked Thóra.

"We order it through the pharmacy that supplies us," replied Dís. "We have a good deal there and get a decent enough discount to allow us not to have to contract with wholesalers. Of course we buy far more goods and drugs than just Botox."

"Who was the clinic's point of contact with the pharmacy?" asked Thóra.

Dís looked at her. "I was. Ágúst a couple of times." She pressed her lips together. "Alda never had anything to do with it," she added.

"You realize that if Alda didn't have Botox in her house, then whoever murdered her took it there?" said Thóra. She allowed Dís to digest this for a moment before continuing. "There aren't that many people with access to those kind of supplies. Certainly not my client."

Dís's foundation partially masked the blush that was spreading over her cheeks again, but it didn't escape Thóra's notice. "I should admit now that I haven't taken an inventory since the end of last month. It may well be that there's something missing from the drug cabinet, but if there is it would be the first time." She cleared her throat daintily. "Neither Ágúst nor I had any reason to wish Alda harm. On the contrary, her death was a great blow to us. That's no secret."

The woman appeared to be sincere. "No doubt the police will be in touch with you," said Thóra. "The results of the drug test have just come back, and I expect they have had more urgent matters to attend to in the light of this. But they will be here sooner or later. They'll go over the inventory with you, which may clear a few things up."

"The police?" repeated Dís. "Yes, of course. I gave a statement after I found the body. They thought it was suicide at the time, and didn't really ask me anything." She shook her head. "Of all the crazy things." She closed her eyes and shuddered slightly. "It's unbelievable how self-centered one can be. When you said that, my first thought was how embarrassing it would be to have the police stampeding through here." She looked away. "Of course that doesn't matter. We have nothing to hide and hopefully that will be proven as quickly as possible."

Thóra saw Dís glance at a little clock on her desk. Her time would soon be up. "Until recently I've heard only good things about Alda, from her childhood friends, her sister, and others. Then I spoke to a woman who worked with her in the A&E and I started to see a different picture emerging. She didn't actually say anything bad about Alda, but she did suggest that something had happened, although I couldn't find out exactly what it was. Do you know what might have happened to make Alda resign?"

Dís shook her head. "No, I'm afraid not," she said. "I thought she didn't want to talk about it, but that she might open up later. Now she'll never have the chance. It's easy to be wise in hindsight." She shrugged unhappily. "I've thought a lot about this and can't say I've reached any conclusions. Plenty of wild theories, of course, but nothing more."

Thóra had the feeling there was more behind this comment. "And do you find one theory more plausible than the rest?"

Dís bit her lip. "I don't know if I should tell you this." She stared at Thóra, who could do little more than look back at her and wait. "I found an unbelievable amount of pornography on Alda's computer. I was mortified. She didn't strike me as that type—generally it's men who get obsessed with it." She took a deep breath. "After I discovered it I started putting two and two together and wondered if she'd had a sexual relationship with someone in the A&E, a doctor or one of the staff. These things do happen."

"Would that be reason enough for her job to have been at risk?" asked Thóra, half wondering if it could have been her ex-husband. "Are workplace romances prohibited at the hospital?"

"No," Dís replied. "I don't think so. Something like that might be kept under wraps, but it's hardly forbidden. Anyway, the material on her computer could hardly be described as romantic. This was hard-core pornography, plain and simple. It crossed my mind that Alda might have had sex with someone on the hospital premises, which would be taken very seriously."

Obviously Thóra would have to phone Hannes again. He wouldn't have missed any gossip that followed in the wake of something like this. "You don't have any idea about the person with whom such a thing might have happened? A doctor, or even a patient?"

"No, I have no idea, this is all just guesswork," said Dís. "The only reason it occurred to me at all is that I also found emails between Alda and a sex therapist on her computer. It crossed my mind that she might have sought their help after her obsession got her into trouble."

"Did the email mention anything like that?" said Thóra.

"No, they were just confirmations of appointments, whether Alda could make it on this or that particular day and so forth."

"Do you remember the name of the therapist, by any chance?" Yet another person Thóra would need to speak to.

Dís nodded. "Yes, she's called Heida. I don't remember her surname, but there can't be many sex therapists with that name working in Reykjavík."

"Did Alda ever speak to you about a tattoo?" Thóra asked as she wrote down the name. "She had wanted to tell her sister something, and it had to do with a tattoo, all a bit mysterious."

"A tattoo?" asked Dís, looking puzzled. Then her face brightened.

"Actually, yes," she said. "Recently a young man came in who wanted to know if we could remove one, and I remember that Alda was particularly interested. She spoke to him for a long time, asking where he'd had it done, and it almost seemed as if she was thinking of getting one herself. But she just laughed when I asked her about it. Then she mentioned it to me and our secretary Kata over coffee, asking if we thought people ever got a tattoo in memory of a bad experience. We didn't know what she was on about." Dís reached for one of her desk drawers. "Since you're here, I may as well show you this," she said, pulling out several pages that were stapled together, as well as a single sheet. "I found these papers among the stuff in Alda's desk after she died. One of the pages is actually a photocopy of a photograph, and it looks to me as though it's of a tattoo." She handed Thóra the single sheet.

"Does it say 'Love Sex' in English?" asked Thóra, reading from the picture. The image was grainy, and hazy from the photocopier, but the tattoo could be seen quite clearly.

"Don't ask me," Dís said, peering at the page disdainfully. "This isn't the tattoo the boy wanted to have removed. That was a Chinese word, as I recall. So I don't have any idea who this came from or why Alda liked it so much. Maybe this man has the tattoo—his photograph was also in her desk drawer. I don't recognize him at all. Is he your client?"

Thóra took the photo, but didn't recognize the young man in it. Although he looked severe, he was very handsome. "No, I don't know who this is." She handed the photograph back to Dís.

Dís took it and handed Thóra the stapled pages. "And then there's this. Who knows, it might be important. At the time I found it I still believed Alda had killed herself, and even thought that this might have been something to do with it." She looked at Thóra. "It was so strange—Alda was unusually happy the day before all this happened. That didn't seem to fit in with the idea of suicide, and I've been racking my brain trying to understand. Now that it turns out to have been murder, these papers might be irrelevant. I'd be happy for you to look at them, since I have no idea what to do with them."

"What are they?" asked Thóra, looking down at the pages.

"It's an autopsy report on an older woman who died six months ago," replied Dís. "I've never heard of her, so I don't know how she's connected to Alda. I thought she might be a close relative and her death might have sent Alda over the edge."

Thóra looked at the top page and read the name of the deceased. Valgerdur Bjólfsdóttir. She had recently come across this name. But where? "May I take a copy of this?" she asked.

Chapter 20

Friday, July 20, 2007

Thóra found the woman's name as soon as she returned to her office. She typed the name into an Internet search engine, and a link came up to a Web site about the houses that had disappeared in the Westmann Islands eruption, the same site Thóra had looked at out on the Islands. There she found the name on the autopsy report that Alda had kept in her drawer. Thóra read her biography on the site: she had lived with her husband, Dadi Karlsson, in the house next to Markús's childhood home. Thóra read through the whole page about this couple, but all she found out was that Valgerdur Bjólfsdóttir had worked as a nurse at a hospital in the Westmann Islands, and her husband had been the captain of a fishing boat. Neither of them had moved back to the Islands after the disaster, and Thóra could see no particular connection to Alda other than their nursing careers. Perhaps Alda had looked up to this woman so much that she had decided to study nursing, but it could just have been a coincidence. At that time it was less common for young women to educate themselves in different fields, but nursing was very popular. The couple appeared to have been childless—at least there were no children accounted for on the Web site. This meant that Alda could not be connected to Valgerdur as a friend of her daughter. Clearly Thóra wasn't going to find an answer on the Internet, so she decided to call Leifur and ask him about the couple. When she'd spoken to him after the detention ruling Leifur had repeated that he wanted to help, and she had promised to let him know if he could assist her in any way.

Leifur answered on the second ring. Thóra allowed him to ask her all about the appeal to the High Court before she turned to the task at hand and asked about their ex-neighbors. His reply surprised her: "Ugh, those old bores." He heaved a sigh. "Why are you asking about them?"

"Valgerdur's name came up in connection with Alda and I'm trying to find out what they had to do with each other. Were they related, perhaps?" she asked.

"Not that I know of," he replied. "They were our neighbors, but I don't know much about them. Valgerdur was from out of town and I don't know how she met Dadi, but he was from here. They stayed on the mainland after the evacuation, so I don't know how you can track them down if that's what you're after."

"Actually, she's dead," said Thóra. "But I don't know about him. As a matter of fact I didn't call to try to get in touch with him, but I was wondering whether there had been any contact between Alda and this Valgerdur. What crossed my mind first was that they were related, but maybe it was something entirely different."

"I don't know whether there was much contact between the two households," said Leifur. "Valgerdur was no particular friend of Alda's mother, as I recall, nor were the husbands friends. That pair were so tedious that I can't imagine any sane man seeking out their company willingly. Dadi was never called anything other than Dadi Horseshoe—with good reason. Picture one upside down on his face. And Valgerdur was nicknamed Horseshoe Two after she entered the picture."

"I see," said Thóra, baffled. "I was thinking Alda might have become a nurse to follow in Valgerdur's footsteps, but that seems unlikely in the light of what you're saying."

"Valgerdur was a school nurse among other things, and I doubt she aroused any great passion for the job in any of the students. She was famous for refusing to send kids home; they actually had to faint right in front of her or puke on the floor to be considered sick. If Alda did know her, I very much doubt she would have been the inspiration for her future career."

This didn't help explain Alda's interest in the woman's death. "There's one more thing you might be able to help me with," said Thóra. "It's to do with some files I'm having trouble getting hold of." She wished she didn't have to ask Leifur for help. "I've been trying to see a copy of the log of objects removed from the excavated houses."

"And who has those records?" asked Leifur briskly, sounding confident that he would be able to get hold of them.

"The archaeologist in charge of the excavations is named Hjörtur Fridriksson," she replied. "He was going to see if he could get them for me, but I haven't heard from him since."

"I'll take care of it," said Leifur, and Thóra had no doubt that he would.

However, she was no closer to a connection between Alda and Valgerdur. She went through the autopsy report Dís had copied for her, but understood almost none of it, other than that Valgerdur had been admitted to the hospital in Ísafjördur with a severe streptococcus infection and had been given antibiotics intravenously, causing a bad allergic reaction which had led to her death the very same night. Alda had neither marked the text nor made notes in the margins, making it difficult to see what had sparked her interest in the death of this woman.

Once again Hannes came to Thóra's mind. He might be able to see something in this that she couldn't. She knew she would have to seek out his help sooner or later, although she would have preferred it to be later. It would have to wait until evening, though, as Hannes didn't take his mobile to work and she didn't feel like having him paged just to listen to him complain that she'd called him out of an operation.

One person she *could* call during office hours was the sex therapist Alda had been seeing. Of course she was unlikely to tell Thóra much, but it was worth a go. After calling and trying unsuccessfully to get the woman to tell her about Alda, Thóra gave up. All she got for her pains was a vehement denial that Alda had been a sex addict, as the Web sites had suggested, and the claim that she had been looking at them on the therapist's recommendation. The woman could not be enticed to reveal what purpose this might have served, and the phone call ended at that.

Next, Thóra decided to go to the police station in the hope of seeing which photos had been shown to the leaflet delivery boy who'd fingered Markús as the man at Alda's house on the night of her murders. Hopefully the police would also give her a log of the phone calls between Markús and Alda that same night.

"You've got to be joking," said Thóra, as she put down the photos. She prodded the one resting on top. "This appears to be a woman, and I can't be sure but it looks as though at least two of these people are over ninety, and one is barely out of adolescence."

Stefán picked up the stack, his face thunderous. As he flicked through it the flush on his cheeks darkened. "These photos were chosen at random, apart from the one of Markús, of course." He put pile the down again. "And this is a man, not a woman," he said, pointing at the photo of the person of indeterminate gender.

"I would like to request that these photos be made available in the High Court," said Thóra doggedly. "This is preposterous, and you know it."

Stefán's expression made it clear that he was seeing the photographs for the first time and was far from happy with the selection. "This is effectively an open-and-shut case," he snapped. "The boy's description alone is enough. These photos were simply dotting the 'i's and crossing the 't's."

Thóra said nothing, but she did not agree. She had read the boy's description, which was rather vague, and in addition had been made many days after he had distributed the flyers. She very much doubted he could remember minute details of a man whom he had passed on the street. "Do you have the phone log?" she asked.

"Part of it," said Stefán, but gave no indication that he was about to fetch the list for her. He straightened up and crossed his arms over his chest. "Markús is guilty," he said, when he thought he appeared sufficiently grave. "I can promise you that."

Thóra smiled at him. "I don't doubt your conviction, but I cannot agree with you." She stopped smiling. "Have you found out where the Botox came from? Markús doesn't walk around with it on him, that's for certain."

Stefán unfolded his arms. "We're working on it. As it is, we're going by the assumption that the drug was already in the house, since she was a registered nurse. But as I said, we're actually still investigating this specific detail."

"I could have told you what her career was and spared you the time that went into investigating that," Thóra said sarcastically, then added: "One of the doctors in the office where Alda worked told me that you haven't even gone to them for information about the drug. They say she didn't have access to it except within the confines of the office." She clicked her tongue. "I'm going to look into that later today. You're not going to help your reputation by focusing so intently on one man that you blind yourself to other possibilities."

"We're not 'blinding ourselves' to anyone or anything," said Stefán crossly. "There are only a few of us here and it takes time. Both of the doctors are coming down later to make statements." He smiled coldly at her. "So we'll be looking into that later today, too. Also, we still haven't managed to find a single soul who saw your client heading east at the time that he claimed to be traveling. We're not just looking for something that proves Markús guilty. Although I'm personally convinced of his guilt, I need to be certain. Conviction alone isn't enough, and it can sometimes let you down—although I don't think that's the case this time."

"Do you have the log or not?" asked Thóra tetchily. "I want to go over it before the hearing begins." She frowned. "Could it be that you're reluctant to give it to me because it shows that Markús spoke to Alda, just as he claimed?"

"It doesn't prove anything," said Stefán, thereby confirming Thóra's suspicion. "Of course you can have the log; it's being photocopied for you right now. I didn't expect you here so soon."

"So Markús did speak to Alda?" she asked, trying to keep the triumph out of her voice.

Stefán's expression was unreadable. "No," he said. "Not necessarily. A call was made from Alda's phone to his. It's not the same thing. Anyone could have answered his phone, and I suspect that he came up with this to create an alibi. We still don't know who helped him, but it'll become clear. In other words, I suspect Markús of having placed a call from Alda's home phone to his own mobile."

"Did you check where Markús's phone was located when the call was made?" asked Thóra, happily. This was all going much better than she had dared hope, despite Stefán's attempts to downplay this good news and turn it to his own advantage.

"Yes," Stefán said reluctantly. "The phone was just outside Hella." He cleared his throat. "But that doesn't mean anything, as I said. Any fool knows it's possible to trace the location of mobile phones. Markús would have done himself a great disservice if he had answered his own phone at Alda's house. That's why he got someone to answer it for him, that party need not have known it was for a criminal purpose."

"This is mind-boggling," she replied. "Markús's photo has been in the papers, and everyone knows he's suspected of murder. Do you honestly believe that if someone had taken it upon himself to answer Markus's phone without any knowledge of this magnificent plot, that this very same person wouldn't have contacted you?"

"I said the accomplice *might* not have been party to the plot. If he *was*, then he would hardly draw attention to himself like that," said Stefán immediately. "Maybe Markús paid him for it, and now he's too scared to report it for fear of being considered an accessory to the crime."

"If you're planning to use this in court, you'd better hope you can find this mystery accomplice. You know as well as I do that it's easy to come up with theories, but without evidence they're not worth anything." Stefán's certainty that Markús was guilty was getting on Thóra's nerves. It didn't bode well, since it meant other possibilities were no doubt being thrown out in the meantime. There was no time to quarrel over this, though. "How are you getting on with identifying the men in the basement?" she asked. "I assume you're in contact with the authorities in Britain?"

"We haven't been able to identify them yet," replied Stefán, without answering her second question. "However, we do have some specific clues that are promising. I actually can't say anything more about them at this point."

"How do these things work?" asked Thóra, but only out of curiosity—she was getting to know Stefán well enough to realize that he wouldn't give in if she badgered him about clues. "Does Interpol have a list of people who vanished without a trace?"

"We've contacted them, among others," replied Stefán, keeping his cards close to his chest.

"It was suggested to me that there were a lot of men from the Defense Force helping out in the rescue operation during the eruption," she persisted. "Could these men have been from the base?"

"No," he replied. "We've already checked, and it's out of the question. As I said, we're hoping this will be cleared up soon, but until then it's not up for discussion."

Thóra could understand his discretion; she wouldn't preach Stefán's own job to him any more than necessary. "Speaking of foreign countries," she said, "has anything been heard from the lab where the cardboard box the head came from was sent for testing?"

Judging by Stefán's face the results of the tests had been received, and were not to his liking. He admitted this reluctantly.

"And?" asked Thóra. "What came out?"

"A rather large quantity of old fingerprints were found on the box," said Stefán. "Most of them were from individuals unknown, since such a box can travel widely." He cleared his throat. "All the fingerprints were compared with Markús's and Alda's and it turned out they had both touched the box at one time."

Thóra grinned broadly. "Which provides strong support for Markús's testimony, as I'm sure you realize."

"The presence of Alda's fingerprints on the box doesn't necessarily mean she touched it while the head was in it. Maybe she simply lent Markús the box when he needed it for something."

"And maybe the moon is made of cheese after all," said Thóra, still cheerful about this latest news. "Well," she said, and pushed her chair back. "I hope I can get all this information more easily from now on. It's a bit of a pain to have to wait for the judge to order you to hand over whatever you've got." The district court judge had reprimanded the police for not having handed over all the case files to her, and Thóra enjoyed reminding him of it. "Is what I received yesterday absolutely everything?" she asked.

"Yes," replied Stefán, gruffly. "Everything that was available at that moment."

"You also still need to speak to Alda's co-workers at the A&E because I didn't see any statements taken from them. Of course you've had a lot to do," Thóra said, standing up. "I believe something came up there that might be connected to the case."

At that moment a secretary entered the office with some papers and handed them to Stefán. He sorted out the originals and handed Thóra the copies. "Here's the report. It's got the phone calls to and from Markús's mobile, as well as to Alda's home phone and mobile. I circled the phone calls that are within the time frame that we're focusing on, Sunday evening, the eighth of July."

Thóra sat back down and looked through the photocopied pages. "Here's the phone call from Alda to Markús," she said, then flipped to the page with information about his phone. "And here is the same phone call received on Markús's mobile," she said, unable to suppress her smile. "And here is another call made to him at around the same time," she continued cheerfully. "You hadn't mentioned that one to me." She looked up from the papers and stared at Stefán. "You know what this means, of course?" she said.

"We would if we knew who called," said Stefán, his expression far from happy. "As you can see, the number is unknown. It could be an unlisted number, or a call from a foreign mobile system that doesn't have an agreement for number sharing with Iceland. It might be possible to dig it up, but that takes time." He sat up straighter in his chair. "While we still don't know who phoned, we've got to assume that it was the accomplice I suggested before."

"What rubbish!" Thóra said, now very irritated. If it were possible to find the second person who phoned, and that person could confirm that Markús had answered, his alibi would be watertight. "Have you made any attempt to ask my client if he remembers who phoned him?"

"Yes, as a matter of fact I have," said Stefán. "It was the first thing I did when I saw this. I made a call to Litla-Hraun Prison and spoke to Markús. He says he doesn't remember who phoned him, which is highly suspicious."

"Could you call to mind exactly who phoned you over a week ago?" asked Thóra. "Of course not." She had had enough. "In fact, it would be more suspicious if Markús *had* been able to remember

who phoned him on the evening in question." She stood up. Before
she left the office she wondered for a moment whether to mention
the autopsy report on Markús's neighbor, but decided not to. In the
light of how everything seemed to be turning against Markús, it
made more sense to check this out in more detail before Stefán and
his colleagues got their hands on the report. She would meet Markús
later, then she could twist his arm in the faint hope that he knew
more about "Horseshoe Two" than his brother did.

Chapter 21

Friday, July 20, 2007

"Markús, sometimes this is just the way it goes," said Thóra encouragingly. "It doesn't necessarily mean that the judges consider you guilty; far from it. I got a strong feeling that they doubted the police's logic and that they were extremely interested when I ran through all the ways in which not only did things not add up, but they actually worked in your favor. I'm convinced that if they had been asked to rule on your guilt or innocence, you would not be here. That decision was not made purely because the police justified keeping you incarcerated during the investigation. It was also because the case is a serious one: it's not every day five people are found murdered. That four of them appear to be foreign citizens doesn't help much, either." Thóra was not exaggerating. She had had a good feeling about the case during the hearing and had been certain of coming out victorious, not least when one of the judges had hesitated over the photo of the feminine-looking man and asked whether it was usual to include both sexes in a photo lineup.

"Well, that makes me feel much better," said Markús dryly. He looked at Thóra, his anger evident. "I sit here, locked up, an innocent man, and find myself wondering if I shouldn't just get myself another lawyer. When I hired you I didn't expect to end up sitting in prison, suspected of murder. Much less serial murder."

Thóra did not look away, but answered him frankly. "If you want to find another lawyer it's no skin off my nose. I can even give you the names of several colleagues who have more experience in penal cases than I do. It's your life and your decision." She refrained from adding that she was convinced a change of lawyer would have had no effect on the High Court's ruling.

Markús nodded, rubbing his face distractedly. He had clearly expected to be released. "It's not really all that long to be locked up," he said, more subdued. "I don't doubt that you've worked your hardest. I'm just going out of my mind over this; I don't know what's what anymore. I don't want to change lawyers." He started rubbing his jaw. "What did my son say?" he asked anxiously.

"Naturally he was horrified, but he seems to be a smart kid so I wouldn't worry too much about him. He understands the circumstances, and I put a lot of emphasis on this incarceration being exclusively during the investigation, and told him it wasn't the same as a prison sentence," said Thóra. "Don't worry about him."

"Maybe you can phone him again for me?" he asked, and Thóra nodded. "Why didn't they accept that phone call as valid evidence?" he asked suddenly. "I thought it would be enough to show that I was far away from Alda's home at that precise time? You said it was obvious that the phone was somewhere on the road between Hella and Hvolsvöllur."

"The police insist you didn't have your phone with you," said Thóra. "They think you had an accomplice, who had your phone with him to provide you with an alibi."

Markús's face turned crimson. "How can they say that?"

"They're grasping at straws," said Thóra. "Shortly before Alda called you, an unknown person also did. He or she unfortunately has an unlisted number, so it will take more time to find them, if that even proves to be possible. Stefán said you don't remember who it was. Is that still the case?"

"Yes," said Markús. "But I don't know what that would change. Isn't it enough that Alda called me?"

"It would change everything," said Thóra. "If we could prove it was you that answered your phone, it would be clear that you were the one on the road to your summerhouse, rather than this imaginary accomplice."

"I understand," said Markús, now rubbing the skin around his eyes. "But no." He closed his eyes. "I just can't remember. Damn it—it was over a week ago."

"Try as hard as you can," said Thóra. "If nothing else, you could give me the names of people who might generally phone you and I could contact them as a last resort. It would take some ammunition away from the police department." She was quiet for a moment. "It would look better for you if we could pinpoint the person in question while you're locked up here. Then no one could claim that you influenced a witness."

"I'll try," said Markús. "For example, it's possible that my brother Leifur called, but he doesn't have an unlisted number as far as I know. I know that I spoke to him some time that day. He wanted me to drop by, since I was coming to the Islands."

"Of course it would be great if it was him," said Thóra. "It would be even better, however, if it was someone a little less connected to you." She couldn't make it any plainer. "Markús," she said softly, "you do understand, don't you, how serious this case is?" She didn't wait for a reply but instead continued: "I think it's extremely likely that the four men who were in the basement were connected to your father in one way or another. I'm not necessarily saying he killed them, just that he's involved in the case. Anything else would be too hard to swallow." She saw that Markús was about to protest, so she held up a hand to stall him. "Just imagine, the bodies are put in your house at the same time as your father is struggling to save his own family. There must have been better hiding places in the Islands, if your father wasn't involved. It crossed my mind that he might even have hidden the bodies for one of his friends. Alda's father, Dadi, or even Kjartan. Even though it's clear to me that Alda is involved in this somehow, it's not possible that she killed all these men."

"My father didn't do it," said Markús, but without the intensity of conviction that accompanied most of his statements. "I just don't believe it."

"Maybe not," said Thóra. "But he knew about it. He had to." She drew a deep breath and gestured around at the narrow prison visiting room they sat in. "You can't let your concern for your father be your shackles now. I suggest that I speak to your mother and arrange to meet your father. Maybe we'll get something out of him; you never know. The oldest memories often survive the longest in people with Alzheimer's. Even if you're released in a few days, this case will hang over you until it's been solved. If the perpetrator is found, at least some people won't always consider you guilty." She gave him a moment for this to sink in. "Think about it, and I'll phone you tonight."

Markús looked up and smiled. "Only sixty-eight more hours of this."

"Did you know that Alda was obsessed with sex?" Thóra changed the subject, not sure how best to phrase the question. "In fact, her computer was full of pornography."

Markús's eyes widened. "No, I didn't know that," he said. "She was always something of a prude. Could it have had something to do with her work?"

"Maybe," said Thóra, although she couldn't really see how this would have helped her work at either the clinic or the A&E. She took out the photos Dís had given her and showed them to him. "Do you recognize this tattoo at all?"

Markús peered at the picture. "No," he said. "Never seen this. Who'd have something this pitiful written on them?" he asked, giving her back the page.

"To tell you the truth, I don't know," she said, passing him the photo of the young man that had also been found in Alda's desk. "How about this man; do you know him?" Markús was visibly surprised when he saw the photo, but he said nothing, simply shook his head and returned the photo to her. "You've never seen him?" Thóra asked.

"No; at first he reminded me of a boy I used to know years ago, but I can see that it was taken recently," said Markús. "Who is he, then?"

"No idea," said Thóra. "I was hoping you'd know." She put away the pages. "When did you next meet Alda after the evacuation?" she asked. "I was told she'd attended Ísafjördur Junior College for a while, but no one knew of her there. Could that have been a misunderstanding?"

"No, not at all," replied Markús. "Alda went west and started school in Ísafjördur after the new year. She then changed schools when she moved to Reykjavík around a year later. That's when we renewed our acquaintance, because I was going to Reykjavík Junior College, where she transferred to." He stared into space, counting under his breath. "It was at the beginning of 1974. I was in my first year then."

"What year was Alda in?"

"She was in the same year as me. We were the same age, and she'd finished the first part of the college year out west."

"The way I heard it, Alda registered for junior college immediately after the eruption," said Thóra. "She started in the middle of the winter term, and so was moved up a year. I found this quite unusual—is that really what happened?"

"I heard the same story," replied Markús. "She was the brightest student in her class, so she'd easily have been able to jump ahead a year."

"But then wouldn't she have been a year ahead of you at Reykjavík Junior College?" asked Thóra.

"Yes, but maybe she hadn't passed her exams the spring after the eruption, or regretted not having been able to take the autumn term," said Markús impatiently. Clearly he thought this discussion a complete waste of time.

"Let's turn to something else," said Thóra. "I understand that the Friday evening before the volcano blew, there was a school dance at which the students in your class all planned to get drunk. Do you remember?"

Markús nodded his head sheepishly. "That's the first time I ever drank alcohol, though it might sound unbelievable," he said. "Most of my friends started experimenting around the time they were confirmed." He looked embarrassed but kept going. "Dad handled alcohol badly, if you catch my drift. So I planned never to drink, because I didn't want to be like him."

"That was an unusually wise decision for a boy of your age," said Thóra.

"It didn't last long," said Markús, and he smiled remorsefully. "Pretty much everyone was going to the party and I couldn't weasel my way out of it. It was the first time I ever got drunk, and I'll never forget that night."

"Do you remember whether Alda was picked up or whether she

made her own way home?" asked Thóra. "Did she perhaps go down to the harbor?"

Markús looked at her, surprised. "She certainly wasn't picked up," he said. "She wasn't that drunk; she was in better shape than the rest of us. On the other hand, I had to get picked up by Dad, which was awful. He wasn't very pleased, that's for sure. But whether Alda went down to the harbor that night, I have no idea. I doubt it. Why do you ask?"

"I've found out that on that same night something happened at the pier. It was completely covered in blood the next morning, which raises the question of whether these bodies had something to do with it. It crossed my mind that Alda might have somehow stumbled into whatever happened and even got hold of the head there."

Markús looked at her blankly. "And then what? Kept it until she asked me about the box on Monday evening? The eruption started on Monday night, so she would have had the head with her for forty-eight hours."

"Did the box smell at all?" asked Thóra, but Markús could only shake his head. "Do you remember whether Alda had been in a bad mood, or in any way different from usual, the weekend of the dance and the following Monday? I'm pretty sure something happened to her the night of the dance, and I imagine it might be somehow connected to the bodies and the head." She told him about the diary.

"I actually didn't see her that weekend," said Markús. "She was ill, so she stayed indoors. She didn't come to school on Monday either, so I was surprised when she called and asked me to meet her that evening and to come alone. It was all very mysterious, but of course I understand the reason now, having seen what was in the box she gave me. She was acting oddly that evening, I know that much. You'd have to ask someone else whether she was like that the whole weekend, because I didn't see her."

Thóra nodded. "And what about the night when Alda's hair was cut off in the school gym?" she said. "I'm sure it's completely unconnected to the case, but you never know."

"I was ill, so luckily I wasn't there," replied Markús heatedly. "I would have been furious. It was a terrible thing to do, and it didn't help that the teachers had no idea who did it. They couldn't even find the hair."

"So you knew who did it?" asked Thóra.

"No, unfortunately. Or fortunately, for him—I would have made him pay for it."

"Are you sure the person in question was male?" she said. "To me it seems very much like something a jealous girl would do."

Markús looked at her, startled. Clearly he hadn't thought of this. "Yes, I just assumed it was a boy. I suspected a boy named Stefán, who kind of had a crush on Alda, but he flat-out denied it and I was forced to believe him, he was so convincing."

Thóra remembered the entry in Alda's diary that had said she had kissed "Stebbi," which was short for Stefán. She assumed this was the same boy. "Could it have been anyone else?"

"No, probably not. Alda was friends with everyone and I don't know of anyone who resented her. I did everything in my power to find out who did it, though. When I discovered the gym had been unlocked the whole night, I stopped trying. It could have been anyone in the Islands, although there weren't many people who would do such a disgusting thing."

It was no use discussing this any further. The only thing she'd accomplished by bringing up the hair story was to annoy Markús. "What do you know about your neighbors from before the volcano went up, Valgerdur and Dadi, who lived next door to you?" she asked. "They were nicknamed Dadi Horseshoe and Horseshoe Two. Could they have been connected to these bodies in any way?"

Markús looked at her flatly. "Definitely," he said. "If the men died of boredom."

On the way into town from Litla-Hraun, Thóra called Reykjavík Junior College and to her surprise someone picked up. The man sighed when she informed him of her business, but promised to find the information she requested. Unfortunately it would take him a little while, he said, so he recommended that she phone back in fifteen minutes, which she duly did. "I've found it," he said breathlessly. "Alda Thorgeirsdóttir was registered in the school in the autumn of

1973 and graduated with honors from the language department in the spring of 1977."

"Did you say autumn 1973?" said Thóra. "Didn't she start her studies after the new year? It was my understanding that she started there with you in the middle of the winter term, having transferred from Ísafjördur Junior College, where she attended the previous term." Thóra decided not to confuse the man any further by adding that Alda was also supposed to have been studying at Ísafjördur Junior College in the spring term, 1973. In any case, the woman at the office there had denied that Alda had been a student there that winter.

"There's nothing here from Ísafjördur Junior College," said the man, and Thóra heard him rustling papers. "She was clearly registered with us that autumn, but was kept out of school that term due to health concerns. It doesn't say what her illness was as that kind of information is confidential, and kept elsewhere. But whatever it was, she was attending school here in good health in January 1974."

Thóra thanked the man and said good-bye. Alda had obviously never attended junior college in the west. That story was a fabrication. The best Thóra could come up with was that Alda had been admitted to a psychiatric ward and it had been a sensitive subject. All those years ago mental diseases were shameful and taboo. Thóra thought it fairly likely that any mental breakdown Alda had suffered had had something to do with the box she'd handed over to Markús. It couldn't have been healthy for an innocent teenager to handle a severed human head.

Chapter 22

Saturday, July 21, 2007

Thóra's mobile rang as she stood at the ship's railing on board the Herjólfur ferry. She had chosen to travel by sea to the Islands since the weather forecast was poor for the next day and she could only afford to be there for one night. She intended during that time to search for information about the Horseshoes, Valgerdur and Dadi, as well as to speak to Markús's mother, and hopefully also his father, which was the main purpose of the trip. Bella had lain down in their cabin; she had been recruited to come along to support Thóra.

It was Matthew, calling from Germany. The ship was sailing swiftly away from all the transmitters on the mainland, and the connection was bad. "Where are you, anyway?" he asked, sounding as if he were calling from inside a barrel.

"I'm out at sea, so the connection could cut out any time," said Thóra. "I'm on my way to the Westmann Islands for this case I'm working on."

"Hopefully it's not the bodies and the head in the basement?" asked Matthew, but apparently some crackling on the line meant he couldn't hear her reply, so he got straight to the point. "How would you like me to come for a visit next week?" he asked.

"That would be great," said Thóra, and she meant it. "Are you coming for work, or just dropping in?" She tried not to show that she was itching to know whether he'd made his decision.

"I'm going for an interview," he replied. "They want to show me around their offices and introduce me to the board. I'll have to make my final decision after this, although I've pretty much made up my mind already."

"And?" asked Thóra, "What are you going to do?"

"I . . . if . . . so . . ." The connection was cut off. Thóra thought about running to the stern of the ship to find a signal and hear what Matthew had decided, but she stopped herself. The ship would be out of phone contact again before she had a chance to select his number. She sighed and stuck her mobile back into her pocket.

"Could you confuse these two houses?" asked Thóra. She was standing with her hands on her hips on the excavation site of Pompeii of the North, looking at Markús's childhood home and the house where Valgerdur and Dadi had lived.

"No," yawned Bella. "They're completely different. That one's actually in ruins." She pointed at the neighbors' house. She wasn't exaggerating: the roof had collapsed beneath the weight of the ash and one of the outer walls resembled the Leaning Tower of Pisa.

"Try to imagine you're in the middle of a volcanic eruption and the house hasn't yet been destroyed," said Thóra. "Could you mix them up?"

Bella regarded her scornfully. "Can't you see that one of the houses has two floors and the other just one?" she retorted. "It's impossible to mix the two up." She pointed at the house on the other side of Markús's home. "No one could mix up that house and the house with the bodies either." Then she turned to scan all the excavated houses. "The house with the bodies is the only one on the street that has two floors."

Thóra looked up and down the street. Her secretary was right: the only house that stood out was Markús's. It was clear that the bodies hadn't been put there by mistake. "So at least we know that," said Thóra thoughtfully. "I really want to get in there," she said, and pointed at the house where the unpopular couple had lived, Dadi Horseshoe and Valgerdur Horseshoe Two. When she saw Bella's expression she felt she had to explain herself better. "The people who lived there are connected to the case, but I still don't know how."

"Huh," snorted Bella. "I'm not going in there. It's about to collapse." She walked closer to it and kicked at some tape that marked the area where visitors were prohibited from entering. "Haven't they already taken everything out of it, anyway?"

"Yes, they have," replied Thóra. "All the same, I want to have a look inside. You never know." She glanced around, though she knew they were the only ones in the area, and followed Bella's example, stepping over the tape and walking up to the house. She peeked in through a crack in the crossed wooden boards that had been nailed over the window, but saw nothing in the darkness inside. She walked up to the door, which was leaning against the doorframe. Bella followed her.

"Are you joking?" said the secretary when Thóra started trying to heave the door out of the way. "Are you going in? It must be off limits." She glanced back along the trench where the excavation had taken place, as though she expected a squad of policemen to come running down its black banks, which were covered with netting to prevent ash from being blown down into the new town.

"This house isn't marked like Markús's house," huffed Thóra, out of breath. "I wasn't supposed to go in there, but there's no police notice on this house saying entry is forbidden."

"What about the sign saying that nonessential personnel are prohibited from entering the houses?" asked Bella, clearly shocked. "I thought lawyers couldn't break the law."

"These aren't laws, they're requests," said Thóra, as the door budged a bit farther. "And the nature of laws is that breaking them is illegal. Not just for lawyers, but for everyone. That's why we *have* laws."

Bella snorted and gave up questioning Thóra. Finally she relented and decided to help her, and by combining their efforts they managed to form a gap just large enough for Thóra to push her way in. "Just shout if something falls down on you," called Bella through the gap, once Thóra was inside. "Then I'll go and fetch help."

Once inside, Thóra was seized by the same feeling that had oppressed her that fateful morning when Markús had discovered the bodies. The stink of the ash was overwhelming, growing stronger the further in she went. There was some light, since the boards over the windows weren't lined up exactly. Light also came in from above, where in several places she could see up to the rafters of the house and the collapsed roof letting in daylight. She moved from the foyer through a narrow doorway leading to the other rooms, and decided to head toward what she assumed was the sitting room. There it was much darker, since the roof was intact, but that mattered little since the room was empty apart from a Coke can and a plastic sandwich wrapper, both of which must have been recently left. On the walls were remains of wallpaper that had mostly peeled off, revealing a spotted and filthy layer of plaster beneath. Two wall lamps still hung in their places, but upside down.

The other rooms were much the same. Everything loose had been removed. Dadi had probably saved most of the contents, and the archaeologist Hjörtur had come and swept up the rest a little more than thirty years later. The house was small, and it was fairly clear from Thóra's inspection that Dadi and Valgerdur hadn't had much money. The bathroom, which was covered with broken tiles, was little more than a cupboard. The couple had lived alone in the house so they hadn't needed more room to live comfortably. When she came to the room next to the master bedroom, Thóra's eyes widened. This room had clearly been a child's, since the peeling wallpaper there was covered with pictures of teddy bears. The broken ceiling light was in the shape of a hot air balloon. The couple had been childless, so Thóra found this most peculiar. In one corner of the room was a pile of rubbish that had been swept together, and sticking out of it was a doll's plastic hand. When Thóra poked at the heap with her foot, the arm rolled out. She kicked lightly through the pile to see whether she could find anything else of interest, but without any results. The doll's arm was by itself and thus had probably not caught the attention of the archaeologist.

Thóra breathed easier after coming back outside. "I have a job for you, Bella," she said as they caught their breath after dragging the door back into place. "You need to find out whether the people who lived here had a child that died, or whether they might have bought the house from people with children."

"How am I supposed to do that?" panted Bella.

"You'll work it out. Maybe the people at the archive can help you."

"I'm sure it's closed," said Bella, and the relief in her voice was plain. "It's Saturday, remember," she added triumphantly.

"The library is probably open, and it's in the same building," Thóra replied, who didn't want to let Bella off so easily. "I'm sure you can get someone to open it for you, especially if you mention that the checking you want to do is for Leifur. Just try to be pushy without being rude." From the secretary's look of surprise, it was clear she had no qualms about being thought either pushy or rude; that it was, on the contrary, harder for her to be only one at a time. "You'll work it out," repeated Thóra optimistically, although she knew it was unlikely.

It looked like Matthew wasn't going to call back, and Thóra was tired of waiting. Twice she'd caught herself looking at the screen, to see if he'd called and to check if she had a signal. Maybe he had tried to phone unsuccessfully throughout the rest of the ferry trip earlier, and had decided to try again later. The easiest way to find out was of course to phone him, but Thóra feared that if she called him first she would seem too excited about hearing his decision, which could then be misread as eagerness for him to move to Iceland. It irritated her that she was thinking like this, because normally she got straight to the point. The problem was that she wasn't entirely sure how she felt. She wanted him to come, but she also didn't want any commitments. Her best friend had taken up with a foreigner and had quickly lost touch with her circle of friends, since the others didn't like speaking English when they got together. Of course that had been many years ago, and Thóra reminded herself that she had very little contact with her old girlfriends now anyway. Most of them had their hands full, just like Thóra, with little time left over to meet for cups of coffee, much less glasses of wine.

She picked up her mobile and called him. She would just have to look desperate. She hung up, irritated, when a female German voice told her that the phone was out of range or turned off. Perhaps Matthew himself was out at sea, or had switched off his mobile because of work. He wasn't the type who spent his work time chatting on the phone to friends and family, unlike Thóra, who took at least ten such calls per day, mostly from her children. As she was thinking this, the phone rang. She grinned.

"Hi, Mum," said Gylfi. "Did you find us an apartment for the festival?"

Thóra rolled her eyes. You couldn't accuse him of giving up easily. "No, sweetheart. I have other things to take care of at the moment."

"Oh." His disappointment was loud and clear. "Sigga and I were starting to really look forward to it."

"All is not lost yet, darling," said Thóra. "I haven't had any 'no's so far." Of course this was because she hadn't made any more inquiries since it had first come up.

"Keep trying," Gylfi said. "It'll be great fun. All the guys are going, you know."

"Are they going to camp?" asked Thóra, who couldn't imagine Gylfi's friends setting up tents without trouble.

"Naw," Gylfi replied. "They're renting people's garages. Maybe you can get us one of those? That'd be fun."

Sure, thought Thóra. To her mind, the word "fun" didn't apply to a weekend spent huddled among spare tires and junk. "No thanks," she said. "You have a small child who could hurt himself, and you'll be dragging around your poor old mother, who needs a shower and a coffeemaker, not a garden hose and a power drill."

She said good-bye after asking how little Orri was doing; his upper teeth didn't want to come out. He was turning out to resemble his father in this as in other things; Thóra had actually considered asking Hannes to cut the little boy's gums open when Gylfi had gone through the same thing. It was getting late, so the phone call to Sóley would have to wait until after she had spoken to Markús's mother. She was supposed to be there at four o'clock sharp, and although the streets in the Westmann Islands weren't numerous, she and Bella had managed to get hopelessly lost just looking for the excavation site, even though it was at the foot of the volcano.

After driving in circles for ten minutes, Thóra finally managed to find the street and the house. It had proven to be even more complicated than the search for the Pompeii of the North site, because this time Bella wasn't there to help her, having gone to the library to try and wheedle her way into the archive and dig around for information on Valgerdur and Dadi. Thóra was therefore slightly late when she parked the car in front of the old woman's house. She carefully smoothed out her trousers and fixed the barely visible crease in the front of them, then smoothed her blouse and headed for the front door. She wanted to make a good impression: people of Markús's parents' age wanted to see respectable individuals working as lawyers, and no doubt preferred them to be men. It was important that the old woman not be shocked by Thóra's appearance when they met for the first time. To that end, Thóra was wearing the best, smart-but-not-fancy outfit in her closet.

Thóra rang the bell and stood stiffly waiting for someone to come to the door. It was Leifur's wife María who opened it. A faint smell of alcohol drifted from her but she didn't appear tipsy at all as she stood there in the doorway, dressed elegantly in a Burberry shirt and skirt. Thóra knew this woman would immediately notice her inexpensive clothing.

"You're late," said María angrily.

"Oh," said Thóra, off guard. "I didn't realize." She looked at the clock on the wall and then her watch and noticed that the latter was off by six minutes. "I got lost."

"Got lost?" said the woman scathingly. "In the Westmann Islands?" She didn't wait for a reply but instead waved Thóra in. "Klara is waiting," she said, and walked into the house.

Thóra followed her sheepishly, and could only think that she hoped her bottom would look that good when she was fifty. Her only physical workout these days was caring for her grandchild, which had given her impressive biceps. She cheered up at the thought that she could at least beat this elegant woman at arm wrestling.

Leifur's wife stopped at a sliding double-door that opened into an old-fashioned but splendid front room. "In you go. She's got so much to tell you." She walked away, adding sarcastically: "As long as you know what to ask."

Chapter 23

Saturday, July 21, 2007

The chilly gaze of the old woman undeniably resembled that of her younger son, Markús, but in other respects they were unalike. She had graying hair, but her face was mostly free of wrinkles. Her skin was the only thing about Klara that seemed young, though; she was wearing a highly patterned, multicolored dress, plainly cut. Her eyes had the watery look of old age, but they did not hide her displeasure at having to sit here and speak to Thóra, who had already asked her several polite questions with little response. Klara was probably around eighty, and wore her age gracefully as she sat there, straight-backed, on the large dark sofa. Carved lions' paws adorned both the sofa's arms and feet. The sofa suited Klara. In fact, she fitted perfectly into the room, whose every surface was dotted with crystal vases. Markús's father, in contrast, didn't look at all at home in this austere, old-fashioned setting. Thóra felt sorry for him. He sat in one of the more modern chairs in the room, an upholstered reclining armchair, and was wearing a tracksuit over a turtleneck sweater, with a fleece blanket wrapped around his shoulders. On his feet he wore sheepskin moccasins. Leifur, who had come in behind Thóra, took a seat next to his father. She wasn't entirely sure why he was here. Perhaps he was meant to act as a kind of watchdog, to protect his mother and make sure Thóra didn't go too far with her questions. He hadn't said anything about coming along when Thóra had spoken to him the night before.

"So you don't remember any foreigners being around at that time?" Thóra asked the old woman, then added: "They were probably British, four of them." The old lady's strong perfume was making her feel a little light-headed.

"No, I don't," Klara replied. "I had enough to worry about at home, and I didn't go down to the harbor much, where any foreigners were most likely to be."

"I see," said Thóra. "And your husband didn't do business with any foreigners?"

"I never paid attention to his work, so I really don't know," the woman replied, looking a little affronted. "Magnús's work was entirely his business, I never got involved—that's how it was in those days." She glanced sideways at her husband, who was sitting looking silently out of the window.

Thóra decided to change the subject and ask about Valgerdur and Dadi. Maybe the old lady would relax if the conversation focused on someone else. "The name of your former neighbor, Valgerdur Bjólfsdóttir, has been mentioned in connection with Alda Thorgeirsdóttir. I'm not sure how they are connected, but I was hoping you might be able to tell me."

"I don't know anything about that," said Klara quickly, almost before Thóra finished speaking.

"Anything about *what*?" asked Thóra, certain Klara was hiding something—she hadn't even tried to remember anything. "About the connection between them?" Without waiting for a reply she smiled sympathetically at the woman, trying to convey that she knew it was a long story. "What little I've heard about Valgerdur and Dadi has all pointed the same way—everyone seems to be in agreement that they were a pretty tedious couple. It would be good to hear your opinion of them."

"How could that possibly be of use to Markús?" Leifur asked, surprised and obviously annoyed. "I was led to believe the purpose of this meeting was to gather information that might help him."

The old woman gave her son a sharp look. "I think I can answer for myself," she said bad-temperedly. She turned to Thóra. "Although I'm in agreement with Leifur in that I don't really understand how this is connected to Markús, it's hardly a secret that both Valgerdur and Dadi were particularly unpleasant people. She was a busybody who enjoyed other people's misfortunes," she said, scowling. "I suppose she was trying to console herself for her own rotten luck."

"What was so rotten about it?" Thóra asked. "I heard she was a nurse and he was a sailor. There are definitely worse jobs."

"It didn't have anything to do with work or money. They met when Valgerdur started at the hospital here as a student nurse. It must have been clear to her even before they'd exchanged rings that Dadi loved the bottle more than her, so it was a loveless and difficult marriage. At first they were no unhappier than the rest of the neighborhood, really, but then things started to go downhill. We could hear everything, because our bedroom window faced theirs. I actually pitied her at first."

"So what changed?" asked Thóra, who had started to feel sorry for poor Valgerdur herself.

"She betrayed my trust so badly that nothing could ever heal the wound," said Klara, pursing her lips.

"Could you go into a little more detail?" said Thóra. "I don't want to pry, but I have to understand what was going on in the neighborhood if I want to help Markús. I'm fairly certain that whoever put the bodies there was known locally."

Klara looked at Thóra without saying anything at first, then raised her eyebrows and let out a low moan. "I don't see how this piece of ancient history could possibly matter today." She cleared her throat. "But nor do I see why I shouldn't entrust you with the information." She sat up straighter. "After listening to Dadi shouting and Valgerdur sobbing for six months, I decided to speak to her and offer her a shoulder to cry on, because she seemed so lonely. All her relatives lived in Reykjavík and in those days people didn't carry around their telephones, ready to discuss things wherever and whenever it suited them. I spoke to her confidentially and told her that she wasn't the only one with a domineering and drunken husband, that it was only too common, and she could turn to me if she needed any help." Klara tapped her nose meaningfully. "She thanked me by repeating the names I had told her, of the other abusive husbands, to anyone who would listen—the men as well as their wives. It took me many months to win back the trust of those women."

"Could she have been so desperate to make friends that she sacrificed you on the altar of popularity?" asked Thóra, trying to imagine being the newcomer in a close-knit community.

"That may well be the case," said Klara crossly. "But it was still unforgivable. She couldn't expect simply to jump into the inner circle here, and after I had cleared up the mess she was as isolated as before. It was most unwise of her." Klara folded her hands demurely on her broad thighs.

Thóra decided there was little to be gained from continuing this line of questioning. "Do you know if the couple lost any children?" she asked instead, although she knew that Bella was at that moment working hard to dig up that information.

"No," replied Klara. "They had no children while they lived here. They tried for a long time, but with no luck. Valgerdur miscarried at least twice and that just made her more bitter. Of course back then there weren't all those psychiatrists people run crying to now, but there's no doubt that her sheer delight in our children's failures was due to her childlessness. She was always ready to spread stories about the kids in the neighborhood, and my boys were no exception because they were quite mischievous."

"There's a child's room in their house," said Thóra, hoping that no one would wonder how she knew this. "Could the people who lived there before Valgerdur and Dadi have had a child?" Again, Bella was hopefully finding out the answer to that very question as she spoke.

"They built that house, so no one lived there before them. The neighborhood was the newest part of town, so some of the houses weren't completely finished even after everyone moved in," said Klara. "I went to their house extremely rarely, only if I couldn't avoid it." She rolled her shoulders gingerly, as if they were sore.

"I never saw a children's room but they may well have set one up. Actually, I heard they had a son not long after the evacuation, so maybe she was pregnant but hadn't told anyone, in the light of her previous experiences. They might have been preparing for the birth of that child. But I can't imagine it, because I heard from a woman I know that rumor had it Valgerdur showed little motherly affection for her newborn at first. It sounds like there were some issues there."

"Did you keep in touch with them after they moved to the mainland?" asked Thóra.

"No," said Klara indignantly. "Why would I? I just told you, they weren't much to my liking. A lot of good people moved away from here and didn't return, and I had enough trouble keeping in touch with *them*."

"I understand," said Thóra politely. "Do you think Dadi and Valgerdur were connected in any way to the bodies found in your basement?"

"I wouldn't know anything about that," replied the woman, still bristling. "I've already told the police I have no idea how this could have happened, and I've said over and over that I had nothing to do with it."

Thóra noticed that the old woman said "I" and not "we." This was something she'd also noticed in the police report—the briefest one in the entire file, written up by Gudni Leifsson. In it Klara had been asked a few questions, and had answered as succinctly as possible. Thóra suspected that Stefán and his colleagues would not be quite so considerate if and when they came to interview her. "But did they have connections to any foreigners here in the Islands?" asked Thóra hopefully.

"Well, yes—Valgerdur worked at the hospital, of course, besides serving as school nurse two afternoons a week," replied Klara. "In school there were no foreign teachers or staff, but the hospital sometimes admitted wounded foreign fishermen, as well as other foreigners, I imagine. You couldn't really call that a connection, though, her taking care of their injuries. As for Dadi, he worked for one of the smaller fishing companies in the Islands. Only Icelanders worked there, to my knowledge. Beyond that it's probably better to direct the questions to their son; I'm sure he could tell you more than I can, since I have never had any interest in them."

"Has Dadi passed away?" asked Thóra. "I know Valgerdur died recently, but I have yet to check on him."

"As far as I know, he died of cirrhosis of the liver a couple of years ago," said Klara crisply. "But I think their son is alive."

"Do you know his name?"

"No, I don't remember. I heard it once but forgot it a long time ago."

Thóra nodded. Maybe Bella would find it in the archive. She had managed to loosen the woman's tongue, so now it was time to change gears again; in any case, she had run out of questions about the neighbors.

"There is something else," she said. "On Friday the nineteenth of January 1973, the weekend before the eruption, there was a school dance here in town that got out of hand. Markús was picked up by his father, since he'd had too much to drink with his friends and schoolmates." She gazed levelly at the woman. "Do you remember that evening?"

From Klara's reaction, you would have thought Thóra had asked for permission to rummage through the family's dirty laundry. "I vaguely remember that," she replied, though she clearly remembered the evening in question quite well. "It wasn't just Markús but the whole class, as I recall. Markús never drank, unlike the other teenagers, so it came as a shock to us."

"I have no interest in Markús's drinking, but I was wondering if you might remember anything else unusual from that evening," said Thóra. "Do you remember whether your husband went out after he brought Markús home, perhaps down to the harbor?"

Klara paled. "Magnús didn't go anywhere," she said. "He brought the boy home and that's all. Magnús wasn't in the habit of wandering off in the middle of the night, and he'd hardly have been in the mood to do so after seeing the state his son was in." She fiddled with the large gold rings on two fingers of her left hand, and looked away.

Thóra didn't believe a word of this. For the first time in the conversation, the woman wore a hunted expression, and she was clearly no actress. She appeared to be just as poor a liar as her son when under pressure. "How about you, Leifur?" Thóra asked. "Do you remember anything from that night?" She smiled brightly at Klara. "Maybe Magnús went out after you were asleep."

Leifur shook his head. "I was in Reykjavík that weekend. Classes had started again after the Christmas holidays. I was in my third year at Reykjavík Junior College and I was living in the city."

Thóra raised an eyebrow. "But you were here the night of the eruption," she said. "And that was in the middle of the week, wasn't it?"

Leifur smiled at her, but unlike his mother's his smile appeared
genuine. The old lady was looking more bored and irritated by the
second. "Markús getting drunk like that really hit the family hard,"
he said. "Mother was in pieces and Father was furious, so I decided
to come home and give Markús a piece of my mind. We were off
school that Monday anyway, so I didn't miss much. I had planned
to go back to town on Tuesday, although I hadn't expected it to be
in the middle of the night, as it turned out to be."

"Is that Sigrídur?" said the old man suddenly. He had stopped
staring out of the window and was now peering in bewilderment
at Thóra.

"No, Dad," replied Leifur gently. "This woman is named Thóra.
Sigrídur is dead." He took his father's hand. "Wow, your hands are
like ice. Should we cover you up a bit better?" Leifur didn't wait for
an answer, since the old man seemed to have tuned out again. Leifur looked at Thóra. "Sigrídur was his sister. He probably thought
you looked like her, although I don't see a resemblance."

Thóra smiled at father and son. "Hello, Magnús," she said loudly,
even though she'd promised herself she wouldn't speak down to the
old man. "My name is Thóra, and I'm a lawyer." The old man
frowned, not taking his eyes off her. "I'm helping your son. Bodies
were found in the basement of your old house on Sudurvegur Street,
and the police think Markús is involved." Leifur and his mother had
agreed that she could try to speak to him, though they both believed
nothing would come of it. Mind you, the look on the faces of both
mother and son indicated that they'd clearly not expected this topic
when they gave their reluctant permission.

"Sigrídur?" repeated the old man quizzically. "Basement?" he
added. Thóra's words were filtering through to him, though possibly not their meaning. The man fell silent and turned back to the
window.

"There's no point trying with him," said Klara, her voice gentler
than before. "He can still speak, but it's not really connected to
what's going on around him. Also, the conversations, the few he
takes part in, go in whatever direction he wants. It's impossible to

manage them." She looked from her husband back to Thóra, and her expression hardened. "I would rather you didn't badger him anymore."

Thóra agreed. She had hoped the man would be in better condition, even though everyone in the family had said that he was suffering from full dementia. "Klara," she said cheerfully, "do you think that your husband could somehow be involved in this case? Even the best of men can end up in situations that bring out the worst in them. No one really knows what happened, and there could even be a natural explanation for the deaths, one that's hard to work out after so many years."

The old woman leaned back as if to distance herself from Thóra as much as possible. The smell of her perfume subsided slightly. "It is my understanding that the men were beaten to death," she said. "My husband was a strong man and a very hard worker. However, he wasn't violent. He couldn't have killed anyone."

"Did he never get into any fights in his youth, do you remember?" asked Thóra.

"Fights?" exclaimed Klara. "He was—" She glanced over at her husband and corrected herself. "He *is* a man. Of course he got into fights in the old days, before the children entered the picture."

"Was he a bit of a handful when he'd had a drink, anything like that?" persisted Thóra, mindful of Markús's assertion that his father had been less than pleasant when drunk. She also knew that seamanship in the old days was usually accompanied by robust drinking. There were many so-called heroes of the sea in her mother's family, and she'd heard tales of their long voyages, where they had worked hard under enormous pressure, then let off steam on shore. Now times had changed, and drunken sailors were no longer in evidence on the streets of the city.

"Magnús wasn't a violent drunk, if that's what you mean," replied Klara sharply. "Nor was he an alcoholic, like some of his colleagues. I actually think that's the reason he did better than them and managed to start a company that is now one of the largest here in the Islands."

"Of course, part of that was because he was also so hardworking," Leifur added. "There are a lot of stories of his diligence when he was a young man—he had to fight hard for everything he got in life." He put a hand on his father's shoulder. "He wasn't born with a silver spoon in his mouth like so many people nowadays."

Thóra didn't wish to point out that Leifur was one of those people: his father's business had been handed to him on a plate. She also decided not to press them concerning Magnús's drinking, since it didn't seem relevant. "Could he have got into something in order to help someone out?" asked Thóra. "Like Thorgeir, Alda's father?"

"Sigrídur?" asked Magnús suddenly, before mother or son could answer her. "Do you know Geiri's girl, Alda?"

"Yes," said Thóra, fearing the old man would retreat back into his shell if she said no.

"How is she?" he asked, picking at a thread on the edge of his fleece blanket. "That was an awful business."

"What business?" asked Thóra calmly, trying not to break the thread of his concentration.

"I wonder if the falcon survived?" said the old man. "I hope so."

"I . . . I think it must have," said Thóra, desperate to say the right thing. "Did Alda kill the man?" she asked, when nothing else came to mind.

The old man looked at her and his mood seemed to darken. "You're always so difficult, Sigrídur. Who invited you here?"

"Klara did," replied Thóra, smiling as gently as possible. When the only response she got was a blank stare, she added: "Klara, your wife."

"That poor child," said Magnús, shaking his head slowly. "Poor child, to have to rely on such people."

"Do you mean Alda?" asked Thóra urgently, because the man appeared to be drifting away again. "Did Alda have a hard time as a child?"

"I just hope the falcon survived," said Magnús, and shut his eyes.

Further attempts to get him to speak were in vain. Thóra sat thoughtfully, unable to make head or tail of anything he'd said. Why was he talking about a falcon? Was it connected to some event in his own life, unconnected to the bodies in the basement or Alda's murder? And which child was he talking about?

Chapter 24

Saturday, July 21, 2007

Bella seemed rather pleased with herself as she sat in the hotel lobby slurping her drink, which could have been plain Coke but seemed more likely to have a shot of rum in it. The sweet odor of alcohol was unmistakable when Thóra sat down by her secretary. "Remember you can't charge alcoholic drinks to expenses," said Thóra. "It's hard to claim a drink as being necessary for work," she added when she saw Bella's expression. Strangely soothing Calypso music floated from the speakers behind them; perhaps it had inspired her secretary to order the drink. Thóra wouldn't have said no to a piña colada herself.

"Oh, do me a favor," said Bella. She took another sip, still smiling smugly. "I've seen Bragi's bills when he goes out of town on business."

Thóra had to admit her partner couldn't enter a hotel without going to the bar, whether he was staying there or not.

"Don't you want to know what I found in the archive?" asked her secretary, sucking at her straw thirstily. "They opened it for me. That Leifur clearly has the town in his pocket. All I had to do was say his name and they pulled out the keys."

"Yes, it's in everyone's interest to keep him happy," Thóra said. "So, what did you find? It's good that one of us is making progress, because meeting Markús's parents did me little good. His father was away with the fairies and his mother was such a dry old stick that she sucked all the moisture out of the air. The only thing I got out of it was some gibberish about a falcon and a child, and a headache from the old woman's perfume. There wasn't anything about a falcon in the files?"

"No," said Bella. "Nothing that I saw, anyway. There are a million files in that archive. You've got to know what you're looking for, and I wasn't thinking about birds."

Thóra sighed. "Oh, they were probably just the ramblings of a senile old man," she said. Suddenly she thought of María, Leifur's wife, who acted as a kind of care assistant for her father-in-law. She must have heard him say all sorts of things. Maybe at some point he'd said something significant, but she hadn't realized. Thóra decided to try to meet her again before they left, and see what she knew. It was entirely possible that he'd come out with something about a falcon or "that poor child," but phrased it in a way that made it easier to determine if it meant something for the case. Her headache was getting worse. She raised a hand to her forehead.

"Guess what?" said Bella, putting down her glass. "I found out that Dadi and his wife Valgerdur built their house, so no one lived there before them."

She seemed surprised when Thóra hardly reacted, but carried on: "And they had no children while they lived there." She watched Thóra, whose face still betrayed nothing. "But after the eruption they had a son, who they christened Adolf."

"Adolf?" muttered Thóra. "Who calls a child Adolf?"

Bella appeared relieved that Thóra was finally showing some interest in her findings. "Well, they did, for starters. He lives in Reykjavík, and when I tried looking him up online I pulled up a blog where there's a warning about him—for being a rapist. It was really hard to piece together—there were a lot of threats made against him in the comments section, by other bloggers who said that they were friends of the victim. In another entry several weeks later the blogger announced that he'd finally been charged."

Thóra began rubbing her forehead, trying to dispel her headache. "Rape?" she said. "Who did he attack?"

"It didn't say, but I figured out when it was supposed to have happened by looking at the date of the first entry. I searched in *Morgunblaðið*'s archives and came across an article that seemed to tie into this. It wasn't interesting enough to deserve much scrutiny, but something rang a bell when I read the article, because the rapist had slipped the girl an emergency contraceptive afterward to stop her getting pregnant."

"What?" exclaimed Thóra, dumbfounded. "Do you mean like a morning-after pill? I don't remember reading about that."

"The case didn't really get much attention, judging by the size of the article, and I doubt the papers would have reported it at all if it hadn't been for that weird detail. It must have been on the news as well, since I recognized it and I never read the papers."

Thóra waved to a passing waitress and ordered a piña colada. To hell with her headache, and to hell with the accountant. "Tell me," she said to Bella after the girl had taken her order, "what did the article say?"

"This Adolf supposedly raped the girl at his house after they met at a bar downtown," said Bella. "She was drunk but she put up a fight, which was clear from the bruises on her body when she went to the A&E a day later."

"A day later?" said Thóra, trying to fight the suspicion she immediately felt. "Why didn't she go there right away, or to the police?"

"The article said she'd been so devastated that she originally planned not to bring charges against the man at all. When she started to bleed heavily although it wasn't her time of the month, she went to the hospital, where the story all came out. The bleeding turned out to be caused by the contraceptive, and when hospital staff pressed her she told them the whole story. She said that she hadn't taken the pill herself, so the rapist must have stirred it into a drink he gave her."

"That wouldn't hold up in court," said Thóra. "How could you prove that she didn't take the pill herself when she regretted having slept with him?"

"Because the drug was found at the man's home when it was searched," said Bella. "In large quantities, according to the report. What's a bachelor doing with contraceptive pills?"

"I see," said Thóra. "I wonder if Alda was connected to this somehow?" she wondered aloud. "When did it happen?"

"The rape itself took place about seven months ago," Bella replied. "It was a Saturday night, but the girl didn't go to A&E until the Monday evening."

Alda was still working weekend and evening shifts at the hospital then, and may well have helped treat the victim. Had she perhaps recognized the name of the attacker because of her ties to the Islands? Thóra didn't see how this could help Markús. This was of course extremely unlikely, but it was hard to be choosy when there was nothing else on offer. "Did you happen to find out where Valgerdur and Dadi moved to after the eruption?" she asked Bella.

"They moved to the Westfjords," Bella said. "The woman in the archive pointed me toward a summary of the new residences of all the Westmann Islands evacuees from about a year after the eruption. She knew who they were, and she thought a relative of Valgerdur's had owned an empty house there that they'd moved into. I also saw in the file that Dadi worked on a trawler outfitted from Hólmavík, but his wife hung around the house, since she'd just had a baby."

Thóra smiled at Bella and decided to skip telling her that you didn't simply "hang around the house" when you had a baby. "Alda moved west with her parents, too," said Thóra. "Maybe they got to know Valgerdur better there. Ex-Islands residents probably stuck together during that period. That might explain why she was interested in the woman's death."

"There was nothing written about the A&E staff in the article, though. All it said was that the girl he raped checked in there."

"It should be possible to find out more. I'm wondering whether this could be related to the trouble Alda had at work; she shouldn't have assisted the victim if she knew the perpetrator."

"Are you sure she knew this Adolf?" asked Bella.

"No," replied Thóra. "I have no idea. Neither Leifur nor his mother remembered his name, so it seems likely that he didn't maintain any ties to the Islands." Thóra sighed pensively. "I don't know the legal ramifications of such a situation, either. Alda probably just took something from the A&E's drug cabinet or something, but maybe it's nothing her fellow nurses want to discuss. The chances are this Adolf has nothing to do with it. He was born after the eruption, so the bodies in the basement can't be connected to him, but I suspect all these things have a common thread."

"Or the two cases could be entirely unrelated," suggested Bella. "Stranger things have happened."

"I don't think so," said Thóra, even though she had little to support her hunch. "The worst of it is, I suspect Markús's family isn't telling me the whole truth. One would expect a mother to put her children's interests before her husband's, especially if the man in question is at death's door while Markús has half his life yet to live."

"I wouldn't know about that," said Bella, sucking on her straw. "I'm single and childless, so I have no idea which I would choose."

A waitress appeared with Thóra's drink. It wasn't the one who had taken her order; this one was much older and looked world-weary. She held a tray bearing a creamy drink in a tall glass, adorned with an umbrella and a dyed-green cocktail cherry. Thóra thanked her and gave her her room number, and as the waitress scribbled it down and turned to leave Thóra detained her. "Do you happen to know of anyone who's particularly knowledgeable about the eruption, and about Islands life at the time?" she asked. "Someone who might be willing to talk to us?"

The woman looked at Thóra. "Couldn't you just go to the theater and watch the film about the eruption? It's very popular." She gestured at the clock. "The next show starts in just under an hour."

"No, that won't be enough," said Thóra. "I'm looking for someone who can answer questions about specific residents." She smiled, hoping the woman wouldn't start asking for further explanations.

The waitress shrugged. "I guess there are plenty of people here who enjoy talking about the disaster. Most of them just want to talk about their own experiences, but I imagine you're looking for someone who can tell you more," she said. Thóra nodded. "I can think of one fellow in particular," she said. "His name is Paddi the Hook, and he knows all about it. The story goes that he's only ever left the Islands once, for the evacuation. He knows more than anyone about the people round here. Besides that, he likes nothing better than a good gossip; you'll have more trouble getting him to shut up. His answers might he hard to understand, but he's not shy about giving his opinion."

"And where can we find this man?" asked Thóra, eagerly.

"He has a tourist boat. Mainly deep-sea fishing. I'd advise you to book one of his trips, otherwise you might not get him to talk to you. He's always out on excursions and I don't think he'd want to miss out on work." She smiled at them. "Do you want me to call and book one for you?"

Thóra thanked the woman and accepted her offer. It didn't matter to her whether they booked a trip for sightseeing or fishing. She sipped her drink and allowed herself to enjoy the sweet coconutty taste for a moment. "Well," she said to Bella, "we'd better put on our wellies."

Leifur sat at his father's bedside in the room that the family had adapted on the ground floor after Klara had decided her husband should no longer sleep in the master bedroom. For some time Magnús had been waking his wife in the night to ask who she was, what time it was or even who *he* was. When his nocturnal behavior had begun to get more angry and violent, she'd had enough. There were two options: they could move him to a health-care facility, or make home-care arrangements so Klara didn't need to look after him twenty-four hours a day. Leifur gazed at the bookshelves, which were all that remained of the original furniture in the erstwhile study. The rest had gone down into the basement, and would be given away after his parents died. Or thrown away. He and María didn't have room for it, and his children had no interest in used furniture, even family heirlooms. It didn't seem to matter to them that it was of far better quality than modern, fashionable furniture, or that it was worth a lot of money. Leifur's son must have replaced his sofas more often in the eight years since leaving home than the old couple had done in all their married life. María was always whining about renovating the house and replacing all the furniture, or else selling it and building a new one. He had managed to avoid making that decision, but he knew he didn't have much time before he either had to give in or run the risk of losing her. Something in her demeanor had changed: she still asked for the same things, but with less conviction. It made him anxious because he knew resignation often preceded some kind of drastic measure. What if this was her first step in the direction of the freedom that she desired so much, and that her mind associated with Reykjavík: the freedom to shop and wander from one café to another, the freedom to let her girlfriends envy all her material possessions? If she divorced Leifur she would be able to buy whatever her heart desired. Prenuptial agreements hadn't been common when they got married, but even if they had been, Leifur would not have asked her to sign one.

He looked away from the old-fashioned set of shelves, which appeared to him to be starting to lean a little. They weren't the only thing in the room that mirrored the family's declining fortunes. Leifur gazed at his sleeping father, but everything that had once characterized the old man's face was now gone. His complexion was pale and his strong jaw hollow, making his lips and teeth seem unnaturally large. There were liver spots on his cheeks and lips. Saliva glistened at the corner of his mouth, and Leifur averted his eyes. This was the reason for everything they had done; his father must live at home as long as he was able. Leifur couldn't picture the old man living alongside people who had known him back when he was one of the pillars of local society, people who would now have to care for him as though he were a small child. He would have none of the child's irresistible charm that makes people happily change their nappies and wipe up their drool and vomit. His wife María had tried to convince him that if they moved to Reykjavík they could put his father in a home where no one knew him. Leifur had pointed out that they couldn't get him into a nursing home in Reykjavík, where the waiting lists were long. They'd be at the bottom of the list, no matter how much they were willing to pay. So it was better this way; they wouldn't gain anything by moving to Reykjavík. Of course, one thing *would* change: María would have more to occupy her time there, and less time for her father-in-law.

There was a lot of pressure on María. She was the one who spent the most time looking after her father-in-law, and although it might have seemed hard to believe, she did it without complaining or demanding any appreciation or credit from Klara and Leifur. She did deserve new furniture, and he would agree immediately next time María raised the subject. It would catch her completely unawares. Maybe he'd suggest they buy an apartment in one of the new apartment blocks on Skúlagata Street, so she could make quick trips to Reykjavík to visit their son and get a brief respite from everything here. In any case, it was time to hire some help; it would be best if he could find a nurse or care assistant, perhaps a foreign one. It wasn't as if anyone needed to spend time chatting to his father—Leifur's mother could take care of that. The nurse could sleep in his room, so they'd no longer need to lock the old man in there at night. Leifur had started worrying that something might happen while they were all asleep, although he wasn't sure exactly what. In his father's room there wasn't much he could easily injure himself on, but his outbursts had become completely unpredictable; just recently he had pushed the family television off its stand, breaking it. When Leifur asked him why he'd done it his father had simply stared at him and shaken his head, like a small child denying he'd made a mess. It had only been a few years since he'd brought home the television and invited Leifur and María round in order to show it off, since Leifur's parents didn't often spend money on luxury items. Leifur still remembered how proud his father had been, how beautiful he'd thought the colors looked on the huge screen.

His father muttered something and Leifur turned back to him. The old man opened his eyes and smiled faintly. His bottom lip was so dry that the smile made it crack, and drops of blood appeared. The blood welled up slowly and did not spill beyond the edges of his blue-tinged lips.

It was as though the blood in his veins was as exhausted as his brain. The smile disappeared as quickly as it had come, and Leifur thought it must be the pain of his cracked lip. But that wasn't the case. He looked straight into Leifur's eyes with rare lucidity, his stare unwavering. "That was a nasty trick we played on her," he said, gripping his son's upper arm tightly. Feeling his bony fingers, Leifur thought that if he closed his eyes it would have been easy to imagine a skeleton had taken hold of him.

"On who, Dad?" asked Leifur calmly. "Were you having a bad dream?"

"Alda," replied the old man. "You forgive me, don't you?"

"Me?" asked Leifur, surprised. "Of course I forgive you, Dad."

"Good," replied the old man. "I know how much you like her, Markús." He shut his eyes. "Don't be late for school, my boy," he said, letting go of Leifur. "Don't be late."

Leifur had long ago given up taking it personally when his father didn't recognize him, though he remembered how much it had hurt the first time it happened. His father had been telling his secretary that he was going to take a week off and that Leifur would fill in for him, but when he came to his son's name he had stood gaping at Leifur, just as surprised as his son at his inability to recall it.

"I won't be late," said Leifur, and went to stand up. His father was already asleep, and it would only upset him to sit with him any longer.

"Do you think the falcon will be all right?" said a weak voice as Leifur was trying to open the door without the hinges creaking.

"Yes, Dad," whispered Leifur. "The falcon will be fine. Don't worry." He shut the door behind him, confused. He'd never known his father to have much interest in birds, with the exception of puffin, which had been his favorite food. Now that they had to force-feed him everything he never got puffin, only whatever was easiest to get into his mouth and least likely to get caught in his throat. Leifur had never heard his father talk about falcons before. It could be random nonsense, jumbled memories, even fragments of some television program that were still floating around in his dusty mind. Whatever this bird meant to him, it was a shame his father seemed unable to forget the bad things in his life and remember only the positive. It certainly wasn't fair that he should have to remember Alda.

Not fair at all.

Chapter 25

Saturday, July 21, 2007

As the boat left the jetty, Thóra waved at two boys who were swimming around the harbor in wetsuits. One winked back but the other, who appeared to be several years older, acted as though he didn't see her and kept swimming after a little boat that had left the harbor at the same time as Thóra, Bella and their guide.

"Haven't they banned puffin hunting now?" Thóra asked the weather-beaten man at the tiller when she saw the pocket-nets lined up in the other boat. "I read somewhere that they were having trouble nesting, for the third year in a row," she added, wondering if she sounded like a resident of the Islands.

"Yes, yes," said the man, clearly unimpressed. "It's not a ban, just a recommendation. People can hunt puffins for their own consumption as long as they don't affect the stock."

"Is that what those men are doing?" she asked, pointing at the little boat about to overtake them.

Paddi the Hook waved at the three men, who lifted their hands in return. None of them smiled or showed any emotion. Thóra watched Paddi at the helm as he stared out to sea. When they met him she had been relieved to see he still had both hands, since she'd been wondering why he had the nickname "Hook." As they sailed past Heimaklettur Cliff they saw a young man sitting at the top, many meters above them. He was surrounded by dead puffins. At his side lay a pocket-net, and he had stuck a yellow flag into a grassy patch just behind him. Puffins were circling all around him. "What's the flag for?" asked Thóra, expecting it to be some sort of security measure.

"Puffins are curious by nature," replied Paddi the Hook, after looking up to see what Thóra was pointing at. "They want to see the flag, which makes it easier for the boy to catch them."

"Does he have a large family?" said Thóra, surprised at the number of birds lying like felled saplings around the young hunter.

"Lining up the dead birds like that calms the fear of the ones still flying around," replied Paddi, choosing to ignore Thóra's snide remark about the number of puffins. "They don't know what happened to their comrades so they think it's safe to come near."

Thóra decided to stop asking about puffin hunting. She knew the man saw her as a typical city mouse who knew nothing about hunting and didn't really have the right to comment. She knew how he felt; it really got on her nerves when foreign whaling activists protested against Icelanders hunting whales. She didn't want to offend the skipper, so she settled for silently watching the boy on the cliff edge as he swept the net in wide arcs over his head. She smiled to herself when the puffin he had his eye on narrowly avoided capture and continued its ungainly flight. She was on the puffin's side; there was something quite appealing about it, the clumsy little thing. The booklet Thóra had read while waiting for Bella to get changed said that the puffin mated for life. In the autumn each member of the nesting pair went its own way, but the male would return several weeks ahead of the female. Thóra was particularly impressed that the male used the time to clean the cave and make it presentable for his spouse. When their palace was fit for a queen, he would sit at the entrance and wait for his mate. She was equally struck by the fact that if the female did not come back the male took a new mate, who he kicked out immediately if the first one returned. "Are we going far?" she asked as they entered open water.

"If you want to catch anything we've got to go a bit farther out," said Paddi, scanning the horizon as if he expected leaping schools of fish to appear any second.

"It doesn't bother me if we don't catch anything," chirped Bella. "I don't eat fish. I think it's disgusting." Thóra turned to her and scowled meaningfully—they had to keep Paddi sweet, and that wasn't the way to do it. Bella gave her a sharp look in return, but added: "I think puffin is absolutely delicious, though." Thóra breathed easier.

Paddi the Hook muttered something unintelligible and continued to scrutinize the calm water. They couldn't have asked for better weather. The rays of the sun bounced off the shallow waves,
creating a glittering sea of light.

Paddi stopped the boat just beyond Bjarnarey Island. On the
tall, sheer cliff walls rising from the sea they could see the ropes
that were used to clamber up to the grassy area at the top of the
island, where there was a handsome hunting shed. Thóra didn't know
what would induce her to climb up there. If she ever did go up, she
would have to live there forever—she would never make it back
down. "Let's try here," said the old sailor, wiping his hands on his
tattered jeans. "We should be able to catch something." A gaggle of
seagulls that had been hovering above the boat drifted down and
settled on the sea, where they rocked in the waves. They were obviously hoping for a free lunch.

"Well then, now the great hunt begins," said Paddi, and he showed
them to the lower deck where several large, powerful rods were set up
next to an open barrel. Paddi handed each of them their own leather
belt with a holster for the rod, and helped them to fasten them. Luckily the belt just reached around Bella, who took all Paddi's comments
about it calmly, without blushing. He showed them how to position
themselves before strapping on his own belt and taking his place next
to them. "You've got to make sure you let the line go all the way to the
bottom," he said, taking a pinch of snuff. "That's where the fish are,"
he said, and watched them critically. Thóra's sunglasses had slipped
down her nose, but she didn't dare let go of the rod for fear that it
would fall into the sea.

Thóra silently prayed no fish would bite her hook, and tried to
avoid letting her line sink all the way to the bottom as Paddi had
recommended. This was difficult, as she had no idea where the line
was located. For all she knew she could be scraping the bottom in
the middle of a hungry school of fish. She looked back at Heimaey,
where the new lava could be seen clearly. "That was quite a disaster," she said, directing her statement at Paddi.

"You mean the eruption?" he asked. His rod jerked slightly and
he started to reel the line in.

"Yes," said Thóra, sweeping her rod clumsily over her shoulder and back out over the gunwale as Paddi had shown them. "Did you live here back then?"

"Yes, I've lived here all my life," he answered, still reeling his line in. "It's been great."

Thóra didn't understand what he meant by this. "What did you take with you from home, in the evacuation?" she asked curiously. What would a man like this choose to save? A fishing rod, or his favorite bottle of whiskey?

"I took my wife," replied Paddi, tautening his line. "And it was a good thing I did, because my house was one of the first to disappear beneath the lava. I would have had a tough time finding a new wife." He leaned into his line and turned the reel with enormous effort. Up came two haddock. Paddi removed the hooks and threw the wriggling fish into the barrel. Thóra and Bella gawped at it as a knocking sound came from inside. They had both expected the man to knock the fish out, not let them die slowly. Paddi wiped his hands on a stained towel tied to the ladder rail and turned back to the women, who were still staring dumbly at the barrel. "You need to grip tighter," he said, and came over to them, whereupon they immediately made a feeble effort to perform correctly. "You don't want me to do it all for you."

Bella let out a shout as her line suddenly tautened. "I've got one!" she yelled, as if she wanted the occupants of the hunting shed to hear them, hundreds of feet above. "What do I do?" The old man went over to her. He was so bow-legged that the fish barrel would have fitted easily between his knees. He helped Bella reel in her catch: a redfish, so small it would barely make a canapé. The seagulls cried out, excited now that something was happening.

"Can't we throw it back?" implored Thóra. "It's so tiny, poor thing." She pitied the poor fish, which dangled from the hook. "Is the wound too deep for it to live?"

"No, no," said Paddi calmly, putting on rubber gloves. Thóra recalled that redfish could be poisonous if they came into contact with an open wound. She had no idea where this poison was to be found on the fish, but judging by how carefully Paddi freed it from the hook, it must have been on its skin. He lifted the gaping fish. "Should I let it go? It's your call."

Thóra and Bella nodded in unison and watched happily as Paddi threw the fish overboard, but instead of darting away it just floated on its side. It seemed to be trying to swim with the fin that was poking up. "Why won't it swim off?" asked Thóra, trying to remain calm. "Is it more injured than you thought?" She was furious at the man.

"Oh," said Paddi, unconcerned. "It's a deep-sea fish, and it fills with air when it comes up from the bottom. It can't sink. I forgot about that. It would have been better off in the barrel."

"How could you not remember that?" cried Thóra.

"I'm not in the habit of releasing my catch, dear lady," said Paddi grumpily. Thóra wasn't sure whether he was irritated with her or with himself.

The seagulls surrounded the wretched fish, which still lay half submerged on its side, trying to swim with the fin that was above the water. They drew nearer. Thóra couldn't help watching, though she had no desire to witness what happened next. She felt uncomfortable, and was beginning to regret having had a drink in the bar. Suddenly the movement of the boat and the smell of the catch in the barrel were making her nauseous. She closed her eyes and breathed through her mouth, which helped a little. Her queasiness erupted again when she opened her eyes and saw that the fish was still locked in a drawn-out but hopeless fight to the death. One of the seagulls stretched out its neck and pecked at the fish's side. The three of them stood side by side on the boat, watching silently.

Thóra wished that either she'd kept her mouth shut when the fish was reeled in or she had a net to fish it out again. Suddenly all the seagulls flocked around the redfish in a feeding frenzy. The fish could be seen twitching a few times before it finally died, much to Thóra's relief. When the seagulls flew up again, full and contented, there was almost nothing left of it. Paddi turned to look at Thóra and Bella, noting their identical expressions of horror. "Are you sure you like deep-sea fishing?" he asked. "We could easily change this into a sightseeing trip if you'd rather."

"Maybe that would be best," replied Thóra, and Bella nodded. "We're not going to make good fishermen." She smiled at him. "Why don't you take us on a short tour? The reason I booked a trip was actually to ask you about a couple of things—we were told that you're the man who knows the most about people in the Islands."

"I see," said Paddi, taken aback. "Why didn't you just say so?"

"I didn't want to deprive you of a tour and I thought we could combine the two, fishing and conversation."

They made their way to the upper deck, which had the best view of the magnificent scenery, and Paddi set sail again. "I expect you've heard about the bodies in the basement," said Thóra. "I'm working for Markús Magnússon, who has unfortunately been linked to the case."

"I have heard," said Paddi, looking straight ahead. "This isn't a big town and when something like this hits the headlines everyone follows the story, me included."

"So you may also know that Alda Thorgeirsdóttir seems to have been murdered, and that Markús is a suspect?"

The old man snorted loudly. "The police in Reykjavík know nothing if they think Markús harmed a hair on Alda's head," he exclaimed. "That boy used to think the sun shone out of her in the old days, and although teenage crushes aren't the kind of thing I'd usually notice, everyone knew about it. With the possible exception of Alda. Even Gudni says the arrest is ridiculous, and he's made a few blunders in his career."

Although Thóra was pleased to hear Paddi's opinion of the case, she wasn't looking for witnesses to Markús's character. "Have you any thoughts on who the men in the basement might have been?" she said. "It's fairly clear that they were foreigners."

"Yes, Brits, I believe," said Paddi. Obviously he hadn't been exaggerating when he said news spread quickly in the Islands. "There were no Brits here the night of the eruption, if that's your question."

"What about shortly before that?" asked Thóra. "Anyone who could have disappeared, but who people thought had simply gone away? When someone disappears, people don't automatically assume they've been killed. Especially not a group of men."

"There were several foreigners in the Islands about a week before the volcano blew," he said. "But they were gone before it went up. Long gone."

"Are you sure?" asked Thóra. "Is it possible they didn't go far, maybe just down into the basement on Sudurvegur Street?"

"No, no," said Paddi, steering toward a gannet that had taken off from the water as they approached. "I watched them sail away. They were a bunch of numbskulls. They sailed out of the harbor in pretty bad weather. Their old tub was a bit beaten up, and I thought they should have repaired it before continuing their journey. So I kept an eye on them. But they definitely made it out."

"I've spoken to a lot of people, and not a single one has mentioned this to me," said Thóra, surprised. "Is it because you have a better memory, or is there something else going on?"

Paddi turned to smile at her. "Naturally, some people have a better memory than others," he said. "In this case there's nothing going on, there's a simple explanation: the smack didn't stop here for long. It came in the evening and sailed away early the next morning, without many people noticing it."

"But you saw it leave?" said Thóra.

"Yes, I always had one foot down at the harbor, still have. Not much has changed. My wife used to suggest that we hire a bulldozer and push the house down there to spare me the to-ing and fro-ing." He looked up at the sky. "May God rest her soul." He resumed his story—much to Thóra's relief, since she never knew what to say at moments like these. "So I was messing around down there, securing my boat because the forecast was bad, as I recall, when this smack came sailing into the harbor. The men were yapping something at me in a foreign language, and even though I didn't understand the words I realized they were asking for mooring. I pointed them to an empty space and that was that."

"Do you know what nationality they were, or how many of them were on board?" asked Thóra.

Paddi the Hook shook his head. "Bloody limeys, I think," he said. "I counted two, but there could have been more as it was quite a big boat."

"And when was it they left, given that it seems no one but you saw them? In the middle of the night?"

"No, love," said Paddi. "They waited out the worst of the weather, since their boat wasn't exactly in the best condition. If I could have spoken to them man to man, in Icelandic, I would have pointed out that they could have repaired most of the damage here, with us. But it didn't get to that stage, because I was up early the next morning and watched through the kitchen window as they sailed away. Although it was dark outside it was clearly them, because the harbor was lit. I recognized their smack as it traveled out to sea. They definitely left."

"Do you by any chance recall the name of the boat?" asked Thóra.

"No, I don't," he replied, avoiding her glance. "I'm not so good at reading, I don't mind admitting. It actually hasn't been too much of a problem—I'm more one for working with my hands, and it's often easier when book-learning's not getting in your way."

She smiled at him. "But you *have* got a good memory. How can you remember this, for example? Hundreds of boats must have been through this harbor; what was so special about this smack?"

"There was nothing that special about it—it was a fairly good-looking boat and all that, but it's true that other, better boats have stopped here." He looked back out over the rudder. "I remember it so clearly because of what happened the next morning, when Tolli discovered blood on the pier where it had been moored."

Thóra's expression revealed nothing, although she was very excited. "I'm guessing you mean the weekend before the eruption?" she asked. "I've heard about this but I understood that no boat had been anchored there for a long time before the blood was found." She decided not to tell him where she'd heard this, since she preferred not to advertise the fact that she and Bella had been snooping through Gudni's files.

"That's because no one knew the smack had been there but me," Paddi replied. "When I left the harbor it was there, but for some reason the men moved it from that pontoon over to one located a bit farther to the east. I watched them sail away, but I've never understood why they moved the boat. Maybe the weather seemed worse in the place I pointed them to."

"Did you tell anyone about the boat?" said Thóra. She was surprised this hadn't come up in Gudni's report, although there was a chance she and Bella had overlooked it in their haste.

"No, actually I didn't," said Paddi. "No doubt I would have

done eventually, but then the volcano went up and I had other things to think about. No one asked me, and then I had the feeling that this information might be used against someone. So I decided to wait and see, and Mother Nature decided for me. I have to admit that since the bodies were found in Maggi's—Markús's father's—house I've often wondered about that blood on the pier, and I expect I'm not the only one."

"Do you mean the harbormaster who discovered the blood?"

"No, he's long dead, the old man," replied Paddi. "I was thinking about Inspector Leifsson, for starters, not to mention all the locals who came down to see it for themselves. You don't see that quantity of blood on the pier just from a large catch of fish."

Thóra thought for a moment. "I'm sure you know who Dadi was," she said. "He was seen there that morning. Do you think he could have had something to do with the blood?"

"That boring old bastard?" said Paddi bluntly. "He may have, though I doubt it. Dadi was a lazy coward who wouldn't say boo to a goose. He was a real drip, not like a proper Islander. His father wasn't born here, you know."

"So do you think he was telling the truth when he denied knowing anything about the blood?"

"I didn't say that. He could have known more than he let on. Actually, he wasn't the only one seen there—just the only one the police knew about."

"Really?" exclaimed Thóra. "There were others there? Why was this kept secret?"

"I should make something clear before we go any further, so there's no misunderstanding," said Paddi. "Maggi was a decent fellow. He was a hard worker from the old school, who wasn't afraid of anything and worked like a dog for his family. He deserves everything that he has, and I don't know of anyone who thinks he got it through any funny business. Leifur is a good man too; Markús I only knew as a child, a cheeky little monkey, good fun."

"But?" said Thóra. "Praise like that is usually followed by a 'but.'"

Paddi smiled at her. "But," he said, no humor in his voice, "when Maggi got ill and started losing his grip . . . Look, everyone knows about his condition although Leifur tries to keep it secret. He took over the company from his dad, and people are getting worried about how it's going. María doesn't bother to hide the fact that she'd rather live anywhere else but here. If they move, the company will be sold and the only ones who'd have the means to buy it would be big-city fat cats. And they would move the fishing rights somewhere where it would be more profitable to fit out the ships and process the catch. You might say Leifur has the whole community by the short and curlies, so everyone tiptoes around for fear of offending him. There are others to whom some of us owe our livelihood, but he's the one who looks like he's leaving."

"I see," said Thóra. She knew that the Islanders' fears were not ungrounded—in such a small community, every employer mattered. "And you think Leifur uses this to keep people quiet?" She was starting to convince herself that Magnús had been one of those seen down at the harbor that fateful night.

"No," said Paddi. "I'm pretty sure he doesn't. In some ways Leifur is a simple fellow, like me, and doesn't care much about what others are thinking. He just does his own thing and is probably pretty happy with how everything's going, and no one argues with him when he suggests something. I predict that if things go on this way, he'll get a big head." Paddi steered the ship closer to Heimaey and pointed out the land formed of new lava, which was impressive when you thought how short a time had passed since it had poured out. "The problem is that different people have different views on what's best for Leifur and Markús, and on what can and can't be said as far as this case goes. Almost all the Islanders will only say what they think will be best for the brothers. Whether that's the right thing to do, that's another question. Some people may actually be keeping quiet about the good things and discussing stuff that could make the brothers look bad, without realizing it."

"And what about you?" Thóra asked. "Don't you fit into that group? You love this place, so you must want to do whatever's best for it?"

Paddi clicked his tongue. "That's not the way I'm made—I don't try to avoid the inevitable. All that does is make things worse. Maggi's company will be sold. Maybe not today or tomorrow, perhaps not until Leifur wants to retire. However, on the evening of the day his children take over, the company will be sold. That much is certain. They've found their calling elsewhere and there's no point ignoring the fact."

"But why didn't anyone mention the blood, since so many people have put two and two together? I don't understand how people could decide that the story makes Markús look bad, or Leifur for that matter?" Thóra wanted to hear what Paddi had to say about Magnús, though she suspected he wanted to leave the story untold and make her read between the lines.

"Let's make one thing clear. People couldn't care less about Markús. In this case he and Leifur are in the same boat and he's the one who's copped it. But if Markús is locked up, Leifur will go to visit him, which might mean Leifur spending more time on the mainland. One thing will lead to another, and in the end Leifur will move away." Paddi glanced at Thóra. "You know what I mean?" She nodded. "Neither Markús nor Leifur was seen there; just their father." Paddi raised a hand to shield his eyes from the sun. "And there's not much left to say, since ever-increasing numbers of those who can remember these events have lost their voices. None of us are spring chickens anymore."

"But even if Magnús *was* seen there, it doesn't mean he had anything to do with the blood," said Thóra, a little lost.

Paddi snorted. "That may be, but it's what people thought at the time, and that hasn't changed." He shrugged. "The one who started the rumor was the same one who told the police about Dadi. He was a grumpy old man," he grinned, displaying his decayed teeth. "Kind of like I am today. He was there for some reason in the middle of the night and stumbled across those two—Dadi and Magnús—in a heated argument, both looking wrung out. When they saw him they were startled, and went off in separate directions. The old guy was surprised they didn't even say hello, but it wasn't until later in the morning that he made the connection. He hadn't noticed the blood, so the first he heard about it was when everyone started gathering down at the harbor to see what the police were looking at."

"How could this old man tell the police he'd seen Dadi without mentioning Magnús?" asked Thóra.

"That's simple," said Paddi, steering the boat in a wide arc.

"Everyone likes Magnús, and this old man was no exception. No one liked Dadi, so the man probably had no qualms about implicating him. It meant he could make things difficult for Dadi, who wasn't a full Islander, and win himself a bit of the Islanders' attention at the same time."

"In other words, he told the police one thing and the rest of the town another?" asked Thóra. "It's not a big town. The real story must have made its way to the ears of the authorities."

Paddi looked at Thóra as if she were a retarded child. "Under normal circumstances it would have," he said, straightening the rudder. "But the volcano erupted a few days later and the Islanders were scattered all over the place. The ones that stayed behind had more pressing business than a puddle of blood on the harbor. And then another man started saying he'd seen Dadi sail into the harbor in a dinghy that night, but most people agreed he made the story up for attention, wanting to play a part in the police investigation." He looked at Thóra. "But do you know what I've never understood?" he asked, rhetorically. "Why that shithead Dadi didn't mention Magnús when the police spoke to him. If the blood had nothing to do with him he could have simply said the two of them were there together, and explained what they were doing. And if Dadi *was* involved somehow, it still makes no sense. If they had been in on it together, surely Dadi would have told the police about Magnús? Then Magnús would either have confirmed Dadi's alibi or gone down with him. And since Dadi was such a mean old bastard, he wouldn't have thought that was so bad." Paddi held Thóra's gaze. "Either way, the question is: why didn't Dadi tell the police he'd been down at the harbor with Magnús?"

Chapter 26

Saturday, July 21, 2007

Tinna's English wasn't good enough to speak to the nurse. Maybe she would have trusted herself to say a few words if the drugs hadn't made her too tired to speak Icelandic, let alone a foreign language. She watched as the woman in white took away the bag that had emptied into her through a needle in the back of her left hand. Tinna couldn't see the needle, which was covered with a dressing. The nurse that inserted it had been Icelandic and had talked constantly throughout the process, afraid that Tinna might find it uncomfortable and start crying or screaming. She had tried to tell the woman that she couldn't care less, that needles didn't hurt, they just felt strange. The nurse hadn't believed her, and when she stuck the needle in for the third time in search of a vein she had raised her voice and talked even faster. Tinna had trouble following what she was saying and understood only every other word, even though the relentless chatter was all in Icelandic. It went in through her ears and didn't seem to go up into her brain, but to somewhere entirely different. Maybe down into her stomach? Hopefully there weren't any calories in words. Tinna's heart skipped a beat. Didn't they say words were food for the mind? Could they change into food for the stomach?

"Okay, now," said the foreign nurse, patting the blanket she had spread carefully over Tinna. "Try to get some sleep."

Tinna stared at her, not replying. She couldn't tell whether the woman had said "sleep" or "sheep." She spoke enough English to know what both words meant, she just wasn't sure. Maybe the woman wanted her to count sheep, like cartoon characters did.

Tinna closed her eyes and tried it. In her mind's eye, one, two, three sheep hopped over a green-painted fence. The door to the room opened and closed with a faint thud. The woman had probably gone, but Tinna didn't want to ruin the sheep-race by opening her eyes and looking. She focused again on the fence and the sheep. It wasn't going well. The sheep were disgustingly fat, and the fourth one couldn't jump at all. It stood by the fence, breathless and panting. Then it started to expand, and soon its snout disappeared into its white belly, which stretched wider until finally there was a loud bang as it burst. Blood and guts flew everywhere. Tinna opened her eyes quickly to rid herself of this vision. She was alone in the room. Her breasts heaved up and down. This was what awaited her if she didn't get out of here. She would get fatter and fatter until she blew up. Tinna turned and looked at the clear bag hanging from a steel frame next to the bed. She watched the drops fall into the regulator, which controlled how much liquid ran into her veins.

She gasped when the first clear thought she'd had all day jumped into her head. The drops were full of calories. Maybe even pure calories, but Tinna had no idea what those looked like. They might be like water, and splash around in her body after they'd gone in. Tinna's hand throbbed beneath the needle, and she felt as if she were burning up. She tried to think more clearly. Heat, calories. The needle was hot because calories were streaming through it now. Hot, evil calories. She felt a tear forming in the corner of her eye. Was it good to cry? Could she empty the evil liquid from her body? Her head started aching from all these thoughts and she pressed her right hand against the spot on her forehead where it hurt. The pain eased a little, but returned as soon as she removed her hand. Should she ring the bell for assistance?

She moved her right hand nearer the bell, which—of course—lay closer to her left hand, the one she didn't dare move for fear that then the calories would start pouring in faster. Also, the stinging she now felt in her hand worsened with movement. Her thumb rested on the chilly button. Tinna was just about to press it when she hesitated. What was she supposed to say to the foreign nurse? She could barely mumble "good day" in English, so she couldn't possibly explain that if the liquid wasn't taken out of her, and immediately, then she would swell up and burst and her guts would be splashed all over the room. Tinna took her thumb off the button. This would get her nowhere. She sat up straighter and tried to focus. The nurse couldn't help her. No one could help her. What should she do?

She looked down at the plaster covering the needle. One of its corners had come slightly loose, probably because she was sweating from the hot needle and all the calories flowing into her. She tugged carefully at the loose corner and listened in fascination as the plaster pulled away from her skin. She pulled it off slowly and watched the skin lifting away from her bones. She looked contentedly at the reddened square where the plaster had been. There was a piece of pink plastic shaped like a butterfly in the center of the square; into one end of it went the tube, and out of the other came the needle that was burrowing under Tinna's skin. She tore off the clear tape that held the butterfly to her skin and grimaced. How could she get the needle out without the liquid going everywhere? She thought and thought but couldn't come up with a solution, so she just pulled the needle out slowly. There was a faint pop and a sucking sound as the needle came free from her skin, and for an instant she could see a tiny black hole in her hand, before droplets of blood welled up and leaked down her wrist. She pushed the needle and the butterfly away, but instead of whipping around the room like a hose, as she had imagined they would, they dropped straight down onto the bed from the weight of the tube. Tinna felt strangely disappointed.

She swept her feet out from under the covers and sat on the edge of the bed for a second to let the familiar dizziness pass. Her stomach rumbled, and she could feel how terribly hungry she was. That was nothing new, but because her head was fuzzy from the drugs, she wanted to eat. Usually she found it easy to handle hunger, and actually enjoyed not satisfying it. That way she was in control, not her greed. The greed that made people fatter and fatter until they burst, like the sheep. She couldn't remember whether a sheep had actually burst or if she'd just imagined it. Tinna stood up, trying to shake off the thoughts of food that pursued her so insistently. She drifted around the room, peered out through the window—nothing worth looking at—then looked into a wall cupboard and saw her parka hanging on a hook next to the clothes she'd been wearing when she arrived. There was nowhere else to look but under the bed or up the tap on the sink, but both of them would require Tinna to bend over, which she didn't like to do. It would scrunch up her stomach and increase her hunger.

A children's rhyme about a cawing crow suddenly flashed into her mind. *Outside sits the carrion crow / Can you hear its croak?/ Beside the old ram's skull and bones / I saw its woolly cloak.* She mustn't eat. She would burst, like the sheep. Why didn't anyone understand that? Tinna suddenly felt as if she were weightless. Indifference overcame her, a feeling that she had things under control and had nothing to worry about. Calories she'd already ingested didn't count. She smiled, then giggled. Where could she find a knife?

Dís sat deep in thought, waiting for Águst. The last patient was in his office, a young woman who was thinking of getting breast implants. Dís had watched her walk in and bet herself that the slender girl would end up with breasts too large to be called beautiful. It was always the same. Dís thought it was tragic—women got breast implants to look better for men, no matter what they said. More often than not they justified it by telling themselves that if their breasts were larger they would be happier and more self-confident. Of course that was true, but that self-confidence was based on the woman feeling more attractive to the opposite sex. That's why it saddened Dís that almost without exception these women chose implants that were too large, which made them more flawed, not more elegant. If the woman was married she often brought her husband to the first consultations; she would be thinking of getting much larger breasts, though the husband often expressed a preference for something subtler. Dís always tried to point this out to the women, usually to no effect: *Why don't you have a think about maybe getting slightly smaller implants? Your breasts will be larger than they are now, but the change won't be as drastic. You'll be happier in the long term.* Neither doctor nor husband could ever persuade the woman to change her mind. Maybe it was the desire to get as much for the money as possible, or the fear that the breasts would get smaller with age; Dís couldn't be sure, nor did she think that the women would be able to answer the question if she put it to them. Not that she was going to start questioning her patients.

Dís looked again at her watch. Why the hell was she thinking about this now? It wasn't her problem, since each individual made the decision, took responsibility for it and had to live with it. Besides, as far as she knew, all the women had been thrilled with their new breasts. Dís looked once more at her watch in case time was passing faster than she thought. But of course it wasn't. Time was creeping by, as it always did when she wanted it to pass quickly. The wait irritated her for more than one reason: it served to remind her that Ágúst was more sought-after than her even though she was just as skilful, if not more so, these days. He was older and more experienced, but he had started to stagnate. She kept up to date with developments in the profession, but he showed less interest. He tried feebly to disguise it, feigning interest when Dís talked about articles she had read—most recently, one about an operation on the ball of the foot that made it easier for women to walk in high-heeled shoes. Yet he didn't need to fake his enthusiasm when it came to conferences abroad. She heard the door to Ágúst's office open and listened to him exchanging pleasantries with the patient, who he clearly intended to escort to the exit. She straightened up when she heard him lock the outer door. Finally.

"I thought that meeting would never end," said Ágúst as he came in to her office. "Sorry for the wait." He plonked himself down, loosened his expensive tie and undid the top button on his shirt. "She wants an apron removal. Just had a baby and can't wait to get into her bikini again."

Dís said nothing. She wanted to go swimming and then home, so she got straight to the point. "I feel awful about the interrogation yesterday," she said. "The police know I took it. I can feel it."

"Oh, come on," said Ágúst, massaging his own shoulders distractedly. "What time do you need to be there tomorrow? I don't have a patient until about ten, luckily."

Dís seethed. He had no idea; there he sat, footloose and fancy-free, while she was falling to pieces. And it was all his fault! "A man is in custody for Alda's murder," she said, as calmly as she could.

"Doesn't that bother you even a little?" Her anger felt pure and crystalline.

Ágúst glared at her indignantly. "Why should it bother me?" he snapped. "I'm thrilled the police have caught the bastard." He looked away from her. "You should be happy too—don't get all worked up over something that's never going to happen."

"Ágúst," said Dís, gritting her teeth to keep herself from shouting. She exhaled through her nose and composed herself before continuing. "I removed evidence from Alda's home, and the police suspect something. This evidence could either prove the guilt of the man in custody, or, even worse, clear his name. Of course I'm worried; only an idiot wouldn't be." She hoped it was clear she meant Ágúst as well as herself.

He didn't react to the taunt. "The police have talked to me too. There was nothing strange about their questions, considering how she died. You can't just grab Botox off the shelf at the chemist's."

Dís rolled her eyes. "You weren't the first one at the murder scene. I was." She realized she was almost lunging at him across the desk and pulled herself back a bit. "That's why the questions they asked you weren't as loaded."

Ágúst seemed unsure what to say. He obviously regretted not having taken the opportunity to slip out with the last patient. "Which questions were you worried about?"

"The questions about the Botox and where Alda might have got it, the questions about exactly what I did while I waited, how much time passed before I called for help, and so forth. How do I know someone didn't see me there, and that they won't find out I did more than I told them?"

Ágúst frowned. "Dís, are you crazy? How long did it take you to remove it from the bedside table? Thirty seconds? Twenty? The police can't possibly have any information like that. Get a grip on yourself and calm down."

Dís had to admit that he was probably right, which she hated. "But where *else* could Alda have got the Botox?" she asked. "They're not going to give up investigating that. Say they get their hands on it in the end—the bottle definitely has a serial number that can be

traced back to the dealer, and from them to whoever originally sup-
plied it. What do you say to that, Einstein? Then you'll be under the
microscope right next to me, I can promise you." She waited, willing him to panic. He had bought the drug, not her. The drugs that
she ordered were on their inventory and didn't ever leave the office.
"And when they start investigating you, other things are going to
come out, you know." She watched him, still waiting for his forehead to crease with worry.

Her hopes were dashed. Ágúst just shrugged, smiling cruelly.
"Not a problem," he said. "I'll never end up under that microscope.
I've already come up with a solution." He was obviously very pleased
with his plan, because he had puffed out his chest. "I told the police
that we might not have checked the inventory closely enough lately,
because we'd been so busy." Ágúst smiled at Dís. "And guess what?
It turned out some Botox was missing."

"Are you going to lie and say it came from here?" said Dís. It
dawned on her that this lie could get Ágúst out of the frame, but
she would still be under suspicion. "But they'll think I took it," she
said, surprised to note that there was no agitation in her voice. "I
told the lawyer of the man they arrested that we check our inventory scrupulously. She's going to suspect something when you tell
a different story," she added.

"Bless you," laughed Ágúst. "That lawyer has no idea what I
told the police." But he looked discomfited. "You shouldn't have
told her that."

Dís was unhappy about being put on the defensive, but there was
little she could do about it. "I thought I could persuade her and the
police to think that this was suicide after all, or at least divert their
attention to the A&E." As she was saying this, she realized how
bad this sounded.

Ágúst rose and placed his hand on her shoulder as she sat with
her palms flat on the desk. "Everything will be all right, Dís. Don't
trouble yourself unnecessarily or do anything rash." He smiled ge-
nially at her, but Dís could feel an edge behind his smile. He soon
proved her right. "Where are you keeping . . . the thing you took
from the bedside table?" asked Ágúst.

Dís tried to hide her distress. "I took it home," she said, and pressed her lips together firmly. She wanted to make this difficult for him.

"And what are you going to do with it?" he asked calmly. "Wouldn't it be best to destroy it?"

"No," said Dís, looking down. "I can't. There might be important fingerprints on the syringe." She stood up. "When I took it from the bedside table I suspected that you'd let Alda have some Botox. I knew she wanted to give herself and her friends injections, and I also knew that you wouldn't say no to her, even though I didn't realize then what interests you were protecting." She crossed her arms so he wouldn't see how much her hands were shaking. "I was afraid she'd made a terrible mistake, a fatal one. Given herself a heart attack, or worse. I was thinking about you, I wanted to protect you if it turned out you'd been careless with drugs. But I never suspected this would turn out to be murder." She looked directly at him. "I wanted to help you, but that doesn't mean I'm going to—"

Ágúst interrupted her. "What? Conceal evidence from the police? You're already doing that." He stared at her, and now she saw fear in his eyes for the first time. "Are you taking this to the police?"

Dís thought for a moment. "I don't know, I haven't decided yet," she lied.

Chapter 27

Saturday, July 21, 2007

The tour had ended with them sailing almost aimlessly through a calm patch of sea around Heimaey and the nearby islands, while the old captain spun his stories. It would have been interesting to see their route on a map, since only fate seemed to determine the course Paddi the Hook took. Now and again he described certain aspects of the landscape to them and informed them of local customs and geography. But it was clear to everyone that this was not the purpose of the trip. He didn't make any particular effort to describe what they were seeing, appearing to slip into tour guide mode only occasionally, out of habit. Thóra would try to appear interested, but with limited success. It wasn't that it was difficult—the scenery was fabulous, especially south of Heimaey—but she thought it looked as though when the Almighty put the main island there, pieces had crumbled off and formed the other islands that lay scattered about. When she and Bella finally disembarked after the three-hour trip, Thóra was much better informed about life in the Islands and the people she thought were tied to the case. Paddi had seemed unwilling to admit that Alda's name had ever been linked with the blood on the pier, and hadn't succumbed to Thóra's badgering. The smack with its foreign crew had sailed away in the night.

Back on land Thóra had tried to show the old sailor the copy of the photo from Alda's desk, in the hope that he could identify the young man. Paddi shook his head and said that he wasn't from the Westmann Islands, and looked more like a foreigner. Thóra thanked him and put the picture back into her bag. What she had, then, was the story about the blood on the pier, and the fact that Magnús had been in the area around the time it appeared. She found it interesting that Magnús's wife was so adamant her husband hadn't left the house again after bringing their drunken son home. Of course it was possible that she hadn't been aware of him leaving, but Thóra suspected the woman had been persuaded to make this statement against her better judgment.

Fresh in Thóra's memory were the descriptions of the violence that had caused the deaths of the men in the basement. It required a particular type of man to attack others in such a way, and now everything pointed toward that man being her client's father. Dadi Horseshoe—and possibly others—must have helped him. This made more sense than the theory that an adolescent girl had been the perpetrator.

Back at the hotel Thóra realized that her cheeks felt warm, and in the first mirror she passed she saw that her face was the color of a redfish. She cursed herself for not using the sunscreen she had so conscientiously taken with her. Bella looked much the same. The secretary yawned and Thóra noticed that she had no fillings in her teeth, although she had had no desire to find this out. "Do you want to take a nap?" asked Thóra, who would certainly have liked to take one herself. "I need to make several phone calls and try to speak to María, Leifur's wife. So you can just take it easy. Then we'll have a late dinner when I come back."

Bella didn't need to be asked twice. Thóra went up to her room, but only to take a shower and put on something a bit cleaner and more presentable than her jeans and sweatshirt. Afterward she felt much better, her fatigue washed away, along with the salt in her hair. It was just as well, because she needed all her energy to make it through the phone calls awaiting her. One of them was to Markús, to tell him the new information about his father, and to let him know that she intended to tell the police Paddi's story about the blood. She also planned to inform the police about the English smack, because she was pretty sure the bodies were once its crew. She couldn't imagine how the men had ended up in the basement of Markús's childhood home after leaving the Islands several days before the eruption, but she had a strong feeling about it nevertheless. Everyone agreed there had been few foreigners in the Islands at the time, so no one else fitted. Right now she couldn't waste time on these speculations, though, because she had plenty of other things to do. She started by phoning her children.

"Have you got an apartment for the festival?" asked Gylfi. No *hello Mum, how's it going?*

Thóra didn't try to explain that she'd been too busy saving an innocent man from prison to make any preparations for the Bank Holiday weekend. It would mean nothing to Gylfi. "No, I haven't heard anything yet," she said honestly. Indeed she hadn't heard anything about empty apartments, since she hadn't asked. "I need to call someone later who may be able to help me." Leifur was on Thóra's list to call, and if he couldn't get them an apartment no one could. The fact that she was about to tell the police his father could be connected to the bodies in the basement might throw a spanner in the works. But her task was to make Leifur understand that it was best for his brother, and that it was Markús's legal right that the truth be told.

"Don't forget to sort it out," said Gylfi doggedly. "We *have* to go."

One has to brush one's teeth, one has to eat healthy food, but one doesn't *have* to go to a festival; Thóra decided not to share this thought with her son, instead asking after Sóley. She then had to pull the phone away from her ear, as Gylfi immediately started yelling his sister's name as though he thought she was with Thóra and he had to make himself heard through the phone. "Hi, sweetheart," said Thóra when her daughter came on the line. "How are things at Grandma's?" The kids were with their father's parents, who often complained about not getting to see their grandchildren enough, but were never free to look after them when Thóra actually needed them. They were well-off and traveled a great deal. Miraculously, this time everything had come together and the kids had gone to stay in their big house on Arnarnes. This was meant to be their dad's weekend, but Hannes and his wife were at a friend's fortieth birthday party that evening. Thóra had never managed to foster a good relationship with her ex-husband's family, though they had never actually had any conflicts. They were simply very different kinds of people, especially her and her former mother-in-law.

"Hello, Mum," said Sóley. "I'm with Grandma in the hot tub. Do you know who's with us?"

"No," said Thóra, hoping it wasn't the nutritionist the couple had recently hired. Thóra didn't want her eight-year-old daughter to have to listen to talk about food and diets.

"Orri!" shouted Sóley, obviously delighted. "He's with us in the hot tub and he *peed*!" She whispered the last bit, then started giggling. Thóra had trouble not doing the same. It had been a long time since she'd laughed and she didn't dare start, for fear that she wouldn't be able to stop. She spoke to Sóley for a few more moments before saying she looked forward to seeing them all tomorrow, and hanging up.

She called Matthew next. Her phone signal had dropped in and out at sea, making it unclear whether he had tried to reach her, but it didn't matter. She wanted to know what he was planning to do. Thóra smiled just hearing his voice.

"Oh, hi," she said stupidly. "I haven't been able to get a good signal for the last few hours, and apparently you haven't either. Otherwise I would have tried you sooner."

"No problem," he said. "I've tried to reach you a couple of times but I haven't had much luck. How's it going? Have you found a body to go with the head?"

Thóra smiled. "No," she replied. "I'm not particularly looking for it; I've got enough on my plate digging around to find out what happened. It's going slowly." She didn't want to waste time telling Matthew the whole sorry story. "And now there's another body."

"What? They found more?"

"Not in the same place. A woman who could have helped my client was found dead. They thought she'd committed suicide, but it turned out she was murdered."

"Ah," said Matthew slowly. "I hope you're being careful. I told you that anyone who could cut off a man's genitals is dangerous."

"We don't know if it's the same guy that killed her," she said. "All the people connected to the old case are either dead or demented, remember?"

"Who says it's even a man?" asked Matthew. "Women can be just

as crazy as men. Maybe this thing with the genitals has something
to do with the man's behavior toward a woman."

It had crossed Thóra's mind that a woman might have done it,
even though a woman surely couldn't have had the strength to beat
several men to death. Especially not a housewife back in those
days, who probably wouldn't have done any training at the gym or
other sports. Of course, a blunt instrument of some sort had been
used, so a very angry woman could have caused the damage, but it
was more likely that a man or group of men had done it. Thóra
grabbed the bull by the horns. "So, tell me what you're planning to
do. I need to know what you're thinking about the job." She closed
her eyes and crossed her fingers. *Please come*, she thought. *Take the
job and come to me.*

"I'm thinking about saying yes," said Matthew. His voice was
cautious, as if he expected her to try to dissuade him. "At least I'm
sort of thinking about it."

"Excellent!" Thóra was startled at the force of her own exclama-
tion, which came straight from the heart. "It's nicer in Iceland," she
added weakly. She counted to ten before going on, so she wouldn't
make even more of a fool of herself. "I'm really glad to hear that.
When are you coming?"

"I still have to get my ticket but I hope to make it over within the
next fortnight, to speak to them one last time. I'll be able to determine from that meeting when I can move there," said Matthew, who
seemed happy with her reaction. "I'm looking forward to seeing
you," he said. "I hope you won't be out at sea or down in a basement the whole time I'm in the country."

"You should try to add a day or two to your trip to be sure," said
Thóra. It would be awful if Markús's case prevented them from
meeting up. "I'm going home tomorrow, but who knows when I'll
have to come back to the Islands."

They said good-bye and Thóra selected the number for Litla-Hraun
Prison with a smile on her lips. After several moments Markús
came to the phone. "I'm really glad to hear from you," he said, out
of breath, after they'd exchanged greetings. "I remembered a phone
call I got while I was driving east, and it's probably the call that
came from the unlisted number." He sounded proud. "I didn't want

to do anything before I'd let you know about it, although of course I really wanted to have the police called here to take a new statement."

"Good," said Thóra, happy with the news, as well as his decision to wait for her. "Who was it, then?"

"I made an offer on an apartment in the Islands for my son. He spends so much time there and has always stayed with Leifur and María. It doesn't really work any more, since he's almost an adult now. I remember that the estate agent called me because the seller's time limit for accepting offers was about to run out. We discussed what I should do, and the upshot was that I asked him to increase the offer. I've done business with him before, so he knows me well and he'll be able to verify that it was actually me on the phone."

Thóra felt like jumping for joy. Now things were starting to fall into place. "Outstanding," she said. "I'll pass this on to the police, and they can talk to him tomorrow when your custody period is over. They'll hardly request an extension if you've got an alibi." She heard Markús sigh with relief.

"That's just as well, because I can't take it here much longer," he said. "I feel like I'm in limbo. I don't know what's happening out in the world, I'm not allowed to read the papers or even watch the news on television. I've got a lot of stocks in foreign markets, and this is completely unacceptable. I could be losing tens of millions."

"It's almost over," said Thóra. "I doubt I'll be in touch with you again about this before tomorrow, because I won't reach anyone from the investigative team today. The last resort would be to talk to Gudni, of course, but I would prefer to speak to Stefán. There was something else I wanted to talk to you about now, though."

"Isn't there any chance of me getting out tonight, since I've got an alibi?" asked Markús, and Thóra wondered if he'd heard what she'd said.

"I'll ask, of course," said Thóra. "But it will be refused, since you're suspected of more than just Alda's murder. They'll detain you as long as they can, because of the other bodies. We're not out of the woods yet, although things are starting to move in the right direction. Actually, that's what I wanted to talk to you about," she added, happy to be able to direct the conversation back onto the right track. "I've received information pertaining to your father and something that happened in the Islands several days before the eruption. It might not have anything to do with the bodies in the basement, but I suspect it's closely related. I need to tell the police what I know." Thóra waited for Markús's reaction, but he said nothing.

"What are you talking about exactly?" he finally asked. "Does it look bad for my father?"

"Yes." Thóra didn't see any reason to lie. "He was seen in the place where the blood was discovered, without any explanation for it. The blood might have come from a fight, or an assault that ended up with the men being put in the basement. Naturally, the truth will come out, but in order to prove or discount anything the police need to know about this."

"Is there any real need for you to tell them?" asked Markús. "If it might not have anything to do with my case?"

"I'm hoping the police will determine whether the events are related," said Thóra. "If it turns out they are, they can investigate what happened and hopefully figure out who these people were and how they met their maker." Thóra took a deep breath. "You need this case to be solved, Markús. The truth won't do you any harm."

"When is Dad supposed to have been seen at this bloodbath?" asked Markús, his voice unreadable.

"The Friday evening before the eruption, the same night you got drunk for the first time," she replied. "Nobody saw him taking part in any violent activity, but he was seen in the place where the blood was found the next morning. Of course that doesn't necessarily mean anything, and maybe a logical explanation will be found, one that has little to do with him." She waited for a moment but Markús said nothing. "Do you remember if your father went out again after he brought you home?"

Markús snorted. "I passed out as soon as we got in. I didn't even make it to my room—I woke up on the sofa, having thrown up on the carpet, to Mum's delight. I doubt that Dad would have been in the mood to go anywhere. It's all a bit of a blur, but I still remember how angry he was."

"So your father could have gone out again after bringing you home?" asked Thóra carefully. "Without you noticing."

"Yes," said Markús slowly. "I guess so." He paused. "But there's no way Dad killed anyone and put them in the basement that night. There were no bodies lying around when I put the box there a couple of days later. So I can't see how it matters, or why you should have to tell the police whether he went out or stayed at home."

"If your father didn't do anything, it'll be fine," said Thóra, although she highly doubted this. Many years had passed since these events had occurred and she couldn't see how anything could be proved after all this time.

"I'm not that keen to clear my name if it means pinning it all on Dad," said Markús stubbornly. "I'm not that kind of man."

Thóra let her head fall back and she looked up at the ceiling. Christ. "Telling the police what I've found out doesn't necessarily implicate him in anything, Markús," she said, then paused for emphasis. "But if he *did* do something, then it's not right to detain you as a suspect, and I believe he wouldn't want that if he understood what was happening. Is that what you'd want for *your* son?"

"No," admitted Markús reluctantly. "Will you talk to my son tonight and tell him I have an alibi for Alda's murder?"

Thóra wasn't going to let Markús off that easily. "I'll do that, but first I need to be sure you understand what I'm saying. I'm about to call the police with information that will help you, but that might be detrimental to your father. You need to realize that I'm doing what is right for you, as you are my client. Your father is not." There was silence on the other end. "Did you know about the blood? It was found on the pier."

"Yes," said Markús, slightly sheepishly. "I remember it vaguely. I had other things to worry about after my drunken night. Of course at school everybody was talking about the dance, so we weren't all that interested in the blood—it seemed trivial in comparison to our troubles."

Thóra suspected Markús recalled this more than "vaguely"; she was sure he remembered everything from the time that it happened, but had not wanted to tell her for fear of incriminating his father. She could understand the sentiment, but the reason wouldn't matter to the police. "This will all come out," she said with finality. "At best, your father had nothing to do with the bodies. At worst, he was involved. Unfortunately, we can't ask him about it."

"But he didn't murder Alda, that much is certain," said Markús.

"No, you're right," said Thóra. "Maybe her murder isn't connected to the other bodies at all." Was that feasible? Who would kill Alda, if it had nothing to do with the head?

Thóra let the stream of words wash over her. Hannes was unstoppable when he talked about himself, especially if he could turn the conversation around to his inspirational ideas about personal morality. In other words, a phone call from him was like a message from heaven. "So you understand why I can't discuss any details that fall under the hospital's confidentiality codes," he said smugly. Thóra had the feeling that he was looking in the mirror as he spoke.

"Yes, yes," said Thóra, suppressing a yawn. "I'll trade you."

"What?" asked Hannes, taken aback.

"You can have your best golf clubs back, in exchange for this information. I'll never tell anyone where I got it, or use it against you," she said, then waited for his response. The golf clubs in question had fallen to her in the divorce settlement, and she had no use for them whatsoever. They weren't annoying her; she would just be happy to get them out of her garage, where they'd been gathering dust ever since Hannes moved out. She had once been adamant about getting them in the settlement, just because she knew how much Hannes wanted to keep them. He believed they were his lucky set, and had often mentioned them to Thóra since the divorce in the hope of getting them back.

"It's a good deal," she added. "I could easily get this information by other means, just a bit more slowly." Like most paragons of virtue, Hannes's conviction was not so strong that he wouldn't betray the sacred trust of his workplace for something he really wanted. Thóra had scored a hole in one.

By the end of the phone call she had all the information she needed about Alda's temporary leave of absence from the A&E. It turned out Hannes never worked evenings or on weekends, so he hadn't known the woman except by sight. He still knew all about the situation, which had been discussed a great deal at work. It hadn't been drug abuse or intimate relations with a colleague or patient, but instead concerned a difference of professional opinion. Alda had turned against a rape victim, a girl she had treated after an alleged assault. As a follow-up, Alda was supposed to have been available to her as a kind of grief counselor. At first, she had been a great help to the girl, and had done everything by the book. According to Hannes, the story went that Alda had supposedly taken this particular case to heart and stood firmly behind the girl. Then something happened that caused Alda to do a U-turn, and suddenly claim the girl was lying about the rape. Hannes didn't know what had caused her to change her opinion, but he knew the nurse in charge of the Emergency Reception Unit had disagreed with Alda that the allegation was unfounded. According to her, Alda was having a nervous breakdown and was clearly not well enough to work. Alda was requested to take a leave of absence, which she did.

Hannes couldn't remember the name of the girl or the alleged rapist. Thóra thought she knew who the latter was. It must have been Adolf Dadason. As well as Alda's familiarity with Adolf's parents, which could explain her change of heart, the time frame fitted. Also, Hannes mentioned that he had heard something about improper work ethics regarding patients in general, but he didn't trust himself to repeat it, since it was unconfirmed and had happened after Alda went off on leave.

Before she let him go, Thóra also asked Hannes about Valgerdur's autopsy report. "Are you talking about what happened in Ísafjördur?" he asked unexpectedly.

"I might be," said Thóra, surprised. "Do you know something about it?"

"Yes, a bit," he replied. "It sounds like you mean the woman who apparently died in the Westfjords hospital there because of a medical error. There aren't many cases like that, and obviously they always attract a great deal of attention within the medical community. The woman's relatives have kept the case going in the hope of a malpractice suit and there's litigation in progress, although a settlement hasn't been reached. It'll be interesting to see how it turns out."

"What actually happened?" asked Thóra, since the only thing

she'd understood from the report was that the woman had died after an allergic reaction to an antibiotic used to treat serious infections.

"The woman was on a trip with the Icelandic Touring Association out west and contracted a serious streptococcus infection. Her fellow travelers didn't respond quickly enough and, among other things, one of her legs had become gangrenous by the time she was transported to the hospital in Ísafjördur. The staff there made the mistake of not asking her whether she was allergic to penicillin before starting treatment. I don't know what kind of state she was in, actually, but they could have checked her history of allergies with a relative if she wasn't able to respond. Anyway, she turned out to have a severe penicillin allergy which had been diagnosed when she was an adolescent, so this could have been prevented. Whether she would have survived the infection is another question, of course."

"But the hospital must have regulations covering these things," said Thóra. "Was her condition so bad that they thought they didn't have time to call Reykjavík or ask her about it?"

"There's the rub," replied Hannes. "The woman had been admitted to that same hospital several decades before and in her medical record, which they had in their hands, there was no indication of any allergies, much less a hypersensitive allergy. So there *was* human error; not then, but many years earlier. Of course I've only heard about this and not read anything myself, but I understand the medical record states that the woman had been treated with penicillin when she was in the hospital the first time with no mention of her having fallen ill as a result."

"Can this allergy come and go?" asked Thóra.

"No, absolutely not," he said. "It was miswritten in the medical record, since they must have given her an antibiotic that didn't contain penicillin. Or it's possible she wasn't even given an antibiotic at all, and that was the mistake in her records. I don't remember how old she was supposed to have been when the first report was written, but she'd been diagnosed with the allergy long before that. No one is born with an allergy to this drug, but once it shows up it doesn't disappear. Things would have gone differently if she'd been given the drug for the first time when she was admitted all those years ago, but that's not important. She'd already been diagnosed, and even carried an allergy alert card in her wallet. You might think that the mistake they made was not looking for the card, but they say she didn't have her wallet with her at the hospital."

"So she just died?" exclaimed Thóra. "Can't something be done in these cases?"

"She suffocated when her trachea swelled shut," said Hannes casually, as if he were describing a runny nose. "Usually it's possible to intervene but it proved impossible in this case, maybe because she was so ill before it happened. I don't know the circumstances."

"How does one get hold of an autopsy report for an acquaintance, rather than a relative?" she asked.

"What? Don't ask me, I don't spend my time wondering about things like that. I wouldn't have thought it was possible, though. Only people with personal ties to an individual can get copies of the reports. You can't just phone up and have it sent to you."

"One last thing—why isn't there a universal database with information on allergies?" asked Thóra.

"That would be a great idea and it's been discussed, but it hasn't become a reality yet," said Hannes. He was quick to turn to another, more important matter. "Are you at home? Can I come and get the golf clubs?"

Chapter 28

Saturday, July 21, 2007

Thóra and Bella were standing on the porch of a little wooden house that had seen better days. It was covered by sheets of corrugated iron that were rusting badly. The windows could have done with a cleaning, and the riot of chickweed in the garden beat Thóra's jungle hands down. "Do you want me to do the talking?" asked Bella, who had been wildly keen on making this visit, while Thóra dreaded it with all her heart. The house belonged to Alda's mother, and Thóra knew it would go down badly when she introduced herself as the lawyer of the man who was suspected of murdering the woman's daughter. It was just a question of how badly.

"No," replied Thóra indignantly, wondering if she'd been right to make Bella come along. She had wanted her there as support if it all went wrong and the woman lost control, or even assaulted Thóra. She wasn't afraid of a woman in her seventies, but she would rather avoid trouble and had thought Bella's strapping build would have a calming effect. "I'll do it. Just try to look sympathetic. This woman is suffering."

They heard footsteps approaching and exchanged a glance before turning back to the door. It was Jóhanna, Alda's sister, who opened it, and she looked surprised to see them. "Hello," she said uncertainly, looking furtively behind her.

"Who is it?" came a shout from inside the house. The voice sounded like an old woman's.

"Just some women I know," called Jóhanna.

"Was that your mother?" asked Thóra, stopping short of standing on tiptoe and peeking over Jóhanna's shoulder. "I came here hoping for a quick chat with her."

"It wasn't a good idea to come here," she said. "Mother won't want to talk to you. She's still absolutely devastated and as long as Markús is a suspect, you're the enemy. I tried to tell her what you told me, that he was innocent, but she didn't want to hear it."

"What women?" came another shout from inside the house, closer this time.

Jóhanna looked miserable. "Just women, Mother," she called back. "Don't worry, you don't know them."

"Nonsense," came the loud reply. The woman had reached the hallway. "As if I don't know all the women here in . . ." She fell silent when she saw Bella and Thóra on the steps. She edged next to her daughter in the narrow doorway, nudging Jóhanna aside, so that only half of her was visible. "Good day," she said, drying her hands on a dishtowel that she was holding before extending one to them. "I am Magnea, Jóhanna's mother."

"Hello," said Thóra, extending her hand. "Thóra Gudmunds-dóttir. I was actually hoping to meet you."

"Oh?" said the woman, and her face darkened. "How can I help you, my dear?"

"I was hoping to be able to speak to you a bit about your daughter Alda," said Thóra, steeling herself. "I am representing Markús Magnússon, who has been wrongly accused of doing her harm."

"Since when is murdering a woman just 'doing her harm'?" hissed the woman. She took a step backward, pushed Jóhanna out of the way and slammed the door with all her might. The house number on the wooden plate hanging over the door came loose from the impact and dangled sideways. Thóra counted herself lucky that neither she nor Bella had already put a foot across the threshold.

She looked at Bella. "Wow," said her secretary. "It must really suck being a lawyer."

Thóra tried knocking softly on the door in the hope that the woman would reappear. From inside a muffled shout told them to go away before the police were called. This was pointless, that much was clear, and Thóra and Bella returned to their car. When

Thóra was about to start the engine, there was a knock on her window. Jóhanna stood outside, and Thóra rolled it down.

"I told you this was a bad idea," she said reproachfully. "Now I've got to spend what's left of the weekend calming her down." She hugged herself as if she felt cold, though it was unusually warm outside. "She's not herself," she said. "She's not usually like that."

Thóra nodded. "I understand, don't worry about it," she said. "I'm sorry to have troubled you, and we wouldn't have come if I had thought it would go like that." This was a white lie, since Thóra had expected precisely this reaction.

Jóhanna stood outside the car shuffling her feet, clearly holding onto something she wanted to say. "What was in the diaries?" she asked suddenly. "I've changed my mind, I want to know." She hesitated for a second and straightened up. "That is, if they said something about Father."

"I've been meaning to let you know, but unfortunately I got caught up in other things," said Thóra, reproaching herself for not having tried harder to get in touch with the woman. "I called once but there was no reply." She smiled at Jóhanna. "The good news is there was nothing bad about your father in the diary."

Jóhanna nodded. It looked as if tears were forming in her eyes. "Good," she said, and smiled. "Good."

"There were various other things that I wanted to talk to your mother about, though. For example, there are a number of inconsistencies about where Alda was after the evacuation." Thóra raised her hand to block the sun, and looked into Jóhanna's eyes. "She wasn't a boarder at Ísafjördur Junior College," she said. "She was never registered there."

"Yes, yes, she was," protested Jóhanna. "I swear it. My memory can't have failed me that badly."

"Did you ever see her there?" asked Thóra. "Did you go to visit her, or did she come home for the holidays?"

Jóhanna seemed to consider the question. "I actually don't remember any visits to her." She brightened. "Oh, yes, Mother went at least once, maybe more."

"But Alda never came home? There are all kinds of breaks when you're at college, long and short," said Thóra, trying to keep her voice upbeat. "You lived in the Westfjords, not so far away. You'd think she would have come to see her parents now and then. Didn't she?" She could tell from Jóhanna's expression that Alda hadn't come home, not for a long or a short break. "Could Alda have been in hospital?" she asked carefully. "Did she have any kind of nervous disorder, perhaps?"

"Not to my knowledge," said Jóhanna, any happiness she had displayed at the contents of the diaries now drained from her face. "I might not have been told, since I was so young," she added sadly.

"I don't have evidence of any illness," said Thóra. "I wanted to ask your mother about it. But I do know for certain that Alda wasn't in Ísafjördur as people suggest, at least not at school there."

"What else did you want to ask Mother about?" asked Jóhanna. She seemed angry now, but not with Thóra. "Maybe I can get her to talk. I'll ask her about the school, at least."

"One of the things I wanted to know, which also concerns you, was whether Alda ever said anything to either of you about being opposed to the excavations. That would help Markús," said Thóra. She didn't tell Jóhanna why Alda wouldn't have wanted Markús's house to rise from the ashes.

"She didn't," said Jóhanna, shaking her head. "Not to me, at least. She might have said something to our mother. Mother and I have a lot to discuss. Is there anything else I might need to know?"

Thóra told her about the peculiar entries in Alda's diary. She decided not to mention what she knew about the rape case, and instead asked whether Jóhanna had heard Alda talk about it. "Did she ever mention a man by the name of Adolf to you? Or his parents, Valgerdur and Dadi?"

"I've never heard them mentioned."

"You aren't familiar with them from your childhood?" asked Thóra. "I had the impression they were friends of your parents for a time. They were from the Islands, and they also moved to the Westfjords—to a farmhouse near Hólmavík, I think. The woman was a nurse."

"We lived in Bildudalur," said Jóhanna. "It's a long way from Hólmavík. I've never heard of these people. Not that I remember, anyway."

Thóra took out the picture of the young man, which she had wanted to show to Alda's mother. "And do you recognize this man at all?" she asked.

Jóhanna took the piece of paper. "Is this a photocopy?" she asked, and Thóra nodded apologetically. Jóhanna held it by its edge and peered at the subject. "No," she said, handing it back. "I feel like he's familiar somehow, but I don't know who he is."

"Do you know what it is about him that looks familiar?" asked Thóra hopefully.

Jóhanna scratched behind her ear. "I have a feeling he looks a little like my cousin, but that's silly." She dropped her hand. "No, I've never seen this man."

"I can assure you that I would remember if my father-in-law Magnús had said anything about people's heads getting cut off," said María, drawing herself up to her full height and trying to look down at Thóra. Thóra, however, was taller than her, and her chair had thicker cushions, which increased their height difference. The two of them sat in the front room in María and Leifur's house, where Thóra had been invited after a drawn-out telephone negotiation with Leifur concerning the wisdom of telling the police about the pool of blood and his father's possible involvement. In the end Leifur had agreed to meet up for the sake of his brother, as Thóra had repeatedly suggested, and had taken it upon himself to tell his mother Klara about the developments in the case. Thóra was enormously grateful not to have that job, since she could get nothing out of the old woman. She seemed determined to hide from Thóra anything that could be considered unfavorable to her husband. Thóra was also relieved that Leifur kept himself at a distance, since it was enough to deal with one irritated person at a time. María, however, had been no happier than Leifur with the suggestion that her father-in-law might have been linked to the case.

Now Thóra smiled icily at María. "That may be," she said. "But you know, there's a difference between remembering something and talking about it. None of you seems to have had much interest in informing me of some very salient facts."

María had twisted her hair up into a bun, which didn't suit her.

"You understand why we have little interest in seeing an old man hounded by the police. It could finish him off. This is just an old story, no one knows what's true or false."

"But what about Markús?" asked Thóra. "You can't expect him to take the blame to protect his father?"

"Yes, actually, I can," said María, almost petulantly. "If it were up to me, Maggi would be kept out of it and Markús would be found not guilty. They're not going to throw an innocent man into prison."

"It wouldn't be the first time," said Thóra, but she resolved to avoid arguing with the woman over the situation between father and son. María was obviously fond of the old man, as anyone could see from the way she looked after him. "I don't know if you realize that though this case may be connected to the blood on the pier, that's not to say that Magnús killed them. If you help me, I might be able to prove that."

María fidgeted for a moment in her seat while she appeared to digest this. She crossed her legs and then re-crossed them. The balls of Thóra's feet began to ache in sympathy again, the woman's stilettos were so high. "I can say with a clear conscience that Magnús has never mentioned a severed head," she said eventually. "What little he says now is all about the past, but he has never spoken about either a bodiless head or a headless body, let alone whole corpses. I believe that's because he had nothing to do with this." Her head drooped sadly. "Whether you believe it or not, Magnús was a wonderful man. When I came here he was the only one who understood me, and very often supported me in my disagreements with Leifur and my mother-in-law. They always knew better than me about everything, be it child-rearing, cooking, politics, buying a car, or anything. Magnús took my side; he realized how lonely I was."

"I don't doubt that Magnús is a fine man," said Thóra. "I came to you simply in the hope that he had said something that could help me in my search for the guilty or innocent parties. He wouldn't need to have said it recently; he could have said something a long time ago that was strange or indecipherable." Thóra looked imploringly at María. "If you could just try to remember anything like that."

María smiled. "Strange or indecipherable," she echoed. "It would be easier to remember the sensible and coherent things Magnús has said since the start of his illness." She shook her head. "Naturally his condition has worsened a great deal in recent years, but even before that he wasn't making much sense. Of course he talked more back then, and understood more; but still, what he said had very little to do with what was happening around him. I could be talking about the weather and he would be on about fishing equipment, or something just as unrelated."

"Do you remember if he ever said anything before like what he was trying to say to me?" asked Thóra. "About Alda, or a falcon?"

"Yes, actually he did," said María. "I don't see how it relates to this, but he's often mentioned birds. Especially falcons. He used to sit at the window—actually he still does—for hours at a time, looking out. If a large bird flies by, he often asks me if it's the falcon. I always say yes, because I think that's the answer he's hoping for." María glanced at the window of the front room where they were sitting. A handsome seagull flew past, as if to order. She cleared her throat delicately and continued. "He hasn't mentioned Alda very often, and there wasn't any way for me to understand what he meant when he did, since I didn't know who she was until recently. I thought he was talking about a relative, or even a childhood sweetheart of his."

"What did he say about her?" asked Thóra. "It might make more sense in the light of everything that's happened." She decided not to ask more about the falcons; any ties this bird had to the case were tenuous at best, and it was more important to hear what María had to say about Alda. "Has he ever said anything clearer about 'the poor child'? Anything clearer about difficulties in her youth, stuff like that?"

María shook her head. "It's been quite a while since he's mentioned Alda, so of course I don't remember it word for word. When he mentioned her name it was always in connection with some sorrow or drama that he never explained properly." María squinted thoughtfully. "Something about making a sacrifice, and how such a thing was sometimes justified. Once or twice I tried to ask him more about it, since it sounded more interesting than his endless stories about sailing and the fishing company, but he always went back into his shell immediately and clammed up. It was actually as if he hadn't realized he'd been speaking out loud until I responded."

"And it never came out what sort of sacrifice he was talking about?" asked Thóra. She couldn't ask if the sacrifice had something to do with the head, since María had been so adamant that Magnús had never mentioned it.

María shook her head. "No, never. Whoever she was, she's stayed longer in his mind than a lot of other things in his life. Actually, he mentioned spirits—I mean alcohol—once or twice in direct connection with the sacrifice. I doubt that this Alda ever had anything to do with liquor, so it's probably not related to the sacrifice, if there ever was any sacrifice."

"Spirits?" asked Thóra. Hadn't the friendship between Kjartan the harbormaster and Gudni fallen apart because of something to do with alcohol? "What did he say about spirits?"

"If I remember correctly it was something along the lines of the spirits making it even, and did I agree? Of course I just said yes, told him they definitely balanced it out. That seemed to cheer him up," said María, shrugging. "But as far as the 'sacrifice' is concerned, I should probably mention that when I realized who this Alda was it occurred to me that she had sacrificed her relationship with Markús, but I've never been able to think of anything that might require such a sacrifice."

"Has your father-in-law ever mentioned Markús in the same breath as Alda, or this sacrifice of hers?" asked Thóra curiously. So far she had been repeatedly led to believe that Markús's crush had not been reciprocated. Maybe that wasn't the case at all. But why couldn't Alda have been with him if she'd wanted to?

María shook her head again thoughtfully. "No, I don't think so. I would have asked Markús about it if I had made the connection between him and this mysterious sacrifice. What sacrifice could such a young woman make?" She scowled. "Sacrifice her education to have a child, or vice versa? Donate one of her kidneys for a sibling? I simply can't think of anything. Nothing serious enough to preoccupy an old man who isn't even related to her." She looked at her watch, then crossed and re-crossed her legs again. Thóra got the feeling she did this regularly in order to prevent varicose veins.

If that were the case, this woman and Thóra's ex-mother-in-law would have got on like a house on fire. "And of course it could be pure nonsense," said María, without much conviction. "He mixed up names a lot, and I find some of what he says turns out to be either daydreams or misunderstandings." She shrugged. "When the brain cracks, a lot of things can go haywire, which is why Magnús sometimes thought scenes from films were memories from his own life. He sometimes talked about how he went parachuting, helped sink some criminals' boat, met Sophia Loren, and other things like that. I don't imagine any of it actually happened."

Thóra sat and thought for a minute. "Has he said anything about the eruption?" she asked. María was right, the testimony of such a sick man could not be taken seriously unless it could be confirmed by some other means. There may have been no sacrifice, or if there had been, maybe it hadn't been Alda who was involved, meaning the incident had no relation to this case.

"Of course he has," sighed María. "Everyone who wasn't an infant at the time of the disaster has plenty to say about it. For a while I feared that I would never be accepted into the community because I hadn't ever breathed in a decent amount of ash." She looked at Thóra sadly. "That fear turned out not to be unfounded. I've never properly adapted to the community here, though I don't think it's entirely because of the eruption."

Thóra sympathized with the woman and her isolation. "What has he said about the eruption?"

"He's mentioned it now and again. Asked sometimes whether I heard a booming noise, as if he were reliving that night. I can almost recite the whole story, he's told me so often. He was one of the first to become aware of the eruption, since he was awake. I understand it was late on a Monday night—"

Thóra cut her off. "I'm not looking for information about what time the eruption began, so much as anything he may have told you about the rescue operation." Thóra could see from the woman's face that she didn't really understand, so she continued, "The bodies showed signs of having been outside after the eruption started, later than the first night. So I wondered whether someone else could have brought the bodies to the basement without Magnús knowing. Maybe someone who helped him clear out the house, and therefore knew when it was safe to bring them in."

"I see," said María. "He mostly talked about how he evacuated residents to the mainland on his ship. I don't remember how long he said he'd been awake at one point, but he talked a lot about it." She smiled. "Fifty, sixty hours, something like that. He was very proud of it. But that may have been a slight exaggeration on his part." She patted her hair before continuing. "He didn't say much about anything that happened while he was trying to salvage the household; he said he'd got out most of what mattered but was still worried about things that he'd forgotten to take: old books he'd inherited from his father, a compass, some coins and other things that it's hard to imagine him missing. He could grumble to himself about this for hours at a time, but those things had been in a store-room, and so they were lost."

"Was the storeroom in the basement?" asked Thóra. If Magnús never went down to the basement, someone could have put the bodies there at any point after the eruption. "One would have expected him to have taken these things from there, since they were dear to him."

María shrugged. "I have no idea where the storeroom is," she said. "It could be in the basement, but that doesn't necessarily mean anything. Maggi still might have gone down there, even if he didn't manage to find everything. It would be impossible for me to remember what was in our storeroom if I had to remove the things I cared about most. None of the objects he mentioned was particularly large, so he could easily have gone down there without finding them."

"But he's never spoken about the basement anxiously, or in any way other than his usual tone?" asked Thóra.

María snapped her fingers. "Yes, now I remember," she said triumphantly. "He did mention the basement in connection with the eruption, but not in the way you described. It was before he got ill so it wasn't that bizarre, but if it's true then he certainly went down there." María drummed her high heels on the floor as she thought back. "Let's see . . . he said he was glad he hadn't taken all the family's possessions down into the basement as he'd first planned, and had even started to do. He was smiling when he said it, because he was laughing at himself for having thought the basement would be safe. So he *did* go down there—is that bad?"

"No, not really," said Thóra, who didn't know whether this meant anything. So Magnús had gone down but probably only briefly, as he had missed things he wanted to salvage. Was that because he knew about the bodies and couldn't bear to stay there very long, or because he thought there was nothing of interest down there? "Do you think it would make him happy to get his hands on those items he was looking for?" asked Thóra.

"Yes, if it could happen soon," replied María. "And if we managed to give them to him when he was in a good mood." Her eyes clouded and she let her hands fall into her lap. "Otherwise, I don't know."

Thóra said nothing, thinking things over. The basement of the house hadn't been emptied yet. If she and Bella went there and found these items, it was entirely possible they would help clear the old man's head when he held them in his hands. Since he seemed to connect them to the eruption, there was a faint chance he would tell Thóra something useful as a result. If they got on the case that evening, they could drop by again in the morning, before catching the boat home. Thóra adjusted her little notebook on her knees and readied her pen. "What was it again that he was looking for?" She wrote the things down and stood up to leave.

"I have some papers for you, from Leifur," said María as they left the room. "I'm to tell you that he got them from the archaeologist." She grabbed a large pile of documents and handed them to Thóra. "I'm also supposed to tell you that no one from the excavation team was aware of Alda having contacted them to try to prevent the house from being dug up." Thóra took the stack and saw that it was the log of everything found in the houses. It would take a while to go through it.

When Thóra left María she realized that she hadn't learned much of interest except that Magnús had sailed overnight to the mainland with refugees, returned immediately the next day and started to salvage what he could. First he had focused on his own house. In doing so he had had the help of several neighbors, who he helped in return, but unfortunately María hadn't known whether this included Dadi from next door. Then Magnús had joined a group of men who went all over Heimaey performing salvage operations, but María didn't know any of their names. After a month or so Magnús had started fishing again, by which time his house was completely buried. Over the following months he'd worked as hard as he could to keep his ship.

Thóra's phone rang, and she answered eagerly when she saw the number of the estate agent Markús said he'd spoken to on his way east. She had talked to him briefly before she'd visited María, but he'd been busy and had promised to ring as soon as his work day was finished, which was usually early on Saturdays. That was clearly not the case today, since it was nearly six o'clock. Thóra got straight to the point after saying hello.

"Okay," said the youngish voice at the other end of the phone, when she had finished explaining what she needed to know. "I understand."

What did he understand? Icelandic? Thóra tried not to let her irritation show, although she had spent longer than was healthy on the phone today. "So, did you have this phone conversation with Markús?" she asked. "It matters a great deal that you tell the truth, and that you tell the story correctly. You won't do Markús any favors by making something up, if he's remembered this wrong. You also need to let me know what phone you called him from, so the police can verify it."

"Ummm," muttered the man. "Yes, I called him. Wait a minute," he said, and Thóra heard a rustling of papers. "It's here somewhere," came the voice over the line, and then: "Ah. Here it is."

"Here what is?" asked Thóra.

"I was looking for the offer we discussed. It expired at eight o'clock on the eighth of July, so that fits perfectly. I called him when it became clear that the sellers wouldn't accept it. That's not strange, because it was quite low. Markús didn't particularly like the apartment, although I understand that his boy was excited about it."

"So you called him," said Thóra, trying to direct the man back to what mattered. "You called him, on his mobile?"

"Yes," said the agent. "That's the only number I have for him, I think."

"And you can confirm that he was the one you spoke to?" she persevered. "Not someone else using his phone?"

"Yes, I spoke to him. Absolutely," said the man resolutely. "We talked a bit about what would happen next, but he was driving, so he couldn't talk for very long."

Thóra looked up at the sky, thrilled. He could not only confirm that Markús had had his phone, but also that he had been driving. "And what number did you call from?" she asked.

"My mobile," the agent replied. "It was after work and I had come home. I have an unlisted number so it wouldn't have shown up on Markús's screen, if that's what you're asking."

"That's great," said Thóra. She explained that he would have to confirm this with the police, and asked him to keep the offer paperwork somewhere safe, in case there was any need for it.

"Do you know if Markús is still thinking of buying an apartment?" asked the young man, sounding anxious. "We weren't able to close a deal that evening. I actually have a lot of new property for sale, damn good places, actually. He wouldn't want to miss this opportunity. I know things are hard for him at the moment and I'll try to keep things open for him, but I don't know how long I'll be able to hold off other buyers."

Thóra smiled to herself. "I'm pretty sure Markús has other things on his mind at the moment, but I expect he'll be thinking about it again soon. You can try to reach him by phone after the weekend. Hopefully all this will be over by then."

After saying good-bye she called Stefán, rather pleased with herself. The only dilemma she had was what to tell him about first: the pool of blood, or her conversation with the estate agent.

Chapter 29

Saturday, July 21, 2007

The excavation site was completely silent, except for the creaking beneath Thóra's and Bella's shoes as they walked through the slag on the pathway. It was as if they were traveling through a deep valley: nothing could be seen of the world around them apart from a clear sky and the faint traces of a street that had disappeared from the surface of the earth a third of a century ago. Thóra couldn't block out the uncomfortable feeling that they were being watched through the broken windows of the empty houses as they walked by. Of course she knew that there was not a living soul here apart from herself and Bella; nevertheless she was plagued by unease. She got goose bumps when a light breeze stirred a loose paper plate lying in front of a little house. The house looked as if it had once been yellow, but the catastrophe that had overwhelmed it had given it a dull green appearance. This decrepit shack looked so sad and neglected that Thóra had to stop for a moment and stare at it. It was easy to imagine a dust-covered middle-aged woman standing at the window in her dressing gown, waiting for life to pick up where it had left off in January 1973. Thóra shook off the image. She wasn't used to letting her imagination lead her astray—it must be the guilt she was feeling over their business in the area. At best, it was immoral. The oppressive silence also played a part. Thóra was so unused to it. In the quiet neighborhood where she lived one could always hear the sound of traffic—even at night an indistinct hum from cars driving down the surrounding streets managed to reach her ears. Here, there was no sound, although the town was just below them and people would barely have gone to bed. Ash and slag clearly swallowed all the noise, even the squeaking of their shoes. It was like watching television with the sound muted. Thóra and Bella said nothing on the way to Markús's childhood home. Their conversation had petered out around the time they reached this street and were met by its silence. Thóra even grabbed Bella's shoulder and pointed when they stopped in front of Markús's house, instead of telling her they had reached their destination. She realized how ridiculous this was and tried to make up for it by breaking the silence: "It's this one," she whispered, even though whispering had not been her intention.

Bella stared silently at the house. "Come on," said Thóra, slightly louder now. She clambered over the tape, and Bella followed. "This'll be no problem," said Thóra, more to persuade herself than her secretary. What if the archaeologists turned up, or had set up security cameras to track any unwelcome visitors? No matter how she tried, Thóra could not think up any excuse for their presence here. They did have a reason for doing this, but wisdom told Thóra that it was a dubious one. The old man would probably stare at the stuff they brought back with the same dull gaze he turned on everything else put in front of him. If they even managed to find what they were looking for.

They came to the door and stood there for a few moments without saying anything, checking to make sure their flashlights were working just as well as when they had set off a quarter of an hour before.

Bella turned her light on and off for the third time. "Are you sure it's safe?" she asked, looking at the door. The oak was deeply scarred and appeared to have bent under weight or heat. Large, slender windows on both sides of the doorway were boarded with dented sheets of corrugated iron, remainders of Magnús's attempts to save his family's home. "I don't like this, and I don't understand why I have to go in. I'll just keep watch, like last time. The house is collapsing." Bella's voice was plaintive and she pushed loosely at an iron sheet to back up her fears. As she had no doubt intended, the sheet fell with a dull crash, and she had to step aside to avoid it hitting her. "You see," she said triumphantly.

"Don't be an idiot," said Thóra. "The sheet was put up in an emergency to prevent ash from coming into the house. The house itself is secure, and it isn't going anywhere." Thóra didn't want to go in again, not at all, and wanted Bella there as backup. She didn't feel comfortable going down into the dark basement alone; if she had someone with her to talk to she could pretend everything was fine. "Let's go, it'll be fun once we're in." Thóra pushed the door with her foot, and it opened with a faint creak. Dust and soot whirled in the beam from her flashlight.

"It must be really dangerous to breathe in this dust," said Bella.

"Since when did you start worrying about that?" asked Thóra. "If you wait outside you'll have several cigarettes, so it'll probably be a nice rest for your lungs in here." She took a few steps into the house, then turned and looked at Bella through the murky air. It was as if she'd jumped inside an old-fashioned coal stove and shut the door. "Come on," she said, beckoning.

The sturdy secretary frowned, but finally let herself be persuaded, turning on her flashlight and walking in to join Thóra. She put her free hand over her mouth and nose and mumbled something indecipherable into her palm, shooting Thóra a look that displayed neither warmth nor admiration. Thóra tried to smile appeasingly, which didn't really work as she didn't want to open her mouth. She walked carefully in the direction of the basement door, happy to hear Bella following close on her heels. The only light came from their flashlights, since all the windows were still boarded up tightly. They fumbled their way along the filthy floor, though there wasn't really anything they could trip over. It appeared that whatever loose items had remained in the house when the police took it over had been pushed to the edges of the room. Thóra tried not to dwell on why they had needed to clear space, but it was obvious. They had to get the three bodies out somehow. She was also trying to forget about the hard hat the archaeologist had insisted she put on the first time she'd come here. She quickened her step.

"Is this the basement door?" asked Bella when Thóra stopped. "Isn't it better if I wait here?" She looked around and coughed. The air hadn't got any cleaner and Thóra knew it would get even worse as they went deeper down, but didn't dare tell Bella in case that was the last straw that sent her straight for the exit. "Then I'd be ready if anything needed to be done up here. For example, I could get help if the floor were to crash down into the basement."

"Enough of that talk," said Thóra, refraining from saying that the floor was more likely to collapse with Bella standing on it. "You're coming with me." She opened the door and shone her flashlight down the stairs. "This won't take us any time at all." She stepped onto the landing and set off cautiously down the wooden steps. When she waved the flashlight around the basement she could see that the police had removed more than just the bodies. Everything from the shelves and the floor was gone. Thóra sighed.

"What?" asked Bella, who had thankfully followed Thóra down. "Is something wrong?" Bella followed Thóra's example and shone her light around the dark cellar.

"They've taken everything," said Thóra. "Damn."

"Wasn't that to be expected?" said Bella. "What if the body that belonged to the head was cut up into little pieces and scattered everywhere? The police would want to make sure they had all the evidence."

"I doubt that," said Thóra irritably, walking farther into the basement. "The objects were removed because this was an atypical crime scene. No one had been down here for thirty-four years, so there was no way of knowing what belonged to the home and what to the possible murderer." She looked around again. "They had to take everything with them, if only to be able to examine it under better conditions."

"Are we finished, then?" asked Bella impatiently. "You said this would take no time."

"No, not at all," said Thóra. "I think there's a storeroom here somewhere, and the police probably haven't cleared it out." She shone her light on the walls, one after another. "Especially not if it's sealed." She walked over to two doors that stood side by side in one corner. "If they'd wanted to remove everything from the house there wouldn't be anything left on the ground floor. There could just as easily be something relevant up there."

"I'm not opening those doors," said Bella, and coughed again. The dust in the air had become extremely thick and every breath was accompanied by a foul taste like musty old books. "The body hasn't been found." Despite this, Bella followed Thóra and took her place at her side.

"Of course the police have already looked here," said Thóra. "It's out of the question that the body is anywhere in this house, let alone in the basement." Nevertheless she felt her stomach muscles tighten. She grabbed the handle of one of the doors and opened it with her eyes closed. She stood for a moment in front of Bella, knowing that the secretary could not see her face. After a few seconds, when Bella still hadn't kicked up the ashes and fled, Thóra knew it was safe to open her eyes. "It's amazing the junk people put in their storerooms," she exclaimed, looking at the jumble of tires, batteries, tools and unidentifiable spare parts. "The police have clearly moved things around," she added, pointing at white rings on the floor from where the tires must previously have lain.

"Do you think they're here?" asked Bella, poking her head through the doorway. "Those books and things?"

"No," said Thóra, shaking her head. "Hardly. The stuff in this storeroom belongs more in a garage than a basement. I don't imagine Magnús would have stored old books along with nuts and bolts." She used her flashlight to make sure there weren't any hidden boxes or shelves where the items might possibly be found. "Let's try the other door," she said, closing the first one. She couldn't figure out whether she'd rather see boxes and other items hidden there, or nothing, which would mean they could get out of the basement. She opened the second door in the same way as the first. When she opened her eyes she knew they wouldn't be leaving here any time soon. It was a full-sized storeroom with shelves on all the walls, each of them full of boxes and other things that weren't fit for around the house but were important enough not to go in the bin.

"Holy moly," said Bella. "Are you going to go through all of this?" She followed Thóra into the storeroom and pointed at the imprint of a box in the dust on one of the shelves. "The police have obviously looked through this stuff, so I doubt there's anything important hidden here."

Thóra opened the first box. "This'll be quick," she said distractedly, pointing her flashlight into the box. "We're looking for books, a compass and money. Coins, I think."

Bella sighed and walked to the shelf farthest from Thóra. "That's easy for you to say," she said, picking up a child's school cap. "It looks like everything's all mixed up here." She reached for a frying pan. "What's wrong with people?" she asked. "Why don't they throw away their rubbish?"

"Times were different when these things were packed up," said Thóra, still examining the box in front of her. She found herself thinking about what was hidden in her own storeroom. She hoped her house would never be buried by ash, so that others would never rummage through her belongings later and make critical remarks. "People had to make do and mend, and most things were more expensive than they are now."

"What, even *hair*?" said Bella. "Ugh."

Thóra couldn't stop to look at what Bella was grumbling about, since she thought she'd seen something that could be loose change glinting at the bottom of her box. "People still keep locks of their babies' hair. It's very common, although I don't understand what one's actually supposed to do with it," she said, as she reached a hand into the box. She pulled out two teaspoons, then let them fall back in. She closed the carton and turned to the next one.

"This isn't from a baby, I can tell you that," said Bella. "It can't be."

"My mother has hair from her grandmother," said Thóra, adjusting her flashlight beam. "She could never bring herself to throw it away, and I believe she may take it with her to the grave." She was glad she'd brought Bella with her. If she'd been down here alone she wouldn't have lasted long. Although the conversation wasn't all that gripping, it helped her forget the foul air and the fear that the house might crash down on their heads. She aimed her flashlight into another box. At the top lay something lacy in a plastic bag that had once been clear but had started to yellow. Thóra pulled it out and saw that it was a christening gown. She set it aside and continued digging through all sorts of children's clothing, for the most part homemade, either knitted or crocheted. At the bottom of the box were two books marked with gold letters: *Baby's First Year*.

Thóra had been given a book like this as a gift when her son Gylfi was born and she had managed to write things in it during the first three months of his life. The book had then been forgotten and never used again. The box also contained various items such as plates for children, silverware and a large old-fashioned baby's bottle. "I just have baby stuff," she told Bella. "Did you find anything besides locks of hair?"

"An old bathing suit," said Bella. "I think it's moldy. It smells bad."

Thóra was removing the last few things from the box, when she noticed the baby's bottle was unusually heavy. She pointed the flashlight at it and saw there was something inside.

"What's this?" she asked herself, unscrewing the top.

"What?" asked Bella, looking up from the bathing suit.

A small mallet dropped out of the bottle with a heavy thud. "Who would keep a salmon priest in a baby bottle?" asked Thóra, grimacing.

"A *priest*?" said Bella.

"Yes, a salmon priest. It's the hammer a fisherman uses to stun the fish, after he's caught it."

"What fucked-up religion do you belong to?" said Bella, coming and looking over Thóra's shoulder. "And what are those marks on it?" The light was stronger now that there were two flashlights. It was a keen observation on Bella's part: the copper mallet was covered with black spots.

"It could very well be blood," mused Thóra. Was this the weapon the unidentified men in the basement had got to know firsthand? She put it to one side and picked up a little shoebox that contained several tiny pairs of shoes, and underneath them an ornate knife. "Look at this," she said.

Bella moved closer to her to get a better look, and when Thóra's phone rang she gave a screech that cut through the oppressive silence. Thóra was equally startled, though she managed to suppress the scream that nearly burst out of her. She fumbled for the phone and answered it. "Thóra speaking," she said, affecting nonchalance. She hoped this wasn't someone from the Islands, asking what she was up to.

"Hi, this is Dís at the plastic surgery clinic," said the voice on the other end. "I have a small problem related to your investigation into Alda's death."

"Really?" asked Thóra, surprised and a little relieved not to have to make up an excuse for where she was.

"Yes. I was hoping you could help me. I need a lawyer."

Chapter 30

Sunday, July 22, 2007

Thóra stared at the paper in front of her. It was not yet eight o'clock. She wasn't usually up and about this early, but tourists eager for a full day's adventures had woken her with their clatter in the corridor at around seven, and she hadn't been able to get back to sleep. She had jumped into the shower and sat down at the little desk in her room in the hope of working out the facts of the case. This was easier said than done, and Dís's phone call the night before hadn't done anything to make it easier. Dís hadn't wanted to say anything except that she had information that needed to be shared with the police. However, her own interests compelled her to speak to a lawyer first; she'd had only Thóra's number, so had called her. Thóra explained to Dís that she couldn't help her since she was Markús's lawyer and he was the only suspect in the case. She asked if Dís would like to speak to Bragi and Dís had taken Bragi's number. When Thóra spoke to him later in the evening, Bragi had told her to prepare herself for new information to appear in Markús's case very soon. He did not say what this information was, and Thóra knew better than to interrogate him about it. He was obligated to protect his client's confidentiality. Thóra had to ask him one thing, though— whether the information in question was likely to be positive or negative for Markús. Bragi had thought it over for a long time but replied that he hadn't actually worked that out yet. If forced to choose, he would say more positive than negative.

Thóra turned back to the paper in front of her and pushed Dís and her mysterious information from her mind. There was no point wondering about that now; all would become clear after the weekend. She lifted her pen. Of everything that she had dug up, how much of it was connected to the case? She lined up the events chronologically in the hope of being able to piece it all together, and then ran down the scribbles on the page one more time.

A damaged fishing smack comes to the Islands January 19, anchors at the pier, moves berths and then leaves during the night. Paddi the Hook watches it sail away.

Teenagers, among them Alda and Markús, get drunk at a school dance that same night. Magnús, Markús's father, goes to fetch him. Alda probably walks home. Something bad happens to Alda, which she decribes indirectly in her diary.

Magnús and Dadi "Horseshoe" are seen down at the harbor that night. A lot of blood is found on the pier the following morning, where the smack was originally moored.

Detective Gudni is called to the scene. He is told of Dadi's presence at the harbor, but not that Magnús was with him.

Dadi denies having been involved in anything illegal and states that he knows nothing about any blood.

Four men, most likely British, are beaten to death—unclear exactly when.

Leifur returns to the Islands to scold his brother for his drinking.

Alda gives Markús the box, and asks him to store it for her. She is in a frantic state.

Eruption during the night.

The residents flee to the mainland, some of them on fishing vessels, and Alda asks Markús what he did with the box. He tells her.

Magnús and his partner Thorgeir, Alda's father, return to the Islands to salvage their possessions. Magnús mostly empties his family home, although not the basement.

Alda, her mother and her sister move to the Westfjords, where she supposedly attends Ísafjördur Junior College—suddenly one year ahead of her previous school year. However, no one at the school has a record of her attendance there.

Markús's mother and her children move to Reykjavík.

Valgerdur and Dadi move west, settle in the vicinity of Hólmavík. There they finally have a child. She wants little to do with the child—perhaps she suffers from postpartum depression?

Some time during the first two weeks of the eruption, the bodies are moved to the basement.

Magnús buys up Thorgeir's shares in the fishing company and continues to run the business alone. He acquires a processing plant for peanuts and lands his catch in the Islands, despite the continuing eruption.

Markús attends Reykjavík Junior College.

Alda is registered at the same school, but for home attendance until after the new year. Markús meets her again for the first time since the eruption and they do not discuss the box.

Alda studies nursing.

Markús marries and divorces, has one son. Markús does not work for his father's company. Maintains his friendship with Alda.

Leifur, Markús's brother, takes over the family business when their father becomes ill. He has worked there since completing his studies in business.

When plans are made to excavate Markús's parents' house, Alda asks Markús to prevent it, but keeps this secret from her sister.

Alda takes a leave of absence from the A&E.

Alda familiarizes herself with Valgerdur's autopsy report.

Alda for some reason keeps a picture of a tattoo bearing the words "Love Sex," as well as a picture of an unidentified young man.

Alda has links to pornographic Web sites on her computer and is seeing a sex therapist.

Markús does what he can to prevent the excavation of his childhood home but settles for being allowed to get the box from the basement after Alda consents to this arrangement. He travels to the Islands.

Alda is murdered.

Markús finds the bodies in the basement and a man's head in the box.

A possible murder weapon is found in a box with children's clothes, also in the basement.

Thóra put down the paper and tried unsuccessfully to recall more details that might possibly make a difference. She also tried to determine how much of this might be unconnected to the murder, but couldn't actually think of anything. It was the same as with the items in the storeroom—if she crossed something off the list it would probably turn out to be the vital clue. She sighed and tried to concentrate. Could Alda have killed the men? It didn't matter how hard Thóra tried to imagine such an attack, with the men rolling drunk and the teenage Alda in a murderous frenzy with a salmon priest on the pier—it didn't add up. What was she supposed to have done with the bodies after such a horrific deed? Thóra didn't know any teenage girl who had the strength to struggle with the body of a full-grown man, still less if she had had to make four trips. If they'd been murdered in the basement, things would look different. Then Alda wouldn't have needed to move the bodies at all. This, however, did not fit, since the murders were committed before the eruption. At least, Markús had put the box with the man's head there before it happened. In addition, there were burn marks on the men's clothing, which suggested that they had been out in the open after the tephra had started to rain down. And Alda had left the Islands by then. Thóra felt the blood on the pier must be connected to this.

Where was the body that was missing its head? It would probably never be found, since it hadn't turned up during the last thirty-four years, even during the excavation. They had already dug up all the houses that they planned to salvage from the ash, so there was no hope of finding anything new that way. In addition, hundreds of houses had been buried beneath lava during the eruption, so the body in question could be inside one of them, and thus gone forever. Then again that could hardly be the case, because why would the murderer or murderers have moved only one of the bodies from house to house? Why move the others from a house that was about to be buried by lava to one that was being buried under ash? She was certain of one thing—if she herself had needed to get rid of a body under such circumstances, she would have chosen the house that would end up under lava. And then, of course, it was possible that the men had not been murdered in the Islands after all, despite the blood on the pier. Perhaps the murderers didn't have ties to the Islands or the Westmann Islanders, but instead were outsiders who had transported the bodies there to hide them. Thóra sighed thoughtfully. If so, it had been a bad plan.

No, everything suggested that Markús's father was the key to the case, not people from the mainland. If the bodies were put there without his knowledge, the murderer would hardly have hidden the mallet and knife in a box in the nearest storeroom, nor left these possible murder weapons next to the bodies. Thóra tried to imagine how Magnús might have played a part in all of this. Maybe he and Dadi had ended up in a scuffle with the crew of the smack, killed the men and brought their bodies to the basement. But that didn't fit with Paddi seeing the smack sail away. Could it be that the paths of these men had crossed out at sea rather than on land, and the blood had ended up on the pier when Magnús and Dadi were dragging the bodies ashore? Thóra frowned. Could the two of them, Magnús and Dadi, have sailed Magnús's ship? She had no idea how many people were needed to handle a boat that size. They would never have managed to get a whole crew of men to keep quiet about something like this. Of course Thóra had seen the ship in a painting at Leifur's house, but that image told her precisely nothing, since she had never even pissed in the sea, much less seen how a fishing operation worked. The trip with Bella and Paddi the Hook could hardly be counted. This led her to something else: if the bodies belonged to the crew of the British smack, then where was the boat?

An unexpected thud came from the door of Thóra's room, snapping her out of her reverie. The sound came again, but now it was clearly a knock. Thóra stood up and went to the door, where she was flabbergasted to see Bella, dressed and ready to go.

"I'm ready," said Bella. She looked at Thóra and appeared to be unhappy with her boss, who wasn't dressed yet. "I couldn't sleep because my room was too quiet."

Thóra looked at the clock and saw that it was almost eight. "I'm coming," she said apologetically. "Would you like to go down to breakfast and get us a table?" She handed Bella the page with her summary of events. "You can look over this while you wait. A second set of eyes." It was apparent from the young woman's expression that she had never heard this idiom before.

"I'll be down in ten minutes," said Thóra, smiling as she closed the door on her secretary.

———————

"Can't I have the list a bit longer?" asked Bella, sipping the black coffee she'd poured for herself. Thóra couldn't count the number of sweet rolls that had disappeared into the girl as they ate their breakfast.

"No problem," said Thóra in surprise. "Did you see anything in it?"

Bella shook her head. "No, not yet," she said. "Actually you forgot to put in about Adolf and the rape." She turned the list toward Thóra. "I stuck it in there," she said, pointing at an illegible scribble in the margin.

"I definitely overlooked a few other things," said Thóra. "If you remember anything else you can certainly add it. It's not sacred."

"I'm also wondering if I should check on this tattoo for you," said Bella, pointing at the list. "*Love Sex*," she muttered. "That's so lame."

A foreign couple at the next table, who had been immersed in a guidebook, finally understood two words of the women's conversation and smiled knowingly at each other.

Thóra thought tattoos were pretty dumb at the best of times, so *Love Sex* was no worse than anything else as far as she was concerned. "What are you thinking of doing?" she asked. "Do you know much about tattoos?"

"I've got three," replied Bella, and she started to fiddle with the collar of her sweater. She pulled it down and Thóra caught a glimpse of a unicorn on the upper slope of the girl's hefty breast. "One," she said, arching in her seat to show Thóra her belly. "Two . . ." The foreign couple were now staring at them.

"It's okay, I believe you," said Thóra uncomfortably. "But what are you going to do with *this* tattoo?"

Bella tidied her clothing and adjusted herself in her seat. "I'm going to see whether anyone recognizes it. There aren't many tattoo shops in Reykjavík, so it won't take long. It's an unusual tattoo, I think," she said. "At least, I've never seen it in any albums."

"Albums?" repeated Thóra, blankly.

"Tattoo parlors have books or folders with drawings of the tattoos that they offer," said Bella, casually. "When I got mine done I had a look at the selection, but I don't remember one saying *Love Sex*."

The young couple at the next table giggled. "Definitely check on it if you feel like it," said Thóra, as she tried to ignore them. "I doubt it will make any difference, but you never know." She looked at her watch and stood up. "We should get going," she said, grabbing her bag from where it hung on the back of her chair. "Now let's see whether we can't score a hit with Gudni."

Bella snorted. "Good luck with that," she said, apparently far from optimistic.

"So you thought you'd left your wallet in the basement when you went down there with Markús?" asked Gudni, clearly not believing a word of what Thóra was saying. He leaned back and glowered at her. He had agreed to meet them at the police station when Thóra called him just after eight in the morning, and she had heard in his voice that she'd woken him up.

"Yes," said Thóra peevishly. "Does it matter?" She pointed at the salmon priest on Gudni's desk. Next to it lay the knife that had been in the same box. "Here you have the possible murder weapons in an unsolved case with four corpses, so I think you should be thanking me for stepping in, rather than questioning my story."

"I just think it's best that we have everything clear," said Gudni calmly. "You and this . . . lady . . ." he pointed at Bella.

"*Lady?*" snarled Bella. Thóra remembered how strange she'd felt the first time someone had called her a lady rather than a girl or young woman, but this was neither the time nor the place to share that experience with her secretary.

Gudni raised an eyebrow at Bella, but continued. "You travel all the way to the Islands, then instead of coming to me or the archaeologists to check if your lost wallet might be in the basement, you wait until the evening, then go to the house yourself?"

"I'm sorry," interrupted Thóra. "But we didn't see any signs saying that it was still a closed crime scene, so we wanted to save you the trouble and just go down there ourselves. I hope you're not saying the house is still under your jurisdiction?"

"No, actually it isn't," replied Gudni. "We finished up yesterday, but that doesn't alter the fact that there's a large notice at the end of the access road stating clearly that people walking through have to remain outside the boundary tape."

"Oh, is there?" said Thóra, smiling innocently at him. "We completely missed that." She pointed again at the objects on the table. "In any case, I have handed over evidence from a serious murder case, but all that seems to matter to you is our little mix-up." Thóra wasn't entirely sure if the warning sign was legally enforceable, but suspected not. "I would like to know whether you consider this a significant discovery or not, and I would also like the mallet and the knife to be taken into consideration if you are thinking of requesting an extension of Markús's custody period. The weapons are not his, and I'm certain that a forensic examination will show he's never touched them." Thóra had contacted Markús and told him about the weapons before going to the police station. Stunned, he had denied ever having laid a finger on them, let alone hidden them in the storeroom.

"You would have to speak to my colleagues in Reykjavík about his detention. They handle these matters," replied Gudni, with sarcastic emphasis on the word *Reykjavík*. "I don't know what their plans are for Markús."

Thóra had hoped Gudni might have been kept abreast of developments in the case and would therefore be able to tell her—or at least give her a hint about—what the police were planning for tomorrow, when Markús's custody period expired. She tried to act unconcerned. Gudni annoyed her just as much every time she met him, and she seemed to irritate him, so she wouldn't give him the pleasure of witnessing her disappointment. She smiled. "But as far as these weapons are concerned . . ." she said.

Gudni laughed dryly. "Weapons?" he said. "These are work tools."

She paused a moment before continuing, "It may surprise you to learn that tools have been used before for acts of violence. I can assure you such a thing is not unheard of."

Gudni stared at her, poker-faced. He leaned forward and glanced at the tools on the desk. "I don't know how you can be so sure these are linked to the bodies."

"It's not natural to keep dangerous tools stored among baby

clothes, especially not a christening gown," she replied. "What's more, I suspect there's blood on both of them. I'm fairly certain these items were put there in an attempt to conceal evidence."

"That would be a stroke of genius," said Gudni, smiling mirthlessly. "Hiding the murder weapons in a box but putting the bodies on display in the middle of the room." He frowned and shook his head. "Do you think the murderer was a raving idiot?"

Thóra turned bright red, but kept her emotions in check. "Now is not the time to conjure up theories about exactly how it happened. First it must be determined whether this is blood, and if so, whether it's from those men. At the same time, it would no doubt be wise to check these items for fingerprints."

"You probably haven't had much call to use tools like these," said Gudni patronizingly, as if no one could call himself a real man unless he went around with a mallet in one hand and a knife in the other. "You do realize there is a natural explanation for why there might be blood on these tools?"

"That may be, but the amount makes me doubt it came from a fisherman knocking out fish—that wouldn't leave so much blood behind on the priest. Wouldn't you agree?"

Gudni narrowed his eyes and his lips thinned. "What are you hoping to get out of this?" he asked, leaning forward on his elbows.

Thóra knew he wasn't talking about her fee. "I thought we were hoping for the same thing," she replied. "To find the murderer. The *real* murderer."

Gudni chose not to reply. He continued to stare into Thóra's eyes, but then he had to blink. He said, "Oh, we'll find him. Without your help."

"Oh, you think so?" muttered Thóra, but decided not to squabble with him. She changed the subject. "What can you tell me about an old case involving smuggled spirits, one that came up here just before the eruption?"

Gudni seemed startled by the unexpected new topic. "What does that have to do with this case?" he asked. Thóra said nothing. "I think you're really clutching at straws if you want to drag that old incident into this." He leaned back and clasped his hands over his chest. "Are you withholding information from us?"

"No, not at all. I've just heard it mentioned twice in my conversations with locals and I wanted to find out more about it, even if only to rule out any links to the current case."

"I see," he said. "It's hardly a secret, I just thought most people would have forgotten that case. It surprises me that anyone brought it up after all these years." He unclenched his fingers and started cracking his knuckles, one after another. "It wouldn't be thought remarkable today, in comparison with all the big drug cases. It became evident that an unusual quantity of grain alcohol was in circulation on the Islands, and all the signs pointed at two residents. The investigation hadn't yet concluded when the eruption occurred, but it was a long way along. Then it was dropped in light of the circumstances."

"Who were the men involved?" asked Thóra. "I know about Kjartan at the harbormaster's office, but who was the other man?"

Gudni cracked the knuckle of his thumb, unusually loudly. "You don't know him."

Thóra named the one man who came to mind apart from Paddi the Hook, who seemed unlikely to be the culprit. "Was it Dadi Horseshoe?"

Gudni couldn't hide his surprise. Thóra had obviously guessed correctly. "I'm not going to speak to you about anyone but your client," he answered. "However, I can tell you that neither of these men was a suspect for long, because a third man turned himself in and confessed everything the morning before the eruption. He got lucky, because as I just said, the investigation didn't go any further."

Thóra knitted her brow. Who could it be? "Was it Magnús?" she asked, and again saw that she had guessed correctly.

"Why don't you ask him about it?" suggested Gudni sarcastically. "If there's nothing more you want to inquire about, it's just a question of telling me whether you found anything else down in the basement. I'm passing this information on to Reykjavík, so now's your chance."

"No," replied Thóra curtly. "That's all." She smirked at Gudni as she thought about what she and Bella had managed to dig up. Several old poetry books bound in leather, an old-fashioned copper compass and gold coins that didn't appear to come from any particular country. Before she handed these things over, she wanted to check whether they could conjure something useful out of Magnús. The evidence was starting to point ominously toward the old fishing tycoon.

"Adolf, the only thing that could justify your continuing existence on the planet would be if you started breathing carbon dioxide and exhaling oxygen." The woman's anger was written all over her face, although her sadness was even clearer. "You know my opinion of you and that's not going to change, so we shouldn't waste time arguing."

Adolf looked at the mother of his child, saying nothing. He wanted to make some retort, something that would sting her, but couldn't think of anything clever. He could tell her she looked knackered and ask if she'd looked in the mirror today, but that was too feeble. Sometimes it was best to keep quiet and settle for a dirty look, which he was rather good at. He didn't even need to try; the expression crept over his face automatically as soon as she sat down and started talking. He shouldn't have opened the door when he saw who it was. He didn't own a car, so she could have concluded that he wasn't at home and left. Adolf couldn't bear her, or the guilt she always tried to make him feel on the rare occasions they talked. It wasn't his damn fault she'd got pregnant. If he'd had any inkling that would happen after their long-ago one-night stand, he would have stayed home that night. He only vaguely remembered the night they had made Tinna, that's how unexciting the sex had been. He'd had better sex with women who were barely conscious.

"Are you even listening to me?" she said, shooting him a dirty look of her own. "I want you to talk to Tinna's psychiatrist. He wants to meet you, but you're not returning his calls. You wouldn't be doing this for me, if that's what's stopping you."

"What the hell am I meant to say to him? If Tinna's in some kind of trouble, it's your fault. You raised her." Adolf shrugged to show how little this affected him. "And what genius came up with the idea of sending her to a shrink? There's nothing wrong with her that a good meal wouldn't fix. You'd be better off giving her something to eat, so maybe you should rethink your cooking. It's hardly

surprising she doesn't want to eat, because you can't cook for shit."
He actually had no idea what kind of cook she was.

"I always knew you weren't that bright, but I hadn't realized you
were retarded," said the woman, her face flushed. She had clenched
her hands into fists. "Do you know anything about this disease?
Have you taken the time to go online and read about what's killing
your daughter?"

"It's all rubbish," said Adolf, feeling his voice deepen to a rum-
ble as it always did when he was very angry. "Everyone knows the
system wants to make out kids have all got something wrong with
them. They're diagnosed with attention deficit disorder, hyperac-
tive disorder, God knows what else, just so the therapists can rake it
in. Tinna is skinny because she doesn't eat enough. Maybe you let
her watch too much TV and read about too many models in maga-
zines."

She sighed. "Will you talk to this man, for your *daughter*, or not?"
She stood up from her armchair and looked around. The look on
her face now beat Adolf's dirty look hands down. "I seriously
doubt any good will come of it, so I don't give a shit what you do.
At least I can tell the doctor with a clean conscience that I told you
to call him."

"What does he want me to say?" said Adolf, suddenly disappointed that she was leaving. It had been a long time since he'd had
a visitor, though he hadn't given it much thought. His friends had
made themselves scarcer and scarcer as his trial date drew closer.
They didn't want to be seen being friends with a rapist. Adolf
didn't like this, but he did understand. He would do exactly the
same in their shoes. "Do you want some coffee? I've got coffee. If
you want."

She looked at him in surprise. "No, no thanks." She adjusted her
handbag on her shoulder and shifted the weight of her slender
body onto one foot. "Will you talk to him?" she repeated.

Adolf shrugged again and looked away from her to the sofa in
front of him. "If I knew what I was supposed to say, of course I
would do it. But I still don't understand what good it would do."

"I don't know what he wants to talk to you about," she said, and
he could hear exhaustion in her voice. "If you're worried he'll start

psychoanalyzing you, you can relax. As far as I know he's simply trying to get a more complete picture of what's going on."

"A complete picture?" asked Adolf, who was having trouble understanding this. Suddenly he wanted to please her and say yes, say he would call the doctor. Still, he didn't want to go. He didn't understand the purpose of this and he didn't like psychiatrists, psychologists, any of that lot. Specialists always confused him and he felt uncomfortable around them.

She looked at him expectantly, obviously keen to get going. Adolf suddenly saw through her: she wanted him to say no, and not go. Then she could continue to be the martyr, the poor single mother with the sick daughter who received no assistance or understanding from the child's dastardly father. She cleared her throat nervously as she realized he'd figured her out. Or maybe it was just tiredness and resignation he saw in her eyes. "A complete picture of Tinna's life, who she was before this disease took over," she said. "If it helps, I've met this man more than once and he's very decent, so it's no hardship at all talking to him. They think Tinna's illness is worse than they had previously realized—that underlying it is a much more serious mental condition." She looked at Adolf for a moment before zipping up her plain, inexpensive jacket. "This doctor can answer your questions about her eating disorder and the other illness, if you have any. It's helped me a lot."

Adolf nodded, pondering his response. He didn't believe in this eating disorder, nor this new illness for that matter. He looked at the mother of his child: her face was so drawn and haggard that she looked much older than she was, but no one said *she* was ill. Tinna had simply inherited her mother's build, and besides she was obviously impressionable. There were often articles in the paper about how much influence skinny models and actresses had on girls, and Tinna had just fallen under the spell of that body image. When she grew up she would get over it and put on a bit of weight. "I don't have any questions about this *disease*," he said. He hadn't planned to say it so sarcastically, but it came out like that.

"She's very ill," said the woman dejectedly. "And you're a fool, Adolf; a total fool, if you can't see it."

He was furious. She was always like this. Nothing was ever good enough for her; all he ever got from her was disapproval and moral lectures. He was a fool, and she was an angel in human form. "You must be a fool yourself, leaving my daughter in the hands of the system for no reason. You're the fool, not me."

She looked at him for a few long seconds. For a moment Adolf thought she might cry, but instead she shook her head in a kind of surrender and waved her hand halfheartedly. "I'm going." She turned and walked away slowly, without looking back.

Adolf stood up and followed her. He had got the last word, but it still felt like she'd won. It was unbearable: he needed every tiny victory he could get before the trial if he wanted to get through it in one piece. "So, you admit you're the stupid one?" he said as she reached the door. He would have liked her to be in more of a rush, and felt again as if she were asserting her superiority through her relaxed pace.

She stopped abruptly but didn't turn round. Her voice was cold. "Adolf," she said. "Your daughter is now on a secure ward, after hurting herself so badly that she can't be trusted to be left alone. If you could speak to the doctor, that would be great; if not, then that's how it'll have to be. His name is Dr. Ferdinand Jonsson. Perhaps you can tell him who this 'Alda' woman is that Tinna's constantly talking about. I don't know anyone by that name, so I expect it's one of your girlfriends."

"What does she know about Alda?" asked Adolf, scarcely recognizing his own voice. "She's not supposed to know anything about Alda."

"I have no idea who she is," replied the mother of his child sadly. "If Tinna knows her, then it must be through you. She's obsessed with her, and goes on and on about how she knows who was at her house." Now she turned to him. "I expect she means you, but she's on so many drugs that it's hard to understand her." She turned back around and grabbed the door handle.

Adolf paused for a moment to regain his composure. He tried to tell himself that he needn't worry about this, he could persuade the girl to stop mentioning Alda. He would tell her that it could look very bad for him, and she should remember that he was her father. She would understand that. Now he had one other thing to worry about.

"What happened to Tinna?" he asked. It must be something very bad, he could feel it as he stared at her mother's tense back.

The woman's shoulders drooped, but she didn't turn round. "Tinna was found cutting herself."

Adolf didn't understand. "Cutting herself? A suicide attempt?"

"No," she replied, her tone defeated. "She was trying to eat her own flesh. She thought she'd already ingested the calories in it, so they didn't count." Now she could hardly speak through her sobs. "As if there were any flesh *on* her."

Abruptly she straightened up, opened the door, walked out and shut it behind her. Adolf stood there openmouthed, too shocked to run after her. Tinna was obviously more seriously ill than he'd thought. He cursed himself for not even having asked the name of the other disease she was thought to have, besides anorexia. Now he knew which of them was the fool.

Chapter 31

Sunday, July 22, 2007

Thóra said good-bye and put down the phone. "Well?" asked Bella impatiently.

"I don't know if he was telling the truth or if he's still hiding something from me," grumbled Thóra. "He might even be out and out lying to me." She had got Kjartan's telephone number from the harbormaster's office and called in the hope of finding out more about the alcohol case and seeing if he had anything to say about the pool of blood. "After a long argument he admitted having been a suspect in the smuggling case, and I'm fairly certain that he did play a part in it even though he hasn't admitted it."

"And this Dadi Horseshoe?" said Bella. "Did Kjartan say he was guilty?"

"Yes, he even gave a little speech about it," said Thóra, staring at her phone in exasperation. "According to Kjartan, Dadi was the king-pin in the smuggling operation, which had actually been going on for quite some time. Dadi was in contact with a couple of sailors on a cargo ship that sailed past here regularly. They would throw the liquor overboard, attached to an anchor line, and it would float there until Dadi came to pick it up in a little rowing boat. When the Cod War started it got harder, since the fishing grounds and the sur-rounding area were supervised so closely. That's how it was uncov-ered, according to Kjartan. He was seen fishing up the containers and sailing away with the unidentified contents. He wasn't actually caught red-handed with the liquor, but the police in the Islands were notified of his mysterious trip and Gudni's investigation ex-posed it."

"And what was Kjartan's part in it supposed to have been?" asked Bella.

"As I told you, he denied any involvement; but he did tell me what he'd been suspected of. The police thought he was the one taking any spirits that didn't sell in the Islands over to the mainland. At the time he was working on a coastal ship for the State Shipping Company."

"That's a sensible division of labor," said Bella, nodding in approval.

Thóra didn't respond. "He said the case fell apart: first the eruption halted the investigation in its tracks, then Magnús turned up at the police station and admitted everything."

"Maybe he was the only one involved," Bella said. "He didn't want his innocent friends to take the blame."

"Kjartan said it was absolutely out of the question that Magnús had anything to do with the smuggling," said Thóra. "I completely believe him about this part, because I think he, Kjartan I mean, *was* tangled up in it. He said he was amazed when this story started going around. But he hadn't had the chance to talk to Magnús or ask what he'd confessed, because the night after Magnús took the blame the volcano blew its top. When they met during the rescue operations a short time later, no one discussed it in the hope that it would simply blow over, which is in fact what happened."

"But surely Magnús was up to his neck in it?" frowned Bella. "Firstly, no one does something like that for his friends—I don't care what anyone says. Secondly, we know he sneaked down to the harbor with Dadi Horseshoe in the middle of the night, which must have had something to do with the smuggling."

"If Kjartan's telling the truth, then it's out of the question. Magnús had his hands full keeping the company going, and he wouldn't have had the time or desire to complicate his life."

"So what did Kjartan say about the blood?"

"Nothing much," said Thóra. "He said he'd heard the story about Dadi and Magnús being down at the pier that night, but knew nothing about the pool of blood. Or about the British fishing smack." She heaved a sigh. "I hope I can get something out of Magnús."

"Do you really think he'll tell you anything?"

"I don't know. But I do know he's one of the only people left alive who know what happened, although it's clearly impossible to tell how much of it is still in his memory."

"If I'd murdered four people, I'd forget everything but that," said Bella. "I'd forget everything about work, everyone at the office, but never that."

Thóra smiled. "Hopefully you're right," she said, crossing her fingers. "We'll see."

Magnús was staring fixedly at the compass Thóra had brought with her. The old books lay in a little pile on a table next to him, but he'd showed no interest in them. His veiny hands gripped the arms of the easy chair tightly. "Why?" he asked suddenly. He hadn't taken his eyes off the compass, so it was unclear who should answer the question. Thóra glanced sideways at María, who simply shrugged her shoulders. Thóra placed her hand on Magnús's gray paw and was startled at how cold and bony it was. "Aren't you happy to have the compass back? I found it in the basement."

The man jerked his head up and glowered at Thóra. "Why?"

She didn't know what to say. "As far as I knew, you regretted having left it behind during the eruption," she said, avoiding his glare. "Isn't that good?"

The old man looked down into his lap and shook his head, his expression melancholy. "You've grown old, Sigrídur," he said. "You were just a little girl."

"Like Alda?" asked Thóra. She doubted the name Sigrídur was significant, since Leifur had told her his father was confusing her with his sister.

"Poor Alda," said Magnús, still shaking his head. "That was ugly."

"What was ugly?" asked Thóra. "I've forgotten what happened." As soon as she'd said it she realized it was a mistake. The man squinted at her and appeared to become confused.

María came to the rescue. "Are you cold, Maggi dear?" she said good-naturedly, and he calmed down at the sound of her voice. "I'll fix your blanket," she said, standing up to pull it over his legs. "There now." She patted his knee. "Be good for Thóra now. She's helping your son, Markús."

"Markús loves Alda," said the old man, nodding happily. "She's a good girl." Then his face darkened. "Ruined."

"Ruined?" exclaimed Thóra. She added, more calmly: "What happened to her? Did she hurt herself?"

"Ruined," he repeated. "The sacrifice." He stared hard at the compass and frowned. "Disgusting. Take it away."

Thóra had to refrain from shaking the man by the shoulders as she put the compass away. Damn it, he had the information she needed. She wondered if it were possible to hypnotize an Alzheimer's patient. "Alda is dead, Magnús," she said. "If I'm going to help Markús, I need to know what happened to her."

"Markús," said Magnús, turning to look out of the window. "Markús loves Alda." He dropped his head again.

"I know," said Thóra, reaching for the roughly made purse Bella had found, full of coins that appeared to be gold. "You see what I've got here?" she asked, showing him the purse. "The coins you were looking for." He tried to turn his head away, clearly reluctant to look at it. She opened the purse and showed him the contents. "Gold, Magnús," she said. "Gold coins." Suddenly he lashed out at the purse, making Thóra lose her grip. The coins scattered everywhere. Several landed in his lap and he reacted as if they were made of burning lava, trembling all over, crying out and trying to shake them off.

María jumped to her feet and tried her best to calm him down. Together they managed to remove the coins. Magnús relaxed a little. "Blood," he said. "Blood money."

"Blood?" asked Thóra, knowing her time here was running out. "Did someone die, Magnús? Did four men die?"

He sat still and looked at her, his expression cruel. "They were evil men, Sigrídur."

"Evil men," he said again, trying to stand. "The falcon is a beautiful bird," he added. "Not like the cuckoo." His face had softened and the dullness seemed to be returning to his eyes. "It doesn't hatch its own eggs," he said. "Other birds do. Remember that."

Thóra promised she would. First a falcon, now a cuckoo. Perfect. Still, at least it seemed clear that Magnús had some connection to the old murders. One step forward, two steps back.

Chapter 32

Monday, July 23, 2007

Time was going by faster than Thóra would have liked. As usual she was worried that she wouldn't make it home in time to prepare dinner. Her stress was exacerbated by the conviction that each passing minute increased the likelihood of Markús's custody period being prolonged by police request. She was in her office waiting for a call from Detective Stefán, who would inform her of their decision about tomorrow's hearing. She should have had the call by now. She hoped the decision had been delayed because the police were still scrutinizing the evidence that had come to light since Markús was locked up, and had found something that implicated others besides him. Of course, it could be exactly the opposite scenario; the police couldn't call her because they were too busy putting together all the evidence against Markús. The uncertainty made her uncomfortable, and Thóra didn't know how to occupy her time. She was reluctant to use the time for phone calls, in case Stefán called then didn't have time to call back. She knew she was being silly, but she didn't want to use her phone. So she sat restlessly at her computer. She knew she should be going over the countless details of the case, but she couldn't concentrate on any of them. The minutes ticked by. To make matters worse, she hadn't been able to make use of her time aboard the ferry from the Islands. Her mobile phone had cut out several miles from shore and didn't regain a signal until just outside Thorlákshöfn. So she had been unable to continue her quest to tie up this case's innumerable loose ends. Instead, she'd been forced to listen to Bella talk about the guy she'd met the night before. If Thóra hadn't known Matthew would soon be on his way to Iceland, she would have thrown herself overboard from the shame of Bella having a better sex life than hers.

The familiar opening notes of "Happy Birthday" rang out from her mobile, and Thóra quickly answered. Sóley had changed the ring tone on her birthday, and although she found it a bit cheesy she couldn't bring herself to change it, since Sóley was so pleased with it. Thóra didn't recognize the number and she crossed her fingers that it would be Stefán. It turned out to be Markús's son, eager for an update. She ran through recent developments for him, and promised to get in touch as soon as she knew more. The boy sounded nervous and mumbled something about his father probably having to stay in prison. Thóra repeated that she would have to let him know, and felt bad for disappointing the poor boy. Things weren't going well for him, and she hoped for his sake that next time she called him it would be with good news.

Thóra went online to check whether anything was being reported on the news Web sites. You never knew, perhaps the media would get the news before her. This turned out not to be the case. The only report she found stated briefly that it was still unclear whether an extension of Markús Magnússon's custody period would be requested before it expired tomorrow. Thóra gave up and decided to call Stefán, so that she could stop wondering when he would call her and get on with something else.

"We're going to request two more weeks of confinement based on his being party to the murders of the men in the basement," replied Stefán brusquely. "The decision will be made before two p.m. tomorrow."

Thóra stifled a sigh, not wanting to betray her disappointment. "But is he no longer a suspect in Alda's death?" she asked hopefully. Even that would be some progress.

"Given the estate agent's statement and the evidence that backs him up, not to mention the information that has recently come to our attention, we no longer consider Markús to have had a hand in that."

Stefán's tone made it clear that he disagreed with this position. He was just as convinced of Markús's guilt as before, but the police department's lawyer had probably made the decision and informed him that there was no way to corroborate his suspicions. It seemed clear to Thóra that the new information Stefán had mentioned had come from the plastic surgeon, Dís. According to Bragi, after their meeting he and Dís had gone together to the police station, where the doctor had told the police some facts pertinent to the investigation.

"What information was this?"

"As your client is no longer a suspect in Alda's case, that is none of your business," said Stefán. "Now he's only a suspect in the small matter of the bodies found on the Islands."

"Do you mean you're going to overlook what I found out about them?" snapped Thóra.

"We don't see that these details of yours make much of a difference," said Stefán. "We'd already received information about some of them from Gudni, including the mysterious pool of blood. Even if Markús's father was involved, that doesn't preclude Markús playing his own part in it."

"I don't understand your reasoning," said Thóra, feeling her spirits start to sink. "There's no indication that Markús isn't telling the truth about the head in the box, and what little evidence has come to light seems to point to other people."

"Your man is involved in the case, whether you like it or not."

"Do you even know who the dead men were? Even if you're in no hurry, it's in my client's interests that the case be resolved quickly."

"Yes," said Stefán, without appearing to register Thóra's jibe. "They were the crew of a boat that disappeared off the coast of Iceland in January 1973. We sent X-rays of the teeth abroad and all the men have been identified."

"What?" said Thóra. She recalled what she had read about two shipwrecks in *Our Century*, one with a crew of Icelanders and Faroese and the other a crew of four British men, one of whom had been found. She had ruled out both incidents, since they didn't seem to fit. "Which boat was it, and when did it sink?" she asked.

"I see no harm in telling you that," said Stefán, and she heard him rustling some papers. "It was a fishing smack named the *Cuckoo*, and it was seen last on the eighteenth of January 1973 off the south coast."

Thóra sat silently, her mind reeling. Magnús had mentioned a cuckoo but she had not made the connection, the vessel's name from the *Our Century* article forgotten. "I read an old news report about it," she said. "It said the body of one of the four-man crew had washed up on shore, along with some other wreckage. If the bodies in the basement are the rest of the crew, then this begs the question: who did the head belong to?" Could it be that there was no connection between the three bodies and the head in the box after all?

"There's no doubt about who the fourth man in the basement was," said Stefán. "Body parts were washed ashore, among them a torso. Its head was missing, and it was thought at the time that it had been torn off by the force of the wreck. The body was in terrible condition and it was missing more than just the head: an arm was gone, and also the body part that was found along with the head." He cleared his throat. "That is to say, in its mouth."

Thóra knew which body part he meant. She was struggling to understand what this new information meant for Markús. The crew had vanished before the eruption, while he was still in the Islands. But she couldn't see how Stefán and his colleagues would prove any link between them and Markús. This must have been the boat that stopped at the Islands on the night Markús was at the school dance, then at home in a drunken stupor. "Did these men have any connection to alcohol smuggling?" she asked.

Stefán hesitated. "Yes . . . you could say smuggling plays a part in this story," he said. "How did you know?" She told him about the alcohol smuggling case, and her suspicion that it was connected to the murders. She also mentioned that she'd already told Inspector Gudni Leifsson about it. Stefán, however, didn't appear to think this significant. "No, it didn't have anything to do with liquor smuggling," he said. "These men were stealing birds, and searching for nesting sites before the spring."

"Bird smuggling?" said Thóra. "Birds of prey, like falcons, maybe?"

"Yes, falcons and eagles, and probably some other species I don't know about," replied Stefán. "I know it's possible to get huge sums for them abroad. At the time, the police had been informed that these men were traveling through the country asking about nesting sites. It seems likely that they planned to return in the summer to steal eggs and hatchlings. If they hadn't sailed away when they did, they would at least have been brought in for questioning. We think the scars on their hands were caused by raptors' claws. They'd been doing it for years."

"Do you know if they had any falcons, or other birds, with them?" asked Thóra, and told Stefán about Magnús's repeated references to a falcon.

"No, not as far as I know," he replied. "But you know you can't take much of what Alzheimer's patients say seriously."

"But it seems obvious from this that Magnús *was* involved," she said, furious at Stefán's contrary attitude. "He also definitely mentioned a cuckoo, so he was probably talking about the boat."

"I'm not going to get into that. Of course we will investigate all potential leads, but your man isn't getting out just because his father blurts out something so open to interpretation, which may or may not be linked to the case."

"So you're not going to investigate Markús's father, or Dadi? I know one of them is senile and the other dead, but there's nothing preventing you from changing the focus of your inquiry."

"Of course we're following every lead, as I said," replied Stefán. "Among other things, we're examining the knife and the salmon priest you found in the basement, although it's too early to know what they will tell us. So there's no point making snide comments about our working methods. On the other hand, nothing has been discovered that proves your client is not involved. Far from it. He's the only one behaving suspiciously. For example, he denies having put the head there."

"You know his explanation for that," fumed Thóra. "An explanation from which he has never deviated, despite countless interrogations and now solitary confinement."

"That may be because he knows no one can confirm or deny it," said Stefán. "And it may be that he himself orchestrated that convenient state of affairs."

Thóra didn't feel like responding to these insinuations. Markús had an alibi for Alda's murder, and besides, Dís's information directed the spotlight away from him. It didn't actually matter how convinced Stefán was of his guilt: no judge would be persuaded that Markús had murdered her. "Obviously I will object vigorously to your request for an extension of custody," she snapped. "For your sake, I hope you have more than just your *opinion* to bring to the table tomorrow."

"Yeah, yeah," said Stefán. "Whatever you say. See you tomorrow, bright and early."

Thóra did not respond to this asinine comment, taking her leave and hanging up. She had allowed her anger to show in her voice, and felt a little bit better. This was not shaping up to be the cozy TV evening with her daughter she'd hoped for. It also looked as though she wouldn't be finished with the case before Matthew arrived. Thóra stood up and started to scrape together the files that she needed to go over to prepare herself. Hopefully she could work on the case at home without upsetting Sóley. If not, she would wait until her daughter had gone to bed and work on it late into the night. Lately her relationship with her daughter had been characterized by too many broken promises. She was torn from her thoughts about Sóley by the realization that she was supposed to call Markús's son, Hjalti. He simply moaned "No" when Thóra told him about the police's decision, then she could hear his rapid breathing. "I should remind you that even though the police are still pursuing this, there's nothing to say that the ruling will go their way," she tried to assure him.

"Yes, there is," said Hjalti, sounding petulant—more like a small child than a young man. "They're going to torture him into confessing."

"Let's not start accusing the police of torture," said Thóra evenly. She knew how to handle children by now, since she had all sizes and shapes of them at home. The boy needed to hear an adult tell him that everything would be all right; that his father would be released from prison, come home shortly, and buy Hjalti an apartment in the Islands, as he had planned. "These cases are very tough while they're going on, and often those who least deserve it end up caught in the slipstream. I have no doubt that your father is one of those. If he didn't murder any of those people, he won't be convicted. I'll make sure of it." She was going to add something about the truth always coming out, but the boy interrupted her.

"But what if someone didn't commit a murder himself, just helped the murderer? What then?" he asked frantically.

Thóra knew that this "someone" was the boy's father, and that Hjalti had realized that Markús might be tied to the murderer or murderers. He was, in other words, not completely clueless, poor boy, although he was deeply troubled. "In my opinion there's nothing to suggest that your father did anything that makes him an accomplice. He might have helped the murderer unknowingly, but that's not a crime." She hoped he wouldn't start asking what she meant, since she didn't want to talk to the boy about the severed head in the box.

"Okay," said Hjalti, his voice still tinged with nervousness. "Maybe I'll come tomorrow at two o'clock. Is that all right?"

"I don't think you'll get to see your father, if that's what you're hoping," said Thóra. "But you can always come and wait outside, if you want. Then I could meet you afterward and tell you how it went, which might make you feel better." The boy agreed to this, although she wished he hadn't. They said good-bye.

The phone rang again, and this time it was Bella. "I've found the tattoo," she said. "You'd better come and see this."

The recent smoking ban hadn't reached the tattoo parlor, Mirror of the Soul; Bella blew a thick cloud of smoke in Thóra's direction. The multicolored man who owned the parlor also had a burning cigarette between his lips, so Thóra couldn't scold Bella. She settled for a glare, wondering what she was actually doing here: Markús was pretty much absolved of all suspicion in Alda's murder, and the *Love Sex* tattoo wasn't linked to the bodies in the basement. However, she didn't want to make light of Bella's investigation of the tattoo's origin, so she acted as though nothing were out of the ordinary. "So you think it's unlikely that this tattoo was put on anyone else?" asked Thóra.

"That would be a pretty fucking huge coincidence," said the man, without removing the cigarette from the corner of his mouth. He took a puff and blew out the smoke, still without touching the cigarette. In the light of Bella's prowess with the men in the Islands, Thóra wondered for a moment whether they'd just been up to something. "A girl made it up from two tattoos I've got in this folder." He lifted his foot and kicked at a tired old folder on the couch in front of Thóra. His black army boot shoved it across to her.

Thóra smiled politely and reached for it. "Why do you remember this so well?" she asked, looking around. Every wall was hung with drawings or photos of tattoos. "It looks like you do a lot of these. You can hardly be expected to remember each and every one." Unless he was a modern version of the old farmers who were said to be able to recognize every sheep marking in the country, she thought.

"Nah," said the man, crossing his muscular arms. When Thóra had first walked into the tiny, dilapidated tattoo parlor she had thought he was wearing a garish fitted T-shirt beneath his leather waistcoat. She was wrong. His arms were covered with colorful pictures from the backs of his hands up: tigers and rain forest foliage that rippled as though in the wind when he flexed or contracted his muscles. "I actually remember a lot of them. Usually the most beautiful ones, but also the really lame ones."

Thóra cleared her throat. "And which group does this belong to?" she asked, pointing at the photocopy of the *Love Sex* tattoo Bella had brought with her.

The man looked at Thóra with disdain. "That's fucked up, Grandma. Absolutely fucked up."

Thóra wanted to keep the man in a good mood, so she didn't waste any time objecting to being called grandma—after all, she was one, albeit prematurely. "And you remember this, even though it's been six months since you . . . did it?" she asked, uncertain which verb one used for tattooing. "I don't see a picture of it anywhere on your wall," she added, though it was impossible to rule out a picture of this particular tattoo being hidden there somewhere.

"I'm not about to hang that on my wall, any more than I would the hundreds of butterflies I've put on girls' ankles over the years," said the man, and he curled his lip in disgust. "If I had to say which I hate most, the butterflies or this disaster, then I would actually say this one. It's one of the saddest ones I've ever done—that girl was an absolute nutter, away with the fairies."

Thóra smiled to herself, thinking she had made a similarly hasty judgment of him just a few seconds earlier. "Did she explain what this was supposed to mean?"

"No," he said. "I didn't ask, either. I tried to talk her out of it, but she wouldn't listen. I even spent some time showing her other, much cooler illustrations, but it was like throwing pearls at swine."

Thóra thought about pointing out that one cast pearls before swine and not at them, but changed her mind. Instead she asked: "Did a woman by the name of Alda Thorgeirsdóttir ever ask you for information about this same tattoo? She was a nurse."

The man nodded his head. "Like I told her . . ." he pointed at Bella. "It's mental that more than one person has contacted me to ask about this horrible thing. I've never had the same reaction to any of the tattoos I'm actually proud of. If you want me to put the same one on you, the answer is no."

"Did Alda want to get the same tattoo?" asked Thóra.

"No," he replied, and smiled to reveal large teeth, stained brown by tobacco. "She wanted to know whether the tattoo had been done here, and when I said yes she wanted to know when."

"And could you answer her?"

"Yeah, yeah, I keep records of my tattoos so I just looked it up. The woman was so incredibly excited about it, I'd never seen anything like it. She said she was working on an investigation for the A&E, and this tattoo had turned up." The man stubbed out his cigarette, which had burned all the way down to the filter. "She pointed out that the investigation wasn't connected to me or my working methods in any way, not that I thought it would be, since I'm really careful with hygiene here."

"I'm sure you are," said Thóra, avoiding looking at a dirty spot on his black leather waistcoat. "Was it long ago that she called?"

"No, not really," replied the man. "Several weeks, two months at most. She said she'd been searching for the origin of the tattoo before but hadn't known about my parlor, since it wasn't in the phone book. She'd recently heard about me from a boy who wanted to get rid of a tattoo that I did." Again the man snarled in disgust. "The little tosser."

"Could we have that same information?" asked Thóra. "We won't use it against you, any more than the other woman did."

"As long as you don't let it get around where this crappy tattoo was done," grinned the man. "Apart from that it's no skin off my nose, provided I can find it quickly. I'm closed now, and I'd rather be on my way home."

The same went for Thóra.

Chapter 33

Monday, July 23, 2007

Sóley was asleep, her head in her mother's lap. Thóra stroked her daughter's hair as she reached for the remote and turned off the television. The show that had sent the little girl to dreamland had also been well on its way to sending Thóra there. She yawned, placed a pillow beneath the girl's head and spread a blanket over her. Sóley murmured a little in protest but did not wake up. Thóra took out the files that she'd brought with her from the office. After coming home from the tattoo parlor, Thóra had whipped up a meal—she boiled some water and poured it over a packet of ramen noodles. Afterward Gylfi had disappeared to Sigga's place, to spend the evening with her and their son Orri. So Thóra and Sóley had spent the evening alone together. They had made themselves comfy on the sofa when Sóley had finished her homework, but the television schedule was so dull that the little girl had fallen asleep during the first program they watched.

Thóra settled into the easy chair next to the sofa and looked at the top page, where she had written the name of the girl who had offended the tattooist's delicate artistic sensibilities: *Halldóra Dögg Einarsdóttir, 26 February 2007*. That was the day the girl had had her tattoo done, according to the man. This didn't tell Thóra anything, so she tried looking the girl up in the electoral register. She was born in 1982, so had been twenty-five years old at the time. Her name sounded familiar, so Thóra tried to search for her on the Internet, but found nothing.

Why had Alda been interested in this girl? Thóra guessed it wasn't because of the tattoo itself. For a moment she wondered if it could have been because of her job at the plastic surgeon's office, or for some unfathomable personal reason. She couldn't understand how the girl could be connected to Alda's murder, even though something told her she must be. Of course, there was one easy way to discover whether and how the girl knew Alda. Perhaps she would turn out to be the one Thóra had searched high and low for—the one to whom Alda had entrusted the secret of the head in the box. Markús really needed that to be the case. Thóra looked at the clock and saw that it was nine thirty, not too late for a phone call. She found the number in the phone book and made the call.

"Hi!" The voice sounded young, in a rather false way, as if the girl were trying to appear childish.

"Hello. Is this Halldóra Dögg Einarsdóttir?" Thóra asked.

"Speaking." The voice still sounded uncomfortably like a little girl's.

Thóra introduced herself and asked whether she might be able to ask her several questions, since her name had come up in a case involving her client.

Nothing could be heard on the other end of the line, but when the girl started talking again her voice was much more mature. "What case?" she asked, all her cheerfulness gone.

"It's a murder case," replied Thóra. "As I said, your name has come up in connection with it, and I wanted to take the opportunity to ask you some questions that might hopefully explain your connection to the murdered woman."

"Who's been murdered?" asked the girl. Her surprise was evident. Then she added, almost excitedly: "I haven't murdered anyone!"

"Sorry for not being clear," said Thóra. "You're not under any suspicion, and besides, I don't work for the police. I'm simply trying to rule out whether you're tied to the case indirectly. In other words, I'm in no way suggesting that you're linked to the murder at all."

"Did you say you're a lawyer?" asked the girl, still sounding very suspicious. "Are you working for Adolf?" Her voice turned shrill on the last word.

"No, not at all," said Thóra, wondering whether to admit she knew his name. She didn't take the risk. "The man I represent is named Markús."

"I don't know any Markús," said the girl angrily. "Are you sure you're not working for Adolf?"

"Absolutely sure," said Thóra. She decided to get to the point of the phone call. "Did you know a woman by the name of Alda Thorgeirsdóttir?" There was a long silence punctuated only by the girl's heavy breaths, and Thóra decided to repeat the question to be certain that the girl had understood her.

The girl drew a breath so sharp that a whistling sound could clearly be heard through the phone. Then she spoke again, her voice betraying her shock at the question. "How could you lie? Lawyers can't lie."

Thóra didn't understand what she meant. "Isn't it easier to answer this with a simple yes or no? I haven't lied to you about anything, if that's what you think."

"You *are* working for Adolf," hissed the girl. "I *know* you are, I should press charges against you."

"Press charges against me?" asked Thóra, flabbergasted. "I think there may have been a misunderstanding." She didn't want the girl to think she was afraid of this threat. "The only thing I'm trying to clear up is whether you knew Alda Thorgeirsdóttir or have heard of her."

A few moments passed before the girl replied. Thóra supposed that she was contemplating whether it would be better to deny this, confirm it or simply hang up. The name obviously rang some bells. "I know who she is," said the girl suddenly, her voice harsh.

"Could you tell me where or how you got to know her, or heard of her?" asked Thóra, pleased finally to be making some headway in this peculiar conversation.

"No," replied the girl. "I don't want to talk about it."

Thóra rolled her eyes. What now? "Did it have something to do with your tattoo? *Love Sex*?"

There was silence on the other end, then the girl hung up.

Thóra put down the thick sheaf of papers. She had had enough of what seemed to be an endless reckoning of every item that could conceivably have been taken from the houses that had been excavated. She still hadn't laid eyes on anything that could make a difference in Markús's case, except perhaps the countless broken bottles that had been found in Kjartan's garage and Dadi's shed. Thóra thought it was obvious that they'd hurriedly tried to hide the evidence of their stash of grain alcohol when the police investigation had started to point toward them. The list did not include Markús's home, since the house was still to be emptied when the list had been written, but Thóra hadn't noticed any bottles there, intact or broken. That didn't mean much; they could have been hidden in a part of the house that she hadn't seen, although she doubted it. Kjartan had been extremely convincing when he told her Magnús hadn't been involved in the smuggling operation. A flash of pain shot through her shoulders. She had to stand up and stretch.

She walked across her office and shook her hands to get the blood flowing better. She didn't know if this actually did anything, but she hoped so. In any case she was tired of this work, and bored. She took her seat again and reached for a piece of paper lying on the coffee table. On it was scribbled the name and telephone number of the defense lawyer in Adolf's rape case. The trial was imminent and Thóra had gone into the private offices of Reykjavík District Court to look up the defense counsel's name. She had hoped it might be someone she knew, so she could ask them for help finding possible links between the rape and Alda's murder. Even though Markús appeared no longer to be under suspicion of murdering his childhood crush, something told Thóra the cases were connected. Fortunately she recognized the name of the lawyer; they had studied together at university. Less fortunately, each time Thóra tried to call her the line was busy. She was starting to think the woman's phone was not turned on, but decided to try one more time before it got too late.

This time the lawyer's husband answered, and sighed heavily before he called her name. A thud indicated that the receiver had been dropped carelessly.

After a short pause Thóra heard the receiver being picked up again. "Svala speaking." The woman sounded out of breath.

"Hi, Svala, it's Thóra," she said. She added, "From the law department?"

"Oh, hi," said the woman, cheerful now. "Great to hear from you. How long has it been?"

"God," said Thóra, trying unsuccessfully to recall. "Far too long." They exchanged stories of what had happened in their lives, then Thóra got to the point. "Anyway, I have an ulterior motive," said Thóra. "I'm sorry to be out of touch for so long then call on official business. I'm working on an unusual case, and the name of your client has come up."

"Oh?" said Svala. "Which one? I have plenty, let me tell you."

"Adolf Dadason," replied Thóra. "It's a strange connection, like everything else in this case, and among other things it concerns a tattoo on a young woman by the name of Halldóra Dögg Einarsdóttir. She nearly threw a fit when I called her just a while ago, because she was convinced I was working for Adolf."

"What case is it actually that you're working on?" asked Svala quickly. "Not the one about the nurse?"

Thóra concurred. "My client is sitting in custody because of her murder, along with the discovery of some bodies on the Westmann Islands. The nurse, Alda, appears to have had some interest in Adolf and this particular tattoo. That led me to this girl, Halldóra Dögg. Is there any chance you could explain this to me? I'm in quite a fix with this case and I'm starting to fear it won't be solved, which would be inconvenient for my client."

Svala clicked her tongue. "I don't know anything about the tattoo," she said. "However, I do know a few things about this nurse and Halldóra Dögg." She took a deep breath. "Halldóra pressed charges against Adolf for rape. He maintains he didn't do it, and even though I've met a lot of assholes in cases like this, who always protest their innocence, I have a feeling he's telling the truth. Don't get me wrong, he's no angel; far from it. He's a nasty piece of work, in fact, but that doesn't mean he's broken the law. Still, everything points toward a guilty verdict, since the girl is so bloody convincing. On top of that, it seems she was drugged with contraceptive pills to prevent pregnancy, and a witness has come forward who says he bought these drugs for Adolf, and not for the first time either. It'll be difficult to get the judge to believe the purchase was made with good intentions—the man is single."

"But how does Alda fit into this?" asked Thóra. "Did she give him the drugs?"

"No, no," said Svala. "She and Adolf didn't know each other. She treated Halldóra when she finally checked into the hospital. This Alda was a kind of therapist to her, providing her with trauma counseling among other things. Alda's testimony looks very bad for Adolf. It deflates our argument that the girl's credibility is questionable since so much time passed between the alleged rape and her reporting it. Alda actually gave the police a statement in which she emphasized how common it was for a rape victim not to come forward immediately. In other words, she wasn't the witness I most looked forward to seeing on the stand."

"You got lucky," said Thóra. "She won't be testifying in this case."

"No, that's the problem. She actually changed her mind suddenly. She got in touch and asked to meet me, saying she had information that could clear Adolf of the charges."

"And what information was that?"

"I'll never know," said Svala sadly. "She died, or to be precise was murdered, before we were able to talk. She didn't want to tell me on the phone, so we'd set up a meeting for the next day. She was being very mysterious and I didn't get much sense out of her, I'm afraid."

"What did you ask her?"

"I was so dumbstruck when she called that I actually didn't know how to respond. At first I thought she'd lost her mind, and I wasn't even sure if I should speak to her. Naturally, I tried to get the information out of her, and when that didn't work I tried to find out the reason for her change of heart. It was a complete about-face, because the woman was really quite merciless about Adolf in her original police statement. Ruthless, even."

"She knew his parents," said Thóra. "Maybe she changed her opinion after she realized the rape suspect was her friends' son. She even knew him as a child."

"If that's the case, then the memory of Alda has completely disappeared from Adolf's mind. He says he's never heard of this woman, and would prefer to hear as little as possible about her."

"But he must have been disappointed that her testimony would never be heard," Thóra said. "There was a lot at stake for him."

"No," said Svala. "It's very strange—he simply shuts down if I try to talk about Alda or her testimony. I understood from Alda that she had tried repeatedly to speak to him, but hadn't been able to persuade him to see her. He didn't turn up when they arranged a meeting, and that's why she contacted me. That same evening, she was dead."

Thóra couldn't work this out. "But you're convinced he didn't know her? Could it be that the reason he's being so stubborn has something to do with an old issue between them?"

"No, I'm sure," replied Svala. "Maybe his parents knew her, but he didn't. They're both dead, so it's too late to ask them about it."

"Here's another strange thing," said Thóra. "Alda had a copy of the autopsy report on Adolf's mother. I don't know why; I wouldn't have thought anyone would be that interested in that kind of information about their friends or relatives. I understand the woman died because of some kind of medical malpractice."

"What?" gasped Svala. "She had the autopsy report?"

"Yes, in her desk at work. The doctors she worked for had no idea why. At least, she hadn't discussed the report with them, even though they could have explained its contents to her. It's not easy to understand at all. I had to get help figuring it out."

"You're telling me," said Svala. "Listen: the report is actually the basis of another case that I'm working on for Adolf. He's in litigation with the hospital where his mother died, and among other things, I've had to go through that same report. It was a medical error, as you said. The woman was given penicillin, but she had a severe allergy. The staff on duty didn't realize it when she was admitted." Svala thought for a moment before continuing: "But I have to confess, I'm really confused. Why was this woman so obsessed with Adolf and his business?"

"I don't know," admitted Thóra. "But I'm starting to think it's linked to her murder."

"Oh, God, no," sighed Svala. "It's more than enough having to get involved in two cases for this man. For God's sake, don't add murder."

Thóra smiled. "But what about this Halldóra?" she asked. "Could it be that she knew or had ties to Alda?"

"That I don't know," said Svala. "I think she's a little cow, actually; not all that bright, and not good-looking at all. So she's got very little going for her. You know, she's one of those girls who goes around with a bare midriff even though she's not exactly a supermodel. She doesn't want to talk to me at all—I've tried to reach her but she always hangs up."

"She hung up on me, too," said Thóra. "When I mentioned the tattoo, she ended the conversation."

"What is it about this tattoo? There's been nothing about a tattoo in Adolf's case."

"Alda had a picture of it in her desk drawer, a tattoo that says *Love Sex*. We found the tattoo parlor where it was done, and they told me Halldóra Dögg had had it drawn on her back. But that's all I know," said Thóra. "When I asked her about it, she responded by putting the phone down."

"Do you know when it was done?" asked Svala. "This hasn't been mentioned in any of the files I've seen, and I think I have everything."

Thóra reached for the piece of paper on which she'd written the information. "The twenty-sixth of February, 2007," she read. "The tattoo parlor is called Mirror of the Soul, if that helps at all."

"What?" said Svala. "What did you say?"

"Mirror of the Soul," repeated Thóra, surprised at the woman's interest in the name.

"No," said Svala impatiently. "When did she get this tattoo?" Thóra repeated the date. "And it says *Love Sex*?" asked Svala, still sounding surprised.

"Yes," answered Thóra. "Not exactly a work of art."

"Maybe not," said Svala, obviously pleased. "But very good news for Adolf."

Chapter 34

Tuesday, July 24, 2007

In front of Thóra sat the man from the picture in Alda's desk, Adolf Dadason. He was older than he looked in the photo, and even better looking. There was something attractive about him, even though Thóra knew he was a waste of space. Svala hadn't tried to make any excuses for his character; she had even offered the opinion that his behavior was typical of the kind of man who put his own interests and desires before everything else. So his charisma didn't come from his personality, only from his physical appearance. Adolf was the living incarnation of a one-night stand, a man who offered sex without emotion. He would no doubt have prospered in prehistoric times. Thóra could feel herself attracted to him in a way, but at the same time she pitied him for existing during the wrong time period. She hastily directed her gaze elsewhere when he suddenly looked up at her from beneath his heavy brow, as if he knew what she was thinking. Before she looked away, she saw one corner of his mouth lift in an ironic smile. She felt as if he were inviting her to go to some out-of-the-way place and have a quickie before they went any further. Thóra was relieved when Svala broke the silence.

"You realize, Adolf, that you owe a great debt to Thóra, and it's only fair that you assist her in return. If she hadn't contacted me, your case would be hard to win, but now it looks as though we may be able to clear your name." Svala hesitated a moment, but then added: "Almost, anyway. We don't know how the judge will react to you having drugged the girl with emergency contraceptives."

Thóra watched Adolf, whose face didn't change as his lawyer spoke. Svala had arranged this meeting at Thóra's request, after their phone conversation the night before. She had been so happy with the information about the date of Halldóra's tattoo that Thóra suspected she would have done even more if Thóra had asked her to. "You do understand how important the tattoo is?" pressed Svala, when Adolf showed no reaction.

He shrugged his shoulders, looking bored. "Yes, yes. It's all the same to me."

Svala put her hands on the desk. They were sitting in her office at the legal firm where she worked. The furniture appeared to be brand-new and very expensive, and even the computer on the table seemed to be from a different generation to the piece of junk Thóra used, with its clunky monitor. Freshly brewed espresso fitted perfectly with the whole image, and it didn't hurt that it was accompanied by chocolates. Visitors to Thóra's firm should be grateful if Bella had remembered to buy milk for their coffee, or the coffee itself, for that matter. This was one of the advantages of working for a large legal firm: decent coffee and better conditions. At the moment Thóra couldn't see any disadvantages, although there must have been some. "No one goes and gets a tattoo that reads *Sex*, much less *Love Sex*, under forty-eight hours after they were raped. This strengthens your declaration that the sex with Halldóra Dögg was consensual."

Adolf sat there silently, expressionless, so Thóra decided to join in the discussion. "It would help me if I could ask you something about Alda's role in this," she said. "As Svala said before, Alda was interested in this tattoo."

Adolf shifted in his seat. "I know nothing about that woman," he said, and glanced out of the window, which had a wonderful view of the city. "She was against me at first, and then all of a sudden on my side."

Svala smiled warily. "That's not entirely true. She told me she contacted you. You even planned to meet up."

"Yes," said Adolf, then added after a brief silence: "Alda did actually contact me. But I changed my mind about meeting her."

"Do you know why she wanted to talk to you?" Thóra asked. "She could just as easily have contacted the police if she only wanted to give them information pertinent to the case."

"No, I don't know why," Adolf replied, still looking out of the window.

"Didn't she mention why, when she called—or did she come to visit you?" asked Thóra, not knowing how Alda had contacted the man. When Adolf did not reply, she added: "You realize that she knew your parents, don't you?"

Adolf shifted again in his chair without saying anything. "How about you answer the lady?" said Svala testily. "These aren't complicated questions."

"I'm not sure I should say anything about it," said Adolf calmly, now looking at his lawyer. "It's not as simple as you think." Svala started to say something, but stopped. "As you know, I'm involved in more than one case right now."

"Do you mean the hospital case?" asked Svala. "Are the two cases connected?"

"No," replied Adolf dryly. "But I need to speak to you in private before we go any further."

Thóra did not object. Adolf was Svala's client and it was right that his interests had precedence over a favor for an old university classmate. She nodded consent as Adólf and Svala left the office together, leaving her with the view. She was happy not to have had to leave the room, as it would have been awkward to wait outside while they discussed things. It also gave her space to consider what this meant, and to try to understand Alda's connection to the death of Adolf's mother. She wanted to ask Adolf if he had any idea why Alda had got hold of his mother's autopsy report. Given how long his corridor conversation with Svala was taking, she was sure he knew the answer. Had Alda also discovered something that could help Adolf get financial compensation for his mother's accidental death? Where could such information have been found? Had Alda spotted something in the autopsy report that Thóra and others had overlooked? Thóra had barely been able to get through the document, so she wouldn't have been capable of noticing anything unusual.

The door opened and Svala stuck her head through the gap. "Who is Alda's next of kin?" she asked.

Thóra looked at the woman in surprise. This seemed an odd

and irrelevant question from someone she had always found very straightforward, but she replied without comment that she imagined Alda's sister or parents must be her heirs, although she hadn't ever checked.

"Precisely, so no children, in other words," said Svala, and closed the door again. Thóra sat and stared at it. She hadn't had time to form an opinion on any of this when the door reopened and Svala appeared in the gap once more. "Do you know anything about her estate?" she asked. "What there is to be divided?"

Thóra raised her eyebrows. "Not in any detail. I know that she owned her house but it's impossible to say how much she owed on the mortgage. It couldn't have been very much, because she bought it long before the prices went up. I believe she'd lived there a long time." Thóra didn't recall whether Alda had any other property. "May I ask why you're discussing this?"

"Give me two minutes," said Svala, and the door slammed shut again. Fifteen minutes later she and Adolf reappeared. Thóra had started to grow uncomfortable. She had a lot to do before going to the courtroom at two o'clock. Luckily she'd managed to get Svala to arrange the meeting for nine in the morning, but if it went on like this it would be almost eleven when Thóra finally made it back to her office. "Well," said Svala, taking a seat at her desk. "It would appear that Adolf has a little story to tell you. It might improve your client's position, but it also might make it worse. We'll just have to wait and see. It's up to you; do you want to hear it, or should we let it go?"

Thóra chose the former. As things stood, any new information could only help Markús. The limbo he was in now was unbearable for him. Even if the court didn't rule against him, a large percentage of the Islands' population would always be convinced of his guilt, particularly if the custody extension was granted.

"Tell her what you told me, Adolf," said Svala. It was clear from her tone that she was not best pleased with him. "I stand by what I told you in the corridor. You'll benefit more by telling your story than by keeping it to yourself."

Adolf did not appear convinced, but began nevertheless. "Alda came to see me," he said slowly. "She rang first, but then came anyway after I refused to talk to her."

"Did she want to talk about the tattoo?" asked Thóra.

He shook his head, his expression just as unreadable as when Thóra had first set eyes on him earlier that morning. "She called me originally to shout at me," he said. "It was shortly after that silly bitch Halldóra accused me of rape, and at first I didn't have any idea who this woman was; I thought it must be her mother, or something."

Thóra looked at Svala. "Did you know this?" she asked. "That the nurse who treated the girl had phoned the suspect to give him a piece of her mind?"

Svala shook her head. "I heard most of this for the first time just now. It'll become clear why he kept it secret." She gestured at Adolf to continue. "There's more. Much more."

Thóra turned back to him. "So she just called you and started yelling without introducing herself?"

"No, she did introduce herself, but her name meant nothing to me," replied Adolf. "After she'd called me several times, just as hysterical each time, I stopped answering the phone." He straightened in his chair. "You can't blame me—who'd want some old fishwife hollering at them day and night?"

"How much time had passed from the date of the alleged rape before Alda first called you?" asked Thóra.

Adolf thought for a moment. "About a month. No, a little longer. Maybe two."

"And did she say anything about why she was calling?"

"No. She was completely crazy" Adolf shrugged. "She probably believed Halldóra, and thought I was a rapist. Maybe she was hoping that if she kept on at me long enough I'd confess to their trumped-up charges."

Thóra knew this hadn't been the first rape case Alda had been involved in, but had no idea whether her reaction was an isolated incident. Perhaps phone calls like these had been the reason Alda had been advised to take a leave of absence. "Do you think she was a friend of Halldóra's, or was it that she realized she knew your parents?"

"She didn't know that lying cow Halldóra," said Adolf. "I actually called her to ask how she managed to get a nurse on her side in her smear campaign."

Svala gasped. "You called the girl? She didn't mention that in the police statement, and the prosecutor hasn't said anything about it either."

"Maybe Halldóra didn't want anyone to know about the phone call. She actually wanted to talk to me, and she offered to drop the charges if I would go out with her." Adolf frowned. "It's like I've always said—her pride was hurt. I don't know what I was thinking dragging her home with me that night, but I was drunk and high and didn't realize what a dog she was. The next morning she clearly thought she'd hit the jackpot and kept going on about our 'relationship' and God knows what else. I got rid of her as quickly as I could, but she came back the next night. I let her in by mistake and it was like she thought we'd become an item. Why couldn't she see how badly we went together, her always talking, talking, talking and me . . . ?" He didn't finish the sentence.

"So when did she decide to press charges against you?" asked Thóra. "You sleep together and the next evening she comes to visit. And after that, just under another twenty-four hours go by before she makes her allegation." Thóra knew she'd gone beyond the limits of what pertained directly to Alda's murder, but she wanted to have everything clear before they discussed the woman. That way she could get a better feeling for Adolf's reactions, and she might be able to tell if he was lying about anything important.

Adolf looked at Svala, who indicated that he should continue. "I gave her pills on her second visit, to stop her from getting pregnant. I thought I'd forgotten them the night before because I was so drunk. That's the only reason I let her in." He didn't even have the decency to look ashamed when he said this. "But it turns out I probably did remember on Saturday night, so she got a large enough—"

Svala interrupted him, either embarrassed by his insensitivity or in a hurry to conclude the meeting. "Anyway, the girl started bleeding heavily and went to A&E. That's where we see what kind of person she is: she put two and two together and started coming after Adolf. After the thing with the morning-after pills came out, she said she'd been raped."

"She called me from the hospital, while she was waiting for the doctor or something," Adolf said suddenly. "She asked whether I'd done this, and what was I thinking since we were a couple. I laughed at her because it was so ridiculous. I probably shouldn't have done that. She went completely nuts and said I would regret it. Then she went and shouted rape after I hung up on her. That's what she's like, she's mental."

Svala cleared her throat. "You didn't tell me about this before," she said. "We could easily check out the phone call."

"I didn't rape her. I thought at least I'd be considered innocent until proven guilty. I didn't *do* anything." Adolf stared at each of them in turn, his eyes shining with the conviction of a simpleton. "I didn't want to have to admit what I did with the drug. I'll get a bad reputation on the scene."

Thóra supposed the "scene" was picking up young women in bars. All the feelings this man had stirred in her before he opened his mouth had long since gone cold. She was glad she never went out on the town, and that it would be many years before Sóley would start doing so; she had heard enough about Adolf and Halldóra's "relationship." "You claim Halldóra didn't know Alda," she said. "But you haven't told me whether Alda realized who your parents were. Was that what inspired the phone call?"

Adolf bared his teeth a little. He reminded Thóra uncomfortably of a snake. "I never said she didn't know Alda; she knew her, but it wasn't her that got Alda to call me. Halldóra said Alda was her counselor or something." He shrugged. "As far as my parents are concerned, you've got to remember that while all of this was going on I was tied up in a lawsuit with the hospital that murdered my mother."

Thóra raised her eyebrows; "murdered" was a bit extreme for a medical error. "I do know about that, yes."

"You'll remember that his mother died when she was given a large dose of penicillin, even though she was allergic to it," interjected Svala. "I'm about to reach a settlement with the hospital, compensating Adolf for their mistake."

Thóra was already aware of all this. "I understand that you brought a lawsuit against the hospital," she said patiently, "but why don't you carry on telling me about Alda?"

"The thing is, I didn't want anything to get in the way of me getting the compensation, so that's why I wasn't pleased about Alda harassing me," said Adolf. "After the first phone call she seemed to give up, so I just stopped worrying about it. But then she started calling me again a few months later, and even though she didn't sound quite as crazy this time she was basically spouting the same old rubbish underneath it all. I didn't want to hear it, which is why I hung up on her. I stopped answering the phone even after she said she had information that could help me, and kept apologizing over and over for having wrongly accused me." He closed his eyes. "Once I humored her and said I'd meet her at a café, but then I changed my mind. I have no idea if she showed up or not."

"Was that shortly before she was murdered?" asked Thóra.

"Yes. Something like that," replied Adolf mysteriously. "I actually saw her several days before she died. She came to my house all smiles and apologies, like I said. I let her talk, then gave up and threw her out. She never called again, and I thought she had finally got the message that I didn't want anything to do with her. Then I saw the obituary in the papers a few days later." He smiled nastily. "The phone calls stopped automatically, in other words."

"Have you ever been to Alda's house?" asked Svala anxiously. Then she added: "Don't say anything if you have."

"No, I've never been to her house and I have no idea where she lives," replied Adolf.

"*Lived*," Thóra corrected him. "She's dead, as we know." She took a deep breath before continuing. Hopefully this would lead to something useful rather than just ending up as a lesson in the psychology of self-obsessed individuals. "Why was Alda so interested in you and this case?" she asked again. "Was it because of your parents?"

Adolf grinned at her. It was as if he suddenly realized that he alone had information that Thóra needed. He seemed determined to make the most of it. "You're in luck," he said, staring at her. "I wouldn't be telling you this if Alda had died penniless."

"In that case, it's certainly lucky that she didn't," said Thóra, unsmiling. "And are you ever going to get around to telling me, or not?" She wasn't going to jump through hoops for him. The police would squeeze it out of him if necessary.

The corners of Adolf's mouth drooped. "Of course I've only got her word for it," he muttered. "It might be bullshit."

"We'll let others be the judge of that," said Svala. "Tell her what Alda said."

"Okay," said Adolf, shifting in his chair to face Thóra. "She said she was my mother." He looked away again. "I'm not the person I thought I was." Then he added nonchalantly: "If it *is* true then I'm her natural heir, of course, so I don't care which of them was my mother. I can inherit from both of them." He shot a sideways glance at Svala. "It's a win-win situation," he said with a grin.

Thóra stared at his swarthy features and pictured Alda, blonde and fair-skinned. Two less similar people were hardly possible to imagine. Had Alda been out of her mind? She didn't have any children: the autopsy report had even stated clearly that she'd never given birth. Thóra's mind was racing, there were so many questions. Could Alda have donated her eggs to Valgerdur, making Adolf a test-tube baby? She couldn't remember when such technology had first made it to Iceland, but it seemed doubtful that it had been available in the 1970s. If Alda were this man's mother, who could the father be? Markús? Did this mean Valgerdur Bjólfsdóttir did not raise Adolf? And if not, where was the son she raised?

Chapter 35
Tuesday, July 24, 2007

Adolf was born on October 27, 1973, so it wasn't hard to estimate his conception at some time around the eruption in January. Could Alda be his mother? After the meeting with Svala and Adolf, Thóra immediately called Litla-Hraun Prison in the hope that Markús would shed some light on Adolf's assertion. She had no idea what Markús was thinking as she told him the story; he hotly denied that it was possible, but then had to admit that Alda had dropped off his radar for precisely the same period as the alleged pregnancy, and actually rather longer, since she wasn't seen for almost a year. He repeatedly expressed his shock at "this bullshit" and wondered aloud who could possibly believe that Alda would have kept this a secret from him. Thóra wasn't as convinced as him, and knew that at least one other person knew the truth of the matter: Alda's mother. She hurried to finish her conversation with Markús but was careful to promise him that they would meet before the district court made its decision on the custody extension. She reassured him that everything pointed toward that decision going his way. Markús was obviously nervous and reluctant to end the conversation, but Thóra finally managed to calm him down and hang up.

Before she tried to talk to Alda's mother, she had to clear up one thing. Was it possible that Alda had actually had a child, even though the autopsy report stated that she'd never given birth? Thóra called Hannes. As she scrolled down to his number she smiled to herself. Since the divorce, this was the second phone call in a row which was not about the children. It was a record. "Hi, Hannes," she said when he finally answered. "I know you're at work so I'll keep this short. Is there any way a woman could have delivered a child, even though her autopsy report says she never gave birth?"

After a drawn-out explanation Hannes finally answered Thóra in layman's terms. The autopsy clarified whether a child had exited through the birth canal; a woman's vagina and other reproductive organs were inspected, especially if death hadn't occurred naturally. A woman could have a child without there being any sign of it in the vagina, if she had a Caesarean section, but that would also be evident in an autopsy, from scarring in the stomach and uterus.

"The report didn't mention scars from a Caesarean section," said Thóra. "Although she had had breast enhancements. Could surgery like that erase traces of a birth?"

Hannes said that he was no specialist, either in plastic surgery or forensic pathology, but thought that such scars could be removed as part of a plastic surgery procedure. But that didn't explain why there had been no scars on the uterus wall.

"Is it possible that the doctor simply overlooked it?" asked Thóra. "The autopsy wasn't primarily concerned with whether she'd had a child."

Hannes wouldn't comment on that, no matter how hard Thóra pressed him. She said good-bye, feeling no closer to the truth. However, it clearly wasn't out of the question that Alda had given birth, so Thóra decided to go ahead and try to arrange another meeting with Alda's mother. If Adolf were Alda's son, it would explain a lot: her reaction when he was accused of rape, and the picture of him in her desk.

Thóra's only hope of getting to Alda's mother was to go through Jóhanna again. The woman would have no more desire than before to meet someone representing the suspect in her daughter's murder. However, Thóra had to hurry; she needed to be finished before Markús's custody hearing at two that afternoon.

The woman who answered at the bank said that unfortunately Jóhanna was not in. She sounded young, and sympathy dripped from every word. When Thóra explained that her business was very urgent and asked where Jóhanna could be reached, the girl's voice became even sadder. Jóhanna was in Reykjavík for the funeral of her sister, and she doubted she would have her mobile turned on, under the circumstances. Nevertheless, Thóra took the number, thanked her and made the call.

An electronic message informed Thóra that the phone was either switched off or out of range. It was ten thirty. Thóra had only attended two funerals in her life, both at Fossvogur Chapel. She tried phoning there, but was told that no one by Alda's name was being buried there that day or indeed that week. The man she spoke to said he unfortunately couldn't guess where the burial was taking place, because there were many other options. He also said that almost without exception, funerals were not advertised; such sacred occasions were reserved only for the next of kin. So it was pointless to look in the papers, which had been next on Thóra's list.

She tried to imagine who might have been invited to Alda's funeral but came up with no one besides Dís. She didn't know whether colleagues were generally considered "next of kin," but tried the plastic surgeon's office anyway. The answering machine announced that calls would only be answered after noon that day due to illness. Thóra couldn't wait that long if she wanted to make it to court by two. In the end the only man that she could think of, when all other doors had slammed shut, was Leifur.

Only seven minutes passed between her saying good-bye to Leifur and his return call to say that the funeral was taking place in the Midtown Church at two o'clock. The location could only have been more perfect if the ceremony had been due to take place in the courtroom itself, as the Midtown Church was right around the corner. Thóra thanked Leifur, without telling him why she needed this information. He didn't ask, though he must have been curious. In fact, she had the feeling he didn't want to talk to her in case she found more evidence for his father's involvement in the murders. If that was the case, it was fine by her—Thóra was happy not to have to discuss the case with him.

She hurried out of Svala's office into the pouring rain. The heavy drops reminded her more of a monsoon in a foreign country than Icelandic rain, and she darted over to the little car she'd bought after selling her big jeep, which she couldn't afford to keep running. Perhaps Alda's mother was already at the Midtown Church, helping to prepare for the ceremony—and if not, the priest might know where she was. She might be at Alda's house, or any hotel in Reykjavík. It was impossible for Thóra to decide if a parent would prefer to sleep among the belongings of their dead child or rest their head on the pillows of an impersonal hotel room.

It was no easier than usual finding a parking space downtown. Thóra decided to drive around near the church until she finally came across someone leaving a parking space, and she waited as the elderly woman pulled out slowly in her Yaris. At first it looked as if Thóra would have to search for another space, but she finally managed to squeeze the car nimbly into the tight space. She allowed herself a couple of seconds in the pouring rain to congratulate herself on her driving ability. In fact the car was a little too far from the curb, but she should be returning shortly so she let it be. She was not at all sure she would do any better on the second try.

She could hear soft organ music through the thick wooden door as she stood in the rain outside the church. She hoped this didn't mean the ceremony was under way. She had no desire to wander into the middle of a solemn moment not meant for strangers. Of course, it was going to be just as tasteless to shoulder her way up to a grieving mother she barely knew, but at least it was for a noble cause. She opened the door cautiously as the organist stopped in the middle of the tune, before starting on finger exercises. Thóra shook rain from her jacket in the foyer before putting her ear against the door to the church itself. The organ notes overwhelmed almost all other noises, but she thought she could distinguish the murmur of voices within. She cracked open the door and peered though. Toward the front of the church sat two women, staring at a white coffin in front of the altar. One of them stood up and walked toward it, and from behind Thóra could tell that it was Jóhanna, Alda's sister. The short, gray hair of the woman still seated belonged to their mother. Thóra slipped in. She was hoping to reach the women before they became aware of her, so she tried to keep the old door from creaking.

"I would have wanted to have the coffin open," she heard Jóhanna say, as she tenderly stroked the gleaming lid of the casket. "I think Alda would have wanted it that way."

As Thóra drew closer she heard the older woman give a snort.

"You wouldn't say that if you knew how her face looked, with all those scratches on it. She wouldn't have dreamed of letting people see her like that while she was alive."

"It could have been fixed with makeup," said Jóhanna testily. She turned to the coffin again, laying both hands on it. They rested there, motionless. "It would have been okay."

"If you want to see her for the last time I'm sure we can get the sexton to take the lid off," replied the old lady, without a trace of sensitivity. "I was here before when they brought her, and I got to see her." She hung her head. "I wouldn't recommend it. This isn't Alda anymore. She's ice cold and I'm sure she's been brought here straight from cold storage. I wished I hadn't been here."

Thóra was just one row behind the two women when she cleared her throat to draw their attention. She didn't want to startle them, and felt uncomfortable to be practically spying on them. The organ music had made it possible for her to get this close, drowning out the low creaking of the floorboards. She would probably have been able to place her hand on the old woman's shoulder before being noticed.

Both of the women turned and stared at Thóra. "What are you doing here?" asked Jóhanna in surprise.

"And how dare you come here?" exclaimed her mother, almost choking. "Don't you know that we're preparing for my daughter's funeral? This isn't the place for someone who defends her murderer." Anger had overcome the sorrow in her voice.

"Markús didn't murder her," said Thóra calmly, suppressing her discomfort at having disturbed mother and daughter at this private moment. "He has a good alibi that proves it was impossible for him to have been anywhere near her at the time."

Until that point Jóhanna had resembled a sleepwalker, but at this she seemed to brighten up slightly. Her face was even more haggard than Thóra recalled; her hair was dirty, and her clothing showed signs of neglect. Her mother, however, had taken the time to fix herself up, and looked respectable. Of course, the difference in their appearance did not necessarily mean that the mother hadn't taken the loss as hard as her daughter. Perhaps she had found it a comfort to have something to occupy herself, even if it were only making herself presentable for the funeral. The corners of her pink-painted lips turned down like a nearly perfect horseshoe, further emphasizing the contrast between mother and daughter. "Of course he has an alibi," said the old woman, adding sarcastically: "His brother Leifur wouldn't have had any trouble sorting that out."

"No," said Thóra, staying calm. "That's not true." She wondered whether she should explain the alibi, but decided not to. They would either accept what she had to say, or not. "Markús is going before the judge today because of a police request that his detention be extended. It's easy to prove that he didn't murder Alda, but it's proving harder to clear him of something that happened out on the Islands." She looked into the old woman's eyes, which were burning with rage. "Most of the people who know what happened there are either too ill to be able to help him, or are no longer with us."

"And why are you looking at me?" asked Alda's mother, putting one hand to her throat dramatically. "I haven't murdered anyone, if that's what you're insinuating."

"Of course not," Thóra replied. "But I think you know, or at least have an idea, who these men were. I'm fairly certain that it was something to do with Markús's father Magnús, and Dadi, who is deceased. Your husband may also have played a part."

The woman stared at Thóra without saying a word. Jóhanna looked from one of them to the other, her eyes wide. "Is that true, Mother? Is Markús locked up for a murder that Father committed?"

"Utter nonsense," her mother spat, without looking at her daughter. She continued to glare at Thóra. "I must ask you to leave. Unfortunately, I cannot help you. If Magnús and Dadi did something, that's too bad, but I cannot answer for it."

"Did Alda have a child?" asked Thóra suddenly. Jóhanna looked almost relieved at this question, perhaps thinking that it confirmed Thóra had a screw loose. Her mother, on the other hand, appeared startled.

"What now? More nonsense?" asked the woman, but she wouldn't meet Thóra's gaze.

"I met a young man this morning who told me that Alda contacted him repeatedly and insisted that she was his mother," continued Thóra. It was best to strike while the iron was hot. "Is he lying?"

"What is she talking about, Mother?" asked Jóhanna, querulously. "Is this the secret Alda was going to tell me?" she said, turning her bewildered face to Thóra.

"I don't know," said Thóra honestly. "All I know is that Alda disappeared for a while. She was supposedly a student at Ísafjördur Junior College for about the same length of time as her pregnancy, if the story is true. But no one there knows anything about her. That's why I'm wondering whether the man's claim might be true."

"Who is this man?" asked the old woman, and added frantically: "I mean, is he mentally ill, or something?"

Thóra shrugged. "That's neither here nor there. I'm not going to discuss him with you if he's *not* Alda's son, as you suggest. If that were the case, he wouldn't have anything to do with you."

The old woman's head dropped. Thóra expected to be chastised again, but instead the old woman's shoulders started to shake, at first slightly, then more rapidly. Jóhanna went to her mother and sat down at her side. She put her arm around her shoulders, and little by little they stopped trembling. "Oh, God," the old woman said, but couldn't continue through her sobs. After a while she said: "I've done so many bad things in my life. So many bad things. I should be lying in that coffin. Not Alda." She still did not look up.

"Everyone makes mistakes," said Thóra automatically. "It's how you learn from them that matters."

The woman shook her head. A moment later she raised her eyes pleadingly toward the white coffin that rested on a low platform before the altar. "That's exactly what everyone fails to do. Everyone." She fell silent and Thóra kept quiet too, thinking it would be best to give her a little time. She was afraid Alda's mother might withdraw into her shell if she pushed too hard to get in. The woman spoke again: "Everything was different back then. Everything young people take for granted today didn't exist. We had to work for everything."

"Did Alda have a child?" asked Jóhanna angrily. "What is this about?" Thóra glared at her, not wanting her to rock the boat. Jóhanna pretended not to notice. "Who was the father?" she demanded.

Fat tears leaked down the old woman's cheeks and fell onto the dark blue shawl she wore around her neck. There they formed a spreading dark stain. "She was raped. By a foreigner." She was speaking to Jóhanna as if Thóra were not even present. "She went to hospital in a terrible state and she was treated there. They called us from there. I've never seen anything like it in my life."

Thóra had no desire to hear the description of Alda after the rape.

"And she discovered she was pregnant after the attack?" she asked, as gently as possible.

The woman gave Thóra a startled look, then nodded. "Yes. Fate can be so cruel, and more often than not to the most beautiful souls. She was just a girl, had maybe kissed one boy, probably not even that. She was so good and obedient that we never had any problems with her, unlike so many kids her age. Just once she does something differently, and then her world falls apart. Once."

Jóhanna sat speechless next to her mother, which prompted Thóra to keep the conversation going. She drew a deep breath. "She drank alcohol that night, didn't she? Like all the kids?"

The old woman nodded. "She wasn't the worst. If she had been any drunker we would have been called and asked to pick her up. Instead, she was allowed to walk home." The woman stared into her lap. "She knew we would find out about it, so she decided to give herself some time to sober up. She went down to the harbor, thinking the sea air would help. There she met that terrible man. He was drunk, and he had his way with her. She couldn't offer any resistance even though she fought back as hard as she could. She was so small and delicate, my darling child."

"And is that monster one of the bodies in the basement?" asked Thóra, hoping that the question wouldn't make her clam up. The woman said nothing, so Thóra tried again. "I have a daughter myself, and I can well imagine what flies through the minds of the parents when something like this happens. The worst of it is that we can't do anything to change it. But Markús has a son, a son who doesn't deserve to have his father locked up for the wrong reason. For his sake, the truth has to come out."

The woman did not look up, but somehow this seemed to move her, and when she spoke again her tone was more determined. "When

Geiri found out from Alda at the hospital who had done it, he rushed out," she said flatly, as if she were reciting a script. "I tried to dissuade him, but it meant nothing. He left me at her bedside and went and got Magnús. One for all and all for one. They caught the men down at the harbor, on their boat, which Alda had described to her father. The men were still blind drunk; there were four of them, and two of them were sleeping. Geiri went into a rage, and Maggi wasn't much better. Geiri was completely covered in blood when he came home."

Thóra said nothing. Thorgeir, Alda's father, and Magnús, Markús's father, were the murderers. According to this account, Dadi had had nothing to do with it. "Did they use a salmon priest and a large ornamental knife?" asked Thóra, certain she knew what the answer would be.

"No," said the old woman, shaking her head gloomily. "They boarded their own ship and fetched a filleting knife and club they had there. They threw them into the harbor afterward."

Thóra didn't react, although this surprised her. She had been so sure that the mallet and knife had been used. This meant there had to be another reason they were kept among the children's clothing in the storeroom. "Did anyone know about this?" asked Thóra. "It couldn't have happened without anyone noticing." She pushed down the image of the beatings that sprang to her mind. They were obviously the source of the pool of blood at the pier.

"Dadi, Valgerdur's husband, went after them," said the woman. "Valgerdur was on duty when Alda arrived at the hospital, and it was she who called and told us what had happened to Alda. I had the feeling she enjoyed giving us the news. Then she hung around the whole time that Alda was crying and telling us what had happened. She offered to call Dadi and get him to find the man, and that's what he did. He stumbled on Magnús and my Geiri at the fateful moment."

"So Dadi was a witness to it?" asked Thóra. The woman nodded. "And he told no one?"

The woman smiled coldly. "No, he didn't."

"The police never heard anything about it, apart from being notified about the pool of blood the next morning?" exclaimed Thóra.

She had always suspected Gudni knew more than he was letting on, but it seemed she had misread him. Maybe he had been trying to hide his suspicions, not his knowledge.

"No," replied Alda's mother. "Naturally they suspected something because of all the blood on the pier, but they didn't find any other evidence so they couldn't do much about it. Then the eruption started, and people had other things to think about."

"But what about Dadi and Valgerdur?" asked Thóra. "I've been led to understand that she was quite a gossip. How were they able to keep quiet about it? Dadi was even questioned about the pool of blood. He was spotted with Magnús at the scene that night, though the police never heard about it."

"Dadi offered to help us," said the woman with a humorless laugh. "Two of the men had died on the boat, and they were left there. Geiri and Maggi had beaten the other two to death on the pier, then dragged them on board. The only way they could think of to hide what they'd done was to move the smack farther out in the harbor. Dadi helped them do that, then came to see us that night—along with Valgerdur, who by then was off duty—and offered to get the bodies and the boat out of there before anyone stirred down at the harbor. Geiri and Magnús were in shock after the incident, and in no condition to clean up after themselves." Thóra nodded in encouragement, her eyes wide. "Geiri phoned Maggi, who had gone home, and he came around. It was agreed that Dadi and Valgerdur would make sure no one would suspect a thing. Then they left, and I don't know what happened next. I didn't want to know anything else. Magnús went with them." The woman shuddered. "I was in shock, though I didn't realize it at the time. Geiri had a job but I wasn't working, and we had two girls to take care of, one of them in a terrible state. If he'd gone to prison, everything would have fallen apart."

"Who cut off the man's head?" asked Thóra. She assumed the one who'd been decapitated was the one who had raped Alda.

The woman looked at Thóra in bewilderment. "That I don't know," she said, and seemed to be completely sincere. "I never saw the bodies, and no one mentioned anything like that. I was absolutely staggered when they were found. But I can't say he didn't deserve it." This last was said without any bitterness or triumph, the words seeming to come out automatically.

Thóra suddenly felt sure that it was Alda who had gone from the hospital down to the harbor and cut off the rapist's head. She did not want to ask her mother about it, but it would explain how the girl had ended up with the head. "Could Alda have left the hospital that night?" she asked, without explaining herself any further.

"I doubt it. She was on sedatives. Valgerdur said she was sleeping when she went off duty. Why do you ask?"

Thóra did not reply, but instead asked how the bodies had ended up in Magnús's basement. "Did he help Dadi move them?"

The woman shook her head. "No, he didn't. Magnús actually went back down to the harbor with Dadi to rescue a falcon he'd seen in a cage onboard the foreigners' boat, and to take any valuables they had there. The finances of his and Geiri's company were in very bad shape. I believe he couldn't bring himself to look into the cupboard where they'd shoved the bodies, so I'm sure he never offered to keep them at his place. The plan was to sink the fishing smack with the bodies still on board."

"Turns out they were bird smugglers," said Thóra. This explained Magnús's rambling about birds. He was still wondering whether the falcon he had freed had survived.

"That's what Geiri said," replied the woman. "In fact onboard they found a map showing some likely nesting sites of eagles and falcons. No one knows whether they already had the falcon, or whether they'd captured him on this trip. Magnús let it go that night in the hope that it would return to the wild."

Jóhanna was staring at her mother. Thóra couldn't imagine what was going through her mind. Was she too angry to speak, or struck dumb with shock?

"Why did Dadi and Valgerdur want to help you?" Thóra asked. "Were they not as unfriendly as I've been told?"

Again a cold smile appeared on the old woman's face. "There's no such thing as a free lunch," she said. "But it's not always the right person who has to pay."

Thóra didn't understand. "What do you mean? Did they want to be paid for keeping it quiet and disposing of the bodies?"

"Yes," she whispered. "In return, Magnús was supposed to take the blame for everything in a case for which Dadi was under suspicion. Smuggling liquor, which he'd been doing for years. Magnús agreed to it, since he hardly had a choice. Murder and smuggling aren't exactly comparable crimes in the eyes of the courts, nor of the public for that matter." The woman paused and drew a deep breath. "Our payment was even higher. Valgerdur had persuaded Alda to tell her at the hospital where she was in her menstrual cycle. If she turned out to be carrying a child, they wanted to take it in secret and bring it up themselves." She looked into Thóra's eyes. "Alda paid her debt to those barbarians; she agreed to it after we worked up the courage to tell her everything. Under normal circumstances, she would have had an abortion. Valgerdur threw out her medical report and made sure Alda was discharged before the doctors came round the wards the next morning. She told the nurses on the night shift that Alda was there to sleep off her drunkenness, that she was the daughter of a friend of Valgerdur and that she was doing her a favor. She asked them to keep quiet about it, which they did. So no one looked in on Alda until we returned early the next morning to fetch her—what was left of her. She was never the same again."

"Did Markús have anything to do with it?" asked Thóra. "Was he connected to the murders in any way?"

"No," said the woman. "He was just one of the kids who drank too much. He was lying at home on the couch dead drunk, according to Magnús. He never came near any of it."

Thóra exhaled slowly and shuddered. She was standing outside the Midtown Church again, but now she relished the unrelenting rain; it felt as if the cold drops were renewing and cleansing her after her conversation with Alda's mother. She took out her mobile and called the police.

"I think we'd better talk, Stefán," she said. "Something tells me that you'll drop your appeal to extend custody when you hear what I have to tell you."

Tinna woke with tears on her cheeks, sobbing weakly. She had no idea why she was crying. She was still in hospital, but didn't recognize the room. There was no dust at the bottom of the lampshade on the ceiling, and the paint on the walls was a different color, but only slightly; this one was just a little more yellow. She tried to turn over but felt a pain in her left arm and breast. The pain wasn't sharp, but felt as if she'd been frozen and was just thawing out. Tinna looked down. She appeared to have bandages beneath her gown, both on her left breast and just below her shoulder. What had happened? Had she been injured in her sleep, but been so tired that she hadn't woken up, either then or when her wounds were dressed? She was still tired and felt dizzy. Had she taken pills? She couldn't remember, and in any case that was irrelevant. There was only one thing that mattered. She had to talk to someone. Someone adult who would listen to her, not just look at her and pretend to pay attention. She could almost see what went through their minds while they feigned interest in her: *She's sick. She's pathetic. We know best. We know best. We'll let her talk but we know best.*

Tinna pushed the red button and waited impatiently for the nurse to come. Why was it taking so long? The hospital corridors were short. It shouldn't take more than a few seconds. Maybe no one cared about her. *What am I going to do with you, Tinna?* Her mother's words echoed in her head. Maybe she had decided to leave Tinna here, and told the people at the hospital not to bother with her. Tinna's breathing was irregular and she felt queasy The door opened and a woman in the too-familiar white uniform appeared. What if this one was foreign? Or deaf?

"How are you feeling?" asked the woman in Icelandic, coming over to the bedside. Tinna relaxed a little.

"I need to talk to my mother," she replied. Her voice sounded whiny, although she hadn't intended it to come out that way. "Now."

"Your mother is coming tonight," said the nurse, leaning over the bed. She lifted one of Tinna's eyelids and stared into her eye. "Are you feeling okay?" *We know best.*

"I want to talk to my mother. I need to tell her about the man. No one knows about this man but me."

"Yes, yes," said the nurse. "We know about that." *She's pathetic. We know best.* "I think it's time for your medicine, dear. You'll feel better afterward." She turned and walked toward the door.

"I need to talk to my mother. I know his name and everything."
The nurse did not react. She quickly returned and put four white
tablets in Tinna's mouth, lifting her head from the pillow and
pressing the glass of water to her lips. She poured the cold liquid in
and held Tinna's chin until she was certain that the girl had swallowed everything. Tinna coughed weakly as the last mouthful of
water got caught in her throat. "We can find out what his name is.
The note fell out."

"All right, sweetheart," said the woman with a smile. "Now you
should sleep for a while, and when you wake up your mother will
be here."

A while later her mother came, but Tinna was still under the
influence of the drugs and was groggy all through visiting hours.
Every time she forced her eyes open she saw the same thing—her
mother crying. "I can find out his name, Mum," she mumbled. Her
voice was as thick and fuzzy as her tongue. She wanted water, but it
was more important to tell what she knew. She had to do it. "He's
called Hjalti," she said. "I couldn't read his last name, it was so
poorly written." Her mother stroked Tinna's forehead, still crying.
"The bad man. He's called Hjalti, Mother."

Her mother wiped her eyes. "Shhh, my Tinna. Sleep. Just sleep."

Tinna gave up and closed her eyes. *We know best.*

Chapter 36

Tuesday, July 24, 2007

Even though not everything had been cleared up, the events from long ago were starting to take shape. Thóra couldn't remember the last time she'd talked for so long—not sober, anyway. Despite the aching in her jaw and the dryness in her mouth, she was happy with her monologue, since her words appeared to have had the desired effect. Stefán and the police department lawyer were on the verge of coming to the same conclusion as her—that Markús was innocent. The three of them sat in Stefán's office, where Thóra had rushed after leaving Alda's mother in the church. Though there was an hour to go before they were due in court, Thóra was fairly sure the custody request would be dropped. Officers had been sent to fetch Alda's mother, but her formal questioning had been delayed because of the funeral. Stefán had settled for speaking to her for long enough to confirm Thóra's story. A plainclothes policeman would accompany her for the rest of the day, in the unlikely event that she should try to get away. Thóra watched as she was brought to the police station. She walked bent over, her face set hard.

There was no way to put yourself in her shoes. How did a woman feel, faced with the knowledge that she had made a terrible mistake in bringing up her child? Thóra was unable to comprehend how she could have sent her daughter with strangers to the Westfjords and forced her to carry a child for another woman; a child that had been created in such an abominable way. Alda's mother had told her how Valgerdur and Dadi wanted Alda to have the child under Valgerdur's name, since they had no chance of adopting a child the traditional way. They had tried before, but had been refused.

At the time there had been no option to adopt children from abroad. And Valgerdur had tried and failed to carry a pregnancy to term herself. For them, this was their only hope of having a child.

In order for the deception to work, Dadi and Valgerdur had to move to an isolated place with Alda and see to it that she had contact with as few people as possible, which meant limited medical checkups. On the few occasions that she was around other people, Alda had to pretend to be much older, so as not to arouse suspicion. According to Alda's mother that wasn't that difficult after the rape; it was as though all the light in Alda's eyes had been extinguished, and she didn't care about anything. In the west the three of them settled on an abandoned farm owned by Valgerdur's relatives. The couple made sure to visit friends and relations in the surrounding area several times with Valgerdur claiming to be pregnant, to back up their story. No one suspected a thing. However, things became more complicated when it came to the actual birth. The plan was for Alda to deliver at home with Valgerdur's assistance, but when it turned out that the placenta was blocking the birth canal they had to rush Alda to the hospital in Ísafjördur. There the child was delivered by Caesarean section.

Alda had been bedridden longer than was usual, to recover from the Caesarean section but also because the site of the incision had become infected. In that time, no one had commented on how young the mother was, or expressed any misgivings as to whether she really was Valgerdur Bjólfsdóttir. The staff at the hospital did notice how peculiarly the new mother behaved toward the child, appearing to care little for it and refusing to suckle it. However, it seemed as if progress was starting to be made by the time mother and child were released. The midwife who visited them in Hólmavík after they'd been discharged informed the hospital that the mother's behavior had improved greatly, although she still refused to breastfeed. This woman was not on the hospital staff, so did not realize that the reason for this change in behavior was that the "mother" was a different person. Dadi had had no trouble keeping visitors away from the hospital, since the couple weren't any more popular in the west than they had been in the Islands. Alda was released just over two weeks after the birth, with Dadi accompanying her and a newborn male child in her arms. She went to the farm to get her things, then left; the boy remained behind with Valgerdur and Dadi. The hospital in Ísafjördur had therefore made no mistake in its drug prescription when Valgerdur was admitted there more than three decades later. In a cruel twist of fate, Alda had been given penicillin for her postoperative infection—an antibiotic to which the real Valgerdur proved severely allergic many years later.

Alda's mother said that Alda had never spoken about the baby, not wanting to know his name or hear anything about him. Thóra did not blame her for that. The child was not welcome in this world in Alda's eyes, and it had never really been "hers." It was understandable that she had shut out the whole experience and looked past it. Mind you, Thóra could well imagine that as the years passed her outlook might have changed, especially when it became clear that she wouldn't have another child. She didn't know if Alda had found out Adolf's name before Halldóra Dögg pressed charges against him for rape, or whether she put two and two together when she found out his surname and age. Either way it must have been a great shock for Alda to discover that her only child, the son of a rapist, was as much of a brute as his father. It must have opened up old wounds. Alda must have harbored some feeling for her son, and may have suffered from guilt over giving him away. This would explain the phone calls to Adolf; first she was accusatory, then pleading. Alda had judged him severely. And when she realized who he was, she must have thought she'd failed him. Thóra wondered whether that had made her want to come clean, to give Adolf the information that proved his innocence and even tell him about his origins. Adolf, on the other hand, had turned a deaf ear and refused to meet her; he thought she would jeopardize his chance of a quick buck from the hospital compensation. Now that he realized he stood to inherit from Alda, everything looked different. But it was too late for Alda.

Thóra had learned while practicing law not to judge others by their actions. They had all made disastrous mistakes—Alda's parents, Dadi and Valgerdur, Adolf, even Markús himself—and none of them had realized the consequences until it was too late. Thóra had seen so many inconceivable things in her work that this didn't surprise her. Most of the missteps her client had taken could be put down to pure stupidity, but the others arose from bad choices, made more often than not in haste or desperation. Alda's fate had been determined by people on the edge of despair, who had reacted the wrong way at the crucial moment. Thóra could only pity those who were left behind and who were now staring their old sins in the face. She felt particularly sorry for Alda's mother, who was actually a victim of circumstance. Her husband Thorgeir, Markús's father Magnús, and Dadi and Valgerdur bore the greatest responsibility, but none of them had been given the chance to repent or atone for what they did. So that left an aged mother who many years ago had become entangled in a sequence of events beyond her control, and now had to bury her daughter.

The same went for Klara, Markús's mother—according to Alda's mother, she had known about the murders. It would, however, be difficult to prove this unless she confessed, and Thóra doubted she would. Klara seemed to have a heart of stone, and with her son Leifur backing her up it was unlikely that she could be made to admit what she knew. Luckily, that was not Thóra's problem. She had had more than enough of this case, with all its corpses.

In the end, though, the question remained: who had murdered Alda? This was the main reason for the police's reluctance to release Markús, despite their previous declaration that he was no longer a suspect in the case. Thóra hadn't expected them to jump for joy at her revelations, but she was disappointed at how forcefully they objected to his release. They were forced to admit that Markús had in all likelihood never been near the men in the basement. How Alda had ended up with her attacker's head in a box would no doubt be explained later, but it had nothing to do with Markús. The unwillingness of the police to admit that Markús was no longer a suspect in Alda's murder was fairly understandable; there wasn't any other suspect, so it was no small matter to admit they had the wrong man in custody. Thóra could feel that the unpleasant sensation in her head, which had started in the church as a faint nagging pain, was getting worse.

"Couldn't the woman simply have committed suicide?" she asked.

"Is there something that clearly suggests she was murdered? Her psychological state can't have been good."

Stefán looked up from the report he'd been going over and frowned. "The autopsy proved that she was murdered," he said. "So I have to reject such speculation."

Thóra sighed deeply. "One of the plastic surgeons Alda worked for contacted me about information that she wanted to give to the police. I understood her to mean that the information concerned Alda and was important for the investigation. Could some of what she had to convey shed light on the case?" She had to pause in her questioning to raise a hand to her forehead and rub it. This dulled the pain, but the headache returned as soon as she dropped her hand. "Is there any new information I ought to be made aware of? I think I have the right to know, since you're starting to direct your attention back toward my client in the case of Alda's death."

"What Alda's colleague told us changes nothing for Markús," said Stefán. "We were given information that might be significant, but at this point we can't say whether it's positive or negative for him."

"Is it possible that Alda's murderer has ties to her work? The drug used to kill her suggests this quite strongly."

"Not anymore," said Stefán calmly. "Whoever killed her didn't need to have access to it."

Thóra gave him an appraising look and cursed her headache under her breath. She was finding it harder and harder to concentrate. The police appeared to have discovered something about the drug that suggested it had already been in Alda's home. Dís must have explained this to them. She settled for saying "I see," since it was clear they weren't going to tell her anything more at this point. "The other thing I want to ask is whether you're planning to speak to the victim in the rape case involving Alda's son. She could conceivably have wished Alda harm, since she could hardly have been pleased when Alda suddenly switched sides."

The police lawyer puffed himself up. He was wearing a dark suit that had no doubt cost a pretty penny, and seemed more than ready to appear in the district court. A wide gold ring on his left hand glittered, and Thóra was sure he had polished it specially. She, however, had not had much time to get ready, and if the police didn't drop their request for a custody extension she would have to stop by her office where she kept a white shirt, dark trousers and comfortable high heels for just such an emergency. It didn't look very good to turn up in court dressed like a tramp, and jeans and a T-shirt hardly sufficed, even though her lawyer's gown covered most of her. At least she didn't have to polish a wedding ring.

"I feel it only right that I point out to you that it is not your role to assist us in the investigation," intoned the lawyer. "We are more than capable of doing our job. You should concentrate on what concerns your client."

"And you think it doesn't serve his interests to find out who really killed Alda?" retorted Thóra. Her cheeks flushed, and her headache was worsening. She felt most of her anger drain away as she realized that if she were him she wouldn't have been pleased to think she had dressed up and polished her jewelry for nothing. She placed her hands on her knees and prepared to stand up. "Can you tell me whether you're going to request a custody extension? If you are, I need time to get ready."

Stefán turned to his colleague and asked him, "Shouldn't we speak privately?" He looked back at Thóra. "I think we've got all the information you could provide," he said, smiling at her. "This shouldn't take long. You can have a cup of coffee outside."

The healing power of the coffee left much to be desired. Thóra had swilled down two strong cups without her pain decreasing. She looked at the clock; just after one. Markús would be on his way into town from Litla-Hraun Prison in the company of the Prison Affairs Transport Officer, so it was not a good time to phone him. But she ought to let Markús's son know that his father might be released without the need for a court ruling. That would save the boy a trip to the district court.

Her conversation with him did not have the effect Thóra was hoping for. He was so beside himself at the news and chattered at her so frantically that it almost made her dizzy. She finally resorted to telling him that someone needed her urgently and she had to hang up. She could no longer endure his noise. If everything went for the best, hopefully Markús would be there for him very shortly. She promised to let him know as soon as it became clear.

Twenty minutes later Stefán came out of his office. He leaned against the doorframe and crossed his arms.

"We've made our decision," he said.

"And?" said Thóra, crossing her fingers. The last thing she needed was to go to court. "What's your conclusion?"

"We're not going to ask for an extension of Markús's detention period, but we will request a travel ban," said Stefán. He wouldn't look her in the eye.

"A travel ban?" asked Thóra calmly. Of two evils, a travel ban was a thousand times better than custody, but at the same time the judge was much more likely to approve it. There was something underhanded about their plan. Release Markús, yet detain him at the same time. She stood up. "I'd better go and get changed," she said, forcing out a smile. "See you later."

How much could she find out about travel bans in a quarter of an hour?

"I don't give a shit about this travel ban, Thóra, they don't even have to discuss it," said Markús triumphantly. "I'm not much of a globe-trotter and even if I was I'm not planning to leave the country any time soon. I'm just thrilled to be out of prison. That's enough for me." He put a hand on her shoulder. "A thousand thanks, and forgive me for any disrespect I showed you. I wasn't myself."

Thóra smiled back at him. Her headache was gone and she felt rather well, even though she'd lost her appeal against the restrictions on her client's movements. She attributed that more to Markús, who had made it clear that it didn't bother him—he had even used the same silly phrase in court as he had to her just now: he wasn't much of a globe-trotter. "If you're happy, Markús, then I suppose I am too. Now we just have to hope that the police find the guilty party, so you can move on to other things."

"Yes, of course, bless your heart," he said happily. "They'll work it out soon enough. If not—then what will be, will be." He took a deep breath; it had stopped raining and the air was clear after the morning's showers. They walked in the direction of Thóra's office on Skólavördustígur Street, where his son was waiting. Thóra had ended up telling the boy to meet them there, since she didn't want him at the courthouse if something went wrong. Even though she trusted Stefán and the lawyer, she wouldn't have fainted with surprise if they had changed their minds and turned up in court demanding an extension of custody.

"This is a great day," said Markús, apparently directing his remark as much at passersby as at Thóra. He had apparently stopped bemoaning the fate of his father, especially since she had told him the old man's condition rendered him unfit to stand trial. It was likely to be hardest for his mother, although she was pretty tough and would survive. Thóra had also been keen to stress that people would not judge the men very harshly, considering they had been exacting revenge for rape. Alda was barely past childhood when this had taken place, and any time sexual assault had been the topic of conversation, she'd heard parents say that if anyone did that to their child, they would kill them. People would find it difficult to condemn them, even though three innocent men had suffered the same fate as the rapist.

"A really great day," repeated Markús loudly.

Thóra was about to agree with him when she saw Alda's mother and Jóhanna walking away from the church.

The funeral had been allowed to go ahead, though the police had set a time limit on the ceremony since they needed to take Alda's body back. Thóra supposed the young man in the blue shirt, following the mother and daughter at a discreet distance, must be the plainclothes policeman charged with keeping an eye on them.

After Thóra had described the sequence of events to the police, it had turned out that Alda's uterus had been removed during the autopsy, and they had simply forgotten to check whether there were any scars from a Caesarean section. At the end of the examination the uterus had been placed back in the abdominal cavity and the body sewn up. This meant that the Criminal Investigation Department needed to have the body back before the burial took place, and as quickly as possible. The shorter the time the body was out of refrigeration, the better.

Jóhanna had a supportive arm around her mother's shoulders.

Thóra hurried to prevent them from seeing Markús, but he seemed not to notice anything unusual when she grabbed him by the arm to chivvy him along. At Lækjarbrekka Restaurant the pair dropped out of sight, and Thóra relaxed her grip. She heard a beep from her mobile and looked at the screen.

"If there is anything I can ever do for you, Thóra, then promise me you'll let me know," Markús was saying as Thóra read her text message.

It was Gylfi, reminding her to check on accommodation in the Islands for the festival. Thóra looked up at Markús, who stood there beaming. "There is actually one thing that would please me no end," she said, returning his smile.

Chapter 37

Saturday, August 4, 2007

Thóra held Sóley's hand so tightly that her daughter winced. She relaxed her grip, but not enough for the girl's little palm to slip from her grasp. The crowd was so dense that Thóra feared if they were separated for just a second she would never find Sóley again. Naturally, she should not have agreed to join the queue at the booth selling festival souvenirs, but it was difficult to say no to Sóley. The girl had been staring enthralled at all the people with flashing sunglasses, masks, hats, necklaces, flags or everything at once, so when she set eyes on the blessed booth Sóley thought she'd hit the jackpot. Thóra adjusted Orri on her hip. He was holding just as tightly to his grandmother as she was to Sóley, and Thóra reassured herself it would take at least four determined festivalgoers to tear the three of them apart.

"I want a rubber nose," said Sóley, as she stood on tiptoe to see what was for sale. "And one of those flashing hair-bands."

After purchasing these essential festival accoutrements they pushed their way back past the queue. Thóra had grown tired of carrying Orri, who was just over a year old and large for his age. She headed toward an empty space below the Islanders' white party tents, standing side by side at one end of the festival grounds, away from the campsite provided for visitors. They took a seat on a little grassy slope, where Sóley removed the decorations from their wrappings and put them on. "Do I look good?" she said, smiling broadly. Thóra smiled back and nodded while Orri stretched a chubby finger in the direction of the red clown's nose. Sóley darted away nimbly and started teasing Orri by pushing the nose toward him, then pulling her face back when he tried to touch it.

The weather was glorious, and Thóra still hadn't seen anyone who looked drunk. The festival had really surprised her and she could only assume that everyone was having too good a time to spoil it by pouring gallons of alcohol down their necks.

She hoped this also applied to Gylfi and Sigga, but she hadn't seen them since they arrived at the festival ground in Herjólfsdalur Valley, on the covered back of one of the trucks used to transport festivalgoers to and fro. There the young couple had met their friends and gone off with them to the concerts, while Thóra stayed behind with the younger generation. She had gone in search of Markús and Leifur's tent, and after threading her way through dense rows of tents that all looked the same, she finally found it.

Thóra enjoyed a hero's welcome in the packed tent, where she was plied with smoked puffin and red wine. Sóley and Orri got as many biscuits as they could eat and as much chocolate milk as they could drink. Thóra's fears that Leifur and María might bear her a grudge were clearly unfounded, and Markús had urged her to drop by. Klara was elsewhere, thankfully—Thóra was fairly certain she would not have shown her the same hospitality. The huge tent was decorated according to local tradition, a semi–living room having been set up inside. It was incredibly well furnished, with three sofas, a refrigerator, a large table, and even pictures hanging from the canvas walls.

María's eyes were watery as she hugged Thóra across the wide table, coming very close to falling across it. *Darling, it's so nice of you to come.* It was more of a surprise to see the brothers drinking. Neither was actually drunk, but both were red-cheeked and spoke louder than usual. Leifur was very generous with the bottle, repeatedly offering to refill the glasses of all the other guests in the tent, whom Thóra did not recognize at all. There was plenty of wine to go around, nonetheless. Leifur had been positioned in the very middle of the tent, but he clambered through the group to plonk himself down on the arm of the sofa where she sat. "You did a good job," he whispered in her ear, grinning foolishly at her. Before Thóra could ask what he meant, he bent down to her again. "Markús is happy, and this was all for the best. Here in the Islands everyone understands what happened, and I don't think I've ever been asked by so many people to give their regards to Father." Thóra nodded and muttered that it was her pleasure. "Here's to the lawyer!" thundered Leifur over the crowd, who lifted their glasses simultaneously.

Markús joined in energetically and grinned at Thóra as widely as his older brother. His travel ban would soon expire, and there was no imminent prospect of it being renewed. He flung his arm around the person sitting next to him and hugged him tight. This was a young man who appeared to be dressed as a garden gnome—the only one inside the packed tent wearing a costume, although these had been a common sight in the throng outside where the crowd was younger. He was wearing a red conical hat, which stood at least half a meter high, a fake white beard and a white wig. It was Hjalti, Markús's son. Unlike the others in the tent he did not seem to be enjoying himself much. Thóra could feel him staring at her from under his bizarre hat, but he looked away when their eyes met. She thought perhaps he was embarrassed by his emotional reunion with his father the day that Markús was released from custody, which Thóra had witnessed. Out of respect for this, she avoided looking too much in his direction. This was easier said than done, since Markús was constantly shouting out to her. One of the things he needed to tell her was that he had now signed off on an apartment in the Islands for his son. A shout was raised for a toast to Hjalti, who looked positively queasy throughout. Finally Thóra herself felt unwell, and she decided to take the kids outside for a while. It was still quite bright outside, and despite the crowds in the tent Leifur had happily offered to store Thóra's covered pushchair. The ground in Herjólfsdalur was far too soft to use it.

Thóra stood and picked Orri back up. He spread out his arms, leaned into her and laid his chin on her shoulder. He was so affectionate that it occasionally worried Thóra, who feared he would have to spend his whole life comforting others. She pushed these thoughts away and tried to attain the carefree joy that seemed to characterize everything and everyone in the valley. Thóra didn't know why she felt so out of sorts, and hoped it wasn't because of the phone call from Bella that morning. The secretary had dreamed about Thóra and found herself compelled to call and tell her boss about the dream. In it Thóra was surrounded by ash, which came out of her ears and mouth, and according to the dream analysis website Bella swore by, ash always symbolized bad luck. It could be an omen of a lawsuit, trouble or adversity. Thóra had a sneaking feeling that if the dream had been given a positive interpretation, Bella would not have called. She said good-bye to her secretary after telling her she didn't believe in that nonsense, and that Bella shouldn't either. Afterward, however, Thóra didn't feel that convinced. She blamed it on a nagging feeling she had had ever since Markús's case was closed. Alda's murderer was still on the loose, and Thóra hated unsolved cases. She had followed the media closely, but according to them the investigation appeared to have run aground.

Thóra found it odd to think that in her pursuit of leads for Markús, she had probably met the murderer. In her mind many people were suspects, some more likely than others. Highest on her list were Adolf, Halldóra Dögg and the plastic surgeon Dís. She hadn't met Dís's colleague Ágúst, so couldn't gauge the likelihood of his involvement.

But this was a festival; people were supposed to enjoy themselves, not wonder about things they couldn't change. Thóra forced a smile.

"Shall we go for a wander?" she asked her daughter. "You should show off your nose a bit."

"I want to visit a tent, like before," said Sóley. The hair-band, which was much too large, had slipped down over her forehead. "They're so cool."

"We can't just drop in anywhere, but we'll walk around and have a look at them," said Thóra. "There are so many of them and we've seen only a small part of the grounds." They walked in the direction of the furthest row of tents facing the slope. "Maybe we'll see Gylfi and Sigga," Thóra said, as she looked hopelessly over the crowd of people on the hillside.

They had come to the tent right at the end. No sound came from it, neither talking nor singing, unlike the other tents. "Can I look in, Mum?" implored Sóley. "Just a peek?"

Thóra nodded, since she couldn't see that it would do any harm. People appeared to be wandering around and peering into tents without anyone thinking it the least bit unnatural. Most of these people were residents of the Islands or had moved away, and were looking for friends or acquaintances. Sóley pulled the white canvas flap wide open, forgetting she had promised "just a peek." This tent was much smaller than Markús and Leifur's, which had been two tents joined together. Nor was it as richly furnished: it had one lopsided sofa and two kitchen stools. On one of them sat Alda's sister Jóhanna, with a heaped platter of flatbread and smoked lamb in front of her. Cling film still covered everything. Jóhanna stared at Sóley then looked past her at Thóra, whom she recognized immediately. "Oh, come in," she said, looking pleased. She stood up and beckoned them in. "I've got plenty of everything." The last sentence sounded even more desperate than the first. Thóra accepted the offer.

"It's really nice to see you," said Jóhanna, as she removed the cling film from the flatbread. "What would the kids like?" she asked, and started to rattle off all the different types of food in the tent.

After Sóley got her Prince Polo chocolate and a glass of fizzy orange, Thóra accepted a piece of flatbread, even though she was far from hungry. She gave Orri another piece to nibble at, though the child had also had enough to eat. She couldn't let the woman go home with her platter of food untouched. "Has anything happened in Alda's case?" asked Thóra after swallowing, more to break the ice than to satisfy her own curiosity. She knew nothing about Jóhanna, and this was the only thing they had in common.

"Well, I don't know what to tell you," said Jóhanna. "A lot of leads turned up, but none of them seems to point to her murderer."

Thóra nodded and took another bite. "I know one of the doctors Alda worked with came forward with information that I had hoped would help." Thóra hadn't tried to persuade Bragi to tell her what it was about, though she had often been on the verge of doing so.

Jóhanna held the plate out to Sóley in case she wanted some flatbread to go with her other snacks. "Yes, yes," she replied, putting it down when the girl declined a slice. "That woman handed over the drug, you know, the Botox, which had been used to . . ." Jóhanna stopped and looked at Sóley. ". . . well, you know. She had taken it from Alda's bedside table when she found her . . . you know . . . I understand that she hadn't wanted her office to become involved in the case, and she thought that Alda had committed . . . you know."

"Was it possible to trace where the Botox came from, and perhaps find some fingerprints on the bottle?" asked Thóra, managing to phrase her question without saying *you know*.

"They only found Alda's fingerprints. That doesn't necessarily mean anything, because the one who . . . you know . . . could have used gloves. They found traces of latex powder, I understand," said Jóhanna, furrowing her brow slightly. "However, they were able to trace where the Botox came from. The other doctor, Ágúst is his name, had bought it. I'm not sure whether they're telling the truth. Alda isn't here any longer to defend herself, and it would be easy for them to make up anything. He says he and Alda had a kind of agreement: she got an unlimited supply of the substance and could do with it whatever she wanted. In return, she used her position at the A&E to put him in touch with patients."

"What?" asked Thóra. "I'm not sure I understand you."

"I'm not surprised," said Jóhanna. "As I was saying, we've only got Ágúst's word on this. He says that Alda sifted out the patients with facial injuries, or who had been wounded or scarred in some other way that might require a plastic surgeon's help. She was supposed to recommend that they have their scars—or nose, or whatever part it was—fixed, and then give them Ágúst's business card. Many of the patients would have been drunk or in shock, and thought that they were being ordered to go to another doctor—that this was a follow-up treatment after the initial examination in the A&E. So they flocked to Ágúst's office."

"And was it not possible to check out this story?" asked Thóra. The police would hardly let such a vague report go uninvestigated.

"Yes, Alda and Ágúst did in fact exchange a number of email messages. Dís passed them on to the police, along with the Botox. The messages proved this was going on. Apparently there was also a rumor about it going round the A&E, but as everyone knows it's not that hard to forge an email, and workplace gossip has never been considered a trustworthy source."

Thóra nodded, even though she had no idea how to send a fake email. Nor did it seem likely that Dís would be able to do so. The A&E gossip mentioned by Jóhanna must have been what Hannes had hinted at but refused to discuss. "Why did Alda need Botox?" asked Thóra. "Couldn't she get them to give her injections for free?"

"She supposedly invited friends and acquaintances home and gave them injections for a fee, but much lower than at the plastic surgeon's, and naturally it was far less trouble for people," said Jóhanna, and she shook her head. "They're saying Alda was getting a fair bit of extra income from this."

"Is that right? Do you believe she did this?"

"No, I can't imagine it. It's one thing to tell your sister she can come and get Botox, and quite another for every old bag in town to be queuing up at her door."

There was no need to discuss this any further. Jóhanna had thought that she was the only one receiving this service, and the same probably went for all the other women. "Has anyone come up with an explanation for why one of the men in the basement was . . . you know . . ." Thóra looked out of the corner of her eye at Sóley, who was intently folding up the wrapper of her chocolate bar. She drew her index finger across her throat.

Jóhanna shook her head. "DNA tests have shown that Adolf is not the son of the man whose head was cut off," she said. "His father was one of the men in the basement who was . . . whole." Thóra grimaced. Had Alda dismembered the wrong man? She dared not speak her thoughts aloud for fear Jóhanna would clam up. She would never accept that Alda had had anything to do with it. "He's put in a claim for Alda's estate, and Mother and I have been told that it will probably be approved. So it won't fall to us," said Jóhanna, who appeared completely unperturbed. "The worst of it is that he doesn't want to talk to us, won't even meet us. He didn't even go to his mother's funeral."

"I'm sure that will improve over time," said Thóra, without

much conviction. It was unlikely that Adolf would mend his ways. "Alda's story is just so tragic."

"Yes, but this does explain some things," said Jóhanna. "Now I appreciate why she and her husband divorced. He was a wonderful man, but from what I understand now she'd never actually been able to have sex after the rape. She had recently started seeing a sex therapist, but to my knowledge the treatment hadn't produced any results. At least, Alda had never been with any men." Orri's head had sunk to his chest, along with the untouched flatbread. He was fast asleep in Thóra's arms. "Is he yours?" asked Jóhanna.

"Not exactly," said Thóra. "He's my grandson." She adjusted the boy in her lap.

"Did you know that Alda was a grandmother?" asked the other woman sadly. Thóra shook her head. "She never knew it, but Adolf has a daughter. She's very ill, unfortunately. Mum has gone to visit her in hospital. She was with her this morning."

"How is your mother?" asked Thóra. "Is she any better?"

Jóhanna smiled unhappily. "She's not very well. She's very unhappy with how slowly the investigation of Alda's murder is going." She looked at her watch. "She promised to drop by, but I don't know if she'll make it. She's been absolutely impossible this afternoon, ever since she returned from her hospital visit. She had some sort of VISA receipt and needed desperately to find out who it belonged to. It was impossible to read the signature clearly but I went into the bank system from my home computer and I managed to dig it up. Hjalti Markússon. She calmed down after that. God knows why. I'm worried about her; I think she's obsessed with Leifur and Markús's family." Jóhanna looked around the empty tent. "Mother and I are more or less invisible these days. She takes it very much to heart, even though she doesn't say so. Leifur and Markús seem to have come out of this as some sort of heroes, along with their father, but it's as if people aren't sure how they should act toward us. I don't get it."

Thóra thought she knew what was going on. People were unsure of the state of the relationship between these two families after everything that had happened. Markús had been locked up, but Jóhanna's mother had neglected to tell the authorities that he wasn't involved at all in the old case. So it was safer to be on the side of the fishing mogul than of the widow and her daughter, the bank clerk. "Well," said Thóra, "I guess I should start making my way back home." She stood up, trying to ignore Jóhanna's mournful look. She couldn't do it. "Will you be here tomorrow?" she asked. "We'll be around, and we'd be happy to drop by." The smile on Jóhanna's face said everything that needed to be said.

It looked as though all the guests in Leifur and Markús's tent had left in a rush, and if Thóra had come just a few minutes later she might have found the place empty. "We're heading over for the singing," said Markús, even more garrulous than when Thóra had left their tent earlier. "A good spot has been reserved for us and I'm sure we can make some room for you."

Thóra declined. "No, thank you, I've got to get home. I just came to fetch the pushchair," she said.

"Bring her the pushchair, Hjalti," said Leifur, his speech even more slurred than Markús's.

The boy stood up without looking at her. He had removed his fake beard but was still wearing the red hat. He seemed very ill at ease, and Thóra was starting to find it peculiar. Maybe he was one of those who couldn't hold his liquor—or perhaps he was ashamed of his father when he drank. He lifted the pushchair and heaved it clumsily across the tent. Thóra could not grab it because of the child in her arms, but María reached for it and after a short struggle managed to open it and set it up for Thóra. Thóra hardly dared to lay Orri in it for fear that it would collapse on him. The woman stood unsteadily next to Thóra, and nearly lost her balance when the tent flaps opened.

Thóra could tell from the look on Leifur's face that the visitor was not particularly welcome. The corners of Markús's mouth had also drooped a little, but otherwise his face was impassive. Thóra had her back to the entrance, but looked around to see who it was. Alda's mother had arrived. She still looked as devastated as when Thóra had seen her after the funeral, but now there was a kind of grim determination in her face. "Perhaps my Geiri and your father were friends," said the old woman, at first hesitantly, but growing bolder with every word. "But I have never really known much about Magnús. Destiny favored him more than most, at least in the beginning. He took a risk and continued his fishing operation, and caught more fish than ever before. He took the blame for Dadi, but because of the eruption the case was forgotten. You, his sons, have lived off your father your entire lives. People tiptoe around you both—especially you, Leifur."

"Shouldn't we talk after the festival?" said Leifur, who seemed to have sobered up in an instant. "I understand there's a lot on your mind, but now is neither the time nor the place."

"No, Leifur," replied the old woman. "You don't get to decide now. I have something to tell you and I doubt you'll be in much of a festive mood afterward."

"*I'll* get back into a festive mood as soon as you clear off," mumbled María. "What's all this about, anyway?" She was clearly not used to people speaking down to her husband. Leifur grabbed her by the shoulder and she stopped talking.

"I was in Reykjavík today, visiting a poor, sick girl," said the old woman. "My great-granddaughter," she added proudly. "I listened to her, and I was the first adult to do that in a long time."

Thóra was so unnerved by the atmosphere in the tent that she instinctively moved the pushchair closer to Sóley, who was yawning on one of the sofas. "What did she say?" she asked, when no one else seemed willing to say anything.

The old woman glared at Hjalti. "Where were you when my Alda was murdered?" She spat out the final word.

Thóra tried unsuccessfully to understand what she was seeing. Markús's son stood gaping at the woman, then grabbed his father's upper arm, a look of terror on his face. "What does that matter?" asked Markús, his face bright red. "Are you suggesting that my son had something to do with Alda's death?"

"Yes, Markús, I am," replied the woman, as if she were speaking to a child. "Hjalti was seen going into Alda's house while she was still alive, then coming out again after she was dead. He and his car were seen there—though he was careful to park it some distance from her house."

"What rubbish," said Markús, putting an arm around his son's shoulders. The boy appeared completely bewildered. "I should remind you that such testimony isn't admissible. Just recently a witness said he'd seen me go past Alda's house, or into it. His testimony was so vague that he couldn't even remember whether I was coming or going when he supposedly saw me."

"We've got more than just a witness," said the old woman. She stared fiercely at Hjalti. "I should kill you, boy. It's what you deserve. I've sat at home and thought about what would be the best way to do it. I'd make sure you'd endure the same agony you put my daughter through, but I'm too old."

"I think that's quite enough," interrupted Thóra. Until now she'd been too surprised to intervene, and everyone else appeared to be struck dumb. "Wouldn't it be best for you to speak to the police if you think you have information about this crime? This is not the proper place for it."

"I've already done that," said the old woman, with a thin smile. "Gudni is on his way. At first he wanted to wait until tomorrow, but he soon changed his mind when he heard what I knew."

"What do you know?" shrieked Hjalti. "You can't know anything."

"You should clean out your car better," said the old woman, still glaring at him murderously.

The boy flinched. "What do you mean, my car?" he asked.

"You opened your car door as you were leaving, and a credit card receipt blew out. It got caught in a bush and the girl who was watching you went and got it. I had Jóhanna look on the bank system to see who the card belonged to."

Hjalti moaned something and his father tried to calm him down. "Don't worry about this, this is bullshit."

"Do something, Leifur," pleaded María tremulously. "You can't let her stand here and say these things."

"I'll pay you well for that receipt," said Leifur levelly. "Neither you nor your daughter would ever need to worry about money again."

Thóra was about to protest, but Alda's mother cut in: "What makes you think I'd want your dirty money? Not everything can be bought. The receipt is not for sale."

"Give me the receipt, or I promise you'll regret it," hissed Markús, advancing toward her. He had trouble pushing between the sofa and the dining table, not least because his son was still hanging off him. The boy appeared to be on the verge of a nervous breakdown. Orri had slept soundly throughout, but Sóley was taking everything in, wide-eyed.

"I couldn't give you the receipt even if I wanted to," said the old woman happily. "I've handed it over to the police."

Markús's son started whining over and over again: *Dad, Dad, you've got to help me, Dad, Dad*. Markús stared desperately at Alda's mother. Thóra felt terribly sorry for him; it was perfectly clear that he loved his son, but he had also loved Alda. He was truly stuck between a rock and a hard place.

The tent flaps swung open again. This time Gudni stood in the doorway, along with another police officer. "Hello," he said to the group, but he was looking at Hjalti. "Hjalti Markússon," he said calmly, "will you come with us?"

The boy continued to whimper the same words as he held onto his father. Markús looked down at him, seemed about to say something, but then loosened the boy's grip on his arm. "My son didn't kill Alda, Gudni," he said. "I did."

Thóra groaned. What now? Did Markús think he could take the blame for his son, as his father had done for Dadi years ago? She wouldn't be surprised if he were hoping for an eruption that very night.

Chapter 38

Saturday, August 4, 2007

"I didn't plan for her to die the way she did. She threw up the drugs, so they didn't work. I didn't have much time and I had to take desperate measures. It was supposed to look like suicide, and I hoped the Botox in her tongue wouldn't be discovered. I left it on her bedside table as a backup—if the drug was found in her body, people might well believe Alda had decided to kill herself that way. Her fingerprints were on the bottle and the syringe. Of course I made sure I wore gloves."

"In other words, you went to her house with the sole intention of ending her life?" asked Gudni deliberately.

"Yes, I did. I had no choice. I had already tried other things. It was her own fault. Of course I was disappointed when the Botox didn't work, but I had to do something. I just wanted to paralyze her tongue. One always hears of people choking on their own vomit. It was supposed to look like that. She was still retching. I knew about the Botox at her house, because she'd got me to try it a few months before. I came that night under the pretense of wanting more. She injected me before I . . . you know."

Thóra closed her eyes. Would this never end? She leaned out to get a view of the corridor, where Orri was asleep in the pushchair and Sóley was sitting playing cards with the police officer assigned to take care of her during the interrogation. Soon Sóley would be too tired to keep playing, and Thóra had decided to leave at that point, no matter what. She had had enough, and the man at her side appeared not to need legal protection. He had decided to confess everything, which meant that there was little use for her. No lawyer could help him now.

There did not appear to have been any mitigating circumstances. Thóra was feeling a little overwhelmed by it all; she felt as though she'd been betrayed and made a fool of. What she wanted most was to drop the case, but her conscience wouldn't let her. Gudni did not appear to feel any better. He had also been deceived, and very publicly. The murderer seemed to have played everyone, except perhaps Detective Stefán. But now the day of reckoning had arrived. "Markús, could you wind this story up?" said Thóra, not looking at him. "I have to go soon." She was still stunned at how easily he had manipulated her.

"Yes, let's tie this up," said Gudni. "Did the estate agent lie for you? Did you pay him to say he'd recognized your voice on the phone?"

"No," said Markús. "He really did hear my voice."

"Now the phone, or the Sim card in it, was traced and found to have been located in the region of the town of Hella, as I recall. You couldn't have been there, Markús, if you're telling us the truth now. So clearly this estate agent didn't speak directly to you. Why did this man lie for you? Because you or your brother are good customers of his? And who answered the phone?"

"I'm telling the truth, and so is the estate agent. I did not have my phone with me," said Markús. He was starting to sober up and kept licking his dry lips. "My son drove my car east to the summerhouse and he had my phone with him. I was hoping that someone would remember having seen my car during the trip, to make my alibi more credible. Actually, no witness to the road trip could be found, but that didn't really make any difference. In any case, I had borrowed my son's car."

"I still don't understand this business with the phone call," said Gudni. "Does your son's voice sound like yours?"

"No, not at all," replied Markús. "I'd prepared everything really well. I bought two mobile phones and put untraceable pay-as-you-go Sim cards in them, which I bought at a petrol station. Then I gave Hjalti two phones, mine and one of the ones I'd bought, while I kept the other one myself. That evening I called my mobile phone from Alda's home phone, pretending to have left it at work so that she wouldn't suspect anything. Hjalti answered and we exchanged a few words. Then we said good-bye and I got down to business." Markús paused for a moment and Thóra wondered whether his conscience was troubling him or if he was simply resting his voice.

He continued: "I'd made a rather low bid on an apartment that I'd chosen randomly, with an estate agent I know a little. I had to be sure that he could tell whether it was me on the phone or someone else. It wouldn't have done me any good to use someone who couldn't confirm it was me he'd spoken to. I let the bid stand until eight o'clock and had the estate agent promise to call me on my mobile immediately afterward to let me know the result. Just before eight Hjalti used the pay-as-you-go phone I'd given him to call the one that *I* had, and we kept the connection open until the estate agent finally called. Then Hjalti answered my mobile there near Hella, and put the phones together so that the speaker of one touched the microphone of the other. That's how I could talk to the estate agent without my real whereabouts being traceable at all. There were some glitches in the connection but I told him that it was because I was on the road near Hella. He accepted that. I'd already tested it out so I knew it would work."

Thóra gaped at Markús. Naturally she wanted to ask him about everything, but Gudni would have to take care of that for the moment. Markús's position was equally dire, whether Thóra attended his interrogation or not. Her job was to support Markús, though it was unclear what advice she could give him at that moment. The only thing she could think of was to try to prove that Markús was unfit to stand trial, although he appeared determined to tell the entire story to save Hjalti.

"Did your son have any knowledge of what was going on?" asked Gudni.

"No, all he knew was that if he did me this favor, I would buy him an apartment out on the Islands. It's been a dream of his for a long time. I'm afraid he won't get the chance to enjoy his new place as he should have. He's been a complete wreck, the poor kid, since he realized what I was up to."

"But why did you do this, Markús? We thought you were in love with Alda. You seemed to be the last person who would wish her any harm." Gudni's question was sincere.

"I told you," Markús replied, indignant. "I tried to avoid it, and I gave her lots of opportunities to sort this out by some other means. It simply didn't work out that way."

"Sort what out?" asked Gudni.

"Oh, this thing with the head," said Markús, as if that explained everything. He looked from Gudni to Thóra and back, but neither of them knew what he was trying to say. He sighed and explained himself better: "I cut off the man's head. Not Alda. I did it for her, but as usual I got no thanks for it."

"You cut off the head," repeated Gudni calmly. "Weren't you in a drunken stupor at home when the murders were committed?"

"No, I wasn't that bad," replied Markús. "I *was* drunk, but not as drunk as the others. I crashed on the couch, but the phone woke me up in the middle of the night. It was Geiri, Alda's father, calling to ask Dad to come over. He wanted to discuss Dadi's offer to help them cover everything up. My mum also woke up and came out of the bedroom. When she saw the blood on Dad, who'd been sitting like a statue in the kitchen since he got back from the harbor, she asked him what was going on. In the end he told her the whole story. They didn't know I was there, but I heard everything. I knew Dad and Geiri had killed the men, and I knew what one of them had done to Alda. I also heard Dad say where the bodies were, in a fishing smack tied to the last pontoon in the harbor. I sneaked out and went down there, after Dad had gone to Geiri's place and Mum had run off crying to the bedroom. I found the boat with the bodies on board, cut off the head and genitals of the one I thought most likely to have raped Alda, and took them with me to show her. I thought it would help her get over it."

Thóra leaned in toward Markús, although it repulsed her to be close to him, and whispered in his ear: "You might want to be careful about mentioning your family members by name. Especially those who are still with us. Of course it's up to you what you say, but you might regret it in the morning."

"And is that when you put the head into the box? To take it home?" asked Gudni.

"No, the box came later," replied Markús. "I put it in a bag and just managed to hide behind a pile of nets when Dad and Dadi came back down to the harbor. They discussed something until some old guy turned up, but they got rid of him quite quickly. Dad went aboard, brought out a birdcage and released the bird. He left shortly after that, but I waited to see what Dadi was up to. He went down into the boat and came up afterward, looking very pale. He'd obviously been startled to see that a head—and more—was missing from one of the bodies. He went and got his pickup, and hauled the other three bodies into it. He spread a cloth over them and parked the pickup a short distance away. Then he pulled a little rubber dinghy on board the smack and sailed off in the smack with the fourth body still on board. He sunk the ship and came back to shore on the dinghy. I hurried home and hid the head in a box down in the basement, and I also put the tools I used to cut it off in one of the boxes in the storeroom, under all the other stuff."

"Why did you use the salmon priest?" Thóra blurted out. She could understand his needing a knife, but not a mallet.

"I took both of them because I thought it might be difficult to cut through the spine." Markús stared at the wall behind Gudni.

"Did you know Dadi had taken the bodies down into the basement?" asked the inspector, trying to hide his amazement.

"No, they weren't there the evening before the eruption. I'm absolutely certain of that. I overheard a conversation between Geiri and Dad on board their ship, *Strokkur*, when I was helping them after school. They didn't know I could hear them. According to Geiri, Dadi had contacted him to say he still had the bodies as leverage if Dad and Geiri didn't keep to their side of the bargain. From what I could understand, Dadi had panicked when he saw the head was missing, and accused Geiri of having removed it in order to pin the murder on him. In other words, Dadi thought that Dad and Geiri were going to bring the head to his house to make it look as if he'd murdered the men. Geiri had no idea what he was talking about, since he didn't know anything about the disappearance of the head, and neither did Dad. They thought Dadi was making it up. They didn't know where he was keeping the bodies, and neither did I, but I do know they weren't in our basement yet."

It took Thóra a while to digest this. Dadi suspected that the two partners, Magnús and Geiri, were going to betray him, and wanted to secure his position by hanging on to the bodies. She exhaled. Clearly this Dadi hadn't been the brightest person in the Islands. How could he think that being in possession of the mens' bodies would prove he *hadn't* murdered them? Maybe he'd planned to put them in Magnús and Geiri's ship, since he thought they were going to hide the head at his house. She nearly laughed out loud. This was so ridiculous. These people must have been desperate. It seemed most likely to her that Dadi would have hidden the bodies somewhere in the vicinity of his house, but not actually inside. When the eruption had started he may have thought it best to move them to Magnús's basement, where they would be buried forever. In the unlikely event that they were found, suspicion would then fall on Magnús, not Dadi.

Maybe he had stored the bodies somewhere they risked being found; the rescuers had wandered freely in and out of all the houses, and someone could easily have stumbled across them. In all likelihood, he had waited until he was certain Magnús would not go back down into his own basement.

Thóra realized she and Gudni were both slowly nodding their heads in response to Markús's last statement. "Yes, it must be easy to lose track of these things," said Gudni, and Thóra had to bite her cheeks so as not to start laughing. For a moment Gudni seemed too stunned to think of any more questions, but then he said: "What about the excavation? Why was Alda so worried about it?"

Markús shrugged. "Actually, she wasn't. I made that up," he said, shutting his eyes. He was clearly getting tired of their questions. "It was like this: during the evacuation to the mainland, Alda and I spoke. She was still in shock, both from the rape and the murders, and it also seemed that seeing the head had scared her. She asked me what had become of it, and I told her; I'd taken the box back home and hidden it in the basement, intending to get rid of it the next day. Her parents had told her the whole story that weekend, and she was understandably afraid that her father would go to jail." Thóra could picture the scene only too well; Alda's parents describing the night's events, persuading her to sacrifice herself to save her father from prison.

Markús had more to say. "No one had mentioned the head, since Geiri didn't know about it until Dadi told him on Monday, and nor did Alda. She never told her parents about it. I suppose she wanted to destroy those memories, and she felt as if she'd got me into trouble. She blamed herself for everything that happened. When we met at Reykjavík Junior College we never talked about it, and it didn't come up again until they were about to excavate the house. Of course I tried to stop the excavation from the first day, but Alda acted as though it didn't matter until a few months ago. Then she said she was going to spill the beans, so I didn't need to pursue the injunction against the excavation. The truth would all come out. I tried to talk her out of it, but it didn't work. I asked her to wait until I had gone down into the basement, and she agreed to that, thank God. Then I made one last attempt to get her to change her mind the night before I had to resort to my final option. I went to her house and begged her to let sleeping dogs lie; I would go down into the basement, get the head, and no one would need to know anything about it. But she wouldn't budge."

Alda had made the decision to confess everything after meeting her son. She wanted to tell the truth because she had nothing to lose. She had just been a pawn in this series of events, a victim. Thóra realized that she herself had believed Markús blindly, and everything he had told her about Alda. She had never doubted him.

"How did you actually think this would work?" asked Gudni.

"I was just going to get the head and get rid of it. Everyone would think Alda had committed suicide, and no one would connect it to the Westmann Islands. Lots of women kill themselves at that age, and she had no family or friends to speak of. I also had an alibi if it came to a murder investigation." Markús sat up straighter. "It all went wrong with the discovery of the bodies. I didn't expect them to be down there, since they weren't in the basement the night of the eruption. I would never have got them past the archaeologists."

"So you turned the story around to pin it all on Alda?" said Gudni.

"Yes, I suppose I did," replied Markús. "I didn't have much time to think; I was down in the basement and I had to come up with something. I don't think it was a bad plan, in light of the circumstances." He looked almost proud of his cunning, and Thóra was convinced at that moment that he was out of his mind. "I decided to say that Alda had given me the box, and years later asked me to remove it from the basement when the house was going to be excavated. She wasn't going to be around to defend herself, so it should have been foolproof. I knew that any investigation of what happened would bring the rape to light, sooner or later. I had to be sure I wouldn't be caught, and make suspicion fall on Alda."

"But why didn't you tell us about the phone call from the estate agent when you were taken into custody?" said Gudni. "You'd had the foresight to prepare an alibi, and then you didn't use it."

Markús grinned. "Of course, I knew the estate agent had an unlisted number. When that was discovered, I didn't want to arouse any suspicion by immediately remembering who had called me. I waited, to make my story more credible. I think it worked beautifully. Also, I didn't want to talk about anything in connection with that night years ago, since I was supposed to have been drunk and unconscious."

"What about the biological samples?" asked Gudni. "The hair that was found on Alda's genitals? Did you forget about that?"

"I loved Alda," said Markús, and there was no doubting his conviction. Thóra gulped. "I always have. But she barely knew I was alive. I just lost control, and I was going to force her—I'd waited for decades, this was my last chance. I pulled down her underwear, but I stopped at the last minute when I realized what I was doing. I put her clothes back on, but the hair must have fallen off me." He looked from Thóra to Gudni. "I swear she was alive when it happened. She was drifting in and out of consciousness, but she wasn't dead. I would never do that."

Gudni did not respond to this, but instead turned off the little tape recorder on the table. "Did Leifur know about the murders?" he asked, looking as though he hoped this was not the case.

"He was aware of them. Dad called him home from Reykjavík for support. He didn't really come to tell me off for drinking, since I never would have listened to him back then. I told him about this thing with Alda afterward. He wasn't very pleased with me."

Gudni nodded. "It doesn't matter what he knew, as long as he didn't take part in any criminal activity. In that case, we don't need to bring him into this." He turned the machine back on and Thóra stared openmouthed at the blinking light on its side. It must be nice to hold all the cards for an entire community. Good for the one who does, not so good for others. As she processed this new information, Gudni took her silence as consent.

"Aren't we finished here yet?" she asked. "I'm not sure I can endure any more right now, and I'm sure Markús has had enough too." In the hallway she could see Sóley yawning widely. "You know where I am if you need me." She wanted to ask Markús about Alda's hair, whether he was the one who'd cut it from Alda's head as she slept in the gym, but decided to let it wait. It seemed a rather trivial detail in the light of other events, and the answer was obvious anyway. Now that she thought about it, the hair in the storeroom that had sickened Bella so much must have been Alda's. Thóra suspected that Markús had been driven to do it by jealousy and anger toward Stebbi, the boy that Alda liked. He had wanted to teach Alda a lesson and show her what happened if she rejected him.

Gudni stood up. "Yes, I think that's all for now. There's a plane on its way from Reykjavík to fetch you, Markús, and I doubt very much you'll be back here in the Islands any time soon. You might want to take the opportunity to admire the view of the cliffs from my window, before you leave."

Thóra walked out without looking back at Gudni and Markús. Thanking the card-playing police officer for his patience, she helped her daughter to her feet. Orri was still sleeping soundly in the pushchair, and she was able to pull up his hood without waking him. The three of them then headed out into the August night in search of a tourist truck to drive them back to their apartment.

"Did the police catch the bad guy?" asked Sóley sleepily, as they walked down the spotless street. They could hear the noise from the festival at Herjólfsdalur, carried on the breeze.

"Yes, sweetheart," said Thóra, trying to look pleased that the case was solved. She still felt she'd been made a fool of.

"And who was the bad guy?" her daughter asked eagerly. In her simple, childish world criminals were easy to spot, like Robbie Rotten or the Beagle Boys in the books Thóra read to her.

"It was the one that I thought was the good guy," replied Thóra, smiling down at her. "People sometimes make mistakes." They waved down a truck and sat on a bench among a group of festival-goers, who were all smiles. She wondered if she could get a babysitter for the following night and allow herself some fun. Maybe she, like Bella, could find herself a handsome sailor and forget everything for a while.

It sounded nice, but Thóra knew it would never happen.

CPSIA information can be obtained
at www.ICGtesting.com
Printed in the USA
LVHW041132150122
708524LV00003B/143